# RESPECT

# MANDASUE HELLER

**LARGE PRINT**

Oxford

First published in Great Britain 2014
by
Hodder & Stoughton
an Hachette UK Company

Published in Large Print 2014 by ISIS Publishing Ltd.,
7 Centremead, Osney Mead, Oxford OX2 0ES
by arrangement with
Hodder & Stoughton
an Hachette UK Company

CIP data is available for this title from the British Library

ISBN 978–1–4450–9922–4 (hb)
ISBN 978–1–4450–9923–1 (pb)

Printed and bound in Great Britain by
T. J. International Ltd., Padstow, Cornwall

# RESPECT

**Staffordshire Library and Information Services**
Please return or renew by the last date shown

| | | Ruce |
|---|---|---|
| 27-8-16 | | NORT |
| 16-9-16 | | |
| NORTON CANES | | |
| | | |
| 2 3 2018 | | |
| 1 3 MAY 2019 | | |

If not required by other readers, this item may may be renewed in person, by post or telephone, online or by email. To renew, either the book or ticket are required

**24 Hour Renewal Line**
**0845 33 00 740**

Staffordshire
County Council

For Karen Brookes,
with love and a million memories.
Until we meet again xx

As always, I have to thank my lovely family for their constant support and love. My man, Win; my mum, Jean; my children, Michael, Andrew, Azzura (and Michael); my grandies, Marissa, Lariah, and Antonio; my sister, Ava; Amber, Martin, Jade, Reece, Kyro, Diaz, Auntie Doreen, Pete, Lorna and Cliff, Chris, Glen, Natalie, Dan and Lauren, Toni, Joseph, Mavis, Valerie, Jascinth, Donna, and their children . . . lots of love to you all.

Thanks, as ever, to my ace editor, Carolyn Caughey, for the brilliant advice and support. Also the rest of the superb team at Hodder: Lucy, Emilie, Emma, Rosie, Francine, Phil — to name but a few.

Immense thanks also to my lovely agent, Sheila Crowley.

Thanks to Nick Austin — your copy-editing has taught me a lot! Also, Cat Ledger, Wayne Brookes, and Martina Cole — for everything.

Love to great friends, Betty and Ronnie Schwartz, The Dysfunctional Duchess: Kimberley Chambers, Liz Paton, Katy and John, Norman Brown and Hilary Devey.

And a special mention to my *Lost Angel* dream-team: Jac and Brian Capron, Ann Mitchell, Rowetta and Chris Coghill. Can't think of a better cast — or nicer people.

A big thank you to Carrie Austin for the invaluable info on the working life of PIs.

And last but never least, a million thanks to the buyers, readers, libraries, and my friends on FB & T. You all make it worthwhile, and I greatly appreciate the support and chats.

Respect!

# PROLOGUE

"Get the fuck out of my house, you stinking, cheating, lying bastard! Go on . . . fuck off — and don't come back!"

"Shut your mouth, you crazy bitch."

"Why? Scared the kids'll wake up and find out what a loser you are? Well, they're my fucking kids, not yours, so don't you be worrying about them!"

"You'd best quit pushin' me!"

"Or what . . .? You gonna whack me again? Go on, then — if you *dare*!"

The words were followed by a loud smashing sound, and Chantelle Booth shivered in her bed on the other side of the wall. She was frequently woken in the middle of the night by the sound of her mum and Jase shouting at each other, and she usually covered her ears and tried to ignore it. But tonight's argument sounded nastier than usual and she was scared to go back to sleep in case something really bad happened.

Jase hadn't long moved in but he was already messing her mum around; staying out for days on end, then walking back in as if nothing had happened. And the silly cow usually welcomed him back with open arms — but not tonight, by the sound of it.

Chantelle was glad about that, because she didn't like Jase. He acted nice, but she had seen through him the instant she first clapped eyes on him. And she had enough experience to know the difference between real nice and fake nice, given how many men her mum had brought into their lives since her little brother Leon's dad had walked out on them. The real nice ones didn't tend to stick around too long, but the fake ones, like Jase, hung around like bad smells, making her mum cry and spending her money on drugs and drink so she couldn't afford to buy food or pay the bills.

A heavy thud on the wall rattled Chantelle's headboard. She sat up and bit her lip when she heard the creak of her brother's bed springs through the wall on the other side. She hoped he wasn't about to wake up. He was only eight, and slightly built for his age, but his handsome baby-face disguised a man-sized temper, and he was bound to fly off the handle if he saw Jase hurting his mum — which would only make everything ten times worse.

Unable to bear it any longer when her mum let out a piercing scream, Chantelle leapt from her bed and rushed into the hall — just as her mother hurtled out of her own room with Jase on her heels.

"Stop it!" she cried when Jase slammed her mother up against the wall and put his hands around her throat. "Leave her alone!"

"Now see what you've done," Mary Booth hissed, using the interruption to regain her footing and push Jase away. "Happy now, are you?"

4

Jase flapped a dismissive hand in Chantelle's direction. "Go back to bed — everything's cool."

"No, it's not," Chantelle sobbed, taking in the bleeding gouges in his cheek which she guessed her mum had raked with her nails, and the bruise that was starting to darken her mum's eye. "You're always hurting my mum, and I don't like it. I don't like you."

Jase narrowed his eyes and stared angrily back at her. "Who the fuck do you think you're talking to, you black bitch?"

"Oi! Don't talk to my daughter like that!" Mary protested, smacking him on the side of his head. "And she ain't black, she's mixed-race, you ignorant bastard, so get your facts right!"

Jase clenched his fist and went to punch her, but hesitated at the sound of someone hammering on the wall that divided Mary's flat from the one next door. "You know what? Fuck this," he sneered. "I've had it with you and your dramas."

"Where d'y' think you're going?" Mary demanded when he turned and walked back into the bedroom. "Don't think you're crawling back into my bed like everything's okay, 'cos it ain't happening. I want you out."

"Don't worry, I'm gone." Jase sat down on the edge of the bed and dragged on his jeans. "I can't hack this shit no more. You're doing my head in."

"Yeah, well, now you know how *I* feel," spat Mary.

Jase stood up, pulled his jumper over his head, shoved his feet into his trainers and, pushing past Mary, strode back out into the hall.

"Where you planning to go at this time of night?" she asked, shaking now because she'd realised that he really was going to leave. "I'm telling you now, if I find out you've been anywhere near that slag Wendy Thompson I'll throw her right over the fucking balcony — and you right after her! Is that where you're going? Is it . . .?"

"None o' your business." Jase grabbed his jacket off the hook behind the front door and shoved his arms into the sleeves. He cast a quick glance back at Chantelle who was still standing there in her nightdress, tears streaking her pretty face, legs shaking visibly. Then, sucking his teeth, he walked out, slamming the door behind him.

Infuriated, Mary yanked it open again, screaming, "Don't you fucking *dare* go to that bitch! I'm warning you, Jase — I'll kill the pair of you!"

"Let him go," Chantelle pleaded, grabbing her mum's arm to stop her from going after him. "*Please*, Mum. We've got each other, we don't need him."

Mary shook her off angrily and stumbled out onto the landing. She'd been sure that Jase would be heading to Wendy's flat eight doors down but the walkway was deserted. Standing there, with the wind lashing her cheeks and whistling down her ears, she picked up the faint slap of footsteps going quickly down the communal stairs and rushed to the balcony.

"Where you going?" she yelled over the rail when Jase emerged onto the path a few seconds later. "Got some other tart lined up already, have you? Some bitch who don't care that you've already got a woman?"

Jase walked on without responding.

"Go on, then!" Mary shrieked at his back. "Go to your whore — see if I care! But don't come crawling back to me when she gets tired of your useless arse and kicks you out, 'cos you've fucked me about for the last time! D'ya hear me, you dirty piece of shit? We're finished!"

"Mum, stop it," Chantelle pleaded, her bare feet freezing on the icy concrete as she tried to drag her mother away from the balcony edge. "You're gonna fall!"

Chest heaving with fury and pain as Jase strolled around the corner and out of view, Mary clenched her fists and pummelled the iron railing. Then the tears came, and she sank to her knees and wailed.

"For God's sake, stop that racket!" a hoarse voice barked. "We're trying to get some flaming sleep here. We haven't all got the luxury of sitting on our backsides watching Jeremy bloody Kyle all day — some of us actually have to *work* for a living."

"Fuck off!" Mary pulled herself together at the sound of her next-door neighbour's voice and lurched back up to her feet. Swiping the tears from her cheeks, she glared at the man who was peering out at her. "Get back in your coffin with that corpse you call a wife before I knock you out, you fat bastard!"

"I'm calling the police," he spluttered, quickly pulling his head in and slamming the door shut when Mary lunged towards him.

"Go on, then — I dare you!" Mary kicked his door. "But don't blame me when all your windows get put through, 'cos everyone already hates you round here, so see what happens if you bring the pigs round, you dirty grass!"

"Mum, come home." Chantelle tugged on her mother's hand again, terrified that she was going to get herself arrested.

Exhausted by now, Mary's shoulders suddenly slumped. She looked balefully out across the estate in the hope that Jase might have changed his mind and be on his way back, but the area was as deserted as the landing she was standing on.

Relieved when her mum walked back into their flat, Chantelle followed and closed the door on the biting cold. She was shivering wildly, but her fear changed to concern when her mum turned the kitchen light on and her injuries became clear. Her eye was so badly swollen that it was starting to close up, and there were livid red marks on her neck from where Jase had throttled her, and scratches and bruises on her bare arms and legs. It was the worst fight they'd had by far, and Chantelle prayed that it really was over this time.

"Shall I make you a cup of tea?" she offered.

"I don't want tea," Mary muttered, pulling the fridge open and taking out a can of Tennent's Super. "Go back to bed."

"I want to stay with you," Chantelle insisted. "You're hurt."

"For God's sake, fuck off and leave me alone!" Mary rounded on her. "You're fourteen, not forty, so stop acting like me bleedin' mother. Do as you're told and go . . . to . . . *bed*!"

Chilled by the fierceness of her mother's tone, Chantelle fled back to her room and climbed beneath the quilt, her heart heavy. Minutes earlier, her mum had been screaming that she never wanted to see Jase again, but Chantelle knew that she would now mope about like a lost soul until he showed up again — which, in turn, meant that Chantelle would be expected to look after Leon while Mary tried to drink and smoke herself to death. And Chantelle would have to do it, or her little brother would end up going to school dirty and hungry, and then the nosy teachers would tell the social worker and all sorts of trouble would break out again. And, even though it wasn't Chantelle's fault, she'd get the blame — just like she always did.

As Chantelle cried herself to sleep in her room, Mary flopped onto a chair at the kitchen table and ripped the tab off the beer can. Aware that it wouldn't be anywhere near strong enough to drown her sorrows, she reached into a drawer and rooted through the junk until she found a strip of tramadol tablets. She'd have preferred temazepam, but she'd sold her last script and the next wasn't due for another week, so the painkillers would have to do.

As the rush of adrenalin subsided and the pain of her injuries began to wash over her, Mary licked at the fresh tears of self-pity and popped two of the little capsules out of the foil strip. Then, thinking *to hell with it*, she pressed out the rest and threw them all into her mouth, quickly washing them down with beer before traipsing miserably back to her bedroom.

She'd never taken so many of the painkillers at one time before, and it crossed her mind as she lay down on the bed that she might overdose and die. But so what if she did? No one would care. They'd probably all be glad to see the back of her. Jase, the kids, her so-called mates . . . none of them gave a flying fuck about her, so it would serve the bastards right if she didn't wake up.

As a drowsy sensation began to creep over her, Mary swallowed the last of her beer. Then, carefully arranging her hair so that it fanned out on the pillow around her head, she crossed her hands over her chest and closed her eyes.

Fuck only knew who would be the first to see her body in the morning, but if it was a fit young copper or ambulance man she was determined to look her best.

# CHAPTER
## ONE

It had just gone eight-thirty and Chantelle was in a rush. She and Leon would usually have left for school by now, but the shirt she'd washed the night before had fallen off the radiator so she'd had to try and dry it with her hairdryer. And now Leon was dragging his feet, so she ordered him to hurry up and brush his teeth while she went into the living room to comb her hair.

Surprised to find her mother in there, she drew her head back and gave her a questioning look. "How come you're up so early?"

"Not long got in," Mary admitted, clamping her lit cigarette between her teeth. "Haven't seen my bank card, have you?" she asked, her backside rearing up into the air as she knelt on the couch and rooted through the junk piled down the side of it. "Can't find it anywhere."

"I hope you haven't lost it again," Chantelle chided, walking over to the fireplace and taking her comb out from behind an ornament on the mantelpiece. "That'll be the third time in a year, and they'll start charging you if you're not careful."

"All right, little miss know-it-all, I can do without a lecture, thank you very much!" Mary straightened up and gave her daughter a dirty look as she teased her thick hair into shape. Chantelle had a beautiful face and a great figure, but it was completely wasted on her because she wasn't interested in anything apart from school. Boring as fuck — just like her father.

Chantelle glanced out of the corner of her eye and frowned when she saw the way her mother was staring at her. "What's up? Have I got dirt on the back of my skirt, or something?"

"As if!" Mary sneered, taking a last drag on her fag before stubbing it out in the ashtray.

Chantelle pursed her lips as she tied the scrunchie around her hair. Her mum acted like it was a crime to want to look presentable, and was forever making sniping remarks about OCD. But Chantelle would rather die than go out in public looking dirty — like her brother happily would if she'd let him.

Mary lit another cigarette and resumed her search for the missing bank card. Chantelle could wind her up on the best of days by just breathing, but with her nerves sparking like live wires — thanks to all the speed she'd done last night — anything the girl said or did today was guaranteed to infuriate her.

When Leon walked in just then, holding his mud-caked football boots out in front of him, Mary snapped, "Don't be fetching them in here. They look like they've been dipped in shit. Get 'em out in the hall."

"They're knackered," Leon told her, as surprised as Chantelle had been to see their mother not only up at this time of the morning but dressed as well. "I need some new ones. Can I have thirty quid?"

"Can you hell! They're not even a year old yet, them. You wanna start looking after your stuff if you want it to last."

"It ain't my fault. And my teacher said —"

"Do I look like I give a flying fuck what your teacher says?" Mary rounded on her son furiously. "He can have his say when he's the one putting food in your greedy gob, but till then he'd better keep his trap shut, or I'll come down there and put my fist in it!"

"All right, Mum, there's no need to jump down his throat." Chantelle leapt to her brother's defence.

"Oh, I wondered how long it'd take for you to stick your beak in." Mary switched the glare onto her daughter. "You know what, I'm sick to death of the pair of you. Give me this, buy me that . . . it's all I ever fuckin' hear round here, and it's doing my head in!"

"Pardon us for being born," said Chantelle, pushing Leon out into the hall.

"Yeah, well, I wish you hadn't been," Mary yelled after them. "The trouble you two have caused me, you'd have been better off leaving me to die that time!"

Chantelle looked back and gave a disapproving shake of her head before following her brother out of the room.

"'S up with her?" Leon whined, stuffing his boots into his school bag.

"The usual," Chantelle muttered. She'd already guessed that her mum was on a speed comedown, because she was always vicious after a heavy session and it always culminated in her saying that she wished they had let her die when she'd taken the overdose a year and a half earlier — even though both she and Chantelle knew that it hadn't been a serious suicide attempt. Given the amount of alcohol she regularly drank, and the cocktail of illegal drugs she'd been feeding into her body for as long as Chantelle could remember, it would have taken a damn sight more than a few poxy painkillers to bring Mary Booth down.

"What am I supposed to tell my teacher?" Leon grumbled when Chantelle hustled him out through the front door. "He says he'll kick me off the team if I don't get me boots sorted."

"You're the best player; there's no way he'll get rid of you," Chantelle assured him. "But if he says it again, tell him I'm going to make sure you get some new ones."

"*BITCH!*" Mary yelled as the front door slammed shut behind them. It pissed her off that Chantelle had gone over her head and promised Leon new boots. But good luck to her if she thought muggins was paying for them, because hell would have to freeze over before Mary dipped her hand in her purse now.

Still fuming, Mary flopped down on the couch and took a deep drag on her cigarette. Almost choking on it when a vibration rattled the back of her head, she grabbed the jacket that was draped behind her and pulled her mobile phone out of its pocket. "That you, Trace?"

14

"No, it fuckin' ain't."

Mary winced at the sound of her dealer's angry voice. "All right, Ricky. Wasn't expecting you."

"No, I bet you wasn't," spat Ricky. "Where's my money, you thieving bitch?"

"I meant to come round," Mary lied. "But things keep cropping up. I'll get it to you as soon as I can, I promise. But it's not easy when you've got kids, you know."

"I don't give a fuck about your kids," Ricky bellowed, forcing her to jerk the phone away from her ear. "I just want my bastard money. You've got an hour — and if I don't see you, I'm gonna come looking for you. You've been warned!"

Mary bit her lip when the line went dead. Shit! Now what was she supposed to do? There was no way she could get her hands on two hundred quid in an hour. But if she didn't, he would kill her.

Almost jumping out of her skin when someone knocked at the front door, she crept over to the window — praying with every tiptoed step that it wasn't Ricky, because she wouldn't put it past him to have been outside the whole time. A man wearing a jacket bearing the E.ON logo was standing on the step. Relieved that it wasn't Ricky, Mary went back to the couch and stubbed out the burned-down cigarette before lighting a fresh one.

The man knocked again, and then raised the flap of the letter box. "Mrs Booth? I need to speak to you about your electricity arrears."

Mary gritted her teeth and stuck two fingers up at the door. Cheeky bastard, shouting out her business for the whole world to hear.

The man tried one last time before shoving something through the letter box and walking away, his heels thudding dully on the concrete landing. Mary went out into the hall, snatched up the letter, and curled her lip when she read that they intended to take her to court if she didn't contact them to make arrangements to pay her arrears. She tossed it onto the hall table along with the rest of her unpaid bills and marched into the kitchen in search of alcohol to soothe her nerves.

They were a load of fucking vultures, expecting her to conjure money out of thin air to pay their extortionate charges. They ought to be chasing the benefits people, not her, seeing as *they* were the ones who had messed up her claim and made her get into debt in the first place.

"*We have strong evidence to suggest that you are living with someone whilst claiming as a single parent,*" the woman from the benefit fraud squad had said when they called her into the office that day, "*and we'll be suspending your claim pending further investigations.*"

Strong evidence, her arse! More like word of malicious mouth. But that was the trouble with living in a place like this: it was chock-full of nosy bastards who had nothing better to do than stick their beaks into things that didn't concern them. Mary wouldn't have minded so much if she and Jimmy had even been serious, but it had only ever been a fling. And, all right, so maybe he *had* more or less moved in — but that was *her* business. She'd kicked him out as soon as it came on top, so that should have been that. But it had taken ages for the stupid bastards to reinstate her benefits, and now, because of their incompetence, everyone wanted a piece of her.

*Fuck them*, she thought, slamming the fridge shut when she saw that there were no beers to be had. They could form a queue to peck the flesh off her bones when she was dead and buried, but until then they could all go to hell.

Chantelle was exhausted when she arrived home from school that afternoon. The walk took fifteen minutes on a good day, but when she felt as lousy as she did today it seemed to take hours. And the weather wasn't helping. It was supposed to be the beginning of summer, but there had been no sign of it yet and the chill air was exacerbating the headache that had started during her last lesson. Her head was pounding, and her neck and shoulders were killing her from the weight of the books she'd been lugging around in her bag all day. All she wanted to do was climb into bed and sleep for a week. But her exams were starting on Monday, and if she were to stand any chance of passing them she was going to have to spend the whole weekend revising.

Inside the flat it was even colder and darker than it was outside, and Chantelle shivered as she dropped her bag on the hall floor. "It's me," she called as she slipped out of her blazer and looped it over the peg.

When no answer came, she popped her head around her mum's bedroom door. Surprised to see that the bed was empty — her mum usually slept for a couple of days after a heavy binge — she wandered into the kitchen to see if Mary had done the shopping before going out.

"Great!" she muttered when she saw that the cupboards were still bare. "So, that's me revising on an empty stomach — *again*. Cheers, Mum."

Chantelle went into the living room and drew the curtains to hide the depressing sight of heavy clouds gathering over the roof of the flats across the way. Then, switching the lamp on, she went back out into the hall to fetch her books.

It was only when she came back that she noticed the note propped on the mantelpiece, and she frowned when she reached for it and a £20 note fluttered to the floor at her feet. No wonder her mum hadn't bothered to do the shopping: she obviously expected her little lackey to do it for her — like Chantelle didn't have better things to do.

*Going to a party with Trace*, the note read, *so you'll have to get our Leon's tea. Don't wait up 'cos I don't know when I'll be back. Mum xxx*

Furious that her mother had gone out on the lash and dumped Leon on her knowing full well that she needed to revise, Chantelle yanked her mobile phone out of her bag and rang her mum's number.

*"Hey there,"* the answerphone message trilled, in the phony American accent that her mum seemed to think was sexy. *"I can't take your call right now, but if you leave your name, number, and cock size, I'll get right back to you . . ."*

Nose wrinkled in disgust, Chantelle waited for the filthy chuckle at the end of the message. Then, keeping as even a tone as she could manage, she said, "Call me back as soon as you get this. I know you've probably forgotten, but my exams are starting on Monday and I need to get my head down, so I could really do without having to watch our Leon. *Call* me."

She'd just finished the message when the door opened behind her. Sure that it was her mum, because Leon didn't have a key, she turned around, saying, "Oh, good, you're back. I just left you a mes —" She trailed off when she saw her brother and frowned. "How did you get in?"

Leon held up her keys and rattled them. "You left them in the lock."

"You're joking!" Chantelle gasped. "God, what an idiot."

"You said it." Leon smirked, tossing the keys onto the table. "Mum still in bed?"

"No, she's gone out." Chantelle followed as he wandered into the kitchen. "And she hasn't been shopping, so don't bother rooting."

Leon looked in the fridge anyway, and then slammed the door when he saw that she was telling the truth. "When's she coming back? I'm starving."

"No idea. But she's left some money, so I'll go to the shops in a bit."

"You're not cooking, are you?" Leon pulled a face. "Can't we have chippy?"

"I suppose so," Chantelle conceded. "But then I've got to revise, so I hope you're going to be quiet."

"I won't be here," Leon told her, walking back out into the hall. "I only came back for something to eat. I'm off to Kermit's."

"I want you to stay in now you're here," Chantelle told him.

"Get stuffed," Leon grunted, still heading for the door. "It's not even five yet; Mum lets me stay out till seven."

"Yeah, but she's not here, so I'm in charge," said Chantelle. "And I've got too much to do, so I want you where I can see you."

"I'll have a sausage when you go to the chippy," Leon said over his shoulder, already opening the door. "And gravy."

"*Leon!*" Chantelle rushed up the hall when he stepped outside and pulled the door shut. "Come back here!" She followed him out onto the landing and gritted her teeth when she saw him legging it for the stairs. "Right, fine, go then," she called after him. "But I'll be coming for you on my way back from the chippy, so make sure you're ready 'cos I'm not hanging round like an idiot if it starts raining!"

Leon raised his hand before disappearing into the stairwell. Chantelle was starting to feel sick by now, and her head was throbbing. Praying that the headache didn't turn into a full-blown migraine, she went back into the flat and swallowed a couple of paracetamol. Then, with an hour still to go before the chippy opened, she lay down on the couch and pulled a cushion over her eyes.

# CHAPTER
# TWO

The Richmond Estate, on the border between Hulme and Old Trafford, was mainly populated by single mothers and their offspring. There was a play area in the centre of the estate, which no child dared go near for fear of getting battered by the hoody boys who hung out there to smoke weed and sniff glue. There was also a car park and a set of garages, which none of the residents ever used, because they knew their cars would get broken into or set on fire as soon as their backs were turned. Of the parade of shops, only two of the original six were still occupied. The owners of the other units had long ago given up on trying to run a business in a place where the majority of their customers had perfected the art of paying for one item whilst walking out with three.

The two units that were still in business sat side by side at the end of the parade. Abdul's General Store had just closed when Chantelle got there at six, but Jimmy's Chippy had just opened. The heat from the fryers smacked her in the face when she walked in, and the delicious scents of vinegar and freshly cooked chips made her stomach growl. The owner, Jimmy, a tiny

Chinese man who could barely see over the counter, beamed when he saw her.

"Ah . . . long time, no see, missy. You had babba now?"

Chantelle smiled when he mimed rocking a baby in his arms, and shook her head. "You must be thinking of someone else. Can I get two lots of sausage and chips and a small tub of gravy, please?"

"Fi' minutes," Jimmy said, his smiling eyes just slits in the deep wrinkles of his kindly face as he stirred his batch with vigour.

On the shelf behind him a portable TV sat between a pyramid of soda cans and a statue of a nodding, waving cat. Chantelle placed her cold hands up against the glass of the warming cabinet and glanced at the screen. It was tuned to the six o'clock news, and flickering images of what appeared to be a riot were flashing across the screen behind the sombre-faced reporter. The volume was too low for her to hear what he was saying, but the subtitles told her that there had, earlier that day in Bury, been a violent confrontation between a faction of the English Defence League and a group of Muslims protesting about a deportation.

"Idiots." Jimmy gave a backward jerk of his head when he saw her watching it. "They need try t'ai chi." He raised a knee and both hands into the air to demonstrate. "Good for chase devil out here." He lowered his leg and patted his chest now, to indicate, Chantelle guessed, that he was referring to the heart. Then, pointing a gnarly old finger at her, he said, "You no have devil; your mama kep' it for hersel' when you born. But your brudda . . ." He trailed off and sucked an ominous breath in through his wonky teeth.

Curious to know what he meant, Chantelle was about to ask when the door opened behind her and a gust of freezing air swirled around her legs.

"It's kicking *right* off out there," the woman who came in declared excitedly as she approached the counter. "That nonce has just walked round the corner bold as brass, and them black lads are having a right go at him. No offence," she added quickly for Chantelle's benefit, "but there's two lots of 'em what hang around outside here of a night, one black, one white."

Chantelle bit her tongue and handed her money over to Jimmy when he placed her wrapped food on the counter.

"Be careful," he cautioned as he pressed her change into her hand. "Go other way, and run run run."

"Don't worry, I'll be fine," Chantelle murmured, hugging the warm parcels to her chest and stepping back out into the cold.

Outside the burned-out TV repair shop at the other end of the row, several youths had formed a circle around the old man who was known locally as Paedo Bob. It was rumoured that he had once been arrested for flashing his bits at some kids in the park, and everyone on the estate hated him even though he'd never actually been charged. Whether or not it was true, Chantelle couldn't help but feel sorry for him now as she watched him turn this way and that, trying to grab back the filthy multicoloured bobble-hat that the lads were tossing to each other over his head. They were all

24

much younger, taller and stronger than him, and they might be laughing now, but Chantelle knew their mood could easily turn. One wrong word and Bob would be on the floor with a flurry of feet aiming at his head.

As she stood there, torn between minding her own business and intervening, Chantelle felt a prickle on the back of her neck as if someone was staring at her. She snapped her gaze to the left and was surprised to see Anton Davis leaning casually back against the wall, smoking a cigarette. A slow smile came onto his lips when their eyes met, and she felt a blush rise to her cheeks. She hadn't seen him around in a while and had heard that he'd been sent down, although she didn't know what for. He'd always been good-looking, and all the girls at school had fancied him. Loads of them had even fought over him, but Chantelle had always steered well clear — partly because of his reputation but mainly because she'd seen enough girls fall for boys like him to know that, whatever kick girls got out of being a bad boy's bitch-of-the-moment, it was never worth the inevitable heartache. They either ended up hitting you, cheating on you, or getting you pregnant — none of which Chantelle was stupid enough to volunteer for.

When the old man suddenly let out a cry, Chantelle turned her attention back to the gang. They had stopped throwing the hat and were now pushing Bob around, and when she saw from their expressions that they were no longer playing, she yelled, "Oi! Pack it in, you lot. Leave him alone."

They all turned and stared at her, and for an awful moment she thought they were going to start on her instead. But then Anton whistled softly between his teeth and, like a pack of dogs obeying a command, the lads backed away. Still smiling, Anton winked at her. Then, jerking his head at his mates, he turned and walked away.

"Thanks, love," the old man gasped as he staggered towards Chantelle, his unshaven face grey, his bloodshot eyes bulging with fear and indignation. "I thought I'd had it there. They want bloody hanging!"

"If anyone wants hanging round here, it's *you*," bellowed the woman from the chip shop, who had just stepped out behind Chantelle. "Blokes like you want your dicks cutting off and rammin' down your throats, if you ask me. Now, *gercha*, before I do it meself, y' dirty auld bastard!"

She swung her bag at him and cackled with jubilation when he fled back the way he'd come. "I fuckin' hate nonces, me," she told Chantelle when he'd gone. "If I had my way, they'd bang the whole filthy lot of 'em up in a cell and let 'em bugger each other senseless — see how *they* like it."

Venom vented, she walked away, leaving Chantelle with a bitter taste in her mouth. She'd lived on this estate her entire life, and most of her neighbours were decent. But for every good one on the left, it seemed there was a replica of that nasty bitch on the right: gobby, bigoted, and ready to attack at the drop of a hat. At times like this, she couldn't wait to leave school and get a good job so she could get the hell out of here.

"Who was that girl back at the shops?" Anton asked his mate, Shotz, when they had left the other lads and were heading up the stairs of their block.

"Some mate of our Teshia's from school," Shotz told him. "Think her name's Chanel, or Chantelle, or something. Why?"

"No reason," Anton said casually, although he was secretly disappointed to hear that she was still a schoolie because he'd thought she looked older. It explained why he hadn't recognised her, though, because he'd never even *looked* at the younger girls when he'd still been at school; too busy working his way through the ones of his own age to bother.

"Coming up to mine for a smoke?" Shotz asked when they reached Anton's floor.

"In a bit," Anton told him. "Just need to jump in the bath and get changed first."

"Laters." Shotz touched fists with him before bouncing up the stairs to his place on the floor above.

Anton was deep in thought as he walked on down the landing to his mum's flat. He hadn't long come home after serving eighteen months of his three-year sentence, and he was finding it hard to adjust. Not because anything had dramatically changed, but because it *hadn't*. Everyone was acting the same as before he'd left, and they all seemed to think that he should be able to pick up where he'd left off without missing a beat. But *he* had changed, so it wasn't that easy. All that shit back at the shops just now, for example. Back in the day, he'd probably have joined in with his mates' game of piggy-in-the-middle with the old nonce, but he just couldn't see the fun in it any more. All he could think about was the shit they could have landed him in if it had got out of hand, as it generally did with those guys. It wasn't their fault that he'd changed, so he knew he shouldn't be too hard on them. But they had to keep that shit away from him while he was on probation, because there was no way he was going back down for them — or anyone.

Just seconds after Anton had gone inside his mum's flat and closed the door, Chantelle came up the stairs and walked to a flat five along from his.

Kermit's mum, Linda, smiled when she answered the door. "All right, love . . . here for your Leon? They're in our Kermit's room playing that *Reverend Evil* — or whatever they call it. Come in while I fetch him."

"No, you're all right, I'll wait here. Need to get home before the chips go cold." Chantelle nodded down at the parcels in her arms to prove that she really did have chips and wasn't just making excuses — although that was exactly what she *was* doing. The one and only time she had made the mistake of going inside, Kermit's little brothers and sisters had leapt on her and by the time Linda had managed to prise them off her blazer had been smeared with snot, and the stench of dirty nappies had clung to her for days afterwards. So now, if she had to come round here, she always stayed out on the landing.

Leon was frowning when he came to the door. He'd been begging for a PlayStation for every Christmas and birthday for as long as he could remember, but his mum always said she couldn't afford it so the only chance he ever got to play on one was when he came round here.

"I've only just got here," he complained, staying put in the hall and talking to his sister through the crack in the door. "I'll come back in a bit."

Chantelle shook her head. "No, the chips will be freezing. Come on."

"I'm not hungry. Kermit made us some toast."

"You knew I was going to the chippy so you should have said no," Chantelle scolded. "Anyway, I told you I'd be coming for you, so stop messing about."

"Can't I just finish my game?"

"No, it's too dark, so just do as you're told — and hurry up."

"I *hate* you," Leon spat, turning on his heel and marching back to Kermit's bedroom to get his jacket.

"Watch it!" Chantelle protested when he came out onto the landing a few seconds later and barged past her. But he stomped ahead without answering.

Leon snatched one of the parcels out of her hand when they got home and marched into his bedroom. "You forgot your gravy," Chantelle called after him, but he muttered, "Stick it up your arse" and slammed the door in her face.

Seconds later, the monotonous *Boom! Boom! Boom!* of the anti-everything rap music that he had recently taken a liking to started blasting out. Chantelle squeezed her eyes shut when her head began to throb along to the beat. She felt like kicking the door open and tossing his cheap stereo out of the window — and him along with it. But she couldn't take any more aggravation, so she bit down on the anger and went into the kitchen to eat her dinner. Then, taking her books into her own bedroom, she stuffed cotton wool into her ears and tried to get on with her revision.

She woke with a start some time later to the sound of someone hammering on the front door. Disoriented by the cotton wool in her ears, it took her a few moments to get her bearings. Then, jumping up, sending the books that had been on her lap flying onto the floor, she ran out into the hall. Leon's music was still pumping out loudly from behind his door. Banging on it as she passed, she peered out through the spyhole and groaned when she saw the irate next-door neighbour standing there.

"I know," she said apologetically when she opened the door, pre-empting the complaint that she knew was coming. "I'll make him turn it off."

"Do you know what bloody time it is?" Stuart Price barked, refusing to be placated before he'd had his say. The music had been booming through the wall since earlier that evening and he'd had a gutful of it. He and his wife were decent, hardworking people, and they shouldn't have to put up with this kind of anti-social behaviour. He'd complained to the council — anonymously — on numerous occasions to no avail; and the police had been no better. This girl had given him a fair few dirty looks over the years but, unlike her mother and brother, at least she had never resorted to being outright abusive. It was the boy who was behind the noise, he was sure. The little bastard was a foul-mouthed, destructive, sly little thug-in-the-making who strutted around the estate as if he owned it. He needed a bloody good slap — and the mood Stuart was in right now, he'd have loved to be the one to administer it.

"I'm sorry," Chantelle apologised again. "I was asleep."

"Lucky you!" snapped Stuart. "Six hours we've been putting up with this racket — *six ... bloody ... hours!*"

"I know," Chantelle repeated guiltily. "And I —"

"Have you any idea what it's doing to my poor wife?" Stuart continued, gesturing angrily back towards his own flat. "She's ill in there, and the doctor said she needs complete rest. But how the hell is she supposed to rest with this going on?"

"I'll sort it out," Chantelle assured him when he paused to draw breath.

"You'd better," Stuart warned, "because I'm this close to calling the police." He held up his hand and squeezed his thumb and forefinger together, before adding, "And then I'll report you to the council, because you're making our lives a living bloody hell!"

His voice had risen in pitch and his face was so red that he looked like he was going to have a fit. Chantelle had never particularly cared for him, because he was such a miserable old git, but she genuinely felt sorry for him and his wife right now.

"I'm really, really sorry," she told him sincerely. "I'll make sure it goes off. And it won't happen again — I promise."

Stuart wanted to go on, but he sensed from the pained look in her eyes that the girl was as distressed as he and his wife were, and it pierced his bubble of anger. Exhaling wearily, he said, "Yes, well, just make sure it doesn't. I know it's not your fault, and I really don't want to cause trouble, but this is unacceptable — you must see that?"

Chantelle nodded and, promising again that she would sort it out, closed the door. Then, gritting her teeth, she marched into Leon's room. Furious to see that he had pulled his quilt up over his head and gone to sleep, leaving his CD on repeat play, she switched his hi-fi off and stood over him. The temptation to wake him and give him what-for was overwhelming, but she knew that would only end up in another row, which was the last thing she needed with Stuart already on the warpath. So, resisting the urge, she went back to her own room, telling herself that their mum could deal with him in the morning.

# CHAPTER
# THREE

When she woke the next morning, Chantelle wasn't impressed to see that her mum still hadn't come home or switched her phone back on. Determined not to have a repeat of yesterday when, thanks to Leon, she hadn't been able to properly concentrate on her revision, she got dressed and pulled her coat on, all set to march round to Tracey's and drag her mum back.

Before she went, she popped her head around Leon's door and sighed when she saw him spreadeagled across the bed. As much as he'd been annoying her lately with his smart mouth and cocky attitude, he was still her baby brother and she loved him to bits. She always had — from the first time she'd ever clapped eyes on him when his dad, Glenroy King, had brought him and their mum home from hospital. He'd been a living, breathing dolly, and Chantelle had insisted on changing his nappies and feeding him his bottles — which had delighted their mum, because it had left her free to run after Glenroy. Not that it had worked, because he had walked out soon after.

A muscular bald-headed Jamaican with a dazzling smile, a husky voice and a smooth line in patter, Glenroy had spread his love freely around every willing female on the estate — Mary's friends included. He'd also had a vicious temper and, as young as she'd been back then, Chantelle still remembered how scared her mum used to be when he'd get in a mood. His eyes would blaze as if there was a fire burning behind them, and his fists would fly with the slightest provocation. Unfortunately, Leon had inherited that temper along with the good looks, and Chantelle sometimes wondered how their mum was going to cope with him when he got bigger and started hitting out — and he would, she was sure, because it was in his genes.

But she didn't want to think about that right now. So, quietly closing his door, she let herself out and walked quickly over to Tracey's flat. After knocking several times and getting no answer, she gave up and headed over to the Saturday market in Moss Side to pick up a few cheap bits for dinner. But if her mum thought she was going to walk in later in the day and find a plateful waiting for her in the oven, she had another think coming. And God help her if she'd spent the rest of the benefit money on booze and whatever else she'd necked with Tracey last night, because then Chantelle would have her guts for garters.

Kermit was on the other side of the Princess Parkway when he spotted Chantelle heading into the market. His mum had made plans to take the younger kids to the carnival in Alexandra Park, but she was skint, so she'd sent Kermit to borrow twenty quid off his nan. He'd begged her to send their Jimmy instead, but she'd said Jimmy was too young to cross the road on his own.

And, anyway, Kermit was his nan's favourite so he had the best chance of making the old girl cough up.

Kermit didn't like his nan. She had see-through skin, a sloppy, toothless mouth, and her room in the sheltered housing unit stank of cat piss even though there were no cats living there. She herself stank of human piss and talc, and she always made him sit next to her so she could *stroke* him and *kiss* him.

The feel of her flesh touching his made him gag, so he'd been in and out of there as fast as was humanly possible today — the £20 note for his mum in one pocket, the half-bottle of whisky he'd swiped off the dresser when his nan turned her back to get her purse in the other. His mum would go ape-shit if she found out, but he considered it payment for the disgusting trail of slime his nan had left on his cheek when she'd kissed him goodbye. Anyway, the old cow was so batty that she'd probably think she'd lost the whisky — if she even remembered she'd had it in the first place.

When Kermit saw Chantelle now, he grinned to himself. She was one of the most beautiful girls he'd ever seen, but she had a way of looking at him that made him wonder if she could read his thoughts and see the dirty things he sometimes thought about her when he was in the bath. He always avoided going round to their place if he knew there was a chance of bumping into her, but it was safe right now so he darted through the morning traffic and ran all the way home.

"Where are you going?" his mum asked when he barrelled through the door and chucked the money at her. "Aren't you coming to the carny?"

"Nah," he called back over his shoulder. "I'm going to see if Leon wants to come round and play on my game."

"Well, don't make a mess," his mum yelled after him. "I've got that woman coming round from the council on Monday, and I don't want to have to spend all day Sunday cleaning up after you."

Kermit waved over his shoulder and slammed the door.

Leon was woken by the sound of someone knocking insistently on the front door. Too cosy to move, he pulled his quilt over his head and waited for his sister to answer it. When she didn't, and the knocking continued, he reluctantly got up and stomped out into the hall in his underpants, all set to give the unwelcome caller a piece of his mind.

"What you doing here so early?" he complained, rubbing the sleep from his eyes when he saw Kermit on the step. "I was having a boss dream, and you've ruined it."

"Soz," Kermit apologised. "Me ma's taking the brats to the carny, and I've just seen your Channy going in the market, so I thought you might wanna come round and get back on the game. I got to level four after you took off last night. It was well hard, but I proper smashed it."

36

"Why didn't you wait for me?" Leon protested, gesturing for his friend to come inside. "I'm gonna have loads of catching up to do now."

"Yeah, well, hurry up and get dressed," said Kermit, following him into his room. "I've got a surprise for ya."

"What?" Leon pulled on a pair of jeans.

Kermit reached into his pocket and brought out the stolen bottle.

"Where'd you get that?" Leon's eyes widened. "Giz it."

"Not here." Kermit stuffed it away again. "I just nicked it off me nan."

"Like your style, bruv." Leon grinned his approval and pulled a jumper over his head. Then, stuffing his sockless feet into his trainers, he said, "Come on, let's get out of here before our kid gets back. Me mum went out last night and our Chan was in a right one. Bitch is lucky I didn't slit her throat, the way she's been talking to me lately."

"Yeah, but she's fit," Kermit said as he followed him out of the bedroom. "I'd slip her a stiff one."

"Shut your gob, y' mong!" Leon pulled a disgusted face and shoved his friend out onto the landing.

Chantelle assumed that Leon must still be sleeping when she got home a short time later. Glad of the peace, she decided not to disturb him and quietly put the shopping away, leaving out the two pieces of chicken she'd bought for tonight's dinner. Leon claimed to hate her cooking, but he'd always loved her curried chicken and rice so she'd thought she would treat him to make up for their row yesterday. And if he was really good, she might make a batch of his favourite homemade macaroni cheese.

Confident that there would be no more trouble from Leon once he saw that she was making an effort, she made herself a cup of tea and went to her bedroom to resume the revision that she'd fallen asleep over the night before.

Leon had never tasted whisky in his life before. But he was a man, and men didn't admit shit like that. So when Kermit — lying through his teeth and claiming to have done it loads of times — offered the bottle to him for first dibs, he fronted it out and took a big swig. His eyes watered when the sharp, bitter alcohol hit his tongue, and he almost choked when it went on to assault his throat. But he forced himself not to spit it straight back out and handed the bottle over to Kermit.

"You all right?" Kermit asked, eyeing him excitedly.

"Yeah, course." Leon shrugged. "Go on — your turn."

Kermit took a tentative sip and pulled a face.

"Ah, you fuckin' lightweight!" Leon crowed, snapping his fingers in the air in a gesture of victory.

"I'm gonna get some pop." Kermit jumped up and rushed out of the room.

Leon scraped at his tongue and coughed to clear the heat from his burning throat when his friend had gone. Composed by the time Kermit came back with a bottle of lemonade and two plastic cups, he gave a nonchalant shrug when Kermit asked if he wanted his next shot neat or mixed, and said, "Not bothered." Then, pursing his lips, he added, "But I suppose I'd best have a bit if you're having it. Don't wanna get pissed on me own while you're having *baby* drinks, do I?"

Kermit ignored the jibe and sloshed two large helpings of lemonade over the inch of whisky he'd already poured into the cups. Handing Leon's to him, he grinned. "You go first."

Leon braced himself and downed his drink in one, then wiped his sleeve across his mouth and held out his cup for a refill. He might be the younger by two years, but he wasn't about to let Kermit get one over on him.

Light-headed by the time they had finished their second drinks, the boys fired up the PlayStation. But it wasn't long before they started squabbling.

"I haven't fuckin' cheated," Kermit insisted when Leon accused him for the third time. "Ain't my fault I'm better at it than you."

"Are you fuck!" Leon argued. "I'm way better than you, and if I had my own console and was on it twenty-four-seven like you, I'd mash you the fuck up."

"I'm hardly ever on it when you're not here," Kermit lied. "I've just got skills — and you're just jealous, 'cos you know you can't touch me."

"That right?" Leon punched him in the arm. "Touched you then, though, didn't I? So what you saying now, shithead? Eh? Eh? Not man enough to fight back?"

Infuriated when Leon started punching him repeatedly in the arm, Kermit threw down the control pad and jumped on him. They rolled around on the bed for several seconds before falling onto the floor in a tangled heap. Then, grunting and wheezing for breath, they grappled until they got themselves wedged between the end of the bed and the chest of drawers. Unable to move, they looked into each other's eyes and burst out laughing.

"Let's have another drink?" Kermit suggested when the laughter had subsided.

"And a smoke," added Leon, pushing his friend towards the door. "Go grab some of your mam's dimps."

Kermit did as he'd been told, and came back with a packet of Rizla papers and a handful of crumpled, black-tipped dog-ends from his mum's bedroom. It was the only room in the flat that she ever smoked in, because she didn't want to pollute the younger kids' lungs, and the place might as well have been a giant ashtray given how many dimps were lying around. Kermit wished she hadn't switched to roll-ups, because he preferred the taste of the proper cigs she used to smoke. But she reckoned she couldn't afford them any more, and beggars couldn't be choosers, so he tore a couple of papers out of the pack, then carefully rolled a couple of fresh smokes from the ashy remnants.

"That's mingin'," Leon complained, spitting out a piece of blackened tobacco after lighting up. "It'd taste well better with weed."

"Yeah, I know," Kermit agreed, squinting as he tugged on his own smoke. "But we ain't got any."

"So let's go get some."

"How? We ain't got no money."

Leon shrugged and reached for the drink he'd poured when Kermit had gone dimp-hunting. "We could go down the canal and see if Damo and the lads are there?"

"I don't know." Kermit gave him an uncertain look. "I don't think they like us."

"They might not like you, but they're cool with me," Leon sneered. "That's 'cos I'm not a wuss like you."

Kermit's heart sank as he watched Leon quickly down his drink. It was all right for him: he didn't go to the same school as Damo and the other lads, so he'd never seen them when they were bullying the smaller kids. Kermit was shit-scared of the lot of them, but Leon thought they were ace and was always going out of his way to bump into them. Amazingly, even though they were all way older than him, they didn't seem to mind; but Kermit had a suspicion that was because Leon was black. If he'd been white, they would probably have battered him by now for being such a pest. And it didn't even matter that most of them were white themselves; they *acted* black, so that *made* them black in their eyes.

"Come on," Leon said impatiently when he'd finished his drink and noticed that Kermit hadn't even touched his yet. "We ain't got all day."

He jumped up now and, shoving the bottle with what was left of the whisky in it into his pocket, headed for the door. Aware that his friend was going to go with or without him, Kermit reluctantly finished his drink. Then, carrying the cups into the kitchen, he rinsed them out so that his mum wouldn't smell the alcohol before following Leon out.

Chantelle only discovered that Leon was out when she took him a sandwich at lunchtime. She was a bit annoyed that he'd gone out without telling her, but he always hung out with his mates at the weekend so it wasn't exactly unusual. And their mum never made a fuss about it, so she supposed she had no reason to either. She had to admit it had been good to have a bit of peace, because the revising had been going pretty well so far and she was beginning to think that maybe the exams wouldn't be too bad, after all.

She spent the rest of the day in her room, only coming out to make dinner at six. Leon still wasn't back by the time she'd finished cooking, so she covered his plate and put it in the oven. When he still hadn't come home by eight she guessed that he was probably at Kermit's and had forgotten the time because he was immersed in that stupid computer game they had been playing. She decided to go and get him.

"Sorry, love, I haven't seen him," Linda told her when she answered the door. "I know he was here earlier, 'cos our Kermit told me he was going to call for him when I went to the carny. But he'd gone by the time I got home."

"What time was that?" Chantelle asked.

"Round six-ish." Linda folded her arms and frowned when she saw the worry in the girl's eyes. "What's up, love? Hasn't he been home yet?"

"No." Chantelle shook her head and bit her lip. Leon had loads of mates, but none of the others' parents were as tolerant as Linda so this was the only place he was ever allowed to hang out for any length of time. But if he wasn't here, where the hell was he? "Can I speak to Kermit for a minute?" she asked.

"Oh, I don't know," Linda said uncertainly. "He wasn't very well when I came in, so I told him to go for a lie-down."

"Well, can *you* talk to him?" Chantelle urged. "Please. I'm really worried."

Linda sighed. Then, nodding, she stepped back. "All right. Come in for a minute."

For once, Chantelle didn't object. Right now, she was more concerned about finding Leon than fending off Kermit's snot-nosed siblings. Fortunately, none of the younger children were up, so she stood in the hall unmolested as Linda went to talk to Kermit. Already edgy, she was annoyed when she heard the boy yelling at his mother to get out and, unable to stop herself, she marched into his room. Kermit was curled up in a ball in the bed with his quilt drawn up around his face. Apologising to Linda for barging in, Chantelle reached down and yanked the quilt back.

"What you doing?" Kermit protested, snatching at it and squinting up at her.

As soon as she looked into his bloodshot eyes, Chantelle knew that he was wrecked, and her concerns intensified. "Where's Leon?" she demanded.

"I dunno," Kermit muttered, his gaze swivelling guiltily.

"You're lying," Chantelle barked.

"Hey, there's no need for that." Linda jumped to her son's defence. "If he says he don't know, then he don't know. And he's not well, so I think you'd better go now."

She gestured towards the door, but Chantelle wasn't ready to leave yet. "Don't protect him," she said sharply. "He's not ill, he's *wasted*."

"What d'you mean?" Linda frowned.

"I mean he's *high*," said Chantelle, wondering how the woman could have lived on this estate for so long and still not know the first thing about drugs.

"Course he's not," Linda scoffed. "He doesn't even smoke — do you, son?"

Kermit's face was already pale, but when it suddenly turned a strange shade of green Chantelle knew what was coming and leapt away from the bed just in time.

"Oh, now look what you've done!" Linda yelped when her son threw up all over the carpet. "I told you he wasn't well, so why did you have to go shouting at him like that? Whatever your Leon's up to, it's not my Kermit's fault. I'm surprised at you, Chantelle, I really am. I thought you were better than that."

Chantelle felt bad for upsetting the woman but she was more concerned about Leon now than ever, and she needed Kermit to tell her where they had been and what they had been doing. It hadn't even crossed her mind until now that Leon might be taking drugs. But if Kermit had been taking them, and they had been together, then Leon must have tried them too.

44

"Kermit, I'm not angry with you," she lied, softening her tone as she gazed down at the boy. "And I'm sorry if I scared you, but I really need to know where Leon is. I don't want to call the police, but if you won't tell me where Leon is, I'll have no choice."

Kermit gazed back at her guiltily and licked his dry lips. "Promise you won't tell him it were me what told?"

"I promise. But please just tell me."

"He was down by the canal when I left him."

"On his own?" Chantelle was horrified. "Oh, God, it's really dark out there. What if he's fallen in? How could you be so stupid?"

"He's not on his own." Kermit flicked a nervous glance at his mother. "He's with some lads."

"Who?" Chantelle demanded.

Kermit swallowed loudly and shrugged. "Just some lads from my school."

"Older lads?" Chantelle asked, frowning down at him. "Is that where you got the weed?"

"Yes." Kermit's voice was little more than a whisper.

"And you've been drinking as well, haven't you?" Chantelle persisted, picking up the bitter scent of alcohol on his breath.

When Kermit nodded, Linda barked, "Oh, you've had it now, boy! You told me you was sick, but you never said nowt about drugs and drinking. You just wait till your dad finds out, he'll —"

Chantelle didn't hang around to hear the rest. Her brother was out there in the dark with some older boys, doing God only knew what. He thought he was streetwise, but it was one thing acting the big man in front of his mates and quite a different matter doing it in front of strangers who had already plied him with drugs and booze. What was to say they hadn't made him sniff glue, or smoke crack, or something, as well? That was the kind of thing teenage lads seemed to get a kick out of doing to younger kids round here lately.

Terrified that she was going to find her brother floating face down in the filthy canal water, Chantelle ran through the estate and down the steps to the towpath. The moon was shrouded in clouds so it was pitch dark, and the sound of the water lapping close to the edge of the path as she made her way slowly along filled her with dread.

As she rounded the wide bend where the canal turned towards the locks, she heard the faint sound of laughter up ahead and quickened her pace. The clouds momentarily shifted and she caught a glimpse of several silhouetted figures in the near-distance. They were laughing and jeering, and her heart leapt into her throat when she got closer and saw that a safety barrier had been untethered from the locks' mechanism and pushed out over the water. Leon, with his arms outstretched at the sides, was walking slowly along it, urged on by prods from the big stick that one of the lads was jabbing into his back.

"Oh my *God!*" she gasped, pushing her way through the boys. "Get him down before he falls, you idiots!"

"Yo! What the fuck . . .?" the lad with the stick protested, scrabbling to keep his footing when Chantelle nearly sent him flying. Righting himself, he turned and glared at her. "See if these garms get wet . . ." He sucked his teeth, before adding in a Jamaican accent, "Man, me haf' fe shoot yuh, t' raas!"

Unimpressed, Chantelle glared at him. He only looked to be about fifteen, judging by the fluff on his upper lip, and he was white, so the bad-boy posturing left her cold. "Get . . . him . . . *down*," she ordered. "He's only a kid; you should be ashamed of yourself."

"He's having fun," the lad informed her, with a grin. "You wanna chill out, sis."

"I am not your sis," she spat through gritted teeth. "I'm *his*!" She pointed at Leon. "And if you don't get him down right now, I'm going to call the police and tell them you've been giving him drugs."

The grin was gone in a flash, and the lad stepped right up to her. "Wouldn't do that if I was you, darlin'."

Chantelle's stomach was churning, but she forced herself to hold the boy's gaze and pulled her phone out of her pocket. "One . . ." she said, pressing her thumb down on the 9 button.

"Leave it, man," one of the others said, tugging on his friend's arm. "Let's chip, yeah?"

But the aggressive one hadn't finished with Chantelle yet. "Nice phone," he drawled, a nasty glint in his eye. "Giz it here."

"Get real!" Chantelle snapped, jerking it out of reach when he made a grab for it. "What you gonna do — beat me up for it?"

"That what you want, is it?"

"Think you're a proper hard man, don't you?" Chantelle sneered, standing her ground even though her legs were shaking wildly. "Go on, then. *Do* it!"

Before he could make a move, one of the others, who had until then been sitting watching, stood up. "Right, that's enough," he said. "Get the kid down, and let's get out of here."

Chantelle sobbed with relief when one of the lads pulled Leon off the barrier and brought him back to the path. She ran over to him to make sure he was okay, but he shoved her away.

"What do *you* want? Coming here shootin' your mouth off, spoiling everyone's fun."

"Don't you dare talk to me like that!" Chantelle yelled, grabbing him by the front of his jacket and shaking him roughly. "Have you any idea how dangerous that was? You could have *died*! It's pitch black, and you're off your head!"

"*Yo!*" Leon spat, twisting free and brushing at his jacket as if she'd smeared it with shit. "Gyal mekkin' pure mess of man's garms."

"Stop talking like a moron and get yourself home," Chantelle barked, completely unimpressed.

"Make me!" Leon jerked his chin up in defiance.

Unable to stop herself, Chantelle swung out her hand and slapped him hard across the face. Then, with the gang's laughter ringing in her ears, she gripped him by the back of his collar and, almost lifting him clean off his feet, marched him back up the path.

Anton Davis lit his spliff and took a deep toke, relishing the feel of the smoke rolling down his throat. He'd had a long, boring day at work and couldn't wait to jump in the bath. But he'd be going straight back out as soon as he was dry, because there was no way he was sitting around watching his mum and her boyfriend make goo-goo eyes at each other.

Phil Green had moved in while Anton was locked up, and the flat reeked of the dude's cheesy socks and cheap aftershave. But it was the fact that he didn't work that really pissed Anton off. Even when he'd still been at school, Anton had always done his bit to keep the family going. The money might not have always come from the most legitimate of sources but it had paid for the TV that the lazy bastard seemed to think was his now — *and* the couch he spent the majority of his life sprawled out on.

Anton couldn't wait to get a place of his own, but he'd put his name down with the council when he was released so all he could do was wait until something came up. Until then, he was staying out of his mum and Phil's way in case the temptation to knock the dude out became too strong to resist. His mum had had a tough time after Anton's dad had died, and none of her subsequent relationships had lasted very long. The last one had resulted in the birth of Anton's little sister, Rachel. She was almost five now, and there had been no one in his mum's life since Rachel's dad had done a flit. Until Phil came along, that was. And, as much as Anton didn't like him, his mum did, so he wasn't about to ruin it for her.

As long as the dude behaved himself.

First sign that he was stepping out of line, Anton would be all over him.

He had just reached his mum's block when two shadowy figures emerged from the side of the bin cupboards. Stepping aside to let them pass, he hesitated when he saw that one of them was Chantelle. He'd been disappointed to hear that she was still at school, but that hadn't stopped him from thinking about her since. Tall and model-slim, she was the spit of the young Whitney Houston, from the creamy butterscotch complexion to the sexy long-lashed almond-shaped eyes. He'd been with more girls than he cared to remember in his younger days, but none — and he meant *none* — had been a patch on her.

He gazed at her now as she marched past with a young scowling boy in tow, and asked, "Is everything all right?"

"Mind your own business!" she muttered, walking on without so much as glancing at him.

Anton watched as she dragged the boy through the flats' main door and up the stairs. The boy complained loudly all the way up through the floors, and Anton couldn't help but smile when he heard the girl warn him to hush his mouth or she would give him licks. She was a feisty one, all right — but not trash-talking feisty, like so many of the other girls on the estate. There was something kind of dignified about her and, while he'd only been half-joking when he'd told Shotz over a spliff last night that he was going to get off with her, now he meant it. One way or another, that girl was going to be his.

# CHAPTER
# FOUR

Monday dawned bright but Chantelle was in no mood to appreciate the overdue sunshine. Her mum still hadn't come home, and her phone was still off, so even if she'd seen the numerous messages that Chantelle had sent she obviously had no intention of replying to them.

She could be lying dead in a ditch for all Chantelle knew, and if this was the first time that Mary had gone awol Chantelle might have been tempted to call the police. But her mum's best mate Tracey was also nowhere to be found, so her instincts told her that they had most likely hooked up with some losers at that party her mum had said they were going to and had spent the weekend with them.

Pissed off about that — and sick to her stomach at the thought of sitting her first exam without preparation, thanks to Leon playing up and stopping her from revising — Chantelle struggled to shake off her foul mood as she got ready for school. It had taken every ounce of self-control to keep from throttling Leon after finding him down by the canal on Saturday night, and she'd had to keep such a close eye on him after that to make sure he didn't sneak out again that she hadn't retained a single word from the tiny bit of studying she had managed to do. She just knew she was going to fail her exams, but there was nothing she could do about it now except try her best — and pray for a miracle.

Still mad at Leon, and convinced that he was dawdling to spite her, she was yelling at him to hurry up as she opened the front door. But the words died in her throat when she found herself face to face with a man she'd never seen before.

Ricky Benson's eyebrows twitched in surprise as he looked the girl slowly up and down. He'd known that Mary had kids, but she was as white as they came so it hadn't occurred to him that her children might be black — or as old as this. If he'd thought about it — which he hadn't — he'd have pictured some snot-nosed pasty-faced little brats. But this girl was stunning.

Already unnerved by the way the man was looking at her, a shiver of apprehension coursed down Chantelle's spine when Leon came out and the man's gaze flicked onto him. "Go on ahead," she said, giving her brother a shove in the direction of the stairwell. "I'll catch up in a minute."

When he'd gone, she reached behind her and pulled the door firmly shut. The man was wearing a leather jacket, jeans and trainers. He didn't look like a copper or a social worker, but she wasn't taking any chances. For all she knew, someone could have sussed that their mum had left them on their own and grassed them up. It had happened before, and there were enough nosy people around here for it to happen again. The next-door neighbours, for example. They rarely spoke apart from to complain, but their net curtains were forever twitching so they had to have noticed that her mum hadn't been around.

"Mum still in bed, is she?" Ricky spoke at last. When Chantelle didn't answer, he smiled. "Tell you what, why don't you open up and I'll go in and see for myself, eh?"

"I don't *think* so." Chantelle jerked her head back when his breath breezed across her face.

"Give us the key, then." Ricky held out his hand. "I'll let myself in."

"My brother's got it," Chantelle lied. "But I wouldn't let you in even if I could," she added, recovering some of her sass. "I don't even know you."

Ricky put his hand on the wall behind her head and gazed down at her. He could see her chest rising and falling, and could almost smell the fear that he could see in her eyes. He could so easily force her to open the door if he wanted to, and if she genuinely didn't have the key a swift boot would soon gain him entry. But people in the surrounding flats were starting to go about their daily business and he didn't need to be clocked pushing his weight around in broad daylight. So, smiling again, he backed up a step.

"Don't panic, darlin', I'm just an old mate of your mam's. When you see her, tell her Ricky's looking for her, yeah?"

Eyeing him warily, Chantelle nodded.

"Good girl." Ricky winked at her and then strolled away.

Chantelle leaned heavily back against the door when he'd gone and released a shuddering breath. Her legs felt like jelly and her stomach was in knots. She had been angry but now she was scared. The man had said he was an old friend of her mum's but she didn't believe him. There had been something really menacing about the way he had looked at her and Leon, and she had a horrible feeling that it wouldn't be the last she saw of him.

When a hot tear trickled slowly down her cheek, she swiped it away with the back of her hand and looked around to see if anyone was watching. Things were difficult enough without letting people see that she was distressed. Telling herself to get a grip, she raised her chin, pushed herself away from the door, and trotted down the stairs to join Leon who was waiting at the bottom.

Mary popped her head around the corner of the bin cupboards at the exact moment when her son and daughter walked out of the stairwell. She pulled back quickly and took a last drag on her fag before dropping it on the floor and grinding it out with her heel. Then, taking another peek, she saw that the coast was clear and nudged Tracey.

"They've gone. Let's go."

Teeth chattering, Tracey dragged her feet as she followed Mary up the stairs and into the flat. Every step hurt because her inner thighs were so badly chafed, and her head was banging from all the boozing and coke-snorting that they'd done over the weekend. It was Mary's fault; she was the one who had insisted they go back to the grotty hotel with the blokes they had copped off with at the party on Friday night. Tracey had been all for going home when it finished, but Mary had wanted to carry on partying. And it hadn't mattered that the blokes could barely speak a word of English, or that the one Tracey had got landed with had been a proper munter. Mary's man was good-looking, and he had drugs in his pocket, so that was as good as marriage material in her eyes.

But it was one thing spending a raunchy sex-and-drug-fuelled weekend with the guys, and quite something else to run away to Spain with them.

Sure that it was a joke, Tracey had laughed when the men had invited them last night. But Mary had taken it seriously and was now searching her bedroom for her passport.

"You do know they ain't gonna be waiting for you when you get to the airport, don't you?" Tracey cautioned from the bed as she watched her friend pull everything out of her drawers. "If they had money they wouldn't have been staying in such a shit hotel, so how they gonna afford to buy you a ticket?"

"I'm paying for my own," Mary told her, shoving knickers and bras into a bag after finding her passport. "I've still got the shopping money in my account, and the child benefit goes in on Wednesday."

"What about the kids?"

"What about 'em?"

"Aren't you going to tell them?"

"And have our Chan go off on one?" Mary pulled a face. "No chance."

"What about money? You can't just take off and leave them with nowt."

Mary rolled her eyes and carried on packing. Tracey had been moaning all the way back in the taxi and it was doing her head in.

"You're out of order," Tracey said disapprovingly.

"If you're that fucking worried about them, *you* look after them," Mary said. "I've done my bit, now I'm putting myself first for a change."

"What am I supposed to say if your Channy asks where you are? She's been ringing me all weekend an' all, you know."

"Tell her I'm having a break." Mary zipped her bag up. "And if she moans about money, tell her to go and get some off Leon's dad. It's about time that selfish bastard dipped his hand into his pocket instead of leaving it all up to me."

Tracey shook her head. "You're mad, you. Anyhow, you can't get on a flight just like that. You have to book tickets and get a visa, and all that."

"Not for Spain, you don't," Mary informed her, with a knowing smile. "I've been there before, don't forget."

"I still think you're mad," Tracey said, getting up and traipsing along behind Mary when she picked up her bag and headed for the door. "There's no way them blokes'll be waiting. You were just a shag."

"We'll see," Mary said unconcernedly as she stood in the hall and phoned the local taxi rank. Tracey could think what she liked. Miguel knew a good thing when he saw it, and Mary knew he'd been serious about her going home with him. The sex had blown his mind, and he'd have to be an idiot to turn his back on that. No . . . Tracey was wrong. He *would* be waiting for her — Mary could feel it in her bones.

The taxi pulled up a couple of minutes after the women walked down the stairs. Mary threw her bag onto the back seat and turned to Tracey. "Last chance to change your mind?"

"Nah, I'm too tired." Tracey folded her arms. "See you in half an hour — when you realise they've gone without you and come home with your tail between your legs," she added sarcastically.

"Whatever," Mary said tartly.

Tracey stood and watched as the taxi drove away. Then, shaking her head, she went home.

# CHAPTER
# FIVE

The permanent stench of rotten vegetables lingered in the air inside Abdul's, and many a shopper had been scared half to death by the sight of a mouse jumping out at them from between the goods on the shelves. Most of the estate residents had avoided it in favour of the nearby Netto, but since that store had closed down a few months earlier they'd had no choice but to come back. Either that, or stump up to travel to the bigger, more expensive supermarkets on the outskirts of town.

Abdul had been delighted to welcome his customers back. But along with the surge in trade had come an increase in shoplifting, and when his takings had started to suffer he'd been forced to hire a security guard — which had brought a whole new set of problems of its own. Those who came from outside the area couldn't handle the intimidation from the gangs who hung around outside the shop, so they rarely lasted for more than a few days. And those who lived on the estate who *could* take the stick were often as sticky-fingered as their neighbours.

Still, at least the local ones were tough enough to provide a deterrent to the protection racketeers who preyed on small stores like his, so Abdul was prepared to turn a blind eye when they left with bulging pockets at the end of a shift. But he refused to overlook his customers' thieving ways — especially those whom he had previously caught red-handed. So when Tracey Smith walked into the shop this afternoon he folded his arms over his fat belly and stared at her as she made her way up the crowded first aisle.

Tracey wasn't about to let a little thing like being watched deter her. After Mary had left that morning, she'd gone straight to bed. She needed a drink now and, in her world, if you wanted something but didn't have the money to pay for it, you took it — simple. And all the better if the shopkeeper was foreign, like Abdul, because that wasn't really theft in her eyes: it was her *right* as a British citizen to reclaim what the bastards had been stealing from her country for years.

She weaved slowly through the other customers now and made her way round to the second aisle, pausing here and there to examine the contents of the freezer cabinets. Picking out a box of fish fingers that she knew she could afford to pay for if challenged, she dropped it into a basket and carried it round into the third aisle, where the alcohol was housed.

Tracey made her way slowly down this aisle until she reached the section she wanted. Then, keeping her back to the bottles, she leaned forward and peered at the cereal boxes opposite as if trying to decide which she fancied for breakfast tomorrow, whilst surreptitiously reaching behind her to lift what she'd come for. Mission accomplished, she dropped the basket and turned to leave.

"Jeezus!" she squawked when she bumped straight into Chantelle. "You scared the shit out of me!"

"Sorry," Chantelle apologised, looking past the woman with hope in her eyes. "Where's my mum?"

"Don't ask me," Tracey muttered, her gaze fixed on the security guard who had just strolled onto the shop floor. The door had been unmanned when she came in, and she'd thought that she would easily get out again. But this complicated things.

"I thought she was with you?" Chantelle frowned.

"Yeah, she was," Tracey said distractedly, her focus on Abdul now as he pointed the guard in her direction.

"Well, she's not at home, 'cos I've just been there," said Chantelle. "So, where is she?"

"For God's sake, get off my back!" Tracey snapped, backing away when the guard turned and started heading their way. "It's got nowt to do with me."

"Hang about," Chantelle called when Tracey suddenly turned and legged it.

The guard was about to give chase but changed his mind when he spotted Chantelle. Keeping it cool, he sauntered towards her. "All right?"

"Fine, thanks," Chantelle murmured, going up onto her tiptoes to keep track of the top of Tracey's head as she dodged through the shoppers in the centre aisle.

"You don't look it," the guard said, adding quietly, "Don't worry, I won't drop you in it."

"For what?" Chantelle snapped her head around and looked at him for the first time. Her cheeks reddened when she saw that it was Anton.

"Abdul saw your mate nick the booze," he told her. "But I'll tell him it had nothing to do with you."

"And you'd be *right*," said Chantelle, offended that he could even think such a thing. She had never stolen anything in her life, because she had seen her mum get arrested enough times to know that she would rather go without than suffer the shame of being branded a thief.

Anton's eyes twinkled with amusement when he heard the indignation in her voice. She was even prettier up close, and she smelled real good.

"Anton!" Abdul's voice suddenly boomed out over the tannoy. "Get back to work!"

"You work here?" Chantelle raised an eyebrow in surprise.

"You don't think I dress like this for fun, do you?" Anton nodded down at his black trousers and bomber jacket. "I'm only here 'cos I've got to be," he went on, casting a dirty look in his boss's direction. "Probation," he added, pride refusing to allow him to let her think that he was the kind of loser who would take a shit job like this of his own accord.

Chantelle was disappointed. For a moment there she had thought that maybe he wasn't as bad as people made out. But if he was only working because he had no choice, then he obviously hadn't changed.

"I've got to go," she said, conscious that she was trapped between him, the shelf, and another shopper's loaded trolley. "Excuse me."

Anton stepped aside, waved for her to go past, and watched as she went to the till and paid for the bottle of milk she'd come in for before walking quickly out of the shop. He wasn't stupid; he had seen the veil fall over her eyes at the mention of probation. She obviously thought she was better than him, but that was okay. He was out now, and there was no way he was ever going back inside, so there was plenty of time to win her over.

He made his way back to the front of the shop now, intending to take up his post at the door. But he hesitated when he heard his boss mouthing off. "You talking to me?" he asked, turning to face the man.

"Yeah, I said you're bloody useless!" Abdul's tone was scathing. "That was a full litre of vodka that thieving bitch got away with while you were busy chatting up that girl. I should take it out of your bloody wages."

Aware that customers were listening, and especially conscious of two teenage girls who he'd previously messed around with who were now giving their toddlers free rein to run riot while they watched to see what he would do, a smile came onto Anton's lips. "Say again," he said, walking calmly up to the counter behind which his boss was standing.

"I said you're an *idiot*," Abdul repeated, raising his voice for the benefit of his audience. "This is what I get for hiring low-life criminals, but you wait till I speak to your probation officer, 'cos I'll —"

Anton seized him by his shirt-front before he could finish the sentence and dragged him over the counter until they were nose to nose. "You ever mug me off like that again," he hissed, "I'll string you up by your ankles and slice your fucking throat open, then sit and watch while you bleed to death. "Y" gets me?"

Abdul let out a strangled squawk of terror when he saw the icy look in Anton's eyes and quickly nodded his agreement. Satisfied that he wouldn't make the same mistake again, Anton let him go and wiped his hands on his trousers.

*Just a few more months*, he reminded himself as he strolled to the door . . . All he had to do was stick this shit out for the remainder of his sentence to keep the probation officer off his back, and then he'd be free to get his life back on track. And the first thing he was going to do was kick this poxy job into touch.

Scared that Abdul might send the security guard after her, Tracey ran all the way home. Out of breath when she got there, she fumbled her key into the lock and fell into the hall. Hands shaking, she rushed into the kitchen, twisting the cap off the stolen bottle as she went, and slopped a large measure into a cup before carrying it and the bottle into the front room.

That was the closest she'd come to getting caught in ages and her nerves were frazzled. Abdul didn't faze her; he was too fat and soft to do anything. But that new security guard lived on the estate, and he looked like he wouldn't think twice about giving her a good hiding.

Almost jumping out of her skin when someone suddenly started hammering on the front door, she crept to the window and peeked out through the gap in the curtains. Relieved to see that it was only Chantelle, she went back to the couch and flopped down to finish her drink in peace.

Chantelle knocked a few more times. Then she raised the flap of the letter box, and shouted, "I know you're in there, Tracey, I saw you go in — and I'm not going away till you tell me where my mum is. I mean it . . . I'll stay out here all night if I have to."

As another volley of knocking echoed around the uncarpeted hall, Tracey squeezed her eyes shut and hissed, "Oh, piss off and leave me alone. I've got enough problems of me own to deal with."

Outside, Chantelle moved from the door to the window. She was sure that she'd seen Tracey going into the flat but the room was pitch dark when she peered through the thin gap between the curtains, so maybe she'd got it wrong?

Too cold to carry out her threat of staying there all night, and scared that Leon might take off if she left him alone for too much longer, she gave up and went home. Her heart had soared when she'd seen Tracey in the shop just now; she'd been made up to think that her mum was back to pick up the reins. But Tracey's words had given her an uneasy feeling. She and Mary were usually glued together at the hip, so why didn't she know where Mary was? Or *did* she know, and was lying to cover for her? Something was going on, and if her mum still hadn't turned up by the time Chantelle got home from school tomorrow she was going to go back round to Tracey's — and *keep* on going back until Tracey told her the truth.

# CHAPTER
# SIX

"Okay, settle down!" the form tutor, Lynn Foster, called, struggling to make herself heard over the cacophony of chair scraping and excited chatter. "Those of you who are coming back for sixth form, remember what I said and try to have a bit of fun during the holidays, because it will be a difficult year ahead. For those who are going straight to college, I wish you the very best of luck. And those of you who are leaving, please try to do something positive with your lives, because you're all capable if you put your minds to it."

Aware that her pupils weren't listening as they noisily pushed and shoved their way out of the classroom, desperate for the freedom that lay beyond the door, Lynn sighed. Then, locating Chantelle at the back, she caught her eye and said, "Could you stay behind for a moment, please?"

"Aw, what's she want now?" Chantelle's friend Immy muttered. "Hope she's not gonna give you one of her epic lectures or you'll be here all day."

"Go on ahead," Chantelle said, a sinking feeling already settling over her. "I'll try not to be too long."

"I'll wait by the gate," Immy said, flashing the teacher an unimpressed look. "But I promised my mum I wouldn't be late, so I'll have to go if you're not out in ten."

Chantelle nodded, and hung back as the classroom quickly emptied. When they were alone, the teacher closed the door and waved for her to sit down.

"I'll try not to keep you," she said, taking her own seat and linking her hands together on the desktop. "I just wanted to speak to you before the summer holidays, because I'm a little concerned about you." She paused now and smiled before continuing. "Nothing to worry about — you just haven't seemed yourself lately, and I wondered if there was anything worrying you?"

Chantelle shook her head and dipped her gaze. "Everything's fine."

"Are you sure?" Lynn probed gently. "I know you struggled with your exams, and that wasn't like you because you usually do so well. If there's something wrong, I hope you know that you can talk to me?"

Chantelle inhaled deeply and bit down hard on the inside of her cheek. "I'm fine," she insisted. "Honestly. I'm just tired, that's all."

Lynn nodded slowly. "I understand that; it's been an arduous few weeks. But you're one of our brightest students and you don't usually have so much trouble with tests. I know you're not the kind of girl who likes to talk about your feelings, but it's my job to help if you're having difficulties."

The teacher stopped talking and Chantelle knew that she was waiting for a response. But she didn't dare speak for fear of what might tumble out. Everything was a mess, and it was getting worse by the day. It had been three weeks now since her mum had disappeared, and not only was she struggling to keep Leon under control but the money that her mum had left was long gone, so she'd been forced to break into her savings — which she really hadn't wanted to. Ever since she'd first started high school she'd known that she wanted to go to college so, while her friends spent their pocket money on magazines, make-up and clothes, Chantelle had put every penny she'd ever managed to get her hands on straight into her bank account. She was determined not to end up like her mum: struggling through life on benefits, with unwanted kids to feed and an insatiable appetite for fags, booze and drugs to cater for. It had been hard, but she had managed to accumulate just under £300 and she resented having to spend it on food. But what choice did she have? She wasn't old enough to sign on, and she definitely couldn't ask anyone for help because then the authorities would know that their mum had abandoned them and it would be game over.

"I wish you'd talk to me." Lynn tried again, watching as the troubled thoughts flashed through the girl's downcast eyes.

Chantelle shook her head and inhaled deeply. "There's nothing wrong. I'm absolutely fine."

Lynn sighed. As she'd already said, Chantelle was one of the school's brightest students, and yet she looked set to do badly in every one of the exams that she had sat. It didn't make sense.

"Maybe I should talk to your mum?" she ventured.

"*No!*" Chantelle's head shot up. "Please, don't. She's not very well at the moment, and I don't want to worry her."

"Ah . . ." Relieved to have finally got an insight, Lynn leaned forward. "Would you like to talk about it?"

"No, we're all right." Chantelle dropped her gaze again.

The teacher's voice was so soft and kind that she felt like bursting into tears. She had always liked Mrs Foster best of all the teachers in the school, and she knew that the woman was fond of her, too. But, in her experience, the kindest adults were often the most easily shocked, and if Mrs Foster were to discover the truth she would feel duty-bound to alert the social worker.

"It's just a bit of flu," Chantelle lied, forcing herself to look the woman in the eye now as she rose from her seat. "Sorry, but I've got to go or I'll be late picking my brother up." She reached for her bag. "And I said I'd go to the doctor's on my way home and get my mum's prescription."

"Okay, well, try to relax during the holidays." Lynn stood up and came around the desk. "And don't worry too much about your exam results. If they're not up to par we can talk about re-sits when the new term starts."

Chantelle nodded and pulled the door open. Then, forcing a smile, she fled down the corridor, determined to get out of there before the tears came.

When the girl had gone, Lynn gathered her own things together. Chantelle had always been reserved but she'd been even quieter than usual of late. And she'd lost weight, which was a definite indicator of stress. As she made her way to the staffroom Lynn wondered again if she ought to call the girl's mother. But she quickly decided against it. Chantelle had asked her not to, and she didn't want her to think that she'd gone behind her back. Apart from which, Mary Booth was hardly the most approachable of women — as Lynn had discovered to her cost on the one occasion when the woman had actually bothered to turn up for parents' evening, eyes glazed and reeking of alcohol. Lynn had only spoken to her once since then: eighteen months ago, after Chantelle and her brother returned home after being placed in temporary care. She had called to offer the school's support, but Mary Booth had made it quite clear that she neither needed nor wanted their help.

So, no, she wouldn't be making that mistake again.

As much as she suspected that something was bothering Chantelle, she sensed that no good would come of interfering. All she could do was be here when — *if* — Chantelle decided that she wanted to talk.

Chantelle was glad to see that Immy had gone when she reached the school gates. They had been best mates for years and always walked home together, but Immy would be bound to ask what was wrong if she saw how upset Chantelle was, and Chantelle couldn't risk telling her. She couldn't tell *anyone*. It was too dangerous.

She had more or less pulled herself together by the time she reached Leon's school, but her heart sank all over again when she turned the corner and saw her brother standing at the gates with Anton Davis.

"What's going on?" she asked, quickening her pace when she saw Leon's ripped shirt and the thin trail of blood that was dribbling out of a little cut above his eye. "Oh my God, what have you done? Have you been fighting?"

"Everything's cool," Anton assured her, shifting the little girl he had in his arms onto his other hip. "Your bro was having a beef with some older kids, but it's sorted now. Ain't that right, Champ?" He ruffled Leon's hair.

Leon nodded and grinned, and Chantelle frowned when she saw the adoring look in his eyes as he gazed up at Anton. It was bad enough that he'd been smoking and drinking and hanging around with a gang, without him adopting Anton as his new hero as well.

"Right, well, thanks for looking after him," she said, pulling Leon away. "But I'll take it from here."

"It was no probs," Anton said, falling into step beside her as she started walking away. "Didn't realise him and my little sis went to the same school. Small world, eh?"

"It's the closest primary to the estate," Chantelle replied frostily. "Where else are they going to go?"

Amused by her feistiness, Anton grinned. "Haven't seen you at Abdul's in a while; been shopping somewhere else?"

"Yeah, the market, where they don't bump up the prices from one day to the next," said Chantelle. "Why

**70**

aren't you there, anyway?" she added snipingly. "Don't tell me you've been sacked already?"

"Day off," Anton told her, frowning now. He was only trying to be friendly, and he seriously didn't know what her problem was.

"If you don't mind, I need to talk to my brother," Chantelle said. "In *private*."

"Cool. No problem." Anton slowed down. "See you around sometime."

"See you," Leon said, glancing back at Anton wide-eyed. He was a legend among the lads on the estate, and Leon was chuffed that his sister was mates with him. Not that she was letting on, but Anton had told him they were so it had to be true.

"Get moving," Chantelle snapped, pushing Leon roughly on ahead of her. "And what the hell do you think you were playing at, fighting at school?"

"It weren't *my* fault," Leon protested. "I was just waiting for you and they started on me. Anton stuck up for me," he added proudly. "And then he stopped with me till you got there in case they came back. He's well cool."

"No, he's not, he's a thug," said Chantelle. "And I don't want to catch you talking to him again."

"I like him," Leon grumbled. "Anyhow, why can't *I* talk to him if you can?"

"I don't," Chantelle retorted sharply. "And I meant what I said, so stay away from him."

"Get lost!" Leon turned on her angrily. "You can't tell me who to talk to."

"Yes, I can," Chantelle hissed. "I'm doing my best here, but don't you think I've got enough on my plate without having to chase around after you to keep you out of trouble?"

"Who says I'm getting in trouble?"

"You were fighting. What if one of your teachers had seen you?"

"It weren't my fault."

"Do you think your teachers would believe that?"

"I don't care what they think."

"Well, *I* do!" Chantelle yelled, annoyed that he wasn't taking this more seriously. "What do you think would have happened if they'd called the police? You'd get put back into care, that's what! Or is that what you want?"

As she glared down into his eyes, Leon dropped his gaze and scuffed the toe of his trainer on the ground. There was no way he wanted to go back into care, but he wasn't lying about the fight. He hadn't started it, and he thought Anton was ace for stepping in.

"You've got to stop this," Chantelle said now, an edge of desperation creeping into her voice as tears began to glisten in her eyes. "I've already made a mess of my exams 'cos I'm so stressed out."

"'S not my fault you're thick," Leon grunted, offended that she was blaming him for that as well.

"It's your fault I couldn't revise properly," she shot back.

"No, it ain't!" Leon screamed up into her face. "It's mum's fault, so blame her. And stop having a go at me all the time, 'cos I've done nowt wrong. You're a bitch, and I *hate* you!"

When he pushed past her and ran off down the road, Chantelle stayed where she was and blinked back the tears. He was right: none of this was his fault. But he definitely wasn't helping the situation. The six weeks' holiday was going to be a living nightmare if their mum didn't come back, and she had no idea how she was going to cope. But, for Leon's sake, she would have to try.

Leon was nowhere to be seen when Chantelle got home, but Tracey was standing on the step and Chantelle's heart leapt at the sight of her.

"Is she back?" she gasped, pulling her key out of her pocket and rushing to open the door.

Unable to look her in the eye, Tracey shook her head. "No, but I have heard from her. Can I come in for a minute?"

"Where is she?" Chantelle stumbled into the hall. "When's she coming home? What did she say?"

"Look, don't have a go at me," Tracey said, shuffling her feet when Chantelle switched on the light and gave her an expectant look. "But she's not coming back. Not yet, anyhow," she added quickly when she saw the disappointment wash over the girl's pretty face. "I'm sure she will — eventually; but she's just not ready yet."

"What do you mean, she's not ready? She's been gone for ages. How much longer does she think she can stay away?"

"If it's any consolation, I told her she's out of order. But you know what she's like. You can't tell her nothing."

"She can't do this," Chantelle croaked. "She's *got* to come back. I can't deal with this on my own any more."

Unable to look her in the eye, Tracey pulled a £20 note out of her pocket. "She asked me to drop this round for you. I know it's not much, but it's all I could manage. At least it's something, eh?"

"Not *much?*" Chantelle squawked. "It won't last two minutes. I've been using my savings, but what am I supposed to do when they're gone? Look . . ." She snatched a pile of envelopes off the hall table and flapped them in front of Tracey's face. "Bills! Electric, water, phone . . . Who's going to pay them? *I* can't."

When Tracey gave an awkward little shrug, Chantelle threw the bills back onto the table and buried her face in her hands. "She can't do this to me. It's not right."

"Aw, don't cry." Tracey extended a hand but quickly withdrew it when the girl snapped her head up and glared at her.

"Where is she?" Chantelle demanded. "I need to talk to her."

"In Spain," Tracey told her. "She reckons she tried to call you, but you must have been at school, eh?"

Chantelle yanked her mobile phone out of her pocket and checked it for missed calls. "She's a liar," she said accusingly when she saw there were none.

"Hey, don't blame me, babes." Tracey held up her hands in a gesture of innocence. "I'm just the messenger."

Teeth gritted, Chantelle clenched her fists. "Well, you've done your bit, so you can go now."

"She, er, asked me to check if any letters have come for her," Tracey said quietly. "She reckons this week's money hasn't gone into her account, and she needs to know if they've found out she's not here and cut her off. If they have, she wants me to . . ." She trailed off and swallowed deeply before finishing, "Well, she wants me to make a new claim — in her name, like."

Chantelle's jaw dropped and she stared at Tracey in utter disbelief. This was a joke — it had to be. Her mum was living it up in Spain, leaving Chantelle to look after Leon, and yet she thought she was entitled to keep all of the benefit money for herself.

"I think that might be it." Tracey pointed at a brown envelope that was sitting on top of the pile. She stepped forward to reach for it, but jumped back when Chantelle slammed a hand down on top of it.

"Don't you dare! If anyone's going to claim that money, it's *me*, not you."

"I won't be getting any of it," Tracey assured her. "It'll go straight into your mam's account."

"Will it now? We'll see about that." Chantelle shoved the envelope into her pocket and pulled out her phone again. "I'm going to ring her and find out what the hell she thinks she's playing at. Her phone must be back on if she's waiting for you to call."

"She's changed her number," Tracey said, shrugging as she added, "Something to do with international signals, or summat. I don't really understand all that stuff myself."

"Give me her new number, then," Chantelle demanded, phone poised.

Tracey sighed. "I can't, babes. She told me not to."

*"What?"*

"She knew you'd be fuming, and she can't face it just now," Tracey explained. "Look, try to see it from her point of view, eh? She's happy for the first time in years — surely you can't begrudge her that? Not after all the shit she's been through."

"I'm her *daughter* — what about the shit *I'm* going through?" Chantelle cried incredulously. "And what about Leon? What kind of woman walks out on her ten-year-old son?"

"You're doing all right," Tracey argued, desperate to finish this and go home for a drink, because the girl was starting to wear her out. "Your mam knew you'd cope, or she'd never have left him with you."

"Are you *crazy?*" Chantelle yelled at her. "What's my mum even *doing* in Spain, anyway? And how did she get there without her passport?"

Cheeks reddening, Tracey took a step back in case Chantelle decided to smack her one. "She came round for it a few weeks back — when you and Leon were at school."

"Are you kidding me?" Chantelle's eyes widened. "I've been going out of my mind worrying about her.

Why didn't she wait till I got home so I'd know she was okay?"

"'Cos she knew you'd try to stop her from going."

Chantelle shook her head slowly from side to side as she tried to digest what she'd heard. But she just couldn't accept that her mother could be so callous.

"It's a man, isn't it?" she gasped when a light suddenly went on in her mind. "She's met a man, and she'd rather be with him than with us. Tell me I'm wrong."

Tracey shrugged. Chantelle was spot on, but Tracey wasn't about to let on that she'd known all along. She hadn't even heard from Mary until she'd rung this afternoon, begging for help to sort out her benefits. Apparently, Manuel, or Miguel, or whatever the hell his name was, couldn't afford to keep them both on his part-time-waiter wages, and Mary was terrified that he would dump her if she didn't get her money reinstated. And what kind of a friend would Tracey be if she didn't at least *try* to help her loved-up mate?

"God, I'm right," Chantelle murmured sickly, guessing from the look on Tracey's face that she had hit the nail on the head. "That's low, even for her. And you're just as bad — standing there making excuses for her."

"Look, I've told you what your mam said, and that's all I know," Tracey said, fed up with taking stick for Mary's actions. "Here . . ." She slapped the £20 note down on the table. "She said if you want more you'll have to get it off Leon's dad, 'cos she's done her bit and it's time he started doing his."

"Are you serious?" Chantelle screwed up her face in disbelief. "Glenroy hasn't shown his face in years. How am I supposed to find him, never mind get money off him?"

"I'm sure you'll figure something out." Tracey shrugged and opened the door.

Shocked to the core, Chantelle stayed rooted to the spot for several long minutes after Tracey had gone. Still there when Leon knocked on the door, she snapped out of her daze and, swiping at the tears that she hadn't even realised she was crying, let him in.

"What's for dinner?" he asked, shouldering past her and dropping his blazer on the floor.

Relieved that he was home, because she had half expected him to go awol to punish her for shouting at him, Chantelle followed him into the kitchen. Now that she knew for sure that her mum was alive but had no intention of coming home any time soon, it was more important than ever to get things sorted between her and Leon. If they didn't start pulling together, it wouldn't be long before they were pulled apart — for ever.

"I'm going to make spaghetti," she told him when she found him rooting through the fridge. "And then we need to talk."

"Whatever." Leon closed the fridge and looked in the cupboard. Disappointed to find nothing that he could eat which didn't need cooking, he slammed the door shut. "How come you never buy biscuits? You never get nothing nice, you."

"We can't afford it," Chantelle said guiltily. "Have you got any homework?" she asked then. "Why don't you make a start on it before you get too tired?"

"I'm on holiday," Leon reminded her, shrugging her hand off his back when she ushered him towards the door. "I'm going to watch telly."

"Okay." Chantelle sighed. "But don't have it on too loud. Oh, by the way . . ." she added, keeping a casual edge to her voice. "Remember when you thought you saw your dad going into that house that time? Did you say it was opposite the precinct?"

Leon curled his lip. "Yeah, why?"

"No reason." Chantelle smiled. "Just crossed my mind, that's all. I'll give you a shout when dinner's ready."

When she heard the TV come on in the front room, Chantelle took the mince out of the freezer and put it into the microwave to defrost. Then, chopping an onion, she mentally reran the conversation she'd just had with Tracey.

She was furious that her mum had rung Tracey and not her, and in hindsight she wished she'd taken Tracey's phone off her and got the new number for herself. But she'd been too shocked to think about it at the time, and now she doubted she'd get the chance again because Tracey would no doubt go back to avoiding her. It was particularly upsetting to know that her mum was more concerned about keeping her hands on the benefit money than she was about her kids. But as for telling Chantelle to get money off Leon's dad, that was a joke. Leon claimed not to care that his dad had abandoned him, but Chantelle remembered how heartbroken he'd been when, a couple of years ago, he'd come home in tears after spotting Glenroy going into a house in Stretford with a woman and a child.

"*I leaned right out of the bus window and shouted at him,*" he'd sobbed. "*And I know he heard me, 'cos he looked right at me. But he just blanked me and shut the door.*"

"*Probably wasn't him,*" their mum had said. "*It's been years since you saw him; you wouldn't have a clue what he looked like.*"

But Leon had been adamant. "*It was him, I know it was. He just don't want me no more. I hate him!*"

Now that she thought about it, Chantelle realised it had been around that time when Leon's behaviour had started to deteriorate. Before then, he'd just been a bit cheeky; but afterwards, he'd become sullen and argumentative — and it had got far worse when he came home after being in care.

They had never spoken about his time with his foster parents because Leon flew off the handle whenever she tried to raise the subject. But Chantelle suspected that he'd been beaten, because he had been covered in bruises when he came home.

And that was why she couldn't let him get taken away again.

She was his big sister; it was her job to look after him. And that was exactly what she would do, even if, as a last resort, she had to beg for money from a man who hadn't cared enough about him to check if he was alive or dead over the last few years.

Leon was watching reruns of *Top Gear* when Chantelle carried their dinners through to the living room. She had less than zero interest in cars, especially ones that were being driven by idiots who seemed to be in competition to see who could kill themselves fastest. But Leon had always been fascinated by anything with an engine, so she let him watch it.

After they had eaten and she had cleared their plates away, she waited for the programme to finish and then switched the TV off.

"What you doing?" Leon protested. "The next one'll be on in a minute. They're going to Iraq — it'll be well bad."

"You can put it back on when we've talked," Chantelle told him.

"About what?" Leon slumped back and pulled a face.

"Mum."

"What about her?"

"She's in Spain," Chantelle said, choosing her next words carefully because she didn't want to upset him. "She rang Tracey and said to let us know that she'll be coming back soon. I just don't know exactly when."

"So?" Leon shrugged and reached for the remote.

"Don't you care?" Chantelle asked.

Leon looked at her as if she was stupid for even asking. "She doesn't give a toss about me, so why should I give a toss about her?"

His attitude saddened Chantelle; he was too young to be so jaded. But she supposed that she couldn't blame him, because he was right. Their mum had always put her own needs and wants before theirs.

"Will you do me a favour?" she asked.

Instantly suspicious of her softer tone, Leon drew his head back and peered at her through narrowed eyes. "Depends what it is."

"Just stop fighting me," she said wearily. "I know you think I'm bossy, but I'm only trying to keep us together. If anyone susses that mum's not here, we've had it. That's why I keep telling you to turn your music down, so next-door don't call the police. And that's why I don't want you hanging around with that gang, 'cos I don't want you getting caught up in anything you shouldn't be doing." She paused when Leon suppressed a yawn, and sighed before adding, "I just want to know we're on the same page, or there's no point me trying."

"Yeah, whatever." Leon made another grab for the remote.

"Do you mean it?" Chantelle snatched it out of reach.

Leon rolled his eyes. "I said yeah, didn't I?"

"And you do know I'm doing this because I love you?"

"Ewww, shurrup!" Leon grimaced.

Chantelle smiled and handed the remote to him. As tough as he acted, he was still her baby brother.

# CHAPTER
# SEVEN

As hard as Chantelle tried, the money seemed to be going down at an alarming rate. They were already eating the cheapest food she could buy, but Leon was a growing boy with a huge appetite, and as fast as she bought it he ate it.

It was the end of the first week of the holidays now, and the cupboards were once again bare. Determined to get down to the market before all the bargains were snapped up, Chantelle got up early and, leaving Leon to sleep, slipped her coat on. But just as she started to open the front door, it was pushed violently from the other side and she was thrown back against the wall.

"What are you doing?" she gasped when a man rushed in. "Get out or I'll scream!"

"Make one sound and I'll put my fist down your fucking throat," Ricky Benson snarled, kicking the door shut. "Where is she?"

Recognising him now that she could see him, Chantelle backed away. "You'd better get out before my dad gets home," she warned. "He's only gone to the shop. He'll kill you if he finds you here when he gets back."

"Don't play games with me, darlin', you ain't smart enough." Ricky pushed past her and reached out to open Leon's bedroom door. "In here, is she?"

"That's my little brother's room," Chantelle cried. "Please don't hurt him."

"Do I look like the kind of freak who gets a kick out of hurting kids?" Ricky sneered, looking inside to see if she was telling the truth before pulling the door shut and moving on to the next room. "I just want what I'm owed, that's all. Your mam's taking the fucking piss, and I've had it with her."

"She's not here," Chantelle told him, wringing her hands as he checked the rest of the flat.

"So where the fuck *is* she?" Ricky grabbed her by the hair and slammed her up against the wall. "You know, and if you've got any sense you'll tell me before I get *really* mad."

"She's in hospital," Chantelle lied, blurting out the first thing that came into her mind.

"Oh yeah?" Ricky narrowed his eyes. "Since when?"

"A f-few weeks ago." Chantelle's heart was pounding crazily in her chest as his hot breath wafted over her face.

"What's up with her?"

"Cancer."

"Is she dying?" Ricky asked, pissed off to think that Mary might have taken that last lay-on of speed when she'd already known she was ill.

Mentally asking God to forgive her for the lie, and unable to bring herself to worsen it, Chantelle guiltily dipped her gaze. "They're still doing tests."

"Good, so she can pay me as soon as she comes home, then, can't she?" Ricky said coldly. "And just so she knows I'm not messing about no more, I'll have whatever you've got on you."

"What are you doing?" Chantelle squawked when he started patting her down. "Get your hands off me!"

"You'd best keep still, unless you want a fuckin' slap," Ricky hissed, dragging her purse out of her pocket and unzipping it. He smiled when he saw the folded wad of notes inside. "That'll do — for starters."

"Please don't take that," Chantelle pleaded, tears springing into her eyes as she tried to snatch it back. "It's all I've got."

"Tell someone who gives a shit!" Ricky stuffed the wad into his back pocket and tipped the loose change into his hand. Then, pursing his lips thoughtfully, he gazed at Chantelle for a few seconds before dropping it back into the purse. "Just so you don't think I'm a complete cunt," he said, pushing it back into her pocket. "But I still want the rest, so don't forget to tell your mam what I said."

Terrified by the leering look in his eyes, Chantelle pressed herself closer to the wall.

"What you acting like that for?" Ricky asked, a slow smile coming onto his lips as he placed one hand on the wall behind her head and ran the other over her slim hip. "I said I wasn't gonna hurt you, and I haven't, have I?"

"N-no," Chantelle croaked, shuddering at the feel of his hand. "But can — can you go now, please?"

Still peering down into her eyes, Ricky said, "You're a bit of all right, you. That mam of yours thinks she's pretty special, but she ain't got nothing on you. How old are you?"

"F-fifteen." Chantelle could barely speak.

"Shame," Ricky murmured disappointedly. "When's your birthday?"

Before Chantelle could answer, a knock came at the door and, seconds later, the letter-box flap was raised and a pair of eyes peered in. "Channy, it's me . . ." Immy called through. "I've been trying to call you."

"*Ssshhh!*" Ricky placed a finger over Chantelle's lips and pressed his body right up against hers.

Chantelle squeezed her eyes shut and held her breath.

"Oh my God, I can actually *see* you, you know." Immy's voice was dripping with indignation. "Are you actually *hiding* from me — for real? If you don't wanna be friends, why don't you just big up and tell me?"

Chantelle's heart sank. But, just as she feared that her friend was about to give up and leave, Ricky's mobile phone bleeped. He pulled it out of his pocket and glanced at the screen, then pushed himself away from Chantelle.

"Got to go. But I'll be back, so don't let me hear you've been bad-mouthing me or it'll be *you* I'm coming for next time, not your mam. Understand?"

Chantelle nodded and stayed frozen to the spot as he strolled up the hall and opened the door.

"About time!" Immy complained. "I was about to —" She stopped speaking when she saw the man and drew her head back. "Oh, sorry . . . thought you were Chantelle."

"No worries, darlin'." Ricky winked at her. "She's in there."

Immy watched him go, and then turned to Chantelle. "Who the hell was *that?* Don't tell me your mum . . ." She trailed off and cast a furtive glance at Mary's bedroom door before whispering, "She isn't, is she?"

"No." Chantelle waved for her to come in. "Hurry up!"

"What's going on?" Concerned now, Immy stepped into the hall and quickly closed the door. "Are you okay?"

Chantelle swallowed deeply and staggered into the kitchen. Her legs felt like jelly, and her head was swimming.

"God, what's happened?" Immy rushed after her and pulled out a chair from under the table. "Did that man do something to you?" she asked, pushing Chantelle gently down onto it. "Do you want me to call the police?"

"No." Chantelle squawked. Then, biting her lip to keep the impending tears at bay, she took a deep breath and said, "He didn't do anything. I'm fine."

"You don't look it," Immy told her. "You're as white as a ghost."

"I'm just due on," Chantelle lied, forcing a weak smile.

Immy frowned, unsure whether to believe her. But she knew Chantelle well enough to know that there was no point trying to force her to talk, so, sighing, she said, "Right, I'm going to make some tea. See if we can't get some colour back into your cheeks."

As her friend filled the kettle and prepared the cups, Chantelle scolded herself for having let her guard down. Immy was her best friend, but she knew from bitter experience that the girl couldn't keep a secret to save her life, so there was no way she could let her know what was going on or *everyone* would know.

When the teas were made, Immy handed a cup to Chantelle and sat down across from her. "So how come you haven't been answering my calls? I haven't seen or heard from you since school broke up. I was starting to think you'd fallen out with me."

"Don't be daft," Chantelle murmured guiltily. "I've just been busy."

"Doing what?"

"This and that." Chantelle shrugged, and gripped her cup between both hands. "Not been in the best of moods, to be honest. I did really badly at my exams, and my PMT's been pretty bad, so I've been up and down like a yo-yo."

Immy nodded sympathetically. "Have you seen your doctor? My mum had to go on the pill when hers got bad. You might need to try it."

"Yeah, maybe." Glad that her friend seemed to have bought the lie, Chantelle took a sip of the hot tea.

"Good excuse to get protection without anyone accusing you of wanting to sleep around," Immy added, grinning slyly. "Although *my* mum would have an absolute fit if she thought I was even *thinking* about sex. I'm sure she's determined to keep me a virgin until I get married."

"Lucky you," Chantelle murmured, wishing that *her* mum felt that way about her. But the truth was her mum would probably be thrilled if she went on the pill, because she'd never understood why Chantelle wasn't as man-hungry as she was and had told her on many a drunken occasion to start using what she'd been given before it shrivelled up and nobody wanted it any more.

"Hey, did you know Anton Davis was out?" Immy asked suddenly, a dreamy look coming into her eyes. "I saw him the other day, and he's fitter than ever. God, what I wouldn't give to kiss those juicy lips of his. And his eyes . . . oh, don't even get me started on his eyes. They're like melted treacle dipped in sex."

"All right, settle down," Chantelle snorted. "He's only a lad."

"*The* lad," Immy corrected her. "He's working at Abdul's, so guess where *I*'ll be shopping from now on?"

As her friend gazed wistfully off into her dreams, Chantelle rolled her eyes and took another sip of tea. Immy was crazy if she thought she stood a chance with Anton. She might be white, blonde and pretty, which seemed to be the main criteria for bagging a lad round here; but there were plenty of prettier, sexier girls on the estate, and Anton could have his pick of them.

"Oh, did I tell you about my dad's new girlfriend?" Immy said now, a sneer twisting her lip. "Her name's *Carolina*, and she looks younger than me. Obviously

**89**

she's not, 'cos my dad's not a perv, or anything; but she might as well be, the way she dresses. My mum acted all cool when he brought her round to pick our Josh up yesterday. She was all like, *Oh, hello, it's so nice to meet you*, but I could tell she wasn't impressed. I said to her after they'd gone, God, you're a right one, you, butter wouldn't melt, or what? And she says —"

Chantelle couldn't take any more. "God, is that the time?" She looked pointedly at the clock on the wall as she pushed her chair back. "I didn't realise it was so late. Promised my mum I'd go to the market."

"Oh, right." Disappointed to have her story cut short, Immy stood up. "Want me to come with you?"

"No, it's probably best I go on my own," Chantelle said, checking that her purse was still in her pocket. "No offence, but you walk too slow."

"I know, I'm terrible, aren't I?" Immy admitted. "My mum hates going shopping with me; says it takes three times longer than going on her own. Should I come back later? Or you can come round to mine, if you want? You'll see the Barbie doll when my dad fetches our Josh home."

"Not sure what I'm doing yet." Chantelle ushered her down the hall and out of the door. "My mum keeps finding jobs for me to do, so I'd best give you a ring when I'm free."

"Make sure you do." Immy pouted and wrapped her jacket tight around herself as the wind whipped her hair across her face. "I've not seen you for ages, and I've missed you."

"I've said I'll ring, so I will," Chantelle said firmly. "See you later." She pulled the door shut now, and gave Immy a quick hug before rushing away.

Head down, she walked quickly out of the estate — and carried on walking until, half an hour later, she found herself in Stretford.

A small patch of grass separated the dual carriageway from the single row of terraced houses facing the Arndale Centre. Chantelle bit her lip as she stared at the doors — one of which Leon claimed to have seen his dad going into that time. It was a good six or seven years since she'd last seen Glenroy, and she wasn't sure how he would react to her turning up out of the blue. Sometimes, on the very rare occasions when she thought about him, she recalled a handsome man with twinkling eyes and a dazzling smile, always dressed up to the nines and flirting and charming his way through life. But in darker moments, she recalled a monster with a vicious face and enormous fists.

Losing her nerve at the thought of coming face to face with *that* man now, she turned to go home and banged straight into a woman who was coming the other way carrying several bulging shopping bags.

"Oh, sorry," Chantelle apologised, reaching out to steady the woman. "I didn't see you."

"No worries." The woman smiled and blew a lock of sweaty hair out of her eyes. "I was in a world of me own. You looking for someone?" she asked then. "Only you've been standing here staring at the houses the whole time it's taken me to cross the road."

"I, er . . . *yeah*," Chantelle said, figuring that she might as well at least ask now that she was here. "Glenroy King. I don't suppose you know him, do you?"

"Glenroy?" the woman repeated thoughtfully. "Black fella?"

Chantelle nodded, her heart starting to pound.

"I've only lived here a few months, so I don't know many of them by name yet," the woman told her. "But I've seen a black fella going in a house down that side." She pointed along the row. "Third from the end."

Chantelle thanked her and made her way to the house she'd pointed out. The curtains were closed at the downstairs window, but she could hear the faint sound of a TV inside. Hands shaking, she reached out and pressed the bell.

The curtain twitched and, a few seconds later, the door opened a crack and a woman with messy blonde hair and sleepy eyes peered out at her. "Yeah?"

"Sorry for disturbing you," Chantelle said, guessing from the dressing gown she was wearing that the woman had not long got up. "I'm looking for Glenroy King, and one of your neighbours told me he might live here."

"Who are you?" the woman demanded sharply. Then, before Chantelle could answer, she drew her head back, and said, "Oh, don't tell me . . . Bloody hell, you're a bit young, aren't you? What did he do, bribe you with a lollipop?"

"Sorry?" Chantelle was confused.

"Oh, I bet you are," the woman sneered. "Not half as romantic once it's all out in the open and they're under your feet twenty-four-seven, is it?"

"I think we've got our wires crossed," Chantelle said politely. "I haven't seen Glenroy for ages, and I'm only looking for him because I need —"

"Oh, he's left you already, has he?" The woman snorted softly and gave Chantelle a gloating look. "Can't say I'm surprised, 'cos I told him it wouldn't last. Never does. Bet you thought you were special, didn't you? Well, sorry to disappoint you, darlin', but you're just the latest in a very long line. And now he's left you, he'll be back here before the day's out, begging me to take him back. See, that's what you little tarts don't realise when you're falling for his sweet talk. You might give him a temporary thrill, but I've got his kid, so he *always* comes back to me in the end."

"Look, I don't know who you think I am, but I haven't seen Glenroy in years," Chantelle blurted out when the woman stopped ranting at last. "If I wasn't desperate, I wouldn't be here; but he's my brother's dad, and I —"

"Okay, you can stop right there." The woman held up her hand. "My Glen hasn't got any kids apart from our Lennox. You must be looking for a different one."

"Oh," Chantelle murmured, feeling guilty for having upset her for nothing. "I'm sorry. It's just that Leon — that's my brother — thought he saw his dad here a few years back. I really am sorry. I won't —"

Before she could finish the sentence, a young boy emerged from the shadows of the hallway and tugged on the woman's dressing gown. Chantelle's mouth fell open when she looked at him. He was the absolute image of Leon when he'd been younger: same silky curls, same deep dark eyes, and same cute dimples in his pudgy cheeks.

The woman saw the recognition in her eyes and pushed the child roughly back, ordering him to go and watch TV. Then, turning back to Chantelle, she hissed, "Whatever you're after, forget it, 'cos you're getting nothing off me. If your mam was stupid enough to get herself knocked up, that's her problem, not mine. Glenroy might mess around, but he's Lennox's dad and I'm not having anyone come between them."

"Look, I can see this has upset you, and I wouldn't have come if I wasn't desperate," Chantelle said quietly. "But he's Leon's dad as well, and we need help. Please just tell me where he is, and I promise I won't bother you again."

"I don't know where he is, and I don't care," the woman spat. "Now get lost!"

Chantelle jumped back when the door was slammed in her face. She didn't understand why the woman was so mad at her; it wasn't *her* fault that Glenroy had lied about having another kid — and, by the sounds of it, he could have plenty more dotted around, so it should hardly have come as such a big surprise.

She raised her hand to press the bell again, but quickly changed her mind. What was the point? The woman clearly didn't know where Glenroy was, and she obviously had enough problems without Chantelle adding to them.

94

Anton was on his way to work when he saw a familiar figure up ahead. Smiling, he flicked the cigarette he'd been smoking into the gutter and ran up behind her, clapping a hand down on her shoulder.

Almost jumping out of her skin, terrified that it might be the man who had forced his way into the flat earlier that morning, Chantelle turned around. "You idiot!" she spluttered when she saw who it was. "You almost gave me a heart attack!"

"Sorry." Smile slipping when he saw the fear in her eyes, Anton tipped his head to one side. "You okay?"

"Absolutely fine," Chantelle said through gritted teeth.

"You don't look it," said Anton, going after her when she started to walk away.

Chantelle flicked him an irritated side glance and quickened her pace. Frowning when he did likewise, she said, "Are you following me?"

"Yeah, course," Anton chuckled, thinking that she was joking.

Chantelle tutted and walked on.

"How's your bro?" Anton asked, keeping up. "Has he had any more trouble with those lads?"

"He's fine, and no," Chantelle muttered, wishing that he would leave her alone, because she really wasn't in the mood for small talk.

"That's good," he said. "But if you have any trouble in the future and need a hand, just give us a shout, yeah?"

Chantelle stopped walking and turned to face him. Blushing when he walked right into her and she caught the musky scent of his body-spray, she stepped quickly back. "Look, I'm not being rude, but don't you think this is starting to get a bit weird?"

"How so?" He gave her a bemused smile.

"I don't know!" Chantelle flapped her hands. *This.* It's like I can't go out without bumping into you."

"And you think that means I'm following you?"

"I don't know? Are you?"

"Whoa, girl!" Anton stepped back and peered at her. "You need to check that ego, for real. I'm on my way to work — ain't nothing weird about that. Unless you think I timed it specially to bump into you — even though I couldn't have known you'd be out here?" he added facetiously.

Chantelle's blush deepened, and she wished the ground would open up and swallow her whole for saying such a stupid thing. They both lived on the estate so it was inevitable that their paths would cross from time to time, but now she'd made a complete fool of herself she would never be able to look him in the face again.

"I'm sorry," she mumbled, tears springing into her eyes. "I didn't mean it like that. I just . . ." Unable to finish the sentence as the lump that was forming in her throat threatened to choke her, she rushed away.

"Yo, wait up," Anton called, running after her. "I didn't mean to upset you. What's up?"

"It's not you," Chantelle sobbed, wrenching her arm free when he caught up and grabbed her.

"Nah, I was out of order," Anton said. "I'm sorry. I just thought you were joking."

Chantelle wiped her nose on the back of her hand. "I asked for it. It was a stupid thing to say."

"No harm done." Anton dipped his head and looked up into her downcast eyes. "Deffo no need to cry about it, anyhow."

"I'm not," Chantelle lied, trying to step past him. "Please let me go," she implored when he didn't move. "My brother's on his own; I've got to get back."

"Hey, no worries." Anton held out his arms and backed off. "Just wanted to make sure we were cool."

He frowned when she hurried away, and looped his hands together behind his head as he stared after her in confusion. That girl had issues, for sure; bitching one minute, crying the next. A dude wouldn't know if he was coming or going with a girl like that — but, man, it'd be worth the ride.

Leon was out when Chantelle got home, and she guessed he'd gone round to Kermit's. She was glad, because he would only be worried if he saw how upset she was and she didn't want to ruin his holiday any more than she already had. He was only a kid; he deserved to have some fun.

Not that either of them would be having too much more of that if she didn't find a solution to their money troubles.

As fresh tears began to stream down her cheeks, Chantelle went to her room, lay down on the bed and pulled the pillow over her face. She'd tried so hard to hold it together but she wasn't sure how much longer she could carry on. All she had wanted to do was protect Leon, but she had totally let him down. Maybe it would be better to just let him go now — before things got really bad?

# CHAPTER
# EIGHT

Leon had left the flat a few minutes before Chantelle arrived home. Unaware that she was back and worrying herself sick over him, he strolled happily down the canal towpath. She thought he'd been going round to Kermit's all week, and he hadn't set her straight because she would only go off her nut if she knew what he had really been doing. As it was, he hadn't even seen his old friend since the night when she'd caught him with Damo and the crew. He knew it was Kermit who had grassed him up, but the shitbag hadn't dared to show his face since, so he'd escaped a kicking — for now.

It was good to have Chantelle off his back, because she'd been seriously doing his head in these last few weeks. She'd always been bossy, but it was like she now thought she was his mum, always telling him what to do and who he could and couldn't hang around with. But she could fuck off if she thought she was stopping him from hanging out with the gang, because he was old enough to make his own decisions.

Damo and the lads were in their usual spot, down by the locks. They all nodded and touched fists with him when he reached them, but Damo's best mate, Acky, didn't. Lounging on the grass bank with a bottle of White Stripe in his hand, he kissed his teeth and said, "Not you again. Thought I told you to do one, y' little dickhead."

"Leave him alone," Damo said, grinning as he pulled Leon into a headlock and rubbed his scalp sharply with his knuckles. "He's a good lad — ain't ya?"

Leon's face was already going red with the pressure of the stranglehold but he grinned and nodded, glad to have Damo on his side.

"I think he should fuck off home and stop trying to play with the big boys," Acky sniped, giving Leon a dirty look. "Wouldn't want sis to come looking for him again, would we? She might get herself hurt."

Damo released Leon and gave his friend a hooded look. "Zip it, yeah?"

When Acky sucked his teeth again and took a swig from the bottle, Leon gave Damo a grateful look. He didn't know what Acky's problem was, but the lad really seemed to have it in for him. He was the one who had made Kermit sick by forcing him to smoke too much spliff that night. And then he'd made Leon walk the plank, and had nearly gone for Chantelle when she'd taken the piss out of him for acting black. He definitely didn't want Leon hanging around with them. But Damo was the leader, not him; and if Damo said it was okay, Acky would just have to deal with it.

Damo's mobile started to ring just then. He looked at the name on the screen and moved away from the others to answer it. "Wha'pp'n, man?" Eyes narrowing as he listened to what the caller was saying, he nodded

**100**

a few times and then said, "No probs, we're on it. Laters."

Acky jerked his chin up. "Who dat?"

"Big T," Damo told him. "Couple of foots from the Longsight Gees need settling." He turned to the others now, and grinned. "Time to kick some arse, boys."

Chantelle woke with a start when her phone started ringing. She rolled over and tugged it out of her jacket pocket, shocked to see on the screen display that it was three p.m. She must have cried herself to sleep, and now she'd missed half the day. That wasn't like her at all. She must be even more stressed than she thought.

"Hiya, babes," a laughing voice trilled when she answered it. "Have you missed me?"

"*Mum!*" She sat bolt upright. "Is that really you? Where are you?"

"España!" Mary giggled. "And guess what? . . . I'm getting *married!*"

"*What?*" Chantelle gasped. "Are you drunk?"

"Aw, don't go and ruin it for me," Mary groaned. "Miggy told me not to bother telling you, but — stupid me — I actually thought you'd be happy for me."

"Who the hell's Miggy?" Chantelle rubbed her eyes, sure that she must still be dreaming.

"His full name's Miguel Ra — . . . Ram — . . . hang on a minute." Mary's voice was muffled for a few seconds as she covered the phone. "Ramirez!" she announced when she came back on. "Miguel Ramirez — your new stepdaddy-to-be."

When Chantelle stayed silent for a few seconds, Mary said, "Well, ain't you gonna say nothing?"

Chantelle gritted her teeth. She wanted to cut loose on Mary for abandoning them, but her mum would only hang up if she came down too hard on her — and God only knew when they would hear from her again if that happened. So, taking a deep breath, she said through tight lips, "Congratulations, I'm really pleased for you. How long have you known him?"

"Long enough to know he's the one," Mary said dreamily. "Honest to God, babes, no one's ever treated me like this man does. And he's handsome like you wouldn't believe. My dreamboat Spaneesh lov-er."

Chantelle grimaced as her mum's voice took on a supposedly Spanish accent. But a cold shiver ran down her spine when, in the background, she heard a man with the real accent order Mary to hurry up.

"Don't go!" Chantelle blurted out. *"Please . . . I need to talk to you."*

"Aw, soz, babes, but it's his mate's phone so I can't stay on too long. I'll ring again soon, though."

"I don't want you to ring, I want to *see* you," Chantelle sobbed, swiping at a tear she could feel rolling down her cheek.

"Aw, me an' all," said Mary. "Here, where's our Leon? Put him on for a minute."

"He's out," Chantelle told her. "But never mind him. I need to know when you're coming back, 'cos I've got no money."

"I told Trace to give you some. Don't tell me the stupid bitch forgot?"

"No, she gave me twenty quid, but that Ricky came looking for you and took it."

"Bastard!" Mary spat indignantly. "You wait till we get home and Miggy gets hold of him!"

"That doesn't help me right now, does it?" said Chantelle. "I'm scared our Leon's going to get taken away if you don't come back soon."

"Don't you *dare* let anyone take him," Mary said fiercely. "I mean it, Chan. If I lose my boy, I'll never forgive you."

"It won't be *my* fault," Chantelle protested. "I'm the one who's here looking after him — or *trying* to."

"Oh, that's right, make me feel guilty, why don't you?" Mary tutted. "God, anyone'd think I was never coming back, the way you're going on."

"Well, are you?"

"Yeah, course. In a few weeks."

"A few *weeks?*" Chantelle repeated incredulously. "Haven't you been listening? I haven't got any money. How am I supposed to feed Leon for a few more weeks?"

"I told Trace to tell you to find Glenroy," Mary said irritably. "It's about time he started doing his bit."

"I already tried, this morning," Chantelle told her. "But his girlfriend doesn't know where he is."

"No change there, then," Mary snorted. "Bastard never could keep it in his pants. What was she like, then — the girlfriend? Bet she wasn't as pretty as me!"

"Never mind her," Chantelle snapped. "What about me and Leon? You're either going to have to come back, or you'll have to send some money. And don't say you haven't got any, 'cos I know the dole sorted out that mistake. They sent a letter saying they were backdating it and paying it into your account."

"What you doing reading my letters?" Mary demanded. "You've got no right."

"Are you serious?" Chantelle was shouting now. "Don't you think I've got a right to know what's going on, seeing as I'm the one who's trying to keep a roof over your son's head? I need money, and I need it *now!*"

"God, you're such a drama queen," Mary said scornfully. Then, sighing, she said, "Right, I'll see what I can do. But I can't promise it'll be much, 'cos I've got the wedding to pay for."

"You're having a laugh," Chantelle gasped. "What's more important, a stupid wedding or your kids?"

"Oh, will you get off my fuckin' back," Mary yelled, losing patience. "I've just told you I'll be coming home soon — what more do you want?"

"*Money!*" Chantelle bellowed.

"Get it off your dad," said Mary. "He's another one who's had it easy for too long."

"Oh, yeah, 'cos it's that easy to get to Jamaica, isn't it?"

"Who said he was in Jamaica?"

"*You.*"

"Did I?" Mary sounded confused. "I don't remember saying that."

"Well, you should, 'cos it's what you've been telling me for as long as I can remember," said Chantelle. "So, what are you saying now? Is he, or isn't he?"

"Not as far as I know," Mary said. "Last I heard he was in Moss Side."

"*What?*" Chantelle felt as if she'd been kicked in the stomach. "You said he went home before I was born."

"Yeah, to his own *house*," said Mary. "Well, I wasn't having him living with me. He did my bleedin' head in, boring bastard."

"How could you?" Chantelle gasped. "All this time I've been thinking he was in a different country, and you never told me any different. You're unbelievable."

"Oh, I've had enough of this," Mary said snappily. "I only rang to tell you my good news but you're obviously not interested. You never are — unless it's about *you*, you self-centred bitch."

When the phone went dead in her hand Chantelle tried to ring her mum back, only to find that the number was withheld. She screamed in frustration, threw her phone down on the bed and pummelled the pillow with her fists. She couldn't believe what she'd just heard, although she didn't know why she was so surprised, because this was just typical of her mother. She'd been lying to Chantelle her whole life, but now, just because it suited *her*, she'd landed a bombshell like this — and wondered why Chantelle was so pissed off.

Agitated, Chantelle jumped up and walked over to the window. If it was true, then her father had been living less than a mile away this whole time. So why had he never tried to contact her? They had always lived in this same flat, so he would have known exactly where to find her, but Chantelle had never seen him in her life. And that made him an even worse father than Glenroy, who had at least stayed in Leon's life for the first few years.

As fresh tears began to sting her eyes, Chantelle rested her forehead against the cold glass. Was she really so unlovable that the people who had created her found it so easy to turn their backs on her? Leon was rude, disrespectful and downright defiant, but in their mum's eyes he could do no wrong; whereas Chantelle, who always strived to be polite and helpful, just seemed to rub her up the wrong way. And now, despite everything that she had put Chantelle through, all the support that Chantelle had given her throughout her numerous failed relationships and drug-fuelled meltdowns, her mum claimed that *Chantelle* was the self-centred one.

But what was the use of letting it get her down? Her father obviously didn't care if she was dead or alive, and her mum cared more about herself than she did about her kids. Maybe she should just give up and phone the social services now, before things got even worse.

Leon's heart felt like it was on fire as, head thrown back, he belted along behind Damo and the gang who were running hell for leather across Alexandra Park. After walking around and around Moss Side for the last few hours, Acky had just spotted the lads they had been looking for going in through the side gates on mountain bikes, and they had to get to the fence that ran down the far side before the lads spotted them and made their getaway.

A narrow path separated the park perimeter from a school field, and it was hidden from the view of the park and the road beyond. Here the boys pulled their scarves up to cover their faces and hunkered down to wait.

"Get over there and keep a lookout," Damo hissed at Leon. "Anyone comes, whistle."

Head down, Leon shuffled off to hide at the side of the bush that Damo had pointed out, from where he could see both ends of the path and a bit of park through the fence. He was gasping hard, trying to catch his breath, but when he heard a squeak of brakes he inhaled deeply and held it in, then listened to the two boys talking quietly as they manoeuvred their bikes out onto the path.

The boys had barely had time to remount and get their feet back on the pedals when Damo and the others swarmed out from their hiding places, and Leon almost threw up with shock as he watched them drag the boys off their bikes and lay into them. He had heard the gang talk about fights they'd had, but this was the first time he'd seen them in action and it totally freaked him out. He'd had plenty of fights himself, at school and on the estate, but nothing as vicious as this. It was six against two, for starters, which didn't seem fair. And they weren't just using their fists and feet. Acky had found a thick branch and was lashing the lads' bodies with it as they lay curled up on the floor, their arms wrapped around their heads to protect their faces. Everyone else was kicking and punching, and Leon buried his face in his arms when he saw the blood. He peered out for a second, and had to bite down on his sleeve to keep from crying out when he saw Damo pick up a rock and, after holding it high in the air with both hands, dash it down on one of their victims' heads.

Leon saw a movement in the distance behind the lads and tried to whistle, but nothing happened because his throat seemed to have closed up. Unable to attract their attention any other way, he jumped up and started waving his arms.

It worked. Damo stopped what he was doing and looked around. When he saw the two men walking slowly towards them from the far end of the path, he hurled the rock as far as he could over the fence and then called his boys off. "Yo, leave it. Someone's coming."

As one, the lads started running the other way down the path, heading for the dual carriageway ahead. One of them grabbed Leon's arm as he passed and hauled him along. As Damo sped past them all, Leon glanced back, wondering where Acky was, and was sickened all over again to see him sticking the boot into the side of one of the fallen lads' heads before coming after them, even though both boys were clearly unconscious already.

The gang burst out onto the pavement at the end of the path and, dodging the traffic, ran across the busy carriageway. On the other side they hurtled around corners and ducked through a maze of alleyways, running without stopping until they reached the broken section of fence at the rear of the derelict pub they used as a hideaway.

"Block it," Damo ordered when they had all squeezed through the pub's back door and piled into the old kitchen area.

As two of the lads hauled an old sink unit up against the door, Leon slid to the floor to catch his breath and watched as Damo peered out through a hole in the metal sheeting covering the window. After several tense minutes, during which Leon was convinced that the gang must all be able to hear his heart thudding as loudly as he himself could, Damo exhaled loudly, and said, "All clear."

"Man, that was close," Acky gasped, sitting on an upturned box and pulling a pack of cigarettes out of his pocket. "I *well* thought we'd been clocked."

"Yeah, well, we weren't," Damo said, flopping down beside him and snatching a cigarette out of his hand. He lit up and took a deep drag, then laughed, and said, "That was *mint*! Did you see the way that rock bounced off the dude's head? Like, *BOOM!*" He slammed his fist into the palm of his other hand. "Out for the fuckin' count!"

"Hope he weren't dead," Dubz, one of the two black lads in the gang, murmured worriedly. "I know his fam; they'll be well gutted."

"Shame," Damo sneered.

"He weren't," Acky said, sucking loudly on his own smoke. "I give him the boot before I left, and he made a noise."

"*Shame*," Damo said again, grinning slyly. "Would have been a buzz seeing that on the news."

"Fuck off, you'd have been well brickin' it if we'd done for 'em," Acky sneered. "Anyhow, Big T only told us to rough 'em up, so you're lucky we didn't do them in, or you'd be in the shit *big* time, bwoy."

Leon was sitting across from them with his back against a damp, peeling wall. As his breathing began to settle, he drew his knees up to his chin and gazed at the floor. He was really struggling to get his head around what had just happened, and he listened in silence as Acky and Damo bantered about which of them had done what. The others were all laughing, which made it seem worse, somehow. All except Dubz, who was sitting beside Leon with his own eyes downcast and a troubled look on his face.

Leon wasn't the only one who had noticed that Dubz wasn't involving himself in the banter. Acky had stopped talking and was staring at him. "Yo, what's up with you?" he asked.

Dubz raised his eyes slowly. "Nowt."

"Don't look like it," Acky persisted. "You've always got a slap-arse face on you lately. If you've got a problem, why don't you just spit it out?"

Dubz pushed his lips out and nodded several times, as if he was chewing it over, then said, "All right. If you really wanna know, I'm sick of settling Big T's beefs."

Acky gave a scornful snort. "Knew you was turning pussy. Told you, didn't I?" He nudged Damo. "Every time it comes on top, *he's* always first to bottle it."

"I'm not bottling nothing," Dubz said angrily. "I just don't see why we're always taking orders from T, all of a sudden. He's got his own crew; let *them* deal with it."

110

"They got more important shit to take care of," Damo informed him. "Anyhow, what's the prob with us helping them out now and then? It's good for our cred."

"How?" Dubz demanded. "Come on, man, I'm serious. This ain't doing *shit* but get us caught up in their battles. Rate we're going, we're gonna have G's from all over Mane gunnin' for us."

"And?" Damo gave an unconcerned grin. "Least they'll be knowing about us. Nowt worse than being part of a crew no one's heard of and got no respect for."

"But that's just it, we *ain't* a crew," Dubz said, gazing steadily back at him. "We're just mates who hang out together. We ain't got no business to take care of, like the real G's. We ain't defending a patch, or running drugs, or nothing."

"No, but we soon will be," said Damo with confidence. "Soon as Big T sees we're loyal enough to trust us with the bigger shit, he'll set us up proper."

"Told you that, did he?" Dubz gave him a doubtful look.

"Not in so many words," Damo admitted. "But it's obvious, innit? Why would he call on us all the time if he ain't planning on bringing us in?"

"Let me think . . ." Dubz drawled. "Mebbe 'cos he knows we're stupid enough to do his dirty work without axing questions."

"Yo! Who you calling stupid?" Acky demanded.

"I'm right, though, innit?" Dubz stood up and brushed the dust off the back of his jeans. "He's

**111**

treating us like joeys, and we're gonna be the laughing stock of the Moss if we keep rolling over every time he whistles."

Acky sucked his teeth loudly. "Fuck you, man. I don't roll for *no* one. We're building cred here, and if you don't like it, you can fuck off."

"Man, you're deluded," Dubz said bluntly, looking Acky in the eye. Then, turning to Leon, he said, "You wanna get out while you still got a chance, kid. This ain't for you."

"Aw, there he goes pulling the old race card," scoffed Acky. "See how he's only bothered about the *black* kid? Talk about looking out for your own, eh?"

"That don't even come into it," Dubz argued. "He's a baby, that's all I'm bothered about. He don't need to be getting tangled up in all dis bad-man shit."

"He ain't no baby," Damo countered, grinning at Leon as he spoke. "Might be little, but he's got heart." He clenched his fist and bounced the back of it on his chest. "Good little lookout, he is. Loyal. More than I could say for *some*," he added, switching his gaze back to Dubz.

Dubz looked from Damo to Acky to Leon. Then, kissing his teeth, he turned and dragged the sink unit away from the door.

"Man best watch 'im back," Acky warned. "If'n him ain't with us, 'im against us, innit."

"You sound like a knob," Dubz jeered, flashing Acky a dirty look before yanking the door open and strolling out.

**112**

Leon saw something on the floor where Dubz had been sitting and reached for it.

"What's that?" Acky demanded.

"A knife," Leon told him, standing up. "Dubz must have dropped it. I'll go after him and give it him back."

"Fuck that," Damo snorted. "If he can't look after his shit, he don't deserve to have it. It's yours. Put it away."

"You deaf, y' muppet?" Acky said when Leon hesitated. "He said put it away."

Leon slipped the knife into his pocket. He liked Dubz, and appreciated the way he'd spoken up for him just now. But he also kind of liked the thought of having his own knife. He'd had one once before that he'd nicked from the corner shop: a tiny penknife with a pearl handle that doubled up as a nail file. He had thought he was the hardest kid on the estate with that knife in his possession — until it had snapped the first time he'd ever tried to use it. But there was no danger of *this* knife snapping, because this was the real deal. Heavy, with a cool black rubber-grip handle: a man could do some serious damage with a knife like this — and Leon already felt powerful just having it in his pocket.

# CHAPTER
# NINE

"Leave him alone!" Chantelle screamed, struggling to break free from the policeman who was holding her arms behind her back. "Get off me! I need to help my brother!"

"You know it's for the best", the social worker said as she ushered Leon out onto the landing where a policewoman was waiting to escort him to the car that was parked below. "If you'd told us what was happening, we could have helped you. But you lied, so now we've got no choice."

"Nooooo . . ." Chantelle wailed. "I can look after him! He's my responsibility."

"He's ours now," the woman replied firmly. "And so are you, so stop being silly and come along quietly, or we'll have to — "

Chantelle didn't hear the rest of the sentence. Woken by the sound of heavy knocking on the front door, she jerked upright in her bed and swiped at her tear-soaked eyes. It was almost a week since her mum had called and there had been no word from her since — and no sign of the money that she had promised to send. Chantelle had resigned herself to the thought that they might never hear from her again, and was numbed by the realisation that their mum cared so little for them. But now she was having these horrible recurring dreams about Leon being taken into care, and it was killing her.

Terrified that it might be her mum's dealer, Ricky, when another round of knocking echoed through the hall, she pulled on her dressing gown and crept out of her room. She jumped when the letter-box flap was pushed open and pressed herself back against the wall.

"It's E.ON," a man's voice called through. "We've got a warrant to enter, so you can either let us in or we'll break in. And if you try to obstruct us we'll call the police. You've got two minutes to decide how you want to do this."

Chantelle's legs were shaking so badly that she thought she might collapse. But she knew she had no choice but to let them in. If they broke the door, she and Leon really would be in trouble because there was no way she could afford to have it repaired.

"Mrs Booth?" one of the two men who were standing outside asked when she opened the door.

"No, she's out," Chantelle told him quietly. "I'm her daughter. Can — can you come back later?"

"Sorry, love, we've got a warrant." He showed her the paper he was holding and then flashed his ID card. "If you're on your own and would feel safer having the police here, we don't mind waiting outside till they come."

Chantelle sighed and shook her head. "No, you might as well just do it," she murmured, stepping aside.

"Sorry about this." The man gave her a sympathetic smile as he walked in. "I hate this part of the job, but there's nowt I can do about it once it's gone to warrant stage, I'm afraid."

"It's all right," Chantelle said miserably, opening the meter-cupboard door for them. "It's my mum's fault, not yours."

As his colleague quickly got to work ripping out the old meter and fitting the new one in its place, the man gave Chantelle the electronic card and explained how it worked. She nodded as if she was taking it all in, but her mind was reeling as he told her that the portion of the payment that represented the debt was to be set at ten pounds per week. On top of that, she would have to put in at least the same again in order to maintain the supply — and choosing to go without wasn't an option, because missed payments would clock up a whole new debt, which would result in a new warrant, only this time it would be bailiffs who executed it.

"And, believe me, they're a lot less understanding than us," the man warned. "Proper heartless bastards, that lot — pardon my French."

Thoroughly depressed by the time the men had cleared up and gone, Chantelle went into the kitchen and sat at the table with her head in her hands. The local free newspaper was lying in front of her, and when her gaze fell on it she had a sudden vision of her mum and Tracey sitting here indulging in the weekly pastime that they had used to enjoy: taking the piss out of the "sad bastards" who posted in the lonely-hearts column. Those ads, she remembered, were in the same section as the job vacancies. But while her mum and Tracey had never been remotely interested in *those* ads, it occurred to Chantelle that a job might be the answer to all her problems.

After scouring the vacancies and jotting down the numbers for the four she'd found which hadn't asked for experience or qualifications, her eye was drawn to the *For Sale* ads and another thought occurred to her. A thought that brought her to her feet and made her run into her mum's room.

She had already long ago found all the loose change that had ever fallen down the sides and backs of the sofa and chairs, and had emptied every pocket and old handbag in the flat. But it had never even crossed her mind to think about selling her mum's old jewellery. And, for a woman who had always claimed not to have enough money to feed decent food to her kids, she sure had enough of the stuff. By the time she'd finished gathering it all together, Chantelle had bagged three gold chains, a couple of chunky sovereign rings, another ring with a chipped amethyst in its centre, four pairs of Creole earrings, and numerous studs and sleepers. None of it was particularly good quality but it was all gold, so she was sure she would get *something* for it.

After getting dressed, she rushed over to a pawnbroker in Moss Side. A tiny twinge of guilt flared inside her as she accepted the £120 that the old man had offered her for the lot, but she pushed it firmly out of her mind, reminding herself that she wouldn't have had to do it if her mum hadn't left them to fend for themselves.

Chantelle stashed the money in her bra before she left the shop, determined not to let Ricky get his hands on it if he came round again. Then, feeling more positive than she had in a long time, she headed over to the market to do some shopping before walking home with a new spring in her step.

A few days later, Chantelle got up early and ironed her best skirt and blouse before polishing her least-scuffed shoes. After making the mistake of telling the first of the employers whose ads she had answered that she was only fifteen and currently on holiday from school, she'd lied to the other three and had managed to secure interviews with them all. It was going to be a bit of a mad dash, because the first two were in Chorlton while the third was in Cheetham Hill. But she wasn't going to complain about a little thing like that. She was just grateful that they had all agreed to see her on the same day.

Dressed, she went into her mum's room and picked through the clutter of make-up on the dressing table until she found mascara, lipstick and foundation. She had never been one for wearing make-up, and she felt awkward as she applied it. She didn't want to cake it on like her mum did and end up looking like a clown; she just needed to look eighteen.

Pleasantly surprised by the results when she'd finished, she stepped back to view herself in the mirror from every angle before going out into the hall and

**118**

slipping her coat on. Then, reaching for her handbag, she tapped on her brother's bedroom door.

Leon was lying in bed admiring his knife. He'd had it for a while now, and it still gave him a major buzz whenever he held it in his hand. But he knew that Chantelle would have a fit if she found out about it, so he quickly shoved it under his quilt when she knocked and looped his arms behind his head.

"'S up?" He smiled innocently up at her when she popped her head around the door.

"I've got to nip out for a few hours," she told him. "Will you be all right on your own till I get back?"

"Yeah, course." He stretched his arms and yawned. "Where you going?"

Chantelle had decided there was no point telling him that she was looking for a job until she managed to get one — after which they would have to have a serious talk; so she lied and said, "Just to the library. I'll come straight back as soon as I've finished. But if anyone calls while I'm gone, don't answer the door without checking first."

"I'll be going round to Kermit's," Leon told her, sitting up. "Can I have some money for chips?"

Chantelle took two pound coins out of her purse and tossed them onto the bed. "I'll see you in a bit. Make sure you behave for Linda."

"Always do," Leon murmured, flopping back down onto his pillow after picking the money up. "Have fun with your *books*."

"Wouldn't hurt you to start taking an interest in reading," Chantelle said, smiling as she closed his door.

When she emerged at the bottom of the stairwell a couple of minutes later, Anton Davis was walking past. Still mortified by her behaviour the last time they had spoken, Chantelle blushed when their eyes briefly met, but then felt strangely deflated when he just nodded and walked on. He was the best-looking boy on the estate and all her friends fancied him like crazy, so it had been kind of flattering to think that he'd been making an effort to talk to her lately. Not that she'd had any intention of trying to take it any further, or anything, because she had always vowed never to follow in her mother's footsteps and get hooked up with a man who would inevitably cheat on her, beat her, or have the police raiding her house every two minutes. But still . . .

Annoyed with herself for having let him get under her skin, Chantelle shoved Anton resolutely out of her mind, raised her chin, and went on her way.

The first interview was at a small bakery in the centre of Chorlton. It was packed with customers when Chantelle walked in, and the women who were working behind the counter looked flustered and sweaty as they tried to serve without getting under each others' feet. Chantelle waited at the back of the shop until the rush had died down, then stepped forward and told one of the women she was here to see Mrs Jones.

"That's me." The woman wiped her face on her sleeve. "You the girl I'm supposed to be interviewing?" She pursed her lips when Chantelle nodded and raised the flap at the end of the counter. "You're late."

120

"I've actually been here for ten minutes," Chantelle corrected her as she followed her through the shop and into a room at the back. "But I thought I'd best wait for the shop to clear."

"If I say you're late, you're late," Mrs Jones snapped, flopping down into a chair behind a messy desk. "And if you're already arguing, is there any point me even interviewing you?"

"I'm sorry," Chantelle murmured. "I'm just a bit nervous."

Mrs Jones sniffed, then waved her hand, indicating for Chantelle to sit down on the chair facing hers. "What did you say your name was again?" she asked, shuffling through the paperwork on her desk.

"Chantelle Booth."

"And you've never worked in a bakery before, right?"

"No, but I'm a quick learner."

Mrs Jones gave up her search and sat back. "I know I wrote it down somewhere, but never mind, I'll get what I need off your CV."

"I, er, forgot to bring it," said Chantelle, blushing, because it wasn't as easy to lie face to face as it was over the phone.

"What about your references?"

Chantelle clutched her bag tightly in her lap and shook her head.

Mrs Jones peered at her through narrowed eyes. "Have you even actually worked before?"

"Not exactly," Chantelle said quietly. "I've, er, been at college since leaving school."

"Studying what?"

"Art."

Mrs Jones rolled her eyes. "Fat lot of good *that*'s going to do you in the real world." Then, sighing, she said, "Look, I'm sorry, love, but I can already tell this isn't going to work out. I've got other people to interview, and some of them have got experience."

"Oh." Chantelle was deflated. "I thought the ad said experience wasn't required?"

"It isn't," said Mrs Jones. "But if it's a choice between someone who knows their way around an oven, and someone who's spent the last couple of years painting pretty pictures . . ." She left the rest unsaid and shrugged. "I'm sure you get my drift."

Chantelle nodded and stood up. "Thanks for seeing me," she said politely. "Bye."

Tears of disappointment stinging her eyes, she made her way back out onto the street. It would have been the perfect location, and she reckoned it wouldn't have been too hard to learn the ropes. But she doubted she'd have enjoyed working for that woman, so it was probably just as well.

With plenty of time to spare since the first interview had ended so quickly, Chantelle walked to the second address on her list. This one was for a part-time position at a newsagent's, and now that she'd had a taste of the kinds of things she might be asked she felt a little more prepared.

The interview went quite smoothly, and they said they would contact her within the week to let her know if she'd got it. But Chantelle wasn't sure she would accept it even if they wanted her, because they wanted

**122**

someone who could start at 5.30a.m. and that would cause problems with Leon. He'd been spending most of his days round at Kermit's lately, and she had mentally arranged her work schedule around that. But if she had to leave before he got up in the morning, he would have to let himself out. And if he left the door open, or that horrible Ricky burst in like he had on her the other week, they were screwed.

Chantelle caught the bus to the third interview in Cheetham Hill and walked around for half an hour before she found the road that the café where she'd been told to meet the man was situated on. It was set right back off the main drag, and she shivered when she walked around the corner and saw how run-down everything looked. Most of the buildings that had once stood on the road had been demolished, leaving a vast expanse of rubble that stretched out as far as she could see. Of the four buildings that remained, one was boarded up, and the second, a scruffy MOT service station, stank of old grease and oil. The third building was an ancient office block, most of the windows of which were either broken or had handwritten "To Let" signs propped up in them. The café was next door to this, and the smell of the greasy food when she pushed open the door was almost as bad as that emanating from the MOT station.

A tired-looking woman with straggly hair was perched on a stool behind the counter, picking at her nails. Three customers were seated at separate grimy tables, and Chantelle looked at each of them as she entered, wondering which, if any, was Bill May. It clearly wasn't the only female customer, who was at a table by the window tapping on a laptop; but both of the two men looked too old and scruffy to own a business.

"Chantelle?"

She turned at the sound of the voice and found the lone female customer smiling at her. "Er, yes." She approached the table. "Are you the lady I spoke to about the interview with Mr May?"

"*Mr May?*" The woman chuckled. "Afraid not, dear. *I'*m Bill." She held out her hand. "Short for Belinda," she added with a grimace. "Far too twee for my liking."

Chantelle didn't know what "twee" meant, but she smiled as if she did and shook the woman's hand.

"Take a pew." Bill used her foot to push out the chair that was facing hers. "Coffee?"

"Yes, please." Chantelle perched on the edge of the seat.

"Two coffees, Maureen," Bill called to the woman behind the counter. Then, clasping her hands together on the table-top, she said, "So, Chantelle, tell me a little about yourself."

Thrown, Chantelle gave a nervous little shrug. "What would you like to know?"

"How old are you?" Bill's pale blue eyes seemed to be boring into hers.

"Eighteen."

"Are you currently working?"

"No. I've been at college since I left school."

"Are you planning to go back after the break, or have you graduated?"

Chantelle licked her lips, wondering if it was a trick question. If she said no, the woman might think she was a dropout; but if she said yes, then Bill might think there was no point taking her on in the first place. She stumped for, "I haven't decided yet."

Bill nodded, and said, "I ask because, if I take you on, the work may not be as regular as you're hoping for. I said in the ad that it was part-time, but it will actually be more of a flexible arrangement — as in, if I need you, I'll call you. So if you're looking for something more stable, then you should probably look elsewhere."

"Oh, right," Chantelle murmured, wondering now if this was the woman's way of letting her down easy because she'd already decided that she didn't want her.

Maureen of the straggly hair carried their coffees over to the table and plonked them down, splashing liquid out of both cups. Dabbing at the mess with a napkin, Bill said, "The hours will be irregular, and it will involve night work. Would that be a problem?"

Chantelle hadn't even considered working at night, but now that the subject had been raised she realised that it might actually work out better. One of her main concerns had been the thought of Leon getting into trouble if he was left to his own devices all day, but if he was already tucked up in bed before she went out it would greatly reduce the risk.

"No, it won't be a problem," she said.

"Good." Bill plucked a crust off a plate that was sitting on the table and fed it to a dog that Chantelle hadn't noticed which was lying at her feet. Then, wiping her hand on her trousers, she looked Chantelle in the eye and said, "I'm going to lay my cards on the table and tell you that I was really looking for someone a little older. But you're the only applicant, so I'm going to suggest a trial run — see how we get on before I say yea or nay. Is that okay with you?"

Chantelle was disappointed, but she reasoned that at least she was being given a chance; and if she did well, Bill might give her the job. So, smiling, she said, "Yes, that's fine."

"Good girl. Now, it'll be cash in hand until we decide where we're going, and I'll cover your expenses on top of that. I've operated pretty much solo until now, but I'm neither as agile as I used to be, nor as inconspicuous as the majority of the jobs which seem to be coming my way lately require, hence my need of an assistant."

"To take calls and make appointments?" Chantelle ventured, assuming that these were the main duties of a receptionist.

"No, dear, that's my department," Bill said, peering at the laptop screen. "All I need you to do is look pretty and take some photographs. Or rather, a video, from which I will extract stills — providing you've managed to capture anything remotely usable."

"Sorry?" Chantelle was confused. "I thought the ad said you needed a receptionist?"

"If I had been upfront in the ad, I'd have been inundated with applications from every would-be James and Jemima Bond in Manchester," Bill said cryptically. "But I need someone I can trust, who is also attractive, and preferably female. Unfortunately, the law prohibits me from specifying the latter, so I was forced to word it in such a way as to guarantee that few if any men would bother to answer. As it happens, *nobody* did, apart from yourself."

"So what do you actually want me to do?" Chantelle asked, frowning now.

"Covert surveillance."

"Pardon?"

Bill looked up and smiled. "I shan't divulge too much at this stage, as I'll need to get the measure of you to ascertain as to whether I can rely on your discretion. But, basically speaking, I want you to videotape somebody — without them knowing that you're doing it."

"What, like, *spying?*"

"In a manner of speaking. You'll be in a public place, so you'll be in no danger; and I'll be waiting around the corner to make sure you get home safely. Are you still up for it?"

"Er, yes, I guess so," Chantelle murmured, wondering what on earth she was letting herself in for.

"Excellent," Bill said approvingly. "Let's get some details, then, shall we?" She turned her attention back to the laptop. "Here we are . . . Chantelle Booth, aged eighteen. Address and contact number . . .?"

Chantelle gave Bill the details she wanted. Then, shifting in her seat, she said, "I don't have a CV, or references, or anything."

"Not necessary at this stage," Bill assured her, saving the file and closing the laptop. "Now, the fee will be fifty pounds per job . . ."

"*Fifty pounds?*" Chantelle's jaw dropped.

"Depending how long it takes," Bill went on. "I anticipate it should only take two to three hours, but if it should go beyond that, we'll reassess. Is that agreeable?"

"*Yes!*" Chantelle said without hesitation.

"Splendid." Bill picked up her cup and swallowed a large mouthful of the hot coffee. Then, slapping a £5 note down on the table, she gathered up her laptop and reached for the dog's lead. "Nice to have you on board." She rose to her feet.

"When do you want me to start?" Chantelle asked, guessing that the interview was over when Bill headed for the door, tugging the arthritic old chihuahua behind her.

"I'll call you when I need you," Bill said, holding the door for Chantelle to follow her out onto the pavement. There, waiting patiently as the dog cocked its leg against the lamppost, she said, "I don't expect it to take too long before a job comes in, so please keep your phone switched on at all times."

Assuring her that she would, Chantelle said goodbye and headed back to the main road. Her mind was in a spin as she walked, and she struggled to make sense of what had just happened. She had never met anyone quite like Bill May before, and with all the secrecy she was beginning to wonder if the woman really owned a business at all, or was just a jealous wife who wanted someone to follow her husband around. But fifty quid was fifty quid, so even if it turned out to be a one-off she wasn't about to turn it down.

Leon was out when Chantelle got back to the flat. She popped her head around his bedroom door when she'd hung up her coat and tutted when she saw his unmade bed and the clothes strewn all over the floor. He'd always been lazy, but he had been getting progressively worse since their mum took off and Chantelle was forever picking up after him. It was her own fault, she supposed. Instead of doing it for him, she ought to put her foot down and make him do it himself. Or, better yet, train him not to do it in the first place.

She snatched up the wet towel that was lying at her feet and carried it into the kitchen. After putting it into the washing machine, she wiped her hands on her skirt and cast a critical eye around the room. Leon wasn't the only one who'd been lazy lately; there were crumbs and bits of dried-up food on the ledges in here, and the lino looked grimy and dull beneath her feet. But it wasn't just the kitchen and Leon's room that needed tackling — the whole place needed scrubbing from top to bottom.

Determined to shake off the cloud of gloom that had been hanging over her head for the past few weeks, Chantelle went into her room and changed into a pair of jeans and a T-shirt, and then got cracking. After blitzing the kitchen and the bathroom, she'd just finished polishing the furniture in the living room and was about to vacuum the carpet when her mobile phone rang.

"Yes?" she answered it snappily, brushing her sweaty hair out of her eyes.

"It's Bill," the caller said. "I've just pencilled in your first job."

*"Really?"* Shocked by the speed of it, Chantelle sat down heavily on the edge of the couch.

"It appears the fates must have been eavesdropping, because the phone rang not half an hour after you left," Bill said with a chuckle. "I've just finished speaking with the client, and she'd like us to do it tonight. I take it you're available?"

Chantelle felt suddenly nervous, but the thought of the fifty pounds she'd been promised overrode her doubts.

"Yes, absolutely."

"Excellent." Bill sounded pleased. "I'll pick you up at eight-fifteen on the corner of Upper Chorlton Road. Please don't keep me waiting, and dress appropriately for a wine bar. I have a photograph which you'll need to study on the way, and I'll show you how to use the camera before you go in. Oh, and no alcohol while you're working."

"It's all right, I don't drink," Chantelle assured her.

"Good. Well, I shall see you later, then."

When the call was finished, Chantelle chewed on her lip. Bill had told her to dress appropriately for a wine bar, but she'd never stepped foot inside one in her life. The nearest she'd ever come was when she'd had to go into the local pubs in search of her mother when Leon was a baby and she needed help. But it shouldn't be too hard to figure out. She'd seen enough of the older girls from around here done up for a night on the town, so all she had to do was fashion herself on them — and then tone it down a bit.

She smiled now, and shook her head. In a few short hours she would have fifty quid in her pocket: more than enough to pay this week's meter charges *and* fill the fridge. She just hoped she could pull it off — and that she wouldn't be asked to produce ID when she got to the bar, or it would be game over.

Brought back to the here and now by a knock at the front door, Chantelle went out into the hall and peeped through the spyhole. Surprised to see Leon standing outside, she opened up. "How come you're back so early?"

"I was hungry." He walked straight past her and went into the kitchen. "What's for dinner?"

"It's nowhere near dinner time," she said, following him. "And I've just cleaned that floor, so don't go scuffing it up with your dirty trainers. Get an apple for now."

"I hate fruit." Leon pulled a face and opened the cupboard door.

"It's good for you," Chantelle said. Then, folding her arms, she pushed her lips out thoughtfully. "Tell you what, I'll do you a deal."

"What kind of deal?" Leon looked back at her over his shoulder with suspicion in his eyes.

"If you promise to behave yourself while I nip out for a couple of hours tonight, I'll treat you to a chippy dinner. But I haven't got much money, so don't go mad."

"I only ever have sausage, chips and gravy," Leon reminded her, reaching for the apple he'd turned his nose up at and taking a big bite. "Where you off? Got a *date?*"

"As if!" Chantelle snorted, resisting the urge to hand him a towel to mop up the juice that was running down his chin. "Immy asked me to go to the pictures with her."

"Can I come?" His eyes lit up.

"No, it's a girly film; you'd hate it. Anyway, she's paying, so I can't just turn up with you in tow, can I? Go back round to Kermit's, if you want. I'll call for you on my way home."

"Nah, he's going out with his mum," Leon said dejectedly. "I'll just stop in and watch telly."

Chantelle felt guilty — although she'd have felt even worse if she really *had* been going to the pictures, knowing that he wanted to go too. But he'd been behaving since their talk, and she wanted him to know that she appreciated it, so she said, "Look, how's about we pick out another film to go and watch tomorrow — just you and me? *Or*, if you're *really* good, we could go bowling."

She'd thought that Leon would be delighted by this, because he loved ten-pin bowling, but he just narrowed his eyes, and said, "Thought you said we didn't have much money?"

"We haven't."

"So how come you can afford to take me out tomorrow, but not tonight?"

"I was going to ask Immy to lend me some."

"Why don't you just ask her to pay for me tonight instead?"

"'Cos it's too late to change our plans," Chantelle said irritably, annoyed with herself for getting caught out.

"You just don't want to take me," Leon said accusingly. "You're just like mum; you don't give a toss about me so long as you're having fun."

"That's not fair," Chantelle retorted. "I've always looked out for you."

"When it suits you."

"Right, enough," Chantelle snapped, fed up with his attitude. "If you must know, I'm going out on a job tonight. *That*'s why you can't come, and *that*'s how I'll be able to afford to take you out tomorrow, 'cos it's cash in hand."

"Why didn't you just say that instead of lying about it?" Leon pulled a face.

Chantelle sighed. "Because it might not come to anything, so I didn't see the point. Anyway, I didn't want anyone to find out, because we'll get into trouble if they find out I'm leaving you on your own."

"I ain't gonna tell no one, am I?" Leon said, as if she should have known that all along.

"I suppose not," Chantelle conceded. "But it's probably a one-off, so I'm not going to start worrying about it. I just need you to promise you won't mess about while I'm out tonight. No loud music, or running in and out leaving the door open."

"I'm not a kid," Leon informed her indignantly.

"I know." Chantelle smiled fondly and ruffled his hair. "You're growing up fast; guess it's time I started trusting you, eh? The offer's still there for bowling tomorrow, though — *if* you can face being seen in public with your big sis."

"*Ewwww!*"

Leon made a gagging face, but his eyes were sparkling, and Chantelle laughed and gave him a playful shove. "Watch it, you! Anyone'd think you were starting to like me, or something."

# CHAPTER
## TEN

Chantelle was already standing on the corner when Bill May pulled up at 8.15 that night. Her nerves had resurfaced with a vengeance, and her legs felt wobbly as she climbed into the car's passenger seat. The smell of dog hit her as soon as she closed the door, and she grimaced when she caught sight of the animal lying on the back seat with its tongue hanging out.

"You'll have to excuse Mitzy," Bill apologised as she handed over the photograph she wanted Chantelle to look at. "In dog years she's almost as old and decrepit as me, and I'm afraid she's developed a little flatulence problem."

Chantelle smiled politely and, trying not to inhale through her nostrils, gazed at the picture. It was a head-and-shoulders shot of an ordinary-looking man with brown hair and eyes. "Who is he?" she asked.

"Names aren't necessary," Bill said, peering over her shoulder to make sure that she was clear to proceed. "You just need to remember the face. The recording equipment is in the glove compartment," she added as she pulled out onto the road. "Take it out and I'll tell you how to use it."

Chantelle looked, but all she could see was a mobile phone.

"That's it," Bill told her. "It's actually a video recorder designed to look like a smartphone. It's very simple to use, and it's fully charged, so you'll have at least three hours of battery life. Just try not to run it until you've identified the subject. Oh, and I've loaded that picture into it, so you can double-check if you need to."

As Chantelle studied the photograph and checked out the buttons on the fake phone, Bill drove to a deserted side street off Deansgate's main drag. Parking up, she switched off the engine and had Chantelle do a test run with the video recorder, showing her how to adjust the contrast and zoom.

"Right, you'd best get going," she said when she was satisfied that Chantelle had got it. "The client said her hubby usually leaves the house at around eight-thirty, so you should have plenty of time to get yourself a drink and find a good position before he arrives. Take this." She handed Chantelle a £20 note. "And if you have any concerns, or you think you've been rumbled, leave immediately."

"How do you know he'll turn up?" Chantelle asked, pushing the money into her bag along with the phone.

"We don't," said Bill. "But if he hasn't shown in two hours, we'll call it a night."

"Where am I going?" Chantelle asked, unclipping her seat belt.

"Ah, silly me." Bill rolled her eyes. "It's a wine bar called The Fallow Field; third business down when you turn the corner onto Deansgate. Ready?"

Chantelle nodded and inhaled nervously. She had spent a long time getting ready and had thought she looked fine, but now she wasn't so sure. Had she put on too much make-up? Was the skirt she'd borrowed from her mum's drawer too short, or the top too low? Did she look like a woman, or a little girl playing dress-up? Was everyone going to stare at her when she walked into the bar and see right through her act?

"Stop worrying." Bill reached across and patted her hand reassuringly. "It'll be over in no time, and I'm sure you'll do a grand job."

Chantelle wasn't convinced, but she gave a fake-confident smile and stepped out of the car. On the pavement, she squeezed her eyes shut and made a silent plea to God not to let her cock it up. Then, raising her chin, she walked down the road and around the corner.

A roped-in smoking area took up most of the pavement outside the wine bar, and Chantelle saw several groups of people sitting and standing in there as she approached; the smoke from their cigarettes swirling around their heads, their faces glowing from the light of a free-standing patio heater. She blushed when three young men who were sitting at the table nearest the door gave her the eye, but she pretended not to notice and strolled up to the door.

Soft music was playing when she walked inside but she could barely hear it for the noise of chatter, laughter, and glass-clinking. It was still relatively early and she was surprised that the place was so packed. But she supposed that was good, because at least she wouldn't stand out quite so much. Although it might make it difficult to get a good viewpoint, given that there didn't seem to be any vacant chairs anywhere.

Her nerves stepped up a gear when she approached the bar. This was the bit she had been dreading. She had never in her life ordered a drink at a bar, and she was terrified that the bartender would take one look at her and know she was too young to be there.

Two bartenders were darting back and forth, filling orders, when she finally found a space. Waiting her turn, she gazed casually out around the room, surreptitiously scanning the faces of the other customers. When she spotted one who looked similar to the subject, she slid the fake phone out of her bag and tapped into the archived photos.

"Hi, there — what can I get you?"

Almost jumping out of her skin at the sound of the voice, Chantelle quickly closed the screen and turned back to the bar. "Erm, Coke, please."

"Ice and lemon?" The bartender was young, blond, and handsome in a bronzed surfer-boy kind of way — and he obviously knew it and traded on it, Chantelle guessed, judging by the super-cool smile he was giving her.

"Yes, thank you," she murmured, giving a small nervous smile in return.

"Waiting for someone?" Surfer-boy reached for a tall glass and pressed it up against the cola pump.

"I'm meeting a friend."

"Boy or girl?"

"Boy." Chantelle glanced at her watch, hoping that he would take the hint and back off. The last thing she needed was for her suspect to walk in while she was chatting, because if she missed him she wouldn't get paid.

"Shame," the bartender drawled, laying a serviette on the counter before placing her glass on it. "On the house," he said quietly when she held out the money Bill had just given her.

"Thanks, but I'd rather pay," Chantelle said, guessing that he'd take it as a green light to carry on chatting her up if she accepted.

He dipped his head in an *if you insist* motion and carried her money to the till, coming back a few seconds later with her change. "I haven't seen you in here before." He rested his elbows on the bar. "First time?"

"Mmmm." Chantelle took a sip of the drink and glanced back out across the room. Then, as if she'd seen someone she recognised, she said, "Excuse me" and walked away.

She made her way to a dark corner from where she could see the door and, sipping on her drink, held up the fake phone. The lighting was dimmer in here than it had been in the car, and when — *if* — the man arrived, she wanted to make sure that she got a good clear shot of him.

An hour passed, and Chantelle was seriously regretting her decision to wear heels. Her feet were killing her, she'd already had to fend off two men who had tried hitting on her, and she was beginning to feel extremely self-conscious, sure that everyone in the room must have noticed her standing there and was secretly laughing at her. She knew it was ridiculous, because she wasn't really waiting for anyone, but her pride was smarting at the thought that the other customers might assume that she'd been stood up.

She was just checking her watch to see how long she had left to suffer when the door opened and her target walked in. She recognised him immediately, and her heart began to beat a little faster as she watched him walk up to the bar. He was alone, but he was looking around as if expecting to see somebody. Seconds later he smiled, and when Chantelle followed his gaze she saw a blonde woman waving at him from a table in the far corner. Hands shaking, she moved into a better position and, pretending to be sending a text as Bill had instructed, framed the table in the screen.

Leon was slouched on the couch with the TV remote in his hand. He'd been flicking through the channels for ages, but there was nothing on that he was remotely interested in. Chantelle had changed the parental lock code, so he couldn't access any of the sex channels; and the DVD player was broken so he couldn't even watch a decent film.

Bored off his skull, he wandered over to the window when he heard a whistle outside. Shocked to see Damo and Acky standing down below, he quickly pushed the window open and leaned out.

"What are you doing here?"

"Come down," Damo said. "I've got summat for you."

"Can't," Leon called back. "Our kid's out, and I haven't got a key to get back in."

"What number you at?"

"Four thirty."

"Be up in a minute."

Leon closed the window and rushed to open the front door. He'd been upset when Damo had sent him home earlier in the day, convinced that Acky had finally got his way and had him kicked out of the gang. But now they were both here, calling for him, so they must still like him.

"All right, kidda." Damo touched fists with him when he strolled up to the door a couple of minutes later.

Leon grinned and stepped back to let him in.

"Wha'pp'n." Acky nodded and followed Damo in.

"Fuck me, it's colder in here than out there," Damo complained when they were in the living room.

"My sis don't like having the heating on too much," Leon muttered, embarrassed to admit that they couldn't afford it.

"Bit of a bossy fucker, her, ain't she?" Damo sneered, walking around the room. "Got a right gob on her, an' all."

"I'd soon fill it for her," Acky said, grinning lewdly as he thrust his hips forward and mimed holding a head in front of them. "I'd be like, yo! Suck on this big boy, baby."

Leon didn't like that, but he kept his mouth shut, scared that Acky might turn on him if he said anything. "What've youse been up to?" he asked instead, following with his eyes as Damo picked up ornaments and leafed through the letters Chantelle had propped behind the clock on the mantelpiece.

"Just some stuff for Big T," Damo said evasively. "That's why you couldn't come with us, 'cos some jobs ain't safe for little 'uns. Gotta look out for our baby soldiers, innit?" he added, flicking Acky a sly grin.

"Yeah. Can't have you getting hurt 'cos of us," Acky agreed, flopping down on a chair and draping his legs over the arm. "Got owt to drink?"

"Tea?"

"Behave. I ain't your fuckin' dad! *Tea*, me arse."

"You'll be *some* fucker's dad before too long if you don't start watching where you put it," Damo jibed. "That Julie you've been knocking off must have had about ten abortions this year. You wanna knock it on the head before she gets caught for one of yours, mate."

Acky sucked his teeth in disgust and pulled his fags out of his pocket. Leon frowned when he sparked up, but didn't dare ask him to put it out. Chantelle was bound to smell it as soon as she came in, but he'd rather have her go off on one because she thought he'd been smoking than risk pissing Acky off again.

"Here, catch." Damo pulled something out of his pocket and tossed it to Leon before flopping down on the couch.

"What's this for?" Leon asked, looking down at the mobile phone in his hand.

"So I can reach you when I need you," Damo told him. "We're going into business, and I'm gonna need you to step up and do your bit."

"Is it mine?" Leon gasped. "For real?"

"Nah, it's for your kid," Acky said sarcastically. "So I can make dirty calls to her in the middle of the night."

"Course it's yours," Damo said, clicking his fingers at Acky to pass his smoke over. "But don't be giving the number to no one, 'cos it's just between us, yeah?"

Leon nodded and gazed down at the phone again. Chantelle had got her mobile ages ago, but his mum always said he was too young whenever he asked for one. It was ace.

"I'm gonna need you to look after something," Damo said now, blowing a smoke ring as he pulled a plastic bag out from the inside of his jacket and chucked it to Leon. "Put it somewhere safe. I'll give you a call when I need you to fetch it to me."

Leon caught the bag and gave Damo a questioning look. "What is it?"

"None o' your business," Acky said sharply. "Just do as you're fuckin' told and put it away."

"Leave the boy alone," Damo said quietly. "He knows not to ask questions — innit, Leon?"

"Yeah, course." Leon nodded. "I won't say nothing to no one."

"Course you won't." Damo smiled.

"Better not," Acky said, taking his knife out of his pocket and staring at Leon as he flicked the blade out. "Wouldn't wanna have to cut your little cock off, would we?"

Leon's mouth went dry when he saw the glint in the older boy's eyes, and he clutched the bag to his stomach. "I'll hide it somewhere safe," he promised.

Bill had Mitzy on her lap when Chantelle came back to the car. Eyes closed, she was humming along to some classical music that was drifting out from the radio. But she sat up straight when Chantelle tapped on the window, and popped the dog onto the back seat before releasing the door lock.

"How did you get on?"

"Okay." Chantelle climbed in and flopped her head back against the headrest. "I'm exhausted."

"Adrenalin," said Bill. "The rush when you locate your very first suspect is a knockout, but it's not quite as bad the second time around. So let's have it, then." She held out her hand.

Chantelle passed over the video recorder. "I didn't think he was going to come, 'cos I was in there for over an hour before I saw him. He was on his own when he came in, so I thought he might just have nipped in for a quick drink. But then I saw him smile at this woman."

"Mmm-hmm," Bill murmured, nodding as she attached a USB lead to her laptop. "And?"

"He bought a couple of drinks and carried them over to the table. But you'll see what happened, because I started filming just before he sat down." Chantelle craned her neck to see the computer screen as she spoke. "It might be a bit shaky to start with," she admitted. "But I think I managed to get some good shots."

Bill had loaded the film by now and was watching the screen intently. She pressed pause a few times and squinted closely at the screen before moving it along.

**144**

Then, a slow smile lifting her lips, she jabbed her finger down on the stop button. "Bingo!"

Chantelle looked at the screen, and saw that Bill had stopped it on a frame that showed the man and his companion kissing. But it was the position of his hand which had brought the smile to Bill's lips, because it was clearly cupping the woman's breast.

"That, my dear," Bill closed the laptop with a flourish, "is what we call the money shot."

"So, is it all right?" Chantelle asked.

"Marvellous." Bill took an envelope out of her pocket and handed it to Chantelle. "*Bloody* marvellous, actually, considering it was your first time. You're obviously a natural."

Chantelle felt so proud of herself that she couldn't stop smiling. She had really thought she was going to mess it up, but it had turned out to be surprisingly easy. So easy, in fact, that she had been convinced she must be doing it wrong: that the film would turn out too dark, too shaky, or, worse, blank because she hadn't pressed the right buttons. But Bill seemed delighted with the results so she couldn't have done too bad a job. And she hadn't even looked out of place standing there with her phone in her hand for so long, because loads of the other customers had been equally attached to theirs.

"What will you do with it?" Chantelle asked, slipping the envelope into her bag.

"Take a few of the best stills and upload them onto my database," Bill told her as she started the engine.

"Then I'll provide my client with a pin number, so she can log in and view them."

"What will *she* do with them?" Chantelle clipped her seat belt into place.

"That's her business," Bill said, manoeuvring the car out onto the main road. "But, in my experience, if a client has reached the point of contacting a private investigator it generally spells divorce."

Chantelle snapped her head around and peered at Bill with wide eyes. She hadn't thought to ask what kind of business Bill actually ran, but she would never have imagined that it would be a detective agency.

"Wow," she said, seeing the old woman with new eyes. "I never knew women did that. You only ever see men doing it on TV, don't you?"

"That's because those shows are generally penned by overgrown schoolboys who fancy themselves as real-life Sam Spades," Bill said scornfully. "But I assure you the reality is quite different. I have yet to be involved in a supercharged car chase, all guns blazing."

Chantelle smiled and gazed out of the window. Bill had really shocked her; she looked nothing like Chantelle's idea of a private investigator. Not that she'd ever really thought about it, but if she had her vision would have been of somebody a lot younger, and far more glamorous.

"Here we are." Bill interrupted her thoughts.

Chantelle blinked when she realised the car had stopped, and was surprised to see that they were back at the corner where Bill had picked her up. "That was fast," she said. "We were still in Deansgate last time I looked."

"You've been in a world of your own for the last few minutes," Bill told her, smiling knowingly as she added, "Adrenalin comedown. Go home and put your feet up — you've earned a rest. I'll give you a call when the next job comes in."

"Does that mean I passed the test?" Chantelle asked, climbing out.

"You'll do for now," Bill said, patting her vacated seat. "Goodnight."

Chantelle quickly closed the door when the dog dragged itself through the gap between the front seats and landed with a plop on the passenger seat. Then, waving Bill off, she walked home.

Two lads strolled out of the stairwell as she headed in, but she was too busy thinking about the events of the night to notice them. Leon was washing a cup at the kitchen sink when she let herself into the flat a couple of minutes later, and she could smell air freshener.

"What's got into you?" she teased. "I should leave you alone more often if it's going to have this effect on you."

"It's only a cup," he grunted, giving her a funny look.

"Yeah, but . . . Oh, never mind." Chantelle smiled and decided not to push it. "How come you're still up? It's nearly twelve, you know."

"I was watching telly," Leon said, wiping his hands on a tea towel. "But there's nothing on, so I'm off to bed."

"See you in the morning," Chantelle said. "Oh, and have you decided if you want to go to the pictures or bowling tomorrow?"

"Not sure." Leon shrugged. "Might just go round Kermit's. Night."

Chantelle frowned as she watched him go up the hall and disappear into his room. That was strange. First, washing up after himself, which she had *never* seen him do before; then opting to go to Kermit's rather than bowling, even though he could go to Kermit's any day — *did* go *every* day, in fact. But bowling was a rare treat, and he absolutely loved it, so she'd thought he would have been really excited about it.

The frown deepened as it occurred to her that he might have been spending so much time at Kermit's because they had been getting stoned again. But she quickly dismissed the thought. Linda had gone mad the last time, so there was no way they would dare to do it in the flat while she was there. If they had been going out, maybe; but they had been holed up in Kermit's room playing computer games for the last few weeks. Which wasn't good in one way, but was infinitely better than him roaming the streets getting into trouble.

Satisfied that she had nothing to worry about, that Leon's computer addiction was normal for boys of his age, Chantelle checked that all the plugs were switched off around the flat and then went to bed.

In his own room, Leon smiled when he heard Chantelle's light go off, followed by the squeak of bed springs as she settled down for the night. He slid his

148

hand under his pillow and pulled out the phone that was lying next to his knife. The glow from the screen lit up his face in the dark when he turned it on. It was one of the most basic models so it didn't have a camera or internet access, or anything like that. It also didn't have credit, so he couldn't make any calls or send texts. But it was his, and he loved it.

Grinning happily, he turned the phone off and slid it back under his pillow. He couldn't wait to get his first text or call, and it was going to be totally cool showing it off when he went back to school. Some of the other kids already had phones, but his was different. His was a *gang* phone, not some dumb-ass kid phone.

As his eyes began to feel heavy, he leaned over and stuck his hand under the mattress to check one last time that the bag was properly hidden. He hadn't dared to look inside after Acky's warning, but it smelled like weed and he guessed that they must have got it off the man they called Big T, because Damo had been saying for ages that he would set them up to deal for him one day. Leon had never seen the man, but he knew from what Damo had said that he was the leader of an older gang in Moss Side. And now that Damo was part of that gang, Leon was, too, by association. And that was so cool.

Chuffed to think that he was becoming a somebody instead of just a kid, Leon closed his eyes and snuggled down beneath his quilt.

# CHAPTER
# ELEVEN

Anton had taken the morning off work. Abdul had complained when he'd told him he wouldn't be coming in but the fat fucker moaned about everything, so Anton couldn't care less. When he'd put his name down on the housing list he'd thought it would be ages before he heard back from them, so he'd been surprised to receive a letter a few days ago telling him that a flat had become available on his block. He had made up his mind that he was going to take it before he'd even finished reading the letter, and he would have gone straight down to the office and signed the tenancy agreement there and then if they had let him. But the council liked to do it by the book, so he'd had to make an appointment to meet up with the housing officer this morning to do a formal viewing.

The flat's front door opened into a small hallway, the kitchen to its left, the tiny cramped bathroom to the right. One of the bedrooms, which was only marginally bigger than the hall cupboard, sat between the kitchen and the living room. That room and the master bedroom were at the back, their large windows overlooking the car park.

"Sorry about the smell," the housing officer apologised, her stiletto heels clipping loudly on the uncarpeted living-room floor as she rushed to open the window. "The maintenance team did a thorough clean-up, but there's not a lot else we can do apart from wait for it to die down. It'll be less noticeable when this has been replaced." She gestured towards the faded age- and tobacco-stained flock paper. "We used to redecorate before reletting, but we don't do that any more, so you'll have to do it yourself if you decide to take it on. But there's a grant for materials, so it won't cost you anything."

Anton nodded and looked into the master bedroom. It was twice the size of the other and he was already visualising how it would look after he'd put his stamp on it. It would take a while to get everything exactly how he wanted it, because his wages were shit. But he didn't care how long it took, so long as it meant getting out of his ma's place.

In the bathroom the woman pointed at a damp patch around the base of the toilet. "That's been sorted, so don't worry about it; it just needs to dry out. I think we could probably do with a new shower head." She wrinkled her nose at the filthy article hanging limply from the wall above the bath. "But everything else seems okay."

"It's all cool," Anton said, squeezing past her to get back out into the hallway. The smell was starting to get to him and he just wanted to get the paperwork signed so he could go and buy some bleach. The previous tenant had been ancient, so he supposed it wasn't her fault she'd let it get into such a state. He just wished she'd chosen somewhere else to die, because it would take a while before he was able to sleep without visualising her corpse lying beside him.

"So, what do you think?" the woman asked.

"I'll take it," Anton said, walking into the kitchen. All the units were new in there, and the smell was nowhere near as bad as in the rest of the flat.

"Great." She smiled and followed him in. "All you need to do is fill out the paperwork and it's yours."

Anton rested his elbow on the counter top and watched as the housing officer took a folder out of her bag and opened it up on the ledge beside him. She looked to be in her mid-twenties and clearly rated herself, judging by the way she was dressed in pencil skirt and heels, with a low-cut blouse that showed a fair bit more cleavage than he'd have expected of a council official. She'd been giving him flirtatious little looks and smiles since she'd got here, and he knew he could have her if he wanted, but she wasn't really his type.

"If you could just sign here, and here . . ." She held out a pen and pointed to the appropriate places on the form.

Anton scribbled his signature and handed the pen back. "When can I get the keys?"

"Right now." She took them out of her pocket and passed them over. "Your tenancy will officially start a week on Monday, so that's when the first rent will become due. I'll arrange to have the card sent out when I get back to the office. You can pay at any post office, or pop in and pay over the counter. Unless you're in receipt of benefits, in which case you'll need to update your claim with them. Oh, and you'll need to let the electricity board know you're moving in so they can start a new account. It's still connected at the moment, but you don't want to be landed with the previous tenant's debts, so make sure you take a meter reading on the day you move in." The woman paused to draw breath, and smiled. "Any questions?"

"Only about that grant you mentioned," Anton said, slipping the keys into his pocket.

"Ah, yes." She took another form out of her folder and slid it across for him to sign. "Just tick everything and they'll send vouchers. You should get them fairly quickly."

"Thanks." Anton signed the form and pushed it back to her. "Is that it, then?"

"I think so." She closed the folder, then took a card out of her bag and handed it to him. "This is my direct line at the office. And my mobile number's on the back — in case you need to contact me outside of office hours."

Anton looked down at it and smiled. "Thanks, *Jodie*. I'll keep it somewhere safe."

She blushed when he said her name and gathered her things together. Amused, Anton showed her out and made sure that the door was double-locked before walking her up the landing.

Chantelle was coming up the stairs as Jodie started walking down. Anton stayed at the top and waved for Chantelle to come the rest of the way up.

"Thanks," she said when she reached the top step.

"No problem." He smiled. "We're going to be neighbours," he said then. "Just signed for the flat three down from yours."

"That's nice," Chantelle murmured. "Sorry, I've really got to go. Bye."

"Yeah, see you," Anton said, watching as she walked away quickly. When she disappeared into her flat, he shook his head and cursed himself for having blurted that out about being neighbours. He didn't know why he'd said it, or how he'd expected her to respond, but she probably thought he was a complete dick for announcing it like that.

Annoyed with himself, he tried to push Chantelle out of his mind as he trotted down the stairs to see the housing officer off, but it wasn't easy. He'd only ever seen her a few times in total, and he'd always thought she was pretty, but this was the first time he'd ever seen her wearing make-up and with her hair down, and she'd looked amazing. But what was the point of thinking about her like that when she'd made it clear that she wasn't interested?

Chantelle rushed straight into the back room and peered through the net curtain to the car park below. The woman who had been with Anton was bent over, her backside in the air as she peered into the wing mirror of a parked car and fluffed her hair. Chantelle cast a critical eye over her clothes and shoes as she watched. She knew the woman was from the housing, because she'd seen the logo on the badge clipped to the lapel of her jacket, but she was surprised that the council allowed their female employees to dress so tartily.

When, a few seconds later, Anton strolled up to the car, Chantelle jerked back from the window and narrowed her eyes as she watched him give the woman a broad smile. Unimpressed when she gazed coquettishly up at him, Chantelle shook her head in disgust. Whatever he was saying to her, the stupid bitch was obviously falling for it hook, line and sinker. Well, more fool her if she couldn't spot a player. Serve her right if she got pregnant, or had her heart broken.

When the woman had driven away at last, and Anton had walked off towards the shops, Chantelle went to her room and got changed. Then, taking her latest earnings out of her bag, she went into the kitchen and reached to the back of the cupboard beneath the sink for the old coffee jar in which she'd been stashing her money. She had thought it would be safer here than in her own room because it was the last place Leon would ever dream of looking, seeing as this was where the cleaning stuff was kept. Not that she thought he would deliberately steal from her, but it would be a huge temptation if he were to come across it by accident and she didn't want to take the risk.

She smiled as she slotted the folded notes in with the rest. She'd done six jobs to date, and hadn't spent a single penny other than what she needed each week for the meter and food. She was grateful that Bill was still paying her cash in hand, but she knew it wouldn't last for ever. The day Bill decided to make their arrangement formal would be the day when Chantelle would have to walk away — and she was dreading it.

She had never in her wildest dreams imagined that she would get such a kick out of spying on people, but she absolutely loved it. She'd always known that men were devious and deceitful, but it still shocked her how easily and unconcernedly they strayed. That was probably why Bill was single, she supposed. Her boss must have long ago reached the same conclusion: that men were born liars who couldn't be trusted as far as you could throw them.

This morning's job had been the first that Chantelle had undertaken during daylight hours. It seemed that the majority of cheats preferred to operate at night, when they could ply their playthings with alcohol and get up to their shenanigans under cover of darkness; but today's suspect had met his lady friend in a coffee shop, both apparently on lunch breaks from their respective jobs. The broad daylight and the fact that they had been surrounded by shoppers hadn't put them off, and Chantelle had caught some fairly full-on groping going on under the table. She pitied the man's poor wife when she saw the footage but, as Bill always said, it was better for their clients to know the truth than to suffer the uncertainty.

Unusually, because her jobs had so far all been a few days apart, Chantelle had another one lined up for this evening. This client, however, had no idea where her husband might be going, so instead of being *in situ* at a predetermined venue Chantelle and Bill were to start their surveillance outside the suspect's house.

Chantelle had a few hours before she had to start thinking about getting ready and she had planned to go shopping. But she didn't fancy bumping into Anton again, so she decided to stay in and do some cleaning instead. Although she wouldn't be going anywhere near Leon's room, because he'd gone mad the last time he caught her in there. But that was fine by her. He reckoned he was growing up, so he could clean up after himself from now on.

# CHAPTER
# TWELVE

Bill turned onto the suspect's road at eight p.m. and parked in a secluded inlet. When she switched off the lights, plunging them into darkness, Chantelle gazed out at the shadowy houses across the way. They were all detached and fronted by neat hedges, with high wrought-iron gates to keep casual callers at bay. She'd only ever seen houses as grand as these on TV, owned by really rich people and maintained by an army of cleaners and gardeners. She couldn't begin to imagine what it would be like to live in such a massive house, and the area was unusually quiet, too; no teenagers hanging around on the corners, no traffic, doors slamming, or people shouting, arguing or fighting. It was a world away from the life she knew, and she couldn't help but envy the people who could afford to live like this. But girls like her didn't fit into places like this, so there was no point thinking about it.

"Something wrong?" Bill asked when she heard Chantelle sigh for the third time in as many minutes.

"No." Chantelle smiled. "Just wondering what it must be like to live in such a big house."

"Lonely," said Bill, quickly adding, "I should imagine."

Chantelle raised an eyebrow, but didn't say anything. She'd known Bill for a few weeks now and they got along well enough. But the woman never spoke about anything apart from the business, so it was hard to imagine her having a life outside of her office and this car.

She was different from anybody Chantelle had ever met before. She dressed scruffily, and her car was old — and smelly, courtesy of Mitzy's continuous farting. Yet her accent was posh, and she used words that Chantelle, who had always been near the top of her English classes, didn't always understand. For all Chantelle knew, she was from a really rich family and had grown up in a house like those they were sitting outside. But she doubted that she would ever find out, because her boss wasn't the kind to talk about personal stuff.

They had been sitting there for over an hour and the windows were steamy by the time Bill saw movement. "He's off," she said. "Quick, get down."

Chantelle glanced out of the window in time to see a flashy BMW emerge from a driveway up ahead. As it turned onto the road and began to head towards them, she slid down in her seat and held her breath until it had passed.

Bill stared at the tail lights in the rear-view mirror. As soon as they disappeared around the corner, she sat up and started her car, causing Chantelle to hold onto the sides of her seat as Bill quickly turned around and set off after the BMW.

The suspect's car was four vehicles ahead of them when they hit the main road. "Camera ready?" Bill asked, keeping the tail lights in her sights.

"Yeah, just need to press record," Chantelle told her.

Bill smiled to herself. The girl was a quick learner who rarely needed telling twice, and she was far more polite and respectful than most girls of her age who were all too often consumed by a staggering sense of self-importance and entitlement. The best thing about Chantelle was that she had a genuine interest in the work and had quickly picked up a knack for judging when something was about to happen, saving Bill from having to wade through swathes of film before reaching the money shot. All in all, she was proving to be a good addition to the business.

Unaware of Bill's silent appraisal, Chantelle reached into the glove compartment and took out the photograph that the client had emailed to Bill earlier in the day. The suspect was handsome, with short, dark, stylishly cut hair and piercing blue eyes. The picture looked as if it had been taken at a party, and Chantelle guessed from the expression in his eyes that he was intimately connected to whoever had been on the other side of the camera. Maybe his wife in happier times — before the rot had set in and she'd decided to have him followed. He looked fairly young, but he obviously had money to be living in such an expensive neighbourhood, and his car was really classy, too.

As she felt the envy stirring again, Chantelle put the picture away and sat back in her seat.

**160**

The man drove into the city centre and parked up on a backstreet off Deansgate, not far from the wine bar where Chantelle had done her first job. Telling Chantelle to duck down, Bill drove past and pulled over a couple of hundred yards further down. She watched in the rear-view mirror as the man sauntered down the road, one hand in his pocket, the other holding the jacket that was slung casually over his shoulder. When he went into the doorway of a nightclub on the corner, she said, "Game on."

Chantelle took the money that Bill was holding out to her and climbed out of the car. No longer afraid of being challenged about her age, she paused to smooth her skirt, then strolled confidently down the road and into the club.

She gazed around as she entered, and quickly located the suspect being greeted with handshakes and slaps on the back from two men at the far end of the bar. She ordered a Coke and carried it over to a table in a dimly lit corner. Then, taking the camera-phone out of her bag, she surreptitiously kept track of the suspect and his friends as they settled at a table in the opposite corner.

It was more than an hour before anything happened, by which time the club had started to fill up. With her view now partially obscured by people on the dance floor, Chantelle moved to an empty stool at the end of the bar and started the camera rolling when she saw a woman approach the men's table and sit down.

The woman was very beautiful, with long dark hair and a great figure, and Chantelle could clearly see by the way she was pouting and batting her lashes that she was flirting with the suspect. She kept leaning in close to speak into his ear, and he obviously found whatever she was saying amusing because he was doing a lot of smiling and nodding. But just as Chantelle thought that something incriminating was about to happen, the suspect received a call on his mobile phone and excused himself from the table. And when he went back a couple of minutes later, he picked up his jacket, shook hands with his friends and kissed the woman on both cheeks before strolling out of the club.

Chantelle waited a few minutes to see if the woman would follow him, then called it a night.

Bill unlocked the car door and gave Chantelle a questioning look as she climbed in. Chantelle shook her head and handed the videophone to her.

"He met up with some men when he first went in, and they were just drinking and talking for the first hour. A woman arrived after that and it looked like there might be something going on, but then he got a phone call and left."

"So he didn't do anything?" Bill slotted the USB lead into her laptop.

"Nothing." Chantelle shook her head. "The woman was flirting and I thought he might be responding, but I'm not sure now. See what you think."

Bill loaded the film and watched it intently, looking for anything that Chantelle might have missed. There were plenty of telltale signs that even the most cautious of people couldn't avoid giving off: a look, a

**162**

subconscious positioning of the body, or a random gesture that betrayed an intimacy they were trying to hide. But, as Chantelle had said, there seemed to be nothing untoward going on.

"Ah, well, the client should be relieved," Bill said as she disconnected the lead and closed the laptop down. "But I see what you mean about the flirting. She couldn't have been more obvious if she'd stripped naked and waggled her tilly mint right under his nose."

"*What?*" Chantelle laughed and stared at her.

"Well, it's true." Bill chuckled and reached through the gap between their seats to put the laptop on the back seat. "Men are foolish creatures but we'd be out of a job if they weren't so easily led astray, so I shan't complain. Anyway, another job well done — so let's get you home, shall we?"

# CHAPTER
# THIRTEEN

Yvette Knight kissed her husband goodbye the next morning and waved him off from the doorstep. As soon as the electric gate slid shut behind his car, she rushed into the kitchen and switched her laptop on. Then, perching on a stool, she opened the private investigator's page and typed in the pin code she'd received by text when Rob had been in the shower earlier.

She'd been itching to see what the PI had got for her, and when a series of pictures appeared on the screen now she tucked her hair behind her ear and clicked on the first image to enlarge it. It showed Rob sitting in a club with two men and a woman, and Yvette's jaw clenched in anger when she saw the way the bitch was gazing adoringly up at him. Yvette was a natural blonde, but that was the only genuine thing about her: everything else was fake, from her nails to her lashes to her boobs — just the way Rob claimed to like his women. But this tart had long, thick, glossy black hair, naturally tanned skin and, Yvette suspected, naturally large breasts.

Already seething with jealousy, Yvette scrolled through the rest of the pictures. She had been asleep when Rob got home last night, and when she'd asked him this morning where he'd been, he'd said he'd been in a late-night meeting at work. So what the hell had he been doing at a nightclub, with *Vampira* drooling all over him?

The sound of the front door opening made Yvette almost jump out of her skin. Hands shaking, she quickly closed the page she was viewing and opened one from the favourites tab just as Rob strolled in.

"Forgot my wallet," he said, looking around. "Thought you said you were getting a bath?"

"I am in a minute." Yvette smiled. "Just came to make myself a coffee and got distracted by Jimmy Choo."

Rob spotted his wallet on the ledge behind the laptop and reached over her shoulder to get it, glancing at the screen as he did so. "Those are nice." He pointed at a pair of strappy stilettos. "Why don't you order them?"

"Maybe." Yvette gritted her teeth as she wondered if those particular shoes had caught his eye because his *tart* had been wearing something similar last night.

"Go on — treat yourself," Rob said magnanimously, slipping his wallet into his pocket. "Not sure when I'll be back tonight. Adam just called to say he's scheduled me in for an extra meeting this afternoon, and I've got a feeling it might run over."

"Again?" Yvette struggled to keep the accusation from her eyes as she peered up at him.

"Can't be helped." Rob shrugged. "Business is business. Anyway, got to go. See you later."

Yvette tilted her head back when he kissed her on the forehead and smiled as he went on his way. But the smile disappeared as soon as he was out of the door, and she listened for the sound of his car tyres crunching gravel before switching screens back to the private investigator's pictures.

One by one she scrutinised them, the anger burning that bit more brightly with each new detail she picked out. When she could stand no more, she slammed the laptop lid shut and lit a cigarette. She took a deep drag and gazed around the room as she exhaled her smoke through gritted teeth. This house was her pride and joy. She had spent months choosing the furnishings and decor which had turned it from a house into a home, and she made sure the cleaners never missed a speck of dust so it always looked immaculate. Rob might be the emperor of all he surveyed at work, but Yvette was the undisputed queen of this castle, and no tarty little bitch was going to wheedle her way into Rob's life and take her crown away from her. Not without a bloody big fight, anyway.

She took another drag on her cigarette and snatched her mobile phone off the ledge.

"It's Mrs Knight," she said when her call was answered. "I've seen the pictures, but it's not enough. I want you to try again. Only this time . . ."

"I'll see what I can do," Bill said when Yvette Knight had outlined what she wanted. "No, it's no problem; leave it with me and I'll get back to you."

**166**

Bill put the phone down when the call was finished and gazed thoughtfully out over her messy office. She'd just been asked to provide a service she had never before offered, mainly because she had worked alone until recently and was herself completely unsuitable for the role. But now that she had Chantelle it was entirely feasible — as long as the girl felt comfortable with the idea. It would be a stretch as Chantelle had so far had no contact with the suspects she'd been tasked to follow. Looks-wise, she was perfect, but Bill wasn't so sure about the personality side of things. As sweet as she was, and as comfortable as she now seemed to feel in Bill's presence, Chantelle had an innate shyness which might prohibit her from putting herself out there in the way this job would require. But Bill supposed she could only ask.

She picked up the phone again and rang Chantelle's number.

"Hello, dear, are you free to talk? I have a proposition for you."

Chantelle bit her lip when Bill had finished the call. What the hell had she let herself in for? She had just agreed to follow last night's suspect again, but this time she wouldn't just be filming him from afar — she would be trying to orchestrate a meeting. A honey trap, Bill had called it, the sweet term making it sound like an exotic, exciting adventure. But Chantelle had never even dated a boy, or had a conversation with one that could lead him to think she was interested. And, on the very rare occasions when a boy had approached her, she had immediately clammed up — as she had with Anton Davis, who had quickly given up after being stonewalled.

But if the thought of flirting with a boy was alien to her, the idea of doing it with a man filled her with absolute dread. And, judging by his behaviour in the club last night, the suspect, whose name Bill had just told her was Rob Knight, was a highly confident man at that. He had to be extremely smart to have made so much money by the age of 25, and he obviously had no trouble attracting sexy women. So how on earth an inexperienced girl like her was supposed to get him to take her seriously, Chantelle did not know.

Regretting having agreed to give it a go, Chantelle brought Bill's number up on her phone and hovered her thumb over the call button. She wanted to tell her that she'd changed her mind, but she guessed that Bill would probably have phoned the client back by now to confirm the booking and cancelling wouldn't be very good for business.

"What's up with you?" Leon walked into the kitchen just then and gave her a funny look

"Nothing." Chantelle smiled and pushed her phone into her pocket. "Just trying to decide what to make for dinner tonight. What do you fancy?"

"Chippy," Leon said, pouring himself a glass of milk. "Happy birthday, by the way."

Chantelle's eyes immediately welled up. She genuinely hadn't expected him to remember, and it meant the world to her that he had. "Thank you," she said, trying to keep her voice from breaking.

"No need to get all *girly* about it," Leon scoffed, his face creasing with disgust. "I take it you're working tonight?"

"How did you know?"

"Heard you on the phone, and you don't talk to no one else these days so I figured it had to be your boss."

Chantelle chuckled softly. "Not as stupid as you look, are you?"

Leon rolled his eyes and carried his milk back up the hall and into his bedroom. Chantelle sighed when he closed his door. That was probably the last she would see of him until dinner time, but at least he'd remembered her birthday — which made him the only one on the planet whose mind she had crossed today.

Determined not to start feeling sorry for herself, she pulled on her jacket and headed out. If Leon wanted a chippy dinner he could have it, but she still needed to pick up a few bits and pieces from the shop.

Anton had just arrived at his new flat when Chantelle stepped out onto the landing. He nodded at her as he slotted his key into the lock. "Morning."

"Morning," she replied, glancing at the mop and bucket that were sitting beside his door, alongside a dustpan and brush, a small bin, and several bottles of bleach, washing-up liquid and air fresheners. "Moving in?"

Amazed that she had initiated a conversation, Anton couldn't help but smile as he said, "Need to do some more cleaning first. Still smells a bit, and I won't be able to forget she died in there till I've got rid of it. It's freaking me out a bit, to be honest."

"I can imagine." Chantelle pulled her own door shut.

"Best get on," Anton said now, pushing his door open and reaching for the mop and bucket. "See you."

Chantelle said, "Bye" and watched as he went inside. She was surprised he was still talking to her, given how snotty and offhand she'd been with him, and she thought he was actually quite nice. But then, with his past record with girls, he must have perfected the art of being charming by now, so she was probably wrong.

"Hey, birthday girl, where d'you think you're going?"

Chantelle turned on her heel when she heard Immy's voice, and smiled when she saw her friend rushing towards her.

"Sorry it's only a card," Immy apologised, thrusting an envelope into her hand before hugging her. "I was going to get you these gorgeous earrings I saw on the market, but I'm skintaroony, so you'll have to wait."

"Don't be daft," Chantelle said softly, her eyes welling up again. "This is more than enough." She opened the card and felt her chin wobble when she read the message. "Thanks. That means a lot."

"So what did you get off your mum?" Immy asked. "Pressies or money?"

"Money," Chantelle lied, shoving the card into her pocket.

"And now you're off to spend it?" Immy gave her a knowing look.

"You know me too well." Chantelle smiled. "Want to come?"

"Wish I could," Immy said regretfully, "but my dad and the Barbie doll are taking me and the brat brother

170

to Blackpool. I'm only going so I can wind her up," she added, grinning slyly. "She's so possessive, it's unbelievable. You should see the face on her when I go near my dad; it's like she thinks I'm trying to get off with him, or something. It'd be hilarious if it wasn't so tragic."

"Weird." Chantelle shook her head.

"Hey, why don't you come?" Immy suggested. "I'm sure my dad won't mind. And the Barbie will have an absolute *fit* when she cops a look at *you*."

"I can't," Chantelle said. "Said I'd take Leon bowling."

"Ah, that's nice." Immy smiled. "Well, have a great time, babe. I'll give you a ring when I get back, tell you how it went."

"Have fun." Chantelle hugged her goodbye. "And thanks again for the card."

When Immy had gone back down the stairs she'd come up from, Chantelle set off for the stairs at the other end of the block. Anton came back out onto the landing to collect the rest of his things as she passed and, smiling, said, "Happy birthday."

"Thanks," she murmured, blushing. He had already gone inside when Immy arrived, but his door must have still been open for him to have heard that it was her birthday.

A small smile played on Chantelle's lips as she walked on. She'd started the day on a low, convinced that nobody cared enough to remember her birthday; but now three people had wished her a happy one, so maybe the day wasn't going to turn out too bad after all.

Bill had no idea it was Chantelle's birthday when she picked her up in their usual spot that evening, but she noticed that there was something different about her. It was subtle, nothing that she could absolutely put her finger on; Chantelle just seemed a little more confident than usual. She rarely spoke about her life, and never mentioned her family apart from to say they were okay if Bill asked. And she had certainly given Bill no indication that she had a boyfriend, which was surprising considering how sweet-natured and beautiful she was. But she seemed quite happy with her lot, so Bill had never pried — and wasn't about to start now.

They had to wait for over an hour before Rob Knight left his house. When he headed again into the city centre and parked up on the same backstreet, Bill guessed that he was going to the same club and parked on a neighbouring street.

"Nervous?" she asked as Chantelle unclipped her seat belt.

"A bit," Chantelle admitted. "But I'm trying not to think about it."

"Probably for the best," Bill agreed, handing over the money for Chantelle's drinks. "Just remember to keep it casual if he approaches you. Let him do most of the talking and, if you in any way feel out of your depth, pull the plug and get out of there. Okay?"

"Okay." Chantelle nodded and took a deep breath. "Wish me luck."

★ ★ ★

As on the previous night, the club was only half full, so there were still plenty of vacant seats. But rather than try and fade into the background as she usually did, Chantelle perched on a tall stool at the bar and looked around.

She quickly spotted the suspect at the far end of the bar, talking to the same men he'd been with the night before. After ordering a Coke, she twisted the stool around and rested her elbow on the counter before casually crossing her legs. Instantly self-conscious when several men cast admiring looks in her direction, she raised her chin and forced herself to maintain the cool façade. She had applied much more make-up than usual tonight, and her loose hair looked glossy thanks to two hours of conditioning and curling. She'd been quite pleased with the results, and it was obviously having the desired effect. But she knew that the interest she was attracting was based purely on looks, so it meant nothing.

When the suspect and his friends moved to a table, Chantelle stayed put. There was no easy way of getting near to him without actually walking right up to him, but she absolutely wasn't going to do that. He had to come to her, or it would prove nothing.

An hour dragged by and Chantelle had almost finished her second drink, but Rob Knight still hadn't so much as glanced in her direction. Concerned that the woman from the previous night might turn up and ruin her chances if she didn't do something soon, she decided to change seats in the hope of attracting his

**173**

attention. But just as she gathered up her bag and her drink and was about to step down off the stool, the man himself appeared at her side, and her Coke sloshed over the rim of her glass when he knocked her hand with his arm.

"Whoops, sorry!" he apologised, grinning as he reached out to steady her glass.

"It's okay," Chantelle murmured, dipping her head to hide the blush that immediately coloured her cheeks. "It was my fault; should have looked where I was going."

"Let me get you another," he offered, pulling a handkerchief from his pocket and wiping her wet hand. "What are you drinking?"

"Coke," she told him. "But it's okay, honestly."

"I insist," he said, dabbing at a wet patch on his shirt sleeve now. "Sure you wouldn't prefer something stronger, though?"

"No, I'm driving," Chantelle lied. "Sorry about your shirt. You might want to go and rinse it before it stains."

"It's fine." He shoved the hankie back into his pocket and waved the barman over. "A Coke for the lady, and two bottles of white, please."

"Thank you." Chantelle settled back onto the stool as the barman went to fill the order. "But it really wasn't necessary."

"Hey, it was my pleasure." He smiled and pulled his wallet out of his pocket. "Alone?" he asked as he slid two £20 notes out.

"Mmmm." Chantelle nodded and glanced towards the door. "I was supposed to be meeting my friend, but it looks like she's not coming. Ah, well . . ." She shrugged. "Suppose I'll just have an early night instead."

"Looking like that?" He drew his head back and gave her an admiring smile. "What a waste. Unless your other half is waiting at home? In which case I'm sure he'll be delighted that your friend stood you up."

Chantelle smiled and shook her head. "Just the dog — and she's so old I'm not sure she even knows I'm there, these days."

"Poor you." He chuckled and passed the notes over to the barman. When the man went off to get his change, he gave Chantelle a thoughtful look. "Don't take this the wrong way, but have you ever considered modelling? I'm only asking because I have a friend who runs an agency, and I'm sure he'd be pleased to meet you. You have a stunning face."

"Oh, I don't think so." Chantelle dipped her gaze as her heart began to flutter in her chest. If he was going to hit on her, it looked like this might be it.

"Just a thought." He shrugged. Then, "Look, why don't you take my number, then if you change your mind you can give me a bell and I'll arrange a meeting. No pressure."

Chantelle bit her lip. He didn't sound like he was trying to chat her up, but Bill had told her to try and get his number. So, nodding, she took her phone out of her bag.

"Okay. But I really don't think I'll change my mind."

"Totally up to you." He extended his hand. "Rob."

"Julia," she lied, noticing as she shook his hand that he wasn't trying to hide his wedding ring.

"Best get back before my pals think I've abandoned them." He picked up his bottles. "Nice to meet you."

"You, too." Chantelle smiled and reached for her fresh drink. She took a sip and watched through her lashes as Rob went back to his table.

When another half-hour had gone by, during which the suspect didn't so much as glance her way again, Chantelle figured that he wasn't interested and made her way back to the car.

"Anything happen?" Bill asked.

"Not really." Chantelle settled into her seat. "I did talk to him, but he didn't try it on. I'm hoping I pressed the right button." She took the videophone out of her bag and handed it over. "He caught me by surprise, so I had to do it without looking."

Bill pressed play and listened to the recorded conversation. It was a struggle to hear the words clearly, but she got the basic gist of it. "Interesting," she murmured when it had finished. "Definitely didn't sound like a chat-up, but he could have just been playing it cool."

"What's the point of that?" Chantelle asked, wrinkling her nose when the dog farted. She wound the window down a little.

"Could have realised his wife is onto him," Bill mused. "She sounds the emotional type, so she's probably not hiding her suspicions as well as she thinks she is. If he suspects she might be watching him, he's unlikely to bite first time. That's possibly why he gave you his number and disguised it as a good deed."

"What will you tell his wife?"

"That he gave you his number," Bill said, starting the car and doing a U-turn before heading back out to the main road. "And that you're going to give him a tinkle in a day or two; see if he bites when he thinks he's safe to talk."

Chantelle nodded, but she was already nervous. Rob Knight had seemed quite easygoing, but it would be so embarrassing if she rang and he didn't remember her. And to make out like she wanted to speak to his friend about becoming a model seemed so vain. Worst of all, what if she forgot the fake name she'd given him? Then he would definitely smell a rat. But she couldn't back out now.

# CHAPTER
# FOURTEEN

The hall light was on when Chantelle got home, and she could hear calypso music coming from the living room.

"Leon . . ." she called as she slipped her jacket off. "What have I told you about leaving lights on? And why aren't you in bed? You'd best not have been playing that music any louder than that, or —"

"God, don't you ever stop nagging?" A laughing voice cut her off.

"*Mum?*" Chantelle's jaw dropped.

"The one and only!" Mary laughed and ran out into the hall. "Come here and give me a hug, you!"

Chantelle didn't know whether to laugh, cry, or go mad. Her mum had been gone for ages, yet she was acting as if she'd done nothing wrong.

"Come and meet Miggy." Mary broke the embrace and grabbed Chantelle's hand. "You'll love him. Him and our Leon are getting on like a house on fire."

Dragged into the living room, Chantelle frowned when she saw the mess. There were beer bottles everywhere, and the air was thick with weed-smoke. Tracey was sitting on the couch alongside a swarthy man with greasy hair, and they both looked wrecked.

Already annoyed, Chantelle was really pissed off when she saw Leon sitting cross-legged on the floor with a bottle of beer in his hand and a daft grin on his face.

"How many have you had?" she demanded.

"*Six.*" He smirked. It was a lie, he'd only had one, but who cared what she thought? His mum had said he could have it, and she was the boss, not Chantelle.

"Leave him alone," Mary scolded. "He's on his holidays."

"He's only ten."

"So what? They start 'em younger than that in Spain. Anyhow, shut up moaning, and say hello to Miggy."

The man smiled up at Chantelle as his gaze slid slowly down her body. "Very beautiful," he said.

"Isn't he gorgeous?" Mary demanded, nudging Chantelle none too gently. "Didn't I tell you?"

Chantelle's heart sank when she saw the bright, glassy gleam in her mum's eyes and realised that she was high on speed or coke. Her mum always started out giddy and jovial like this, but she could flip at the slightest provocation and get really nasty.

"I'm tired," she murmured, eager to escape before her mum's mood switched. "I'm going to bed. We'll talk in the morning."

"Sod that," Mary scoffed, grinning as if she thought it was a joke. "We're having a party, so go grab yourself a glass before I smack your arse. And you still ain't said hello to Miggy. He'll be thinking you've got no manners."

Chantelle breathed in deeply. Then, forcing herself to smile, she extended her hand to the man. "Nice to meet you."

Miguel grasped her hand and raised it to his lips before rising unsteadily to his feet and pulling her into a hug.

"All right, put him down," Mary blurted out, following it with a laugh to make it seem less like the attack of jealousy that it actually was.

Chantelle prised herself out of the embrace and backed towards the door as the man fell back onto the couch. But Mary wasn't about to let her leave just yet and, shoving a glass of rum into her hand, she pushed her towards the armchair, saying, "Get that down your neck and lighten up, misery guts. It's supposed to be a party, not a bleedin' wake."

Chantelle didn't want a drink, but she knew that her mum would be upset if she refused, so she took the glass and perched on the edge of the seat.

"Our Leon says you've got yourself a job," Mary said, refilling her own glass before handing the bottle to Tracey.

"Just a bit of office work," Chantelle lied, flashing Leon a hooded look of annoyance.

"Sounds like a right barrel of laughs," Mary sneered. "Bit late for offices to be open, though, isn't it?"

"It's an all-night business," Chantelle said quietly.

"Sacked off the idea of sixth form, then, have you?" Mary flopped down on the arm of the couch and draped her leg over Miguel's. "'Bout time, if you ask me. It's a bloody waste, all that studying; never gets you nowhere. Look at me . . . not an exam to me name, but I've done all right. Got me lovely kids, me own flat, and a fit-as-fuck fiancé."

"Fiancé?" Chantelle gave her a questioning look. "I thought you'd got married?"

"Not yet," Mary told her. "It would have been too expensive over there with all his relatives expecting an invite. There's about four bleedin' hundred of 'em," she confided in a loud whisper, as if she thought Miguel wouldn't be able to hear. "But they can fuck off if they think *I'm* shelling out for them to stuff their greedy gobs. Gonna do it here at the registry office instead, then go down the dole office and get him added onto my claim before we go back."

"You're not staying?"

"No chance! And neither are you."

"What do you mean?"

"Youse are coming with us," said Mary. "I'm sick of looking after his mam and dad on me own, so I want you there to help me. Our Leon's well up for it, ain't you, son?"

"Yeah, sounds ace." Leon grinned. "They live right near the beach, and Miggy reckons all the girls are naked."

Disgusted when the man gave Leon a wasted grin and stuck up his thumb, Chantelle frowned at her mother. "Do you really think that's appropriate?"

"Oh, don't start," Mary moaned. "He was only having a laugh. Do you really think I'd be smiling if I thought he was out eyeballing tits all day? I'd smash his bloody face in. *Innit?*" She nudged Miguel, and repeated in a terrible Spanish accent, "I'd smasha your bloody face in if I catcha you looking at girls' titties."

Miguel nodded, but it was clear from his glazed eyes that he was too stoned to understand what she had said. "I need bathroom," he mumbled, edging off the couch and stumbling towards the door.

"Thick git," Mary snorted when he'd left the room. "Good job his dick's got a mind of its own, or he wouldn't have two brain cells to rub together, bless him."

"Thought he was supposed to be the love of your life?" Chantelle sniped.

"He is." Mary reached for the bottle to top up her glass. "I'm only having a laugh."

When a knock came at the front door just then, Tracey said, "That'll be the pizza."

"Go get it, babes," Mary ordered.

"What did your last slave die of?" Tracey grumbled, pushing herself up to her feet.

"I hope you ain't expecting me to pay?" Mary drew her head back when Tracey held out her hand. "I bought the booze, so this is on you, mate."

"I ain't got no money," Tracey informed her. "And you never said nothing about me paying, or I'd have told you not to bother."

"God, you never change, you," Mary sneered. "Happy to sit here supping my booze all night, but come time to put your hand in your pocket and you've got all the excuses under the sun."

"You should have asked before you ordered it," Tracey argued. "Anyhow, you invited me round, so don't start having a go just 'cos I've had a few."

**182**

"God, stop arguing," Chantelle said, pulling a £10 note out of her bag. "I'll pay. Here."

"Wow, wonders never cease!" Mary leaned over and snatched the money out of her hand. "Never thought I'd see the day when *you* coughed up. Best hope you didn't disturb the moths, or they'll be eating us alive in a minute."

Chantelle gritted her teeth as Tracey got up and lumbered out into the hall to pay for the pizza. Her mum had a cheek making out like Chantelle never contributed when she had been keeping Leon the whole time her mum had been gone. And she would tell her so — tomorrow, when Mary was sober.

A loud bang in the hall shook the pictures on the wall behind the couch. Shocked when Tracey let out a terrified yelp, Chantelle jumped to her feet just as the living-room door flew open and Ricky Benson strode in.

He paused in the doorway and looked around. Then, smirking when his gaze landed on Mary, he said, "Well, well. Someone said they'd seen you, but I said, *nah* — she wouldn't have come home without telling me. Not when she knows I've been looking for her."

"I was going to call you," Mary said, sliding off the arm of the couch. "But I —"

"Don't bother." Ricky cut her off. "I can't be arsed listening to lies — just give me my fuckin' money."

"Tomorrow." Mary licked her lips. "I'll get it tomorrow, I promise."

"Ain't good enough." Ricky cracked his knuckles and walked slowly towards her.

"Leave my mum alone!" Leon yelled, jumping up and running at the man, the beer bottle raised in the air.

"Behave!" Ricky lashed out with the back of his hand and laughed when the boy went flying into the wall.

"How dare you!" Chantelle cried, rushing to her brother and squatting beside him. "Get out before I call the police!"

"Oh yeah?" Ricky stalked over and grabbed her by the hair, dragging her back up to her feet. "Thought we'd already had this conversation, darlin'?" he hissed, pushing her up against the wall and staring down into her eyes. "Forgot already, have you? Need me to remind you, do ya?"

"What is this?" Miguel asked, walking in just then.

"Get him out!" Mary cried, rushing to stand behind him. "He's just burst in and started hitting the kids. I don't even know him!"

"Lying bitch!" Ricky spat, glaring round at her as he held Chantelle up against the wall. "You know damn well why I'm here. I want my money, and I ain't going till I get it."

"Let her go and get out," Miguel ordered, squaring up to him.

He was a little taller than Ricky, but he looked ill and weak, and Ricky figured he could easily take him if he had to. "If you know what's good for you, you'll stay out of this," he sneered. "It's got nowt to do with you."

Miguel still felt sick but he wasn't about to let another man order him around in his woman's home.

**184**

"I told you *go*," he snarled, rushing across the room and throwing an arm around Ricky's neck.

Buzzing when Miguel dragged Ricky off Chantelle and they started scuffling on the floor, Mary jumped up and down, crowing, "Not so fucking tough now, are you? Quick enough to push me and my kids around, but you ain't got the balls to stand up to a *real* man, have you?"

"Shut up, Mum!" snapped Chantelle, her stomach churning as she stood back against the wall with her arm around Leon. "*You* caused this."

"Oh, here we go," spat Mary. "Fucking goody two-shoes, sticking up for anyone but your mam. Least my Leon tried to protect me — innit, son?"

Leon didn't answer. Right then, he was on his sister's side.

Ricky had built his rep on verbal intimidation but he was nowhere near as tough as he liked to make out, and he hadn't bargained for a fight when he'd pushed his way in here tonight. He'd expected to find Mary alone with the kids, and had intended to scare the crap out of her, because that was what he did best. Most of the scumbags he dealt with were drug-addled and feeble, and they invariably crumbled at the slightest hint of intimidation. But this crazy foreign bloke was stronger than he looked and, no matter how hard Ricky tried, he couldn't shake the bastard off. Already exhausted, his nose bleeding, he cried out when the man raised his fist to punch him in the face.

"All right, all right, I'll go! I just want what I'm owed."

"You're getting nothing," said Mary, smirking as she looked down at his flushed face. "And if you ever come near me again *he*'ll have you, 'cos he's more of a man than you'll ever be."

"You stop?" Miguel peered down into Ricky's eyes.

"Yeah." Ricky nodded and clutched at his chest, his breath raspy and harsh. "I need me inhaler."

Satisfied that the man had conceded defeat, Miguel stood up. Hands still fisted, he jerked his head when Ricky also rose unsteadily to his feet. "Go, and don't come here again."

Humiliated, Ricky stumbled towards the door. Pausing there, he gave Mary a hate-filled look and hissed, "Watch your back, bitch," before going on his way.

"Woo hoo!" Mary whooped, throwing her arm around Miguel's neck. "That showed the bastard! Thinks he can force his way in here and push *me* around like that? Well, he'll think twice before he tries any of that shit on with me again, 'cos my hero will punch his fuckin' lights out. Innit, babes?" She planted several kisses on Miguel's cheek.

"Stop," he snapped, pushing her away. "I no like have to fight stranger. What was for?"

"Why you having a go at me?" Mary protested. "I only owe him a bit of money, but anyone'd think it was thousands the way he's going on."

"You say you no know him," Miguel reminded her. "You say he hit you and kids for nothing, but you lie."

"Still didn't give him the right to barge in," Mary retorted indignantly. "Anyhow, it's about time you did something for me, after everything I've done for you."

"You've changed," said Miguel. "You come here and act different. Not like at home."

"Oh, what, just 'cos I'm having a bit of fun for a change? It's all right for you, innit? You're out all day; I'm the one who's locked in twenty-four-seven with your mam and dad. Youse have got me running round like a skivvy."

"Is your job. You my woman, you look after family. I'm man, I work."

"I'm no one's *woman*," Mary retorted angrily, pushing him in the chest. "I do what I want, and no man's ever gonna tell me different."

"I warn you." Miguel's dark eyes flashed as he pointed a finger in her face. "You push, I explode like volcano."

"Go on, then," Mary challenged, raising her chin. "Hit me, if you dare. But don't think you'll get away with it, 'cos you're in *my* country now."

"Oh, for God's sake, pack it in," Chantelle blurted out. "Haven't we had enough drama for one night?" She looked down at Leon now, and said, "Go to bed. I'll see you in the morning."

For once, Leon didn't argue. Muttering, "Night," he went to his room.

"Thanks for helping," Chantelle said to Miguel. "But I'm sorry you had to get involved. It wasn't your fight and you shouldn't have had to do that."

"Is okay," Miguel said, backing away from Mary and flopping down onto the couch as the sickly feeling stole over him again. "I do for you and brother. Is not right have man hurt you."

Chantelle looked down at him and felt a bit guilty for having dismissed him as a slimy loser. He'd already shown that he had more about him than most of her mum's previous boyfriends, and he clearly wasn't impressed that her mum had manipulated him by lying about her involvement with Ricky. But, if the past was anything to go by, he wouldn't be in her mum's life for too much longer, because the better men rarely stuck around once Mary started her nonsense.

A knock came at the open front door just then, and a man's voice called, "Pizza."

Tracey still had the money to pay for it, but she was nowhere to be seen when Chantelle walked out into the hall. Irritated that she was being forced to pay for food that she didn't even want, she took another £10 note out of her bag and handed it over. She closed the door when the man had given her the change, and almost jumped out of her skin when she saw Tracey hiding amongst the coats behind it. "God! What are you doing there?" she gasped. "I thought you'd gone?"

Tracey didn't answer; she just stared at Chantelle and pressed herself further back into the shadows.

"She's on a speed para," Mary declared, walking out into the hall. "Just leave her; she'll be all right once it wears off. Me and Miggy are off to bed," she said then, smiling when the man walked out into the hall behind her. "He's got some making up to do, so try not to disturb us in the morning, 'cos it's gonna be a long night. Oh, and I'd best take that." She snatched the pizza box out of Chantelle's hand. "Haven't eaten all day; gonna need it for energy."

**188**

Chantelle grimaced as her mum and Miguel stumbled into their bedroom and slammed the door. Then, casting a look of despair at Tracey, she shook her head and went to her own room.

She was exhausted, but she doubted she was going to get much sleep because she could already hear sex noises coming through the wall. She and her mum were going to have to sit down and have a serious talk tomorrow. She was sixteen now, and that meant she was old enough to make her own decisions. If she decided not to go back to school when the summer holidays came to an end, for instance, then it was her choice. Just as it was her choice not to go to Spain. It wouldn't, however, be so easy to stop her mum from taking Leon, and that worried Chantelle. As badly as she had thought she'd been doing these last few weeks, she had always loved her brother and tried to give him stability, which was a damn sight more than their mum had ever done. He was growing up fast but he was still a kid, so there was no telling what kind of trouble he might get into without Chantelle to keep an eye on him.

As a feeling of despair began to settle over Chantelle, she climbed into bed and pulled her quilt up over her head. She had been dying for her mum to come home, but now that it had happened she was beginning to wonder if they might not have been better off if Mary had stayed away.

# CHAPTER
# FIFTEEN

Tracey had gone when Chantelle got up the next morning, and her mum, Miguel and Leon were still in bed. The living room stank of smoke, so she opened the window to air it out and then set about clearing the empty bottles and emptying the ashtrays. That done, she moved on to the bathroom.

She wrinkled her nose in disgust when first she smelled, then saw the puke that was on the toilet seat, down the side of the bowl, and puddled on the floor beneath the sink. It had to have been Miguel, and she really wanted to leave it for her mum to deal with. But, knowing it would probably never get done if it was left to her, she swallowed her revulsion, pulled on a pair of rubber gloves and set to it.

She had finished the bathroom and moved on to the kitchen when Leon came out of his room at 10.30. Halfway through washing the dishes, she smiled back at him over her shoulder. "Sleep okay?"

Leon nodded and reached for his jacket off the hook behind the front door.

"You're not going out, are you?" she asked, wiping her hands on a tea towel and walking out into the hall. "Don't you think you'd best wait till Mum's up?"

"Why?"

"'Cos she's not seen you for ages, so she'll probably want to spend some time with you."

"I'll see her later," Leon grunted, walking out.

Chantelle shook her head and went back to the kitchen. She'd thought that he would be made up to spend time with their mum and Miguel, especially after they had let him have beer last night. But the night had ended with him getting a slap, so she supposed she shouldn't be surprised that he was in a mood with their mum.

Leon pulled his hood up when he got to the foot of the stairwell and, sliding his hand inside his jacket to make sure the plastic bag was still safely tucked under his jumper, he quickly walked over to Damo's estate.

Damo and Acky were sitting on the wall at the side of Damo's block of flats, and Acky gave him a dirty look as he approached.

"Took your fuckin' time, didn't you? Where is it?"

"Sorry, had a late night," Leon said, pulling the bag out.

Acky snatched it off him and weighed it up in his hand. "Have you been helping yourself? Feels lighter to me, this."

"I haven't touched it," Leon said honestly. "It's probably just squashed 'cos it's been under the mattress."

"You'd best not be a bed wetter," Acky snarled, tossing the bag to Damo. "I'll cut your fuckin' cock off if we get any complaints about it tasting of piss."

**191**

Damo smirked and shoved the bag inside his own jacket, then jumped to his feet. "Let's go. We're gonna miss all our customers at this rate."

Chantelle had finished cleaning and was carrying a loaded bin bag to the front door when her mum emerged from her room fifteen minutes after Leon had gone out.

"Christ, don't you ever stop?" Mary snorted, shaking her head as she looked round and saw how spotless everything was. "I'm gonna make an appointment at the doctor's, see if they've got any pills to cure that OCD of yours."

"Ha ha, very funny," Chantelle drawled, dropping the bag by the front door and wiping her hands on her jeans. "Are you going somewhere?" she asked when her mum reached for her jacket.

"Yeah, round Trace's. Why?"

"I wanted to have a talk," Chantelle said, flashing Miguel a side glance when he lumbered into the hall in his underpants, with his hair hanging greasily down around his love-bitten neck.

"I feel sick," he groaned, rubbing at his stomach and giving Mary a self-pitying look. "You make breakfast?"

"In your dreams," she snorted. "If you're not coming you can make yourself a butty, but I'm not stopping in to look after you. Me and Trace have got some shopping to do."

Miguel muttered something unintelligible and went into the bathroom, slamming the door shut.

"Serves him right," Mary scoffed when the sound of retching filtered out. "He knows he can't handle his booze, so he shouldn't have tried keeping up with me and Trace last night. Got a good shag out of him, though," she added, grinning lewdly.

Chantelle struggled to keep the revulsion off her face and folded her arms. "You're not going shoplifting, are you?"

"What do you think?" Mary smirked, opening the door. "This wedding ain't gonna pay for itself."

"Are you sure you really want to get married?" Chantelle asked quietly. "All I've heard you do since you got back is argue."

"Ah, that don't mean nothing." Mary flapped her hand dismissively. "Me and Miggy are the real deal, babes. Anyhow, best go and see if droopy drawers is ready. See you later."

"Yeah, see you," Chantelle murmured, disappointed that she was going to have to wait to have that talk. At the sound of yet more retching, she pulled a face and went to her room, closing the door firmly behind her.

Leon's eyes were swivelling every which way as he, Damo and Acky walked through Chorlton. He'd never ventured this far into the area before Damo and Acky had brought him here, and he still felt edgy about being so far out of his own territory. Damo was obviously feeling cool about it, though, because he'd been swaggering around like he owned the place since Big T had set him up a spot to deal from down on the Mersey Bank Estate.

They had been at it for a few days now, and had made a pretty good start. But Leon doubted they would be rolling in it any time soon, as Damo seemed to think, seeing as they had to hand whatever they made over to Big T, then take whatever cut he decided to give them. Leon hadn't seen a penny of it so far, so he didn't know how much they had made, but he suspected they would have done it for free if it meant keeping in with the big boys.

Their "spot" was at the far end of the estate, in a little copse of overgrown bushes facing a run-down sheltered-housing complex and several scruffy blocks of maisonettes. A wildly overgrown field stretched out behind them, beyond which ran the canal. As Damo and Acky took up their positions now, way back from the road and hidden from view by the foliage, Leon pulled his hood down around his face and scuttled across the road. He ducked into the tunnel-like walkway between the maisonettes and stood in the shadows beside the huge communal wheelie bin, from where he could see the road clearly and would be able to warn the others if he saw the police coming their way.

It wasn't too bad a day; the sun was shining, and there was only a light breeze. But it was much colder in here, and Leon stuffed his hands into his pockets as the chill air seeped through his jacket. He hoped Damo and Acky weren't planning to stay too long, or he would be frozen stiff by the time he got home.

He saw a movement across the road and glanced over in time to see two young lads heading into the bushes. They came back out a couple of minutes later, obviously satisfied with what they'd bought, because they were grinning as they raced off up the road. As more customers came and went, Leon went back to watching out for the police, but his mind soon wandered and his eyes glazed over as he started thinking about what had happened at home last night.

Like Chantelle, he had almost given up on ever seeing his mum again, so he'd been shocked when she had walked in with her new man and Tracey in tow. They had all been half-cut, but that hadn't bothered him because he was used to adults being drunk around him. He hadn't been too happy about the boyfriend at first, because his mum's fellas tended not to be too nice, but he'd soon cheered up when Miguel had given him a bottle of beer. It had taken him a while to understand what the man was saying, because his English was so bad and his accent so thick, but his ears had pricked up when Miguel had told him what life was like in Spain. Apparently, it was all blazing sunshine and near-naked girls. And, best of all, Miguel worked in a beachfront bar and had promised to take Leon to work with him so he could enjoy the view all day long. It sounded like paradise.

Chantelle hadn't looked too pleased when she'd come home, and Leon had thought she was just being her usual naggy self. She'd really stuck up for him after that man had hit him, though; and Miguel nearly flattening the bloke had been super-cool. But Leon was torn now. Spain sounded great, but if he went he might never see Chantelle again.

Or Damo and the gang.

Stirred from his thoughts when he heard footsteps on the path at the other end of the walkthrough, Leon quickly ducked behind the bin when a youth strolled into view. The boy had his mobile phone pressed to his ear, and he was laughing at whatever the person on the other end was saying. He abruptly stopped laughing when he reached the other end of the tunnel, though, and he jerked back into the shadows just inches from where Leon was squatting.

"Yo, you'll never guess who I've just seen?" he hissed. "Them cunts who jumped me and Gilly in Alex Park the other week!"

Leon held his breath as his heart lurched into his throat. He'd heard that one of the lads the gang had attacked had walked out of A & E with nothing more than bruises and a few stitches, but the other had been much more seriously hurt and he'd been on life-support for a couple of weeks, his brain so badly swollen from all the kicks to his head they had thought he was going to die. He had pulled through but he was still in hospital, and Leon still felt a bit guilty about his involvement in it all. But he tried not to dwell on it too much, reminding himself that his loyalty lay with Damo and the boys.

"I ain't shittin' you!" the youth was saying now in an urgent whisper. "I'm down by the bogs and just spotted some kids sneaking about across the way, then I seen *them*. Round the crew up and get over here — and be quick, case we miss 'em!"

**196**

Leon pressed his mouth against his knees and inhaled slowly and shakily, praying that the lad wouldn't hear him. Damo and Acky were about to get jumped, and it was his job to warn them. But how could he when the lad was standing right in front of him?

A few tense minutes passed before Leon heard the sound of running feet and the distinctive swish of bicycle tyres. Light-headed with terror when several hooded youths joined the first one, he squeezed further back into the corner and listened as they formulated a plan of attack. He couldn't make out much of what they were saying because of the deafening roar of his heartbeat in his ears, but he knew it was going to be hard and fast — and would involve weapons.

Chantelle was reading when a tap came at her bedroom door. It was an hour since her mum had gone out, and she'd heard Miguel shuffling around the flat making little moaning noises. He'd checked the fridge and kitchen cupboards in search of food, and had then gone into the living room where he had spent the last forty minutes flicking through the TV channels. Guessing that he was bored now, Chantelle laid her book down on the bed and opened her door.

"Yes?"

"Not want disturb," Miguel said apologetically. "But I no have cigarette. You have one, please?"

"Sorry, I don't smoke," she told him. "Have you looked in my mum's room? She might have some in there."

"No, she take," he said. Then, smiling pathetically, he shrugged. "What I can do? Is not my home; can't know way to shop. And no have money. Your mom, she take all."

Chantelle sighed. He was obviously struggling with the language, but at least he was making an effort — which was more than could be said for her. "I'll go and get you some," she offered.

"Ah . . ." Miguel spread his hands, a look of relief on his face. "Thank you, thank you. I come, yes?"

"If you like." She shrugged.

"You are angel." He reached for her hand and kissed it. "You wait, I get coat."

Chantelle wiped the back of her hand on her jeans when he went into her mum's room to get his coat, and then reached for her own jacket. He was still a bit slimy, but it couldn't be easy meeting your fiancée's kids for the first time. And it must have been doubly hard for him, because he probably thought they blamed him for their mum abandoning them. Chantelle didn't know how Leon felt about that, but she certainly didn't blame Miguel. Her mum was the one who had chosen to go, and there would have been nothing that he or *anyone* could have said to make her change her mind once she had decided that was what she wanted to do.

"We go?" Miguel came back out into the hall.

Chantelle almost gagged at the strong fumes of the aftershave he'd just plastered on, but she forced herself to smile and quickly pulled the door open.

**198**

Anton was standing on guard by the door of Abdul's when Chantelle and Miguel arrived. He smiled at her, and nodded to the man. "All right, mate?"

Miguel nodded back and pulled his collar up high around his throat. "Is so cold," he complained, rubbing his hands together.

"This is pretty warm compared to the weather we've been having lately," Chantelle told him as they walked inside. "It should get better, but I wouldn't hold my breath if the last few summers are anything to go by."

"Sorry?" Miguel looked confused.

"Doesn't matter."

"He is boyfriend?" Miguel asked, jerking his head back towards Anton who was watching them.

"God, no!" Chantelle blushed.

"Ah, is just friend?"

"No," Chantelle murmured. "He's just . . ." She trailed off, unsure how to describe it. She and Anton were just people who had grown up on the same estate and gone to the same school, whose paths had crossed at various times without a word ever having been exchanged until a few weeks ago. What name could you attach to that? Friend didn't fit it, and nor did acquaintance. They were just people who vaguely knew each other.

Kermit's mum, Linda, was at the till unloading the contents of her basket. It was the first time Chantelle had seen her since the night she'd told Kermit off for leaving Leon on his own by the canal, and she still felt a bit guilty about the way she'd left things.

But Linda wasn't one to hold a grudge, and she smiled when she saw her. "Hiya, love. How are you?"

"I'm all right, thanks." Chantelle smiled back. "You?"

"Be glad when these holidays are over and my lot are back at school." Linda swiped a lock of lank hair out of her eyes before taking her purse out of her pocket. "Driving me up the bloody wall, they are."

"Hope our Leon's not getting under your feet?" Chantelle asked.

"Your Leon?" Linda gave her a questioning look as she handed her money over to Abdul. "Why would he be?"

"Well, it can't be easy having him there all the time as well as your own lot," Chantelle said. "I've told him to behave, but I know he can be a bit daft at times, so if he gets on your nerves just send him home."

"I don't know what you're talking about," Linda said, taking her change and slotting it into her purse. "I haven't seen your Leon since him and our Kermit fell out over all that nonsense that night." She paused when she saw the look of confusion in Chantelle's eyes, and gave her a conciliatory smile. "I'm not blaming it all on your Leon, love; I know my Kermit's no angel. But it's probably for the best that they've stopped hanging round together, 'cos they'd have only ended up getting each other into trouble. Anyway, got to go, or they'll be ripping lumps out of each other. See you."

"Yeah, see you," Chantelle murmured, frowning thoughtfully as the woman took her bag and left. If

Leon hadn't been round to her place since that night, where the hell *had* he been going?

"Yes?" Abdul's loud voice interrupted her thoughts.

Chantelle turned to Miguel. "Which kind do you smoke?"

"Marlboro," he told her, practically licking his lips as he pointed them out.

"Twenty Marlboro, please. And a lighter."

Miguel lit up as soon as they were outside the shop and exhaled noisily. "Ah, thank you," he gushed, smoke swirling from his nostrils. "Very bad, but I like very much."

Chantelle gave him an understanding smile and stuffed her hands into her pockets. She'd never smoked but she knew how hard it was for an addict to go without, because she'd seen her mum almost tear the flat apart in search of dog-ends on numerous occasions.

Miguel chatted about his life in Spain on the walk home, but Chantelle was too distracted to do more than just nod and smile every now and then. Back at the flat she left him in front of the TV and went to her room to think about Leon. He'd been behaving quite well lately, so she hadn't suspected that anything was amiss. But if he'd been lying about where he was going, he was obviously up to something, and she could only hope it didn't have anything to do with that gang, because those lads were trouble. Still, there was no point going out to look for him because he could be anywhere, so she would just have to wait until he came home and then confront him about it.

She had just settled on the bed and picked up her book when her phone rang. Happy to see Bill's name on the screen, she answered with a cheery, "Please tell me you've got a job for me? I'm dying to get out of here."

"Not as such," Bill replied. "I sent last night's recording over to my client, and she rang me almost immediately. I explained that our intention was to leave it a couple of days and then call him, but she doesn't want to wait; she wants it done now."

"What, *now* now?" Chantelle asked, her heart already pounding at the thought of having to speak to the man and pretend that she wanted to become a model. "Oh, God! I can't remember what I told him my name was."

Bill chuckled softly. "Julia, if I'm not mistaken. At least, that's what it sounded like on the recording — what I could hear of it. Does that sound right to you?"

"I think so," Chantelle said uncertainly, wondering why she'd chosen that name when she didn't even know anybody called Julia.

"I'm pretty sure it was that," Bill said confidently. "Anyway, let's discuss what you're going to say when you speak to him . . ."

A few minutes later, Chantelle nervously dialled the man's number. He answered on the second ring.

"Hello?"

"Er, hello . . . is that Rob?"

"Speaking."

"Hi, it's Julia . . . from the club last night."

"Ah." There was a smile in Rob's voice. "How are you? I take it the dog was pleased to see you when you got home?"

"Yeah, really happy," said Chantelle, relieved that he not only remembered her but also sounded pleased to hear from her. Good start. "Look, I'm sorry if I'm disturbing you," she went on, "but it's about that thing you mentioned. The, um, modelling."

"Changed your mind?"

"I'm not sure yet," Chantelle said, squeezing her eyes shut as she spoke because this felt so wrong. "I just thought it might be worth talking to your friend."

"I'm sure he'll be delighted," Rob said approvingly. "Tell you what, I'm a bit busy right now, but why don't you leave it with me? I'll give him a call when I get a chance and set up a meet, then call you back to see if the date suits. How does that sound?"

"Great. Thank you."

"My pleasure. Speak soon."

Chantelle pursed her lips when he abruptly cut the call and stared at the phone for several long moments before calling Bill back.

"I really don't think he's interested," she said. "He remembered me, and even remembered that I'd said I only had the dog waiting for me when I got home. But he wasn't flirtatious in the slightest; just told me to hang fire till he's spoken to his friend and set up a meeting. So what do you want me to do?"

"Nothing, for now," said Bill. "I'll tell the client what happened, and see what she wants to do. But, to be honest, I can't really see anything coming of this. I think he'd have made his move by now if he was angling for an affair. Let me know if he calls back, of course, but just put it out of your mind for now and relax until the next job comes in."

Chantelle had just said goodbye to Bill when she heard the front door open and close. Thinking that it was her mum, she went out into the hall and was surprised to see that it was Leon. She'd had a key cut for him after she had started working for Bill, on the strict proviso that he came home no later than nine p.m. or she would take it back. He'd been home on time so far, but had never come home earlier — and *never* when it was still light outside.

"We need to talk," she said, giving him the look to let him know that it was serious.

Instead of rolling his eyes, as he usually did, Leon kept his head down and muttered, "Leave me alone" before going into his room and closing the door.

When, seconds later, Chantelle heard him shove the back of his chair under the handle, she tutted softly. She had wanted to tackle him about his lies, but if she tried to force the issue while he was in a mood it would only end in a row, and he was likely to walk out again.

Miguel wandered out of the living room just then en route to the bathroom. He paused when he saw her standing there, and tilted his head to one side. "Is okay?"

"Sorry?" Chantelle snapped out of her thoughts and turned to him. "Yeah, fine. Just thinking." She motioned with a finger towards her temple.

"Ah, your mom say you very clever." Miguel smiled. "Book, book, book, she say."

Chantelle nodded. "I love books."

"I like only little." He held up his thumb and forefinger about an inch apart. "Too hard for eye."

"You probably need glasses."

"Glasses?" He gave her a confused look, and then mimed drinking from a glass. "This you mean?"

"No." Chantelle chuckled and, circling her fingers and thumbs, held them in front of her eyes.

"Ah . . ." Miguel understood this. "Yes, I think so." His stomach rumbled loudly just then, and he slapped his hand on it and gave an embarrassed smile. "Sorry, I hungry. When your mom is come?"

"Your guess is as good as mine." Chantelle shrugged. Then, sighing, she said, "I can make you something, if you like?"

Miguel peered at her with gratitude in his eyes. "Mom say you clever but no nice, but *I* say clever *and* nice. Yes?"

"I try," Chantelle murmured, upset to know that her mum had been bad-mouthing her to the man before they had even met. But she didn't know why she was surprised, because her mum had never understood her, and seemed to take it as a personal insult that she'd given birth to a child who actually enjoyed learning. She called Chantelle a snob, but she was wrong, because Chantelle had never considered herself to be better than anyone else. She just didn't see why she should have to settle for whatever life threw at her, like everyone else seemed to.

"I too like cook," Miguel said as he followed her into the kitchen.

"Really?" Chantelle raised an eyebrow and opened the cupboard to see what was in it.

"I look after parents till your mom came do for them. She no like them." He grinned. "Always say they too demand, they too old, she need fun."

"Sounds about right," Chantelle snorted, taking a can of tuna out of the cupboard. "You like?" She held it up so he could see it. "In sandwich?"

"Ah, si." He nodded. "Is taste."

"Tasty," she corrected him, smiling amusedly as she took the bread out of another cupboard and a knife out of the drawer. He was starting to grow on her, and she just hoped that her mum didn't screw it up, like she had every previous relationship.

Miguel took a seat and watched as Chantelle made the sandwich. When she put it on a plate and carried it over to the table, he smiled up at her and reached for her hand.

"You be good wife for man one day," he said, peering deeply into her eyes. "You very beautiful. Very sexy."

"Sorry?" Sure that she'd misheard, Chantelle frowned and tried to pull her hand free. But Miguel held on, and stood up.

"I like very much," he purred, putting his hand on the small of her back and pulling her towards him. "And you like too, no?"

"Not like *that*," Chantelle gasped, struggling to push him away. "Let go," she ordered when he held on. "I mean it!"

"I want you," he persisted, trying to kiss her now. "Just try," he said silkily, holding her face gently in his hand as she jerked her head. "You like, I promise."

Chantelle wanted to scream, but nothing came out when she opened her mouth. Terrified that he was going to try and force himself on her when he backed her into the corner and clamped his lips over hers, she mustered all of her strength and brought her knee up hard into his crotch. When he immediately released her and slid to the floor with a look of agony on his face, she leapt away from him and grabbed the knife she'd just used to butter the bread.

"You ever touch me like that again, I'll kill you," she gasped, holding it out in front of her.

In too much pain to reply, Miguel just groaned and rolled into a ball on the floor. Disgusted, Chantelle threw the knife into the sink and fled from the room. Then, grabbing her coat and keys, she ran out of the flat.

She didn't know where she was going as she walked quickly down the stairs — she just had to get away from that lecherous pig. He was supposed to be getting married to her mum, so how the hell could he *do* something like that? All she had done was try to make him feel welcome; she'd done or said nothing whatsoever to make him think that she was interested in him like *that*. Bastard!

Leon was dozing when his phone vibrated. Awake in a flash, he reached under his pillow and pulled it out, sitting bolt upright when he saw that it was Damo.

"All right, kid?" Damo said. "Got back okay, did you?"

"Yeah," Leon answered sickly. "I — I'm sorry I couldn't warn you, but they were right in front of me, and —"

"Don't worry about it." Damo cut him off. "We saw them coming and got away over the field. Just wanted to make sure you were okay."

"Yeah, I'm cool," Leon said, relieved that nothing had happened.

"Good. Right, well, we've got a few things to do," Damo went on, "but we're gonna need that other bag, so fetch it down the canal at half-six."

"Okay," Leon agreed. "See you later."

Happy again, Leon smiled when Damo hung up. It was good to know they weren't mad at him for not alerting them, but especially nice that they had been concerned about him, because that meant they cared.

# CHAPTER
# SIXTEEN

After a long day in town with Tracey, Mary was laden down with bags when she arrived home later that evening. Shoplifting always gave her a buzz, but where she and Tracey usually targeted things they wanted at the time — like booze, or something to wear for a night out — today's expedition had been about accumulating stuff they could easily sell on in order to get money for the wedding. She had applied for a loan from the DSS, but there was no guarantee that she was going to get it, and with the day drawing closer she was determined not to have to do it on a budget. It might only be a registry-office affair, but it was her first time and she wanted the full works, from the dress of her dreams, to a horse-drawn carriage, to a massive blow-out of a party afterwards.

She'd nicked a whole load of jewellery — some gold, but most just decorative; tons of bottles of expensive perfumes and aftershaves; and heaps of clothes. She had spread the loot out on the living-room floor, and was happily sorting through it when Chantelle walked in at six.

"Hey, babes," she said, looking up. "Where've you been?"

"Round at Immy's," Chantelle lied, noting that Miguel, who was lying on the couch, was studiously avoiding her eye. "What's all this?"

"Wedding fund," Mary told her, grinning happily as she rooted through the still-labelled clothes. "Here, these are for you." She held out two tops and a skirt. "Go and try them on, then give us a fashion show."

"Later," Chantelle murmured, unbuttoning her jacket. "I need to see what's in for tea."

"Me and Miggy are going down the pub to sell this lot; we'll get something from the chippy."

"I'll just make it for me and Leon, then," Chantelle said, eager to get out of the room.

"He's out," Mary informed her.

"Where?"

"How do I know?"

"Didn't you ask?" Chantelle frowned.

"Why should I?" Mary gave her an irritated look. "What's your problem? He ain't a baby."

"I know," Chantelle replied coolly. "I just don't like him wandering around at night. It's not safe."

"Aw, chill out," Mary sneered. "He's tough, he can handle himself. And if he can't, he'll have to learn how, won't he? It's a cruel world out there — he's got to be able to fight his own battles or he'll end up a little wuss."

Chantelle bit down on the concerns that were still rolling around in her mind. Leon wasn't tough, he was a kid, and the last thing she wanted was for him to start fighting and acting like a thug, because that was a fast track to ending up in jail. But her mum obviously

**210**

didn't share her concerns, and now she was back in control there was nothing Chantelle could do if she allowed him to go off by himself.

"Go and try that stuff on," Mary said again. "I wanna see if it fits. She'll look gorgeous, won't she, Miggy?"

Chantelle gritted her teeth when Miguel swivelled his eyes towards her. "I'll try them on later," she repeated, snatching the clothes and walking towards the door.

"You're a right miserable cow, you," Mary spat, lighting a cigarette and giving Chantelle a dirty look. "I've been out all day busting a gut to get the money for the wedding, and I wasn't just thinking about myself, I made an effort to get something specially for *you*, an' all, 'cos I thought you deserved a treat. But there you go again, chucking it back in my face."

"I'm not chucking anything back in your face," Chantelle protested. "I've just got a headache, that's all. I said I'll try it on, and I will. Just not now."

"Yeah, you take your time," Mary said sarcastically. "Never mind me, you just think about yourself — as usual."

"Why are you being like this?" Chantelle asked, a real headache starting up now. "I haven't done anything wrong."

"Apart from being selfish," said Mary. "All I wanted to do was see if they fit so I'll know I've got the right size when it comes to getting the bridesmaids' dresses. But no — you've got to be awkward about it."

"Why didn't you just say that?" Chantelle murmured guiltily.

"Wouldn't have to if you did as you were told and didn't argue about everything."

"All right, I'll try them on."

"Don't bother." Mary clamped the cigarette between her teeth and shoved the perfumes back into a bag. "I don't even know if I want you there now; you'll probably only ruin it."

"Don't be daft."

"I'm not." Mary was unrelenting. "You're a pain in the arse. Nothing's ever good enough for you, and I'm sick of trying to live up to your expectations. I'm your mother; I deserve a bit of respect."

"Respect is earned," Chantelle retorted coolly. "And it goes both ways."

Mary gave her a dirty look, and said, "Miggy was right — we should just do this on our own and fuck off back to Spain without you."

Chantelle was starting to feel sick. She'd done nothing wrong, but yet again her mum was having a go at her. And how dare Miguel try to cut her out of the wedding just because she'd rejected him.

Guessing that she'd been dismissed when her mum turned her back to pack the rest of her things away, Chantelle cast an accusing glance at Miguel and went to her room. The tops weren't her style, but she wouldn't have been happy to take them even if she'd loved them, knowing they'd been stolen. Still, Mary had tried to do something nice, so she should have at least said thank you.

Sad to have upset her mum again by being thoughtless, Chantelle sighed when her phone started ringing. Surprised to see that it was Rob Knight, she answered with an apprehensive, "Hello?"

"Hey . . ." he said, his tone friendly. "Hope I'm not disturbing you?"

"No, it's fine," Chantelle assured him. "What's up?"

"Just wondered if you were free tonight? Only I've spoken to my friend, and he'd be delighted to meet you — if you're still up for it?"

"Oh, right." Chantelle bit her lip. "Yes, I guess so."

"Don't sound too enthusiastic." Rob chuckled. "He's only one of the top agents in Manchester."

"Sorry, I've got a bit of a headache, can't think straight," Chantelle apologised. "Thanks, I'm really grateful. When does he want to meet?"

"Eight-thirty. Sorry it's such short notice but he's a busy man, so we're lucky he had a slot. Anyway, I've told him you're nervous, so he's promised to go easy on you. It'll just be an informal drink to start with, so the two of you can have a little chat and see what you think of each other. If it makes it any easier, I'll be there. Unless you'd rather meet him on your own?"

"No, that's great," Chantelle murmured, feeling sick all over again.

"Lovely. We're meeting at Cloud 23; the wine bar at the top of the Hilton."

"The *Hilton?*" Chantelle's stomach was really churning now.

"Don't worry, it's not as posh as it sounds." Rob laughed. "Just dress to impress, and leave the rest to nature."

Chantelle pondered that last comment for several minutes after Rob had said goodbye, but she couldn't figure out what he'd meant by it.

"Probably nothing," Bill said when Chantelle rang and asked what *she* thought. "But don't worry about it for now. Just get yourself ready, and I'll pick you up at eight. Oh, and I'll do the surveillance tonight," she added cheerily. "I've been to that bar, and I shan't look out of place sitting off in a corner by myself. Quite looking forward to it, actually; it's right at the top, and has the most magnificent views of the city. Now run along and make yourself beautiful."

Chantelle was a little happier to know that Bill would be there to keep an eye on her, but she was still nervous about the meeting. Rob had said it would be informal, but what if his friend took one look at her and asked why she had ever thought she could be a model? It would be so humiliating. And it was all too likely to happen, given how many beautiful women he must be surrounded by day in, day out. Oh, God, why had she agreed to do this?

She shook off the dread thoughts when she heard her mum and Miguel go out, and gazed down at the new clothes. They were quite nice, she supposed; and the blue top would look great with the wedges she'd bought last week. But there was no way she was wearing the skirt her mum had nicked for her; it was way too short and flouncy, and was more likely to make Rob's friend think she was auditioning to be a pole-dancer rather than a model. Not that she intended to become either, but she had to make it *look* as though she was being serious, or there was no point going.

Leon quickened his pace when he rounded the bend on the canal towpath and saw the gang in their usual spot by the locks up ahead.

"All right?" he said, grinning when he reached them, and holding out his hand to touch fists with Damo.

He immediately knew that something was wrong when Damo ignored his fist, and a flicker of fear sparked in his gut when the others turned and stared at him.

"Where is it?" Damo demanded, holding out his hand.

Already shaking, Leon tugged the bag out from under his jumper and passed it over.

Acky had been sitting astride the barrier smoking a cigarette. He flicked the butt into the water now, jumped down and strode towards Leon.

"'S up, guys?" Leon asked, aware that his voice sounded squeaky.

"'S up?" Acky repeated, peering down at him with a nasty glint in his eye. "You've got the nerve to ask what's up after legging it and leaving us to get mashed up, you little *rat!*"

"I — I didn't know what to do," Leon yelped, stumbling as he backed away. "I was hiding behind the bin, and they were right in front of me. If I'd tried to warn you they'd have got me."

"So you decided to run home like a baby and let them get *us* instead?" Acky towered over him. "You know how fuckin' many of them there were, do you?" He jabbed a hard finger into Leon's chest. "Fuckin' *eight*, that's how many. *Eight*, against me and him." He jerked his thumb back at Damo.

"Damo said you got away," Leon cried, tears of fear running down his cheeks.

"No thanks to you," Acky snarled. "And quit fuckin' crying, you little pussy," he added, punching Leon in the mouth before seizing him by the throat. "I've always said you were a liability, and now you've proved it. What d'ya think, lads?" He looked back at his friends over his shoulder. "Reckon it's time to get rid?"

"Please don't hurt me," Leon whimpered, sickened by the taste of the blood that was seeping from his split lip. "I didn't mean to run; I just didn't know what else to do."

"Well, *I* know what to do," Acky growled, tightening his grip. "I'm gonna fuckin' strangle you, then toss you in there." He dragged Leon towards the canal as he spoke. "Get me some bricks," he barked back at the others when they reached the edge of the bank. "I'm gonna mash his face up so no one'll recognise him when they fish him out."

"*Don't!*" Leon squealed, his whole body shaking with terror as he felt the empty space beneath his heels and heard the water lapping behind him. "Please, Acky, *please* . . . I'm sorry, I'm sorry!"

"That right?" Acky jerked him backwards so he almost fell, then hauled him back. "Sorry, are ya? Sorry for almost getting us fuckin' killed?"

**216**

Leon was crying freely now, snot running from his nose as tears streamed from his eyes. He'd never been more afraid in his life, and he was convinced that he was about to get his head smashed in. "Muuuum!" he wailed, clutching at Acky's hands. *"Muuuum!"*

"Yeah, that's right, you cry for your mummy like the baby you are," Acky sneered. "Ain't gonna get you nowhere, though. Think anyone can hear you down here?"

"All right, leave it," Damo said suddenly.

"Eh?" Acky snapped his head around. "What you on about?"

"I said leave it," Damo repeated quietly. "Get him away from the edge before he falls."

"He ain't gonna fall, I'm gonna *push* him," Acky said nastily. "With a fuckin' brick in his gob to make sure he stays under."

Leon peered at Damo through his tears and silently begged him for help. When Acky suddenly pulled him clear of the edge and released him, his legs gave way and he fell to his knees, crying, "I'm sorry . . . I'm sorry."

Damo walked over and squatted down in front of him. "You did a bad thing," he said quietly. "Being part of a crew is all about looking out for each other; all for one, and one for all, an' all that. That's why he's so fucked off with you, 'cos your arse went and you nearly got us killed. Lucky for you, they didn't catch us, or I'd have let him do for you," he went on. "But now you're gonna have to prove yourself if you wanna keep on hanging round with us."

"I'll do anything," Leon sobbed, seizing the lifeline that Damo was throwing him. "Just tell me what you want."

"I had a job for you," Damo told him. "But I ain't sure I can trust you no more."

"You can," Leon insisted.

"Can you fuck," Acky interjected scathingly. "He's a shady little cunt; wouldn't trust him to pick me nose."

Damo held up his hand to tell Acky to stay quiet, and peered thoughtfully down at Leon. "I'll give you one last chance," he said after a moment. "But if you fuck it up, I'll let Acky have you."

"I won't," Leon whimpered. "I swear."

"Better not," said Damo, reaching inside his jacket and pulling out a plastic bag. "See this?"

Leon glanced at it. Something was wrapped in it, but he couldn't make out what it was.

"I want you to take this home and hide it for me." Damo's voice was low and serious. "And when I tell you I need it, I don't care what time it is, you bring it. Got that?"

Leon nodded, and wiped his nose on his sleeve.

"You ain't serious?" Acky said incredulously. "You're letting him take the gun? What the fuck, man?"

"Who's the leader of this crew?" Damo demanded, his eyes still on Leon.

"You," Acky conceded. "But —"

"Ain't no buts about it," Damo said sharply. "I'm in charge, so I decide who does what." Then, talking to Leon again, he said, "Ever used a gun before?"

Leon shook his head.

"I have." Damo's eyes held a weird gleam that frightened Leon almost as much as the thought of having to carry a gun home. "And I liked it. First time's always the best; never get a buzz like that again. Now, Acky thinks you're a bottle merchant, but I've always said you had guts, haven't I?"

Leon nodded and licked his lips.

"Problem is, I'm not so sure any more," Damo went on. "So you're gonna have to prove it."

"H-how?" Leon could barely speak.

"We're taking the leader of that crew down," Damo told him. "And *you're* gonna do it."

"*What?*" Leon's mouth flapped open in shock.

"You heard." Damo grinned. "You're gonna shoot the fucker."

"But I can't," Leon spluttered. "I've never used a gun; I don't know what to do."

"It's easy," Damo assured him. "I'll show you when the time comes. For now, you just take it home and sit on it. Unless you ain't got respect for us?" No longer smiling, he drew his head back and stared at Leon. "'Cos if you ain't, you already know too much, and we won't be able to let you go. So what you sayin'?"

"I've got pure respect," Leon croaked, sure that he was about to piss himself. "I swear."

Damo carried on staring into his eyes for a few moments, and then nodded slowly. "We'll soon find out, won't we? Now, take it and go home." He shoved the package into Leon's hands. "I'll call you when we need you. Don't let me down."

"Or you're dead," said Acky, cocking two fingers and miming shooting Leon through the head.

As Damo and the others walked away, Leon rose unsteadily to his feet and carefully slid the package inside his jacket. It felt heavy as he began to walk slowly in the opposite direction, and he was terrified with every hesitant step that it would go off and shoot him in the stomach.

Chantelle was on her way out when Leon arrived back at the flat. She was standing in front of the hall mirror when he let himself in, giving her hair one last spritz of hairspray.

"Oh, you're back, are you?" She gave him an unimpressed look when he shuffled towards his room with his hood up and his head down.

"Get lost."

"Don't you dare talk to me like that." Chantelle slammed her comb down on the table and placed her hands on her hips. "I've been looking after you for weeks, but now mum's back you think you can backchat me. I'm sick of it!"

"You ain't my boss," Leon snapped. "Just get off my back and leave me alone. And you look like a *whore*," he added, giving her a dirty look before slamming his door in her face.

Chantelle gritted her teeth and balled her hands into fists. If she'd had more time she'd have called off tonight's job and stayed here to have it out with Leon. But Bill would already be on her way, and she couldn't just leave her boss sitting there.

"Right, I've got to go out," she shouted through Leon's door. "But we *will* be having that talk, so make sure you're here when I get back."

When they reached the Hilton, Bill went in first and Chantelle waited a few minutes before following. Her stomach was churning as she rode the lift up to the bar at the top, but when she stepped out and saw the view through the bank of windows that greeted her it took her breath away. As Bill had said, it was incredible; she could see lights and buildings stretching out for miles and miles.

Aware that she was gawping when a passing waitress gave her a curious look, Chantelle snapped her mouth shut and glanced around until she located Bill at a table to the rear of the room. When she spotted Rob Knight waving to her from the bar, she took a deep breath and walked calmly over to him.

"You look beautiful," he said, kissing her on both cheeks.

"Thank you," she said shyly, clutching her bag to her stomach. He looked even more handsome than the last time she had seen him, and his aftershave smelled divine.

"Would you like to sit here, or would you prefer to find a table?" he asked.

"I don't mind."

"Okay, we'll stay here for now," Rob said decisively, holding out his hand to help her up onto a tall stool. "We can always move when Greg gets here. What can I get you?"

"Just a Coke, please." Chantelle settled on the stool and crossed her legs.

"Driving?"

"Er, no, I got a cab. Just don't want to drink before I've met your friend, in case I say something stupid."

"Doubt that'd happen," said Rob, waving the bartender over. "But you've got to do whatever makes you feel comfortable."

After ordering their drinks, he sat on the stool facing hers. "So, how have you been?"

"Fine," she said. "You?"

"Busy." He shrugged. "Nothing new there, though. Never seem to have a minute to myself, these days."

"What do you do?" Chantelle asked, nodding thank you to the barman when he placed her drink on the counter.

"Computer stuff," Rob said, removing the stick from his cocktail. "All very boring. How about you? What's your line?"

"I, er, look after children," Chantelle lied, taking a sip of the icy Coke.

"Rather you than me," Rob chuckled.

"Don't you like kids?"

"Nope. Do you have any of your own?"

"Not yet." Chantelle smiled. "One day, maybe, but there's too much I want to do first."

"And a boyfriend would probably help," said Rob, reminding her that she'd told him she was single.

"Of course," she agreed. "But even if I had one I'd have to know he was the *right* one before I considered having children with him."

222

"Sensible." Rob nodded approvingly.

"So, doesn't your wife want children?" Chantelle asked. Then, blushing, she said, "I'm guessing that's a wedding ring on your finger?"

Rob nodded and took a swig of his drink.

Chantelle noticed that his smile had slipped, and said, "Sorry, that was none of my business."

"Hey, don't apologise, it's not a secret, or anything. I'm just . . ." Rob trailed off and sighed, before adding, "Actually, I'm in the doghouse at the moment. She reckons I *work too hard*." He made quotation marks with his fingers and rolled his eyes. "But businesses don't run themselves, so what can I do?"

"Must be hard," Chantelle said sympathetically.

"Yep. Although I don't hear her complaining when she's splashing out on shoes and weekend spa breaks with her girlfriends." .

"Nice," Chantelle murmured enviously. She hadn't thought that women actually did that kind of stuff in real life, but women with rich husbands obviously did.

"Yeah, nice for *her*," said Rob. "I'm just the mug who slogs my guts out to bankroll it. But enough about me and my high-maintenance wife; tell me about you."

"There's not much to tell." Chantelle shrugged. "I work with kids, and occasionally go out for a drink with my friend. Other than that, I lead a pretty boring life."

"What a waste." Rob shook his head and gave her a teasing smile. "With a face like that, you should be out every night. Still, once Greg gets his hands on you,

you'll need a big stick to fend the fellas off. Subject of . . ." He glanced at his watch. "I wonder where he's got to. If you'll excuse me for a minute, I'll find somewhere quiet and give him a ring."

When he stepped down off his stool and walked away, Chantelle glanced across at Bill. Her boss was studying the videophone and, to anyone who didn't know, she appeared to be reading and sending text messages. Chantelle was pleased about that, because she often worried when she was on a job that she might be being too obvious.

She smoothed her skirt over her knees now and took another sip of her Coke. She hoped Rob's friend was on his way so she could get this over with and go home. Rob was nice, but she had never felt comfortable lying to people's faces, and she was terrified of tripping herself up.

"I am so sorry about this," Rob said when he came back a couple of minutes later. "Greg can't make it."

"Oh?" Chantelle was relieved, but forced herself to sound disappointed. "That's a shame."

"He's caught up in some video shoot on the other side of town," Rob said, sitting on his stool again, "and he reckons it'll be at least another couple of hours before he gets away. If you're willing to wait, he's told me I must buy you dinner."

"Thanks, but I'd best not," Chantelle said. "I've got an early start in the morning."

"No worries." Rob smiled. "I can introduce you to Greg another time."

"Actually, I think I've changed my mind," Chantelle said, figuring that there was nothing more to be gained from this. Rob had already admitted that he was married, so he obviously wasn't going to try it on with her. The job was done, as far as she was concerned.

"Really?" Rob gave her a regretful look. "I'm sorry to hear that."

"I just don't think it's for me." Chantelle reached for her bag. "I'm really sorry for wasting your time."

Rob held up his hands. "Hey, it's totally your choice; I wouldn't dream of making you do something you're uncomfortable with. But can. I at least get you another drink before you go?"

"No, I'm fine." Chantelle smiled. "Maybe you should go home and spend some time with your wife while you've got a chance? Might get you out of the doghouse?"

"She's out with the girls," Rob told her as he stood up. "But not to worry, I've got plenty of stuff to catch up on. Can I drop you somewhere? My car's just across the road."

"Oh, no, really, I don't want to put you out," Chantelle said quickly. "I'll get a cab."

"If you're sure." Rob put his hand on the small of her back and guided her towards the elevator. "But I'll pay your fare."

"There's no need." Chantelle cast a furtive glance in Bill's direction.

"I insist," Rob said, letting her know that he wasn't going to take no for an answer.

"Okay, thank you. But I, er, just need to nip to the bathroom before I go."

Chantelle rushed to the toilets and fell through the door, then paced the floor until her boss ambled in. "He's insisting on getting me a cab home," she whispered worriedly. "What should I do?"

"Go," said Bill. "But if he tries to get in with you, say no. And *don't* give the driver your real address. Get him to drop you by the library in Chorlton; I'll follow and pick you up. Now, stay here for a minute, give me a chance to get to my car."

"Okay." Chantelle felt a little calmer. "See you in a bit. And please don't lose sight of the cab."

"Have I *ever* lost track of a car I'm tailing?" Bill raised an eyebrow. Then, smiling, she patted Chantelle on the arm and made her way back out to the bar.

As directed, Chantelle waited a short time before following her out. "Sorry," she apologised to Rob. "Got something in my eye; took me ages to fish it out."

"Is it okay?" he asked, taking her face in his hands and peering into her eyes.

"Yeah, it's fine," Chantelle murmured, blushing again as she caught another waft of his expensive aftershave.

The elevator door opened just then, and they were forced to step aside as several people poured out. When it was empty, Rob waved for Chantelle to go in ahead of him. Out on the pavement a minute later, he flagged down a black cab and held the door open for her.

"Where to?" the driver asked.

"Barlow Moor Road," Chantelle told him as she climbed onto the back seat.

Rob passed a £20 note to the driver before leaning in to kiss Chantelle on the cheek. "Sorry it didn't work out, but you've got my number if you change your mind again."

Chantelle thanked him and sat back. Then, waving when he closed the door, she breathed a huge sigh of relief when the cab pulled away from the kerb.

No longer in the mood for a confrontation, Chantelle was glad that Leon was asleep when she got home. She didn't know why she was so tired, considering that all she'd done tonight was talk, but she felt totally worn out and couldn't wait to go to bed.

Ten minutes later, having washed off the heavy make-up, changed into her pyjamas and climbed into bed, she had just begun to doze off when the front door slammed back against the hall wall. Scared that it had been kicked in, she jerked upright, but lay back down when she heard her mum's and Miguel's raised voices. They sounded drunk, and it was clear that they were arguing, but she had no intention of getting involved.

Mary had other ideas.

"Oi, you!" she barked, bursting into Chantelle's room and switching the overhead light on. "What've you got to say for yourself?"

"What are you on about?" Chantelle squinted up at her.

"Don't come the innocent with me," Mary snarled, marching over to the bed and glaring down at her.

"Thought you could nick me man from under me nose, did you?"

"*What?*" Chantelle's brow creased deeply and she pushed herself up on her elbows. "I don't know what he's told you, but —"

"He's told me *everything*, so don't bother denying it," Mary spat, weaving now as she towered over her daughter. "I can't believe you'd do that to *me*, your own mother. But I should have known you couldn't be trusted. You act all la-di-fuckin'-da, but you're just a little slag underneath it all. Bet you've shagged your way through half the estate while I've been gone. And how many of me *other* boyfriends did you make a play for when my back was turned, that's what I'd like to know?"

"You're being ridiculous," Chantelle said calmly. "I haven't slept with anyone, never mind one of *your* boyfriends. Do you really think I'd do that to you?"

"Yeah, 'cos you're jealous of me," Mary retorted nastily. "Always have been, always will be, 'cos I'm white, and you wish you was, an' all."

"I have *never* been jealous of you for that." Chantelle was starting to get angry now, too.

"Don't make me laugh," Mary sneered. "You've always wanted to be like me, but you'll never do it, 'cos I'm fun, while you act like you've got a sodding great mop stuck up your arse."

"I don't want to talk about this any more," Chantelle said coolly. "I'll see you in the morning when you've sobered up. You're talking rubbish, and we're just going to end up saying stuff we don't mean."

228

"Oh, so you think you can take me on, do ya?" Mary reached down and seized Chantelle by the hair. "Come on, then, if you think you're hard!"

Chantelle gritted her teeth as the pain burned her scalp. "Get off me," she said firmly. "I mean it, Mum, let go of me right now."

"Or *what?*" Mary tugged at her daughter's hair. "Think you can handle me, do ya? You might be taller, but you ain't harder, and that's a fact."

"I never said I was," Chantelle argued, holding onto her mum's wrists to keep her from tearing the hair right out. "But I am *not* putting up with this, because I've done nothing wrong."

"Apart from try and shag my fella," Mary reminded her. "Well, tough, 'cos he didn't want you. And you know why? 'Cos you ain't all that. You *think* you are, but you ain't. You're ugly and boring, just like your father."

Chantelle couldn't take any more. Tears stinging her eyes, she leapt out of bed and wrenched her head free of her mum's grip, then shoved her forcefully towards the door. "Get out before I do something I regret," she cried. "It was *him* who tried it on with *me*, if you must know, and he got a kick in the balls for it, but I bet he didn't tell you about that, did he? Even if I liked him, which I *don't*, do you really think I'd go near anyone who'd screwed *you?*"

"You fuckin' *what?*" Mary screeched, stumbling as her daughter pushed her out into the hall. "You lying cow! Why would he try it on with you when he's got *me?*"

"Ask *him*," yelled Chantelle, furiously pointing at Miguel who was slouched against the living-room door. "Go on, *ask* him."

"I ain't asking him nothing," spat Mary, straightening herself up. "I know he loves me, so he wouldn't do that to me. But *you* . . ." She looked Chantelle up and down with a hateful sneer on her lips. "You'd do anything to get attention, you. But you ain't getting it off my man, so keep your fucking eyes off him in future."

"Oh, don't worry, I don't *want* to look at him," said Chantelle. "If I never saw him again it'd be too soon. Now leave me alone — I'm going to bed."

"*Bitch!*" Mary spat when Chantelle closed the bedroom door in her face. "I'll be watching you."

Chantelle climbed back into bed and pulled the quilt over her head. She'd been on the verge of dropping off when her mum burst in, but she doubted she'd get any sleep now. Her body felt wired, and her stomach was churning so badly that she was glad she hadn't eaten earlier or she'd have been in danger of throwing up. She couldn't believe Miguel had lied about her like that — or that her mum had believed him. He'd probably thought she was going to grass him up and had decided to get in there first. But God help him if he came near her after this, because she would rip his greasy head off.

# CHAPTER
# SEVENTEEN

The atmosphere in the flat was heavy during the next few days, and Chantelle prayed each morning that Bill would call with a job for her. Nothing came and, rather than stay in her room all day, she took to walking into town and wandering around until she thought that her mum and Miguel were likely to have gone out. Whenever their paths did cross, Miguel couldn't look her in the eye, and Mary made it clear that she still wasn't talking to her. It was unbearable, and so unfair, but there was nothing Chantelle could do about it if her mum didn't believe her.

What upset Chantelle most was the thought that they might not have resolved their differences in time for the wedding. Mary was happily forging ahead with her plans, and Tracey seemed to be a permanent fixture in the flat as they organised everything between them. They had nicked some wedding magazines from the newsagent's, and were always ooh-ing and ah-ing over dresses and rings and hairstyles and flowers and suits . . . Chantelle didn't even know if the date had been set yet, but she couldn't ask because she wasn't even sure that her mum was going to invite her. And Leon was in a world of his own, so she couldn't even ask him.

She was feeling so low when she got a call from Rob one morning that she almost didn't answer. But curiosity got the better of her.

"Hey," he said. "Not disturbing you, am I?"

"No, I was just reading," she told him, surprised to find herself smiling at the sound of his voice. But then, with no one speaking to her at home just now, any friendly voice would have been welcome. "What can I do for you?"

"Just wondered what you're doing tomorrow?"

"I'm not sure," she said cautiously. "Why?"

"Because I'd like to invite you out for a meal," Rob said. "And you'll be doing me a massive favour if you say yes."

"Oh? Why's that?"

"I've got to wine and dine a client and his wife. The missus was supposed to be coming, but she's decided she needs another break," Rob explained. "I was relying on her to keep the client's wife entertained while we get on with business, but she's scuppered that. So I thought, why not ask Julia? She's smart, beautiful, and great company — perfect hostess material. So, what do you say?"

"I don't know. I'll have to think about it."

"Sure, no pressure. But you really would be doing me a favour. And you'll have a great night, I promise. Top-class restaurant, no expense spared. I'll even pay you for your time."

"No, that's not necessary," Chantelle said. Then, taking a deep breath, she said, "Okay, I'll do it."

"You're a lifesaver," Rob said gratefully. "I'll pick you up at eight, if that's okay?"

"No, I'll make my own way there," Chantelle told him, hoping as she said it that the restaurant would be in town and not near his house, which was miles out. "Just tell me where to meet you."

She cut the call after writing down the name of the restaurant, and bit her lip. She supposed she really ought to tell Bill. But she wasn't going to be alone with Rob, so it wasn't like he was asking her out on a date, or anything. And he'd offered to pay her, so he was obviously being honest about it being a business thing. It was flattering to know that he considered her a fitting stand-in for his wife, and she couldn't deny that it would be nice to get away from the horrible atmosphere in the flat for a while. So, no, she wouldn't bother telling Bill.

Happier than she'd felt all week, Chantelle got up and checked her wardrobe for something nice to wear. Nothing seemed quite right, so she decided to head over to the market and spend a bit of her savings on a new dress. Nothing too expensive, just something classy that the wife of a rich businessman might wear for dinner at a posh restaurant.

"Behave," she scolded herself as she pulled her coat on. "It's not a date, it's a business arrangement, and don't you forget it."

Anton was washing out a glass at his kitchen sink when Chantelle walked past. He waved when he saw her but she didn't see him, so he rushed to the door in time to see her disappear down the stairs. He decided there was no point trying to catch up with her because he would need to go back inside and get his jacket and keys first, by which time she'd probably be long gone. Anyway, he was already late for work, and he didn't want to push his luck now that he had rent and bills to pay. He would just have to catch her another time and tell her about the party.

He smiled to himself as he went back into the flat and looked around. He'd moved in properly a few days earlier, and it already felt like home. His stereo and speakers were sitting in pride of place in one corner of the black-and-silver-decorated living room, the flat-screen TV in another. He'd ordered a sofa but it wouldn't be here for a few weeks, so the only seating was a couple of leather beanbags; but his bed was set up, so at least he could sleep in comfort. He had managed to pick up a cheap fridge-freezer and a cooker, and his mum had given him a kettle, some cups, plates, and cutlery. The rest would come in time, but he basically had everything he needed for now.

The party had been Shotz's idea.

"You can't not have a house-warming," he'd said when Anton had admitted that it hadn't even crossed his mind. "Think of all the gals we can fetch in, man; it'd be like twenty-four-seven pussy heaven — with no ma giving them the evil eye. And it might scare the old 'un away," he'd added in a whisper, shuddering as he'd nodded towards the bedroom that he still hadn't dared step foot in for fear of being confronted by the ghost of the previous tenant.

234

Anton was no longer as spooked by the thought of the old woman's spirit as he had initially been, but he guessed that Shotz had a point. A party would christen the place properly and lay down some fresh vibes — clear out the old to make way for the new, and all that.

They had decided to have the party tomorrow night, and Shotz had been on a mad inviting spree for the last few days. Anton had intended to invite Chantelle just now, but he was sure he'd catch up with her again.

Mary had found her perfect wedding dress. She'd picked out about a thousand perfect dresses over the last few weeks, but this one was *the* one. Its sweetheart neckline was smothered in glittery crystals, which would make her look dead classy *and* show off her tits. The skirt was neither too wide nor too flouncy, so she wouldn't get weighed down *or* look a complete mug trying to get in and out of doors; and it had long princess sleeves that would hide her bingo wings and all the ugly marks on her arms from where she'd cut herself in the past.

She wanted this dress, and she was determined to have it. There were just two problems. One: it was priced at £350, which was *way* out of her league since she'd already spent all the money she had made off the perfumes and jewellery; and two: the stupid shopkeeper was watching her like a hawk.

The snotty bitch had clocked them as soon as they walked in and had turned up her nose as if they were a load of dirty pikeys. She seemed to be alone, so Mary could easily have knocked her out and taken the dress.

But she preferred to lift without violence, if possible, because it made everything so much easier in the long run not to have assault and battery added to the rap sheet if she got caught.

Mary had ordered Miguel to keep the woman occupied while she and Tracey did the business and, to his credit, he'd been laying on the charm as if he really meant it. But the bitch wasn't falling for it. If anything, it seemed to be making her even more suspicious, and every time Mary turned around there she was, hovering in the background like some kind of vulture.

Aware that Miguel was getting nowhere, Tracey had stepped in and made the woman move to the back of the shop to show her some bridesmaids' dresses. It was all Mary needed and, as soon as the woman's back was turned, she slid her dress off its hanger, quickly and expertly balled it up, and made a dash for the door.

"*Stop!*" the woman shouted, turning at the sound of the bell and seeing Mary hotfooting it out with Miguel on her heels. "I've still got your friend — I'll lock her in."

"In your dreams," Tracey growled, smacking her in the face before legging it after Mary.

Out on the pavement, Tracey skidded to a halt when she heard Mary's raised voice and saw that her friend had run straight into the path of two police officers, one of whom had a tight grip on her arm. Miguel was nowhere in sight and, guessing that he had done a runner, Tracey decided to do the same. Mary would understand. If she was getting nicked, she wouldn't expect Tracey to offer herself up as well.

When she heard the tinkle of the shop bell behind her, Tracey dived into an alleyway between the shops just as the irate owner rushed out, and quickly made her getaway.

"Arrest her," the shopkeeper demanded, pointing an accusing finger at Mary as she marched up to the group. "She's just stolen that dress from my shop. And her friend assaulted me."

"What friend?" Mary gave her a dirty look. "I'm on my own, you dozy bat."

"Well, you weren't a moment ago," the woman replied icily. Then, turning to the officers, she said, "She had a foreign man and a scruffy woman with her, and you need to alert your colleagues before they get too far, because they're clearly dangerous. Look what she did to me." She turned her head to show them her reddened cheek. "And he was probably an illegal immigrant," she added indignantly.

"Racist bitch!" Mary kicked out at her.

"Pack it in," the officer who was holding her barked.

"Why should I?" Mary demanded. "She's making racist comments. That's illegal — I want her charged."

"I am *not* a racist." The woman bristled. "And give me back my dress, you thief."

"Get lost!" Mary clung onto it. "I've paid for it fair and square."

"No, you haven't."

"Yes, I fucking have." Now it was Mary's turn to address the officers with indignation. "I gave her the deposit weeks ago, and I've been paying it off ever since. We're all straight now, so I came to pick it up — just like we arranged," she added to the woman.

"Oh, you liar," the woman gasped. "I've never even seen you before."

"You're trying to rip me off," Mary gasped back, imitating her.

The officers clearly didn't know who to believe as they looked from one to the other of the women. "Have you got any proof that you've paid?" one of them asked Mary.

"Yeah, I had a book," Mary told him. "But I was going shopping for shoes when I made the last payment the other day and I didn't want to lose it, so *she* said she'd keep it in the safe for me."

"Oh, really?" The woman raised her chin and smiled smugly. "Well, it'll be very easy to prove I don't have anything of the sort when I show these officers the safe, won't it?"

"Yeah, 'cos you've probably chucked it out so you can diddle me," Mary retorted.

"Do you have CCTV?" the other officer asked the woman.

"No," she admitted quietly. "But I shouldn't need it. It's quite obvious who's telling the truth here. Why hasn't she got a bag if this was prearranged?"

"Because you were faffing about, and I needed to catch my bus," spat Mary, feeling more confident by the second. "Bloody missed it now, though, haven't I? Thanks for that. You knew I had to get back or I was going to miss the flower woman."

**238**

"Oh, this is ridiculous," the woman said irritably. "Just give me my dress and get lost."

"What, and let you swan off with my money? I don't think so!"

"You haven't paid any bloody money."

"Prove it."

"You prove you have."

"I can't, can I, 'cos you kept my book."

"There was no book."

"Prove it."

"All right, that's enough," one of the officers said wearily. He looked at the shop owner. "What do you want to do?"

"I just want my dress," she said, folding her arms.

"You don't want to press charges?"

"What's the bloody point?"

"And you?" He looked at Mary.

"Here, take the damn thing, I don't even want it no more, probably jinxed now," she said, shoving the dress into the woman's hands. "But I'll be coming for my money back, so don't think you've got away with it."

"I take it you don't want to press any charges, either?" the officer peered down at Mary with a knowing glint in his eye as the woman marched away with her dress.

"No, I'm too tired," she said, resisting the urge to laugh. He'd clearly sussed that she was as guilty as sin, but there was nothing he could do about it. "I'll just set my solicitor on her," she added self-righteously.

"Whatever." He shook his head and chuckled softly. "Go on . . . piss off before I do you for time-wasting."

Mary smiled to herself as she walked away. She might have lost that dress, but there were plenty of ways to skin a cat — and she knew exactly which little pussy to target.

Back at home, Chantelle copied Leon's trick and shoved the back of a chair under her door handle before taking her new dress out of its bag and laying it out on the bed. Then, slipping out of the clothes she was wearing, she pulled it on carefully and stepped back to view her reflection in the dressing-table mirror.

It had cost more than she'd intended, but she figured it was worth it because it was the kind of dress she could wear for a variety of occasions. Not too fancy, or too low-necked or short-skirted, it was made of soft wool in a gorgeous shade of taupe. It clung to her figure in a really flattering way without making her look tarty, and she was thrilled with it.

She just hoped that Rob wouldn't think she was making too much effort, because it would be so embarrassing if he got the impression that she was the kind of girl who went after married men. He was undeniably good-looking, and she felt comfortable in his presence despite the awkwardness of the situation. But there was nothing more to it than that. He was a nice man, and she was doing him a favour, end of.

A tap came at her door just then, and her mum's voice sing-songed, "Channy . . . are you in there, babes?"

**240**

Chantelle frowned. She hadn't heard her mum come in, and certainly hadn't expected to be spoken to after the freezing-out of the last few days.

"Just a minute," she said, rushing to the door when the handle started to rattle.

"Why have you got it barricaded?" Mary asked when Chantelle opened up. Then, eyebrows creeping up when she saw what her daughter was wearing, she whistled softly through her teeth. "Whit-woo, look at you."

"Do you like it?" Chantelle asked, blushing shyly.

"Like it? I *love* it. Who's it for?" Mary grinned slyly. "Got yourself a date?"

"No, it's a work thing," Chantelle lied. "The boss is taking us out for dinner."

"How old is he?"

"It's a she, and she's in her sixties."

"Oh, well, never mind," said Mary. "There's bound to be a handsome waiter who'll appreciate it. Want a brew?"

"Er, yeah, all right," Chantelle murmured, hoping this sudden thaw meant that Miguel had confessed to lying about her trying it on with him, because it had been horrible living under the cloud of suspicion. "I'll just get changed. Won't be a minute."

Mary was sitting at the table, a cup of tea in one hand, a fag in the other, when Chantelle walked into the kitchen.

"Thanks." Chantelle sat across from her and reached for her own cup. "Where's Miguel?"

"Don't worry about him." Mary tapped her ash into an ashtray. "I've told him to stop round Tracey's for a bit; give us a chance to have that chat you wanted."

"Great," said Chantelle, resisting the urge to wipe up the ash which had spilled onto the tabletop.

"Go on, then." Mary smiled at her. "What did you want to talk about? Love your hair like that, by the way," she chipped in before Chantelle had a chance to speak. "It's really grown, hasn't it? Suits you."

"Do you think so?" Chantelle raised a hand and self-consciously touched her hair.

"Yeah, it's lush, babes." Mary gave her a loving look. "Great this, innit? Me and you having a lovely girly chat. You know you've always been my favourite, don't you?"

Chantelle almost choked on the tea she was sipping. "Since when?"

"Aw, don't be like that." Mary gave her a sorrowful look. "I know we haven't always seen eye to eye, but we only clash 'cos we're so alike."

Chantelle couldn't believe what she was hearing. They were so *unalike* that it wasn't even funny. And her mum had always been the one to say it, so why was she suddenly saying the opposite?

"Have you been drinking?" she asked.

"Have I 'eck as like," Mary scoffed. "Just trying to put things right between us. What's wrong with that?"

"Nothing," Chantelle said cautiously. Her mum had never climbed down after an argument before, so this was a definite first. But she didn't trust Mary one inch.

242

"Guess what I was doing today?" Mary said, grinning. "Looking at bridesmaids' dresses."

"Really?" Chantelle wondered if she'd forgotten that she'd said she didn't want her at the wedding.

"I saw one that I thought would really suit you," Mary went on. "But you know what? I reckon the one you just had on would be absolutely perfect."

"Yeah?"

"Yeah, it looks amazing on you," Mary gushed. Then, giving a sheepish little smile, she added, "And it'd help me out if I didn't have to buy something else. Not that I won't if you don't want to wear your one, but I've not even got the money for my own yet."

"What about the money you got the other day?" Chantelle reminded her. "From all that stuff you sold."

Mary pulled a face and rolled her eyes. "Made the mistake of letting Miggy hold it, and he lost it. It's my own fault; I know what he's like when he's had a drink. But it's all right. I'll wear a bin bag if I have to, so long as I get him up the aisle."

"Didn't you apply for a crisis loan?"

"Yeah, but they turned me down 'cos it's not been a year since the last one." Mary shrugged now and took a sip of her tea. "Just my luck, eh? Biggest day of my life, and it's probably going to end up a rush job in jeans, with a chippy dinner and a can of beer for a reception."

Chantelle peered at her mum over the rim of her cup, but didn't say anything.

"Still, it's not your problem." Mary flapped her hand. "Probably don't deserve a nice wedding, anyway, after all the stunts I've pulled over the years." She

243

paused and took another drag of her fag, then asked, "So, how are you getting on? Job still going well?"

"Yeah, it's okay," Chantelle said quietly, guessing what was coming next.

"I always knew you'd make something of yourself," Mary said proudly. "Always been clever, haven't you? Bet you've saved a fair bit."

"A bit." Chantelle stared down into her cup.

"That's my girl." Mary beamed. "Here, that's a thought . . ." she said then, chuckling as if it was a joke. "Mums are supposed to pay for their kids' weddings, but how funny would it be if I had to borrow money off you to pay for mine?"

Chantelle exhaled wearily. Bingo!

"Not that I'd ever dream of asking you for money," Mary went on insincerely. "Wouldn't seem right, knowing how hard you worked for it. I'll just have to go out on the rob again."

"You need to pack that in," Chantelle said disapprovingly. "One of these days you'll get caught, and what'll happen to our Leon if you get banged up? They're not going to let me keep him when I've only just turned sixteen."

"You're sixteen?" Mary drew her head back. "Since when?"

"Since my birthday last week," Chantelle told her. "The day you came back, actually."

"Shit, I knew there was something special about that day," Mary said. "Ask Miggy. All the way back on the plane I was saying, I'm sure there's something I'm

244

supposed to remember about today. Sorry, babes. I'll make it up to you."

"It doesn't matter," Chantelle said, gripping her cup between both hands. "It's done now."

Mary gazed at her across the table and sighed. "You're a good girl, you; so grown-up and responsible. I don't deserve you."

"Don't be daft."

"I mean it." Mary stubbed the butt of her cigarette out, then reached across the table and placed her hand over Chantelle's. "I know I don't always show it, but I'm proper proud of you."

Chantelle bit down on the inside of her cheek. This was the first time her mum had ever spoken to her like this, and it felt really weird. No, not just weird: *unnatural*.

Mary withdrew her hand after a moment and lit a fresh cigarette. She took a deep pull on it and blew the smoke out into the air. Then, her tone hesitant, she said, "I don't like asking, but it really would help if you could lend us some money, you know? I'd pay you back as soon as they put us on couples' benefits. A couple of hundred should do it," she added tentatively. "But only if you can manage it?"

Chantelle felt as if she'd been backed into a wall. "I'll see what I can do," she said wearily.

"Course, whenever you're ready," Mary agreed. "You'll probably have to go to the bank for it, eh?"

"Mmmm." Chantelle dipped her gaze again. It was a lie, but she wasn't about to tell her mum that the money was already here. She'd probably get drunk and tell Miguel, and he'd already proved that he had no conscience, so what was to stop him from stealing it if he knew it was here?

Mary narrowed her eyes and took another drag of her fag. Then, glancing at the clock on the wall, she said, "Oh, shit, look at the time; Miggy'll think I've forgot about him." She jumped up and took her jacket off the back of the chair. "See you later, babes. And thanks again for that." She leaned down and planted a kiss on Chantelle's cheek, then rushed out.

Disappointed to have been right about her mum having an ulterior motive for talking to her again, Chantelle finished her tea, then cleared the cups away, emptied the ashtray and wiped the table before going out into the hall.

"Leon . . .?" She tapped on his bedroom door. "Are you awake?"

"What?"

"It's dinner time, but I can't be bothered cooking. Fancy something from the chippy?"

"I'm not hungry."

"My treat."

"I said I'm not hungry. Just leave me alone and stop bugging me."

Chantelle rolled her eyes and shrugged in a gesture of surrender. Oh, well, she'd tried. But if he wasn't ready to snap out of his mood, there was no point forcing the issue.

She'd hung the new dress on the wardrobe door, and when she walked into her bedroom now and her gaze landed on it she felt a tickle of excitement in her stomach. If someone had told her a few weeks ago that she would enjoy getting dressed up and putting on make-up, she'd have said they needed their head testing. But it was true; she really was starting to enjoy it. She just hoped she didn't do anything stupid tomorrow and make a fool of herself in front of Rob and his client.

Anton was at the foot of the stairwell when a woman appeared at the top. He stepped back and waited for her to descend.

"It's all right, I don't bite," Mary teased, giving him a flirtatious smile as she sauntered down the steps.

"Superstition," he explained. "My nan reckons it's bad luck to pass someone on the stairs."

"That right?" Mary had reached him by now, and she pouted. "And what does she say about her grandson dating older women?"

"Eh?" Anton recoiled.

Mary saw the look of horror in his eyes and snorted softly. "Don't flatter yourself, darlin'; I eat boys like you for breakfast." She pushed her breasts out now and sashayed away, glancing back over her shoulder after a few steps to see if he was watching.

He was, but not for the reason she thought. He'd just remembered where he'd seen her before: coming out of Chantelle's place a few days earlier.

"Are you Chantelle's mum?" he asked.

Mary stopped walking and turned round. "Might be. Why?"

"I've just moved in a few doors down," he told her, "and I'm having a house-warming party tomorrow. I meant to invite her, but I haven't seen her, so can you pass the message on? Tell her it's at Anton's, and it'll be starting about nine-ish."

"Am I invited an' all?" Mary gave him a sexy smile. Then, tutting when he frowned, she said, "Oh, get a sense of humour, you boring sod. You might be fit, but it takes more than that to keep a girl's interest, you know?"

When she turned and stomped away, Anton shook his head bemusedly and trotted up the stairs.

"What did she say?" Tracey asked when she let Mary in a short time later. "Is she gonna lend you some?"

"Course," said Mary, strolling into the living room and flopping down beside Miguel who was sprawled out on the couch. "She loves her mummy, innit?"

"Have you got it now?" Tracey perched on the edge of a chair. "Can we score?"

"Nah, she made out like it's in the bank." Mary sneered as she lit a cigarette. "But I'd bet my arsehole she's got it stashed in the flat, 'cos the stupid cow couldn't look me in the eye when I mentioned the bank. Thinks she's so smart, but I can read her like a book."

"So what you gonna do?" Tracey was scratching her arms now.

"Wait till she goes out and find it."

"She'll go mad when she finds out," Tracey said nervously, remembering the run-in *she*'d had with

Chantelle when Mary had sent her round for the letter that time. The girl had always unnerved her, even when she'd been a kid, because she had a weird way of looking at you. But she'd been furious that day, and Tracey had been a bit scared of her.

"What's she gonna do about it?" Mary scoffed. "Have me arrested and risk having our Leon put in care?" She took an angry pull on her fag now, her eyes glinting with malice. "Bitch thought she could try it on with *my* man and get away with it, did she? Well, we'll soon see about that."

# CHAPTER
# EIGHTEEN

Anton rushed home from work the next evening and jumped straight into the shower. Abdul's place smelled putrid, and he was always convinced that the stench was on him when he left at the end of a shift. He was becoming so paranoid about it that he'd lost count of how many bottles of shower gel and tins of deodorant he'd bought recently.

"The man 'im turnin' batty," Shotz had joked to the lads when they had gone clubbing the other night. "Me smell 'im comin' way afore me see 'im pretty face."

Anton had taken it in good humour, insisting that he'd rather smell of Lynx and aftershave than stink like Abdul's rancid stock; but he did sometimes wonder if he wasn't going a tad overboard. Still, the girls seemed to like it, so he wasn't about to stop just to shut his mate up.

He had just got out of the shower and was making his way to the bedroom with a towel around his waist when Shotz arrived carrying an armload of bottles for the party. Anton opened his front door and reached out to take some of them from him — just as Chantelle's mother and the man he'd seen at the shop with Chantelle walked past.

"Pwhoar," Mary growled, her gaze sliding from his wet chest to his taut, dripping stomach. "Don't get many of them to the pound these days."

"Hey," Miguel protested, getting the gist even if he didn't understand the actual phrase. "You stop, or we no get marry."

"Aw, chill out." Mary grinned and squeezed his backside. "No harm in looking, is there?"

"I no look at woman," Miguel lied, a sulky scowl on his face.

"Why would you?" Mary snorted. "Only an idiot would go after scrag-end when they've got steak at home."

Anton exchanged a bemused glance with Shotz and quickly closed the door. "How the fuck did *that* give birth to a honey like Chantelle?" he said, following his friend into the kitchen.

"Man 'im got it *baaad*," Shotz teased, placing the bottles he was holding on the ledge alongside the batch they had brought in the day before.

"Whatever," Anton drawled, watching as his friend turned the bottles round to line up the labels. "It ain't even like that."

"So why go out of your way to invite her to the party?" Shotz gave him a knowing look and pulled a pack of Rizla papers out of his pocket.

"She's a neighbour — it'd be rude not to," Anton said, pulling down the blind to stop passers-by from seeing the spliff his friend was building. The last thing he needed was for one of his new neighbours to report him to the police.

Shotz didn't believe that excuse any more than Anton did. "Yeah, man, course," he scoffed, lighting up and grinning slyly. "So you've invited the others, an' all, have you?"

"Fuck off, they're too old. Anyway, I haven't seen her, so she probably won't even come."

"Man 'im want puss-puss," Shotz drawled.

"I'm getting dressed," Anton said, snatching the spliff out of his friend's hand and sucking deeply on it before handing it back. "Labels are out of line." He jerked his thumb at the bottles. Then, smirking when Shotz snapped his head around to see if it was true, he went to his bedroom with a spring in his step.

Smiling when Shotz put on some music in the front room a couple of minutes later, he pulled on a pair of boxers and reached for his new jeans. Tonight was going to be a blast, and he couldn't wait for the party to get started.

Chantelle left the flat at 8.45, and guessed that the deep throbbing music she could hear was coming from Anton's place because none of the other neighbours ever played music as loudly as that. She knew she was right when she heard laughter and saw a couple of dolled-up girls carrying bottles of wine emerge from the stairwell and walk up to his door. It crossed her mind to wonder why he hadn't invited her if he was having a party, but she quickly brushed it aside. Why *would* he invite her? It wasn't like they were mates or anything. He'd tried to talk to her and she'd acted snotty, so it was her own fault that he didn't want to know.

She wouldn't have fitted in, anyway, she reasoned as she walked down the stairs and out onto the path. She was nothing like those girls she'd just seen. They looked to be around his age and, knowing him, he'd probably slept with them both at one time or another.

Irritated with herself for being bothered about not being invited to the party of a man who was everything she professed not to find attractive, Chantelle pushed Anton firmly out of her mind and walked briskly out to the main road where the taxi she had ordered was idling at the kerb.

She climbed into the back and gave the driver the address of the restaurant, then settled back in her seat, her thoughts on Rob Knight now. Now he *was* a good man. Everything that Anton Davis would never be, he was rich and an absolute gentleman who treated women with the utmost respect. And she was looking forward to seeing him again — as friends.

Rob was smoking a cigarette outside the restaurant when Chantelle's cab pulled up. He smiled when he spotted her and, dropping his smoke, stepped forward to open the door for her.

"Wow." He gave her an admiring look when she stepped out. "You look incredible."

"Thank you," she murmured shyly. "I'm not late, am I?"

"No, you're bang on time." Rob smiled and paid the driver, then held out his arm. "Shall we?"

Chantelle took his arm and walked inside with him. It was the first time she had ever been inside a real

**253**

restaurant, and she was terrified that it would be full of rich people who would look down their noses at her. But none of the few diners who were there so much as glanced their way as Rob led her towards a booth at the rear of the room.

"Thanks again for doing this," he said when they had both slid onto the semicircular padded leather seat. "I was dreading having to entertain my client's wife. I've met her before, and she's . . ." He trailed off and narrowed his eyes thoughtfully. "Well, I suppose the polite word would be *flirtatious*. That's why Yvette was supposed to be coming — to protect me. But she ducked out, so here we are. Anyway, enough of that." He smiled. "Shall we order drinks while we're waiting? White wine all right?"

The strongest drink Chantelle had ever tried was the occasional glass of Lambrini at Christmas. She had meant to stick to her usual Coke tonight but Rob knew she wasn't driving, so she couldn't use that excuse again. Anyway, this was supposed to be a grown-up dinner and, if she expected Rob and his friends to accept her as an adult, she guessed that she ought to act like one.

"Yes, that's fine," she said.

Rob ordered the wine and sat back with his arm draped casually along the back of the seat. "Been looking forward to this all day," he said. "The food here is terrific. Have you eaten Italian before?"

"Not really," Chantelle admitted, thinking how handsome Rob looked in the low lighting. She'd thought it when they first met, but he seemed to get more attractive each time she saw him. His jaw was firm, his teeth white and even, and she loved the way his blue eyes sparkled when he talked. And she'd never met anyone who had such an air of self-assurance without the usual look-at-me posturing.

"You'll love it," Rob said, smiling at the waiter when he arrived with the wine. "Here, let me." He took the bottle and poured a little into Chantelle's glass for her to try. "Is it okay?" he asked when she'd taken a tiny sip.

"Lovely," she lied. "Thank you."

"Are you ready to order?" the waiter asked.

"Not yet," Rob told him. "We're waiting for our guests."

When the waiter politely bowed his head and backed away, Chantelle gazed around. "It's really nice in here. Do you come here often?"

"Thought that was supposed to be the man's line!"

"Sorry?"

"It's number one on the list of naff things to say when you're on the pull."

"God, no, I didn't mean it like that," Chantelle gasped. "I just —"

"Relax." Rob chuckled. "I was joking."

His mobile phone rang just then, and Chantelle was relieved when he excused himself and slid out from behind the table to take the call. She'd thought she was acting so cool and sophisticated, but acting it and *being* it were two different things.

"You are never going to believe this," Rob said when he came back to the table a few minutes later. "That was my client. He's had to cancel."

255

"Really?"

"'Fraid so." Rob gave her an apologetic smile as he slid back onto the seat. "Seems his wife's come down with a stomach bug."

"Oh, what a shame," said Chantelle, unsure if she was glad that she wouldn't now have to act as a buffer between Rob and the client's flirtatious wife, or disappointed that the night was going to end before it began. "Hope she's okay."

"Me, too," said Rob. "Still, at least we don't have to wait any longer to order." He reached for the menus and handed one to her. "Don't know about you, but I'm starving. What do you fancy?"

Chantelle smiled and gazed down at the menu in search of a word that she even vaguely recognised, but it was all alien to her. "What are you having?" she asked, closing the menu after a while. "You've eaten here before — you choose."

"Are you sure you want to do that?" Rob asked, a playful glint coming into his eyes. "I'm thinking raw oysters, followed by octopus chowder and kangaroo steak."

*"Really?"* Chantelle grimaced.

"Nah, just teasing." He grinned. "Yvette used to ask me to order for her when we first got together, but she soon stopped when she realised we're complete opposites. I go for white wine, she prefers red; I'll happily demolish steak with all the trimmings, she pecks at fish and salad. And don't even get me started on dessert. She thinks she'll get fat just *reading* the

256

word chocolate. Please tell me you're not on a diet?" He gave Chantelle a pained look.

"No." She smiled and shook her head. The few sips of wine she'd had were starting to kick in, and she was beginning to feel pleasantly light-headed.

"Thank God for that." Rob gave a mock-relieved sigh and looked down at the menu again. "How does lasagne grab you?"

"Absolutely perfect," Chantelle said, relaxing a little more now that she wasn't being faced with the prospect of having to try an unfamiliar dish.

When the meal arrived, Rob kept up a steady stream of conversation as he ate. The computer-software stuff went right over Chantelle's head, but she was fascinated to hear him talk about his relationship with his wife. They had been married for three years, she learned; and while he seemed to work every hour God sent, his wife Yvette, who was an ex-dancer, seemed to live a life of pampered luxury courtesy of his credit card. The more she heard about the woman, the more Chantelle disliked her. Yvette had a great husband, an amazing house, and unlimited cash to buy whatever she desired. But instead of thanking her generous husband, she moaned constantly about his long work hours, and then took off and left him in the lurch as soon as he asked *her* to do something for *him*. And to top it all, she'd had the audacity to use *his* money to pay a private investigator to follow him. But Chantelle was in no position to tell him about that, so she just listened, and nodded, and smiled when appropriate.

Time flew, and before they knew it they were the only two diners left in the place. When he noticed the waiters hovering by the bar, Rob glanced at his watch.

"Wow, how did it get so late? You must think I'm terrible; I've been talking your ear off for hours."

"No, I've enjoyed it," Chantelle told him honestly.

"So have I." Rob waved for the waiter to bring the bill. "It's been a pleasure getting to know you better, Julia. Just hope I didn't bore you too much?"

"Not at all."

"We'll have to do it again sometime," Rob said, sliding off the seat to get his wallet out. "If you want to, that is?"

"I'd love to," she replied, hoping she didn't sound too forward. She'd had more wine than she intended to, and was feeling very mellow.

"Great." He held out his hand to help her up. "I'll give you a call to arrange something soon. But, for now, I think I should get you home."

Acutely conscious of the feel of his skin as his hand enveloped hers, and the gleam of the gold band on his third finger, Chantelle came back to earth with a bang. She slipped her hand free.

"I'll get a cab. You get yourself home to Yvette."

"She's out, and I insist," Rob said. "It's the least I can do after dragging you out on yet another wild-goose chase. Granted, it turned out great, but I absolutely refuse to pack you off in a cab again. We're friends now," he added, peering down into her eyes.

"Okay," Chantelle conceded, reaching for her handbag as butterflies began to flutter in her stomach.

258

Now that she was on her feet, her head was spinning and she was beginning to regret the last glass of wine. She just hoped she didn't throw up, because that really would be embarrassing.

The perfect gentleman, Rob led her out to his car and opened the passenger-side door for her. He helped her in and then went round to the driver's side. "Where to?"

"Do you know Chorlton Road?" Chantelle asked, shivering as the heater kicked in and warm air swirled around her ankles.

"Sure do," Rob said, turning on some music before easing out onto the road. "Which end?"

"Um, the Whalley Range end," she lied, directing him a good half-mile past the estate because she didn't want him to see where she lived. The estate was too scruffy, and that was bound to cloud his view of her. Apart from which, she couldn't risk letting him find out that she wasn't who he thought she was. He was a nice man, and it would upset him to think that he'd been so open with her while all she'd done was tell him a pack of lies. If he found out that his wife was behind their initial meeting, it could potentially destroy his marriage, and Chantelle really didn't want to be responsible for that. And then there was Bill . . . if *she* found out what Chantelle had been up to tonight, she would probably sack her on the spot — and rightly so.

Chantelle sighed as she thought about the tangled web of lies she had woven, and gazed wistfully out of the window. It had been such a lovely night, but it wasn't real, and it could never happen again. Rob was married, and she was a fake. End of.

"You're very quiet," Rob said as the car purred its way out of town. "Feeling okay?"

"Yeah, I'm fine," Chantelle lied. "Just a bit tired."

"Ah, well, at least you can have a lie-in tomorrow. *I*, on the other hand, shall be up at six."

"Oh, sorry. You should have said you had an early start."

"What, and miss out on a great night in the company of a beautiful lady?" Rob glanced at her out of the corner of his eye and winked. "No chance."

As the butterflies stirred in her stomach again, Chantelle inhaled deeply and dug her nails into her handbag on her lap. His wife was so lucky, if only she knew it.

When they reached Chorlton Road, Rob pulled over where Chantelle directed and glanced out of the window. "Are you sure you won't let me take you to your door?" he asked when he spotted two hooded youths on mountain bikes heading their way. "You shouldn't be walking around on your own at this time of night; it's not safe."

"It's not far from here," Chantelle told him, lowering her head as if she was struggling to undo her seat belt, although she was actually hiding her face because she knew both of the lads on the bikes from school and didn't want them to see her. "It's just round the back of those shops, but it's a one-way street so you'd only end up getting stuck. This is fine, honestly."

The boys had passed by now and the road ahead was deserted, so Rob shrugged and said, "Okay, if you're sure." Then, turning in his seat, he said, "Thanks again for tonight, Julia. I know it started out as a favour, but I've had a really great time, and I meant what I said about doing it again."

Chantelle's heart had started to race and she couldn't look him in the eye. "I had a lovely time," she said quietly. "But I don't think we should —"

Before she could finish speaking, Rob leaned forward and kissed her softly on the lips. She was shocked. Apart from the time a few years back when Immy had persuaded her to practise kissing techniques, it was the first real kiss she'd ever had. And she liked it.

"Sorry," Rob said huskily when he broke away after a while. "I shouldn't have done that, but I couldn't resist. You're just so beautiful." He reached for her hand now and, still gazing into her eyes, entwined his fingers in hers. "We can't leave it like this; I need to see you again."

"We can't," Chantelle croaked.

"I haven't stopped thinking about you since the first time we met, and it's driving me crazy," Rob said. "Tell me you don't feel the same way, and I'll never bother you again," he challenged, his face still so close to hers that Chantelle could feel his breath on her cheek.

"I do like you," she admitted. "But —"

When Rob pulled her close and kissed her again, Chantelle closed her eyes and felt herself drift away. But when his hand began to slide up her thigh, her conscience kicked in and she quickly pulled back.

**261**

"I can't do this," she gasped, fumbling for the door handle. "I've got to go."

"Julia, wait . . ." Rob jumped out and gazed after her as she fled down the road. "I'm sorry."

Chantelle ran past the shops and into the alleyway behind the row. She pressed her back up against a wall and held her breath as she listened to hear if he was following. When, after several moments, she heard the purr of his car engine as he gave up and drove away, she exhaled shakily and squeezed her eyes shut. Oh God, oh God, oh *God*! Why had she let him kiss her like that? It was so, so wrong.

Disgusted with herself, she lowered her head in shame and made her way home.


Anton's party was still going strong but he'd come out onto the landing to get some air. Shotz and their mates had been caning the weed all night, but Anton had been working all day and couldn't keep up. He'd also had too much to drink and was tugging on a straight cigarette now, trying to clear his head.

The door opened behind him and a drunken girl staggered out. "*There* you are," she said, lurching towards him. "I've been looking for you."

"Don't," Anton groaned when she looped her arms around his neck. "I don't feel too good."

"Let's go to bed," she said, giving him a seductive smile. "I'll soon make you feel better."

Feeling sick when she pushed her hips up against his, Anton held her off. "Leave it out, Linz; I haven't got the energy for this."

"You've *always* got the energy," she persisted, pouting at him now. "What's up, don't you like me any more?"

"Course I like you," he said, trying to let her down easy. "We're mates."

"We were more than that once," she reminded him. "And you know I've always wanted to get back with you."

"It didn't work," Anton said gently. "We split for a reason, and it's best just to leave it at that."

"You fancy someone else, don't you?" she demanded, her eyes filling with tears. "It's that bitch Simone, isn't it? She's been giving you the eye all night, the slag. What's she got that I can't give you? I'm way better-looking than her."

"You're just being stupid now," Anton said, losing patience. "I'm not looking to get with *anyone*. I just want to get my head together, so go back inside and give me some space, yeah?"

"Just give me a chance," she begged, clutching at his hands. "I love you."

"You're drunk," Anton snapped, snatching his hands away. "And I'm not interested, so pack it in!"

As the girl burst into tears and fled back into the flat, Anton caught a movement out of the corner of his eye and glanced around in time to see Chantelle opening her door. Their eyes met, and his heart sank when he saw the expression of disapproval on her face. She had obviously witnessed the end bit of his confrontation with Linz, and probably thought him a complete bastard for shouting at her and sending her away in tears.

When Chantelle went inside now, closing her door firmly behind her, Anton brought his fists down on the balcony rail. *"Shit!"*

Another girl came out of his flat just then and walked over to stand beside him. "Linz is having a shit fit in there," she said, resting her elbows on the rail. "You okay?"

"Yeah, I'm cool." Anton sighed. "Just tired. Think I might call it a night."

"Want me to stay and help you clear up?"

Her voice was soft, and her perfume smelled really sweet. Figuring that if he'd ever had any chance with Chantelle, he'd totally blown it now, Anton smiled.

"Yeah, why not."

Chantelle leaned her back against the door to catch her breath after letting herself in. She could still hear the faint thud of music coming from Anton's place but, apart from the soft snores coming from Leon's room, it was deathly quiet in the flat. Irritated to see that her mum had left her bedroom light on and the door open, she walked up the hall to turn it off. She shook her head when she glanced into the room and saw the mess. Her mum had always been untidy, but it looked as if she'd met her match in Miguel because it was even more of a tip than usual. But it was their business if they wanted to live like pigs.

She flicked the light off and went to her own room, then undressed quickly and climbed into bed. The night had started off great and ended up horrible, and she just wanted to go to sleep and forget all about it.

# CHAPTER
# NINETEEN

Chantelle had a restless night, haunted by the shame of having responded to Rob's kisses. Woken with a start by the sound of somebody knocking loudly on the front door the next morning, she groaned as she got up and shuffled her way into the hall. Her head was banging from all the wine she'd drunk, and she felt nauseous.

"Delivery for Mrs Ramirez," the delivery man told her when she opened the door an inch and squinted out at him through the crack. "Needs signing for."

Chantelle tutted when she heard that her mum was already calling herself by Miguel's surname despite not yet being married. But she signed for the parcel and brought it in. She put it on the table and was about to go back to her bed, but hesitated when she heard a noise coming from Leon's room. It sounded like he was crying, and she frowned. He hadn't left his room in days apart from to go to the toilet or to get something to eat, and she'd been concerned when their paths had crossed to see that he had developed bags under his eyes. It was clear that something was bothering him, but he had flatly refused to talk to her when she had tried, so she'd been leaving him alone. But she couldn't ignore this.

"Leon . . .?" She tapped on the door. "Can I come in?"

"No," he croaked. "Go away."

"Please," she implored. "I know something's wrong, and I just want to help. Are you in some kind of trouble? Is someone picking on you?"

"Go away," he said again, his voice hoarse.

"I can't," Chantelle persisted. "I'm your sister; it's my job to look after you."

"I don't need looking after," he sobbed. "Just keep your nose out; it's got nothing to do with you."

Irritated when he put his music on at full blast, Chantelle said, "Oh, I've had enough of this," and marched into her room to get dressed. Something was obviously wrong, because he never cried. But if he wouldn't tell her, she would just have to ask Kermit instead. Leon hadn't been himself since their falling-out and she knew he'd been hanging around with that gang she'd caught him with. If they had been bullying him, as she suspected, then she needed to know where to find them so that she could put a stop to it.

Kermit groaned when his mum showed Chantelle into the living room. He hadn't seen her since she'd got him into trouble for drinking and smoking, and her appearance now could only mean one thing: Leon had done something bad, and she was going to blame Kermit — *again*.

"It's got nowt to do with me," he said before she'd even opened her mouth.

266

"Don't be rude," Linda scolded, waving for Chantelle to sit down. "She just wants a quick word."

"I'm watching telly," he protested, annoyed with her for not warning him. If he'd known Chantelle was here, he'd have locked himself in his room and refused to come out until she was gone.

"You *were*," said Linda, reaching down and switching the TV off. "Now find your manners before I find them for you," she warned, giving him a stern look. Then, turning to Chantelle, she smiled. "Can I get you a drink, love?"

"No, thanks." Chantelle shook her head.

When his mum herded the smaller kids out of the room and closed the door, Kermit slumped further down in his chair and rested his cheek on his fist.

"Don't worry, I won't keep you long," Chantelle said, guessing from the way he was staring at the floor that she was the last person he wanted to talk to. "I just need to know if you know what's going on with Leon."

"Why you asking me?" Kermit muttered sulkily. "Haven't seen him, and don't want to."

"Why?" Chantelle probed. "You've been best mates for years."

"Not no more."

"Because of that night?"

When Kermit just shrugged, Chantelle leaned forward in her seat and peered at him. "Look, I know I shouldn't have had a go at you over that, but I was worried about him. I still am," she added quietly. "I think he might be being bullied."

Kermit snorted softly and picked at a fraying hole in the knee of his trousers.

"What does that mean?" Chantelle frowned. "Are you trying to say *he*'s bullying someone?"

"Not now," Kermit said quietly. Then, biting his lip, because he hadn't meant to admit that a kid like Leon had the power to intimidate him, he kicked out at one of his brother's toys.

"Those boys he was with that night," Chantelle said. "Who are they?"

"Dunno."

"Yes, you do. You said they went to your school."

"So? Doesn't mean I *know* 'em."

Chantelle supposed she couldn't blame the boy for not wanting to talk to her after the way she'd gone off on him the last time, but it was frustrating all the same.

"Look, I'm not asking you to take me to them," she said, a little more sharply than she'd intended. "I just need to know *about* them. I've already seen them, so I know they're a lot older than you and Leon, and I don't get why they're letting him hang around with them."

"'Cos he's their joey," Kermit said scathingly.

"Meaning?" She sighed when he didn't answer, and said, "*Please*, Kermit, I wouldn't be here if I wasn't worried. And I promise I won't tell him I've spoken to you."

"You said that last time, but you did, and now I can't go out 'cos he says he'll cut me if he sees me."

"What are you talking about?" Chantelle gasped. "Leon would never say something like that. You were his best mate."

268

Kermit's bottom lip crept out, but he quickly sucked it back in and bit down hard on it to stop the tears from escaping. It was humiliating to be scared of a little kid like Leon, but his ex-mate hadn't been joking when he'd flashed that big knife at him down by the shops the other week, and Kermit hadn't dared to go out since. He was absolutely dreading going back to school after the holidays, because he just knew that Damo and his boys were going to make his life hell on Leon's behalf.

"If you care about him at all, you need to tell me what's going on," Chantelle said quietly. *"Please, Kermit."*

She sounded as if she was on the verge of tears now, and it penetrated Kermit's shell. He breathed in deeply through his nose. Then, voice muffled, he said, "I don't know if it's true, but I heard they've been dealing."

"Who?"

"Damo and Acky. And probably Leon, seeing as he's always with them."

*"Drugs?"* Chantelle was shocked.

Kermit shrugged. "Big T's supposed to have set them up with their own patch."

"Big T?" Chantelle's face creased in confusion. "Who the hell's that?"

Kermit swallowed nervously. He'd said way too much, and it was too late to take it back now "Look, I don't know nothing," he said, pushing himself to his feet. "And if you tell him I said anything, I'll deny it. Just leave me alone!"

He fled from the room and ran into his bedroom, slamming the door behind him.

"What's going on?" Linda rushed out from the kitchen as Chantelle walked out into the hall. "What've you said *now?*" She looked at the girl accusingly. "He's not set foot out of here in weeks so, whatever he's supposed to have done, it wasn't him."

"He hasn't done anything," Chantelle assured her. "I was just asking about those boys our Leon's been hanging round with. I think he's being bullied, and your Kermit knows them, so I thought he might be able to help me find out what's going on."

"Yes, well, he can't," Linda said frostily. "And I'll thank you not to come round here again if you're just going to keep upsetting him. He's a good boy, and I'm not having him dragged down by your brother."

"I'm sorry," Chantelle apologised. "Will you please tell Kermit that I meant what I said — I won't mention his name to our Leon, or *anyone.* I promise."

Linda shook her head disapprovingly. "I'll tell him, but this is the end of it, Chantelle. I said I didn't blame your Leon for all that stuff with the drugs, but I do. My Kermit never did nothing like that before he hooked up with him, and I'm not having any more of it. Just keep your brother away from him in future. Okay?"

Chantelle could have said the same: that Leon had never done anything like that before he'd started hanging out with Kermit. But she doubted it would go down too well, so, nodding her agreement, she went on her way without another word.

270

Leon was in the toilet when Chantelle got back to the flat, and she wrinkled her nose at the telling noises that were coming out through the door. His stomach was obviously upset, and that, added to him crying, convinced her that he was definitely in some sort of trouble. Praying that it wasn't drugs, as Kermit had suggested, she decided to check his room while he was out of the way. He'd go mad if he caught her, but she had to know what she was dealing with.

A quick search of his jacket and trouser pockets yielded nothing but scrunched-up tissues and chocolate wrappers, and the contents of his wardrobe and dresser drawers were spilling out, but there was nothing druglike in any of them. She kneeled down and looked under the bed. Again, there was just rubbish, and she was about to give up when she spotted a piece of plastic bag poking down through the springs of the bed-base. She raised the mattress and was shocked to see a flick knife sitting beside a mobile phone and a charger.

No wonder Kermit had been scared. He'd said that Leon had threatened to cut him if he saw him, so he must have seen this knife to have taken the threat so seriously. But where had Leon got it from?

Aware that he could walk in at any moment, she laid the knife and phone on the floor beside her and reached for the plastic bag that was stuffed at the back near the wall. As soon as her fingers touched it her instincts told her exactly what it was, but her mind refused to accept it. A knife was one thing, anyone could get a knife. But a *gun* . . . ? No way.

She didn't hear Leon walk into the room, and almost jumped out of her skin when he bellowed, "What are you doing, you nosy bitch? Get out!"

"Pack it in," she protested, almost losing her balance when he ran at her and tried to grab the bag out of her hand.

"It's mine," he yelled, jumping up at her when she stood up and snatched the bag out of his reach. "Give it back!"

"Not a chance," she snapped, struggling to hold him at bay. "I knew you were in trouble, but this is way worse than I thought. What the hell do you think you're playing at?"

"It's none of your business," Leon cried, still fighting to get at the bag.

"*STOP* IT!" Chantelle squawked, wincing with pain when he kicked her in the shin. "I don't want to hurt you, but if you carry on, I'm gonna leather you."

"Do it, then," he challenged, his eyes wild. "I'm gonna die anyway, so take your best shot."

"What are you *talking* about? Chantelle grabbed him by the front of his jumper and shook him. "Tell me what's going on, or I swear to God I'm going to call the police. Where did you get this? Did Big T give it to you?"

Leon's face drained of colour, and his mouth fell open. "How d'you know about him?"

"Oh, God, it's true." Chantelle stared worriedly down into his eyes. "What have you got yourself messed up in, Leon? This is really serious."

"You don't know *nothing*," he spat, baring his teeth at her. "You're just a stupid ho who thinks she's in control of everything. But you ain't in control of me and my bros, so keep your nose out before you get hurt."

"Are you threatening me?" Chantelle gasped, wondering who this aggressive creature was. She and Leon had always bickered like normal siblings, but this boy was a complete stranger to her. His eyes were filled with hate, and the disrespectful way he was talking to her was shocking. "What are you on?" she demanded.

"Stupid bitch!" Leon sneered, pushing her so hard that she almost fell back onto the bed. Then, snatching his knife off the floor, he flicked the blade out and jabbed it at her. "Give me my fuckin' gun, or I'll cut your throat. I mean it."

Chantelle was too shocked to speak, and too scared to breathe. Gaze riveted to the blade, she didn't resist when Leon snatched the bag out of her hand and ran from the room. When the front door slammed shut behind him, her legs gave way and she slumped down heavily on the edge of his bed. He'd been so far out of control just then that it was terrifying, but what was she supposed to do now? She couldn't let him run around with a gun, but she also couldn't report him to the police because he wouldn't just get put into care over this, he'd end up in serious trouble. And once he got started on that path, his life would be ruined.

Aware that she needed urgent help, Chantelle ran into her room and snatched up her phone. She'd put it on silent before going into the restaurant last night, and she saw that she'd missed several calls from Rob. He'd also sent a few texts, and the last one was still showing on the screen: a picture of a bunch of red roses, with a message telling her that he was sorry for upsetting her and would have sent the real thing if he'd known her address; and would she please call him so he could explain himself.

Disgusted with herself all over again, she cleared the image from the screen and rang her mum's number. When it went straight to answerphone, she grabbed her keys and rushed over to Tracey's place. Getting no answer after several minutes of knocking and calling through the letter box, she gazed helplessly out over the balcony.

*Anton.*

The name shot into Chantelle's head like a bullet, and she seized it with both hands. *He* would know what to do. Even if he'd never dealt with anything quite like this before, he knew a damn sight more about gangs and guns than she did.

Anton folded his arms when he answered his door and saw Chantelle standing there. After the look she'd given him last night, he had vowed to play it cool with her when he saw her again. He'd gone out of his way to be nice to her these last few weeks, but she had completely rebuffed him at every turn, and he was done with mugging himself off. Yeah, she was hot, but that didn't give her the right to look at him like he was some piece of shit she had stepped in.

"'S up?" he asked.

274

"I'm sorry for coming to you with this," Chantelle murmured, her voice cracking as tears of despair immediately flooded her eyes. "But I need help, and I didn't know who else to turn to."

Anton dropped the act when he saw the tears and stepped back. "Come in."

"I'm really sorry," she sniffled, following him into the living room. "I just don't know what to do."

"What's up?" Anton asked again, waving her to take a seat on one of the beanbags.

"It's Leon," she cried. "He's been hanging out with a gang, and he's been acting weird for days, so I thought they might be bullying him. He wouldn't talk to me, so I asked his friend, and he said he'd heard they've been dealing . . ."

Anton had been listening intently as she poured out her story, but when she reached the part about finding the gun, he drew his head back in disbelief. "Say *what?*"

"I didn't believe it, either," she said, terror in her eyes as she stared at him. "But it's true. And now he's running round with it, and I'm scared he's going to shoot someone, or accidentally shoot himself. He's only ten," she added, her face crumpling. "This shouldn't be happening."

"All right, calm down," Anton said quietly. "Tell me what you know about this gang."

Chantelle took a deep breath and told him the little she knew, starting with the run-in she'd had with the boys down by the canal that night.

"I knew they were trouble as soon as I saw them," she said, "and I couldn't get why they'd be letting a little kid hang out with them. But Leon's friend reckons they've been using him as a joey."

"Probably," Anton said, lighting a cigarette. "Go on."

"Well, his friend said he'd heard they were dealing for someone called Big T, and —"

"Say again?" Anton interrupted, narrowing his eyes.

"Big T," Chantelle repeated, giving him a questioning look. "Do you know him?"

Anton didn't answer. Cheek muscles jumping as he chewed this information over, he took a pull on his cigarette and stared at the floor.

His bedroom door opened just then, and Chantelle was shocked to see a girl peering out at her. The girl had obviously just woken up, judging by her messy hair and smeared make-up, and she was clearly naked beneath the sheet that was wrapped around her.

"I'm so sorry," Chantelle apologised, pushing herself up to her feet. "I'd never have disturbed you if I'd known you had company."

"It's cool," Anton said, also rising to his feet. "Look, go back to yours. If your bro comes home before I get back, keep him there. I'm going to talk to some people; see if I can find out what's what."

"Thanks," Chantelle murmured. Then, glancing at the girl, she gave her an apologetic smile and hurried out.

"Who was that?" the girl asked as Anton walked into his bedroom.

"A friend," he said, picking up his keys.

"Just a friend?" She gave him a teasing smile. "She's very pretty."

"Yeah, she is," Anton agreed, sighing as he reached for his jacket. "But she's not interested, so that's that."

"More fool her," the girl said softly. Then, yawning, she said, "Suppose I'd better get dressed. Thanks for letting me stay; I really didn't fancy walking home on my own."

"Any time." Anton gave her a sheepish smile. "Sorry about — you know. Guess I was too far gone."

"More like you had other things on your mind," she said, giving him a knowing smile. "But you can't blame a girl for trying. Anyway, you go and do whatever you've got to do. I'll let myself out."

Anton winked at her, and then headed out.

# CHAPTER
# TWENTY

Several youths in hoodies and low-slung jeans were gathered in the small front yard outside Big T's house on the Alexandra Park estate. Some were sitting on the wall, and some were standing, while a couple of others were doing wheelies on the pavement on their mountain bikes. They all stopped what they were doing when they spotted Anton, and eyeballed him as he walked towards them.

Jacko had been sitting on the step, but he stood up now and blocked Anton's path as he made to come through the gate. "'S up, bro?" He jerked his chin up aggressively.

"Where's Trey?" Anton maintained a cool façade, but he was on high alert for any signs of movement from the crew. He had been one of them once, but now they considered him an enemy.

The youth motioned with a jerk of his head back towards the door, but when Anton stepped forward he put a hand on his chest. "Nah, man, them days is over. You need an appointment to see the man now."

"For real?" Anton looked down at Jacko's hand, then up into his eyes. "You really wanna go there?"

They stood like this for several tense moments, eye to eye, toe to toe. Then, pushing out his lips, Jacko reached back and pushed open the door an inch, calling over his shoulder, "Yo, T — someone to see ya."

There was movement in the narrow hallway and, seconds later, Trey Berkley's imposing twenty-stone frame filled the doorway. A ripple of anticipation passed between the watching youths when the man saw Anton and something unreadable flashed through his dark eyes. But then a slow smile came onto his lips and he held out a meaty hand.

"Long time no see, blud," he said, pulling Anton towards him and clapping him on the back. "Wha'pp'n?"

"We need to talk," Anton said. "*Alone*," he added pointedly, in case any of the crew decided to try and muscle in.

"What you got?" Big T stepped back and peered down at him.

Anton raised his arms and held his jacket open to let the man see that he wasn't carrying a weapon. Then, snapping his head around when mouthpiece Jacko made to pat him down, he hissed, "Touch me again, I'll rip your fucking head off with my bare hands. This is between me and him; it's got nothing to do with you."

Big T shook his head at Jacko. Then, jerking his chin at Anton, he retreated back into the shadows of the hallway.

Anton flashed Jacko one last cold stare before following Trey inside. Respect was everything in their world and, even though he no longer wanted to be a

279

part of it, he couldn't let Jacko get away with dissing him in front of the crew or his life wouldn't be worth living.

"So, where you been hiding?" Big T asked, leading Anton into the back room and sitting down heavily on an enormous leather recliner armchair. He reached for a spliff that was smouldering in the ashtray on the table and took a deep pull on it. "How come you ain't checked me since you been out?"

"I've been keeping my head down," Anton told him, perching on the couch and resting his elbows on his knees. "No offence, but you wasn't top of my list for catch-ups."

"Weren't my doing, for real, bro," Big T said quietly. "I had your back; it was *you* stopped having mine."

"I'm the one who did time," Anton reminded him. "If I'd stopped having your back, I've have taken you and your cuz down with me."

"True say." Big T tipped his head in a conceding gesture. "Still ain't no excuse for the way you been avoiding me since you been out. If you had beef, you shoulda fronted, 'steada dissing me by blanking me."

"I haven't got beef," Anton informed him calmly. "I dealt with all that shit while I was away, and saw no point in stirring it up again when I got free. You say you wasn't involved, I know different."

Big T took another pull on his spliff and squinted as he blew the smoke out into the air. "So, what you after? Compensation?"

"Nah, man." Anton shook his head. "I'm staying straight. I just need a favour."

"Oh yeah?"

"I hear you set up some little white boys to sell bags, and now they got grief with another crew."

"So?"

"So, they've dragged a kid I know into it, and I want him out. *Intact*."

"Don't know nutt'n about that."

"Maybe not," Anton conceded. "But I'm betting you know about the gun they've had him holding for them?"

Big T's eyes became so tightly slitted when he heard this that Anton could barely see them amongst the folds of his fat cheeks.

"He's ten," he went on quietly. "And right now he's running round with that piece, scared shitless 'cos your boys have been heavying him. If I know you, it'll have history," he said now, pausing to let his meaning sink in before adding, "You need to get it back, and I need the kid home safe."

Big T stared at Anton for several long moments. Then, taking another suck on his spliff, he reached for his phone.

"Yo!" he barked when his call was answered. "Where's my t'ing at?" His nostrils flared when the boy on the other end said it was safe, and he slammed a massive fist down on the arm of his chair. "What you lyin' for, you lickle cunt? Y' t'ink I don't know nutt'n about nutt'n? Fetch it," he ordered now, a murderous edge to his voice. Then, glancing at Anton, he added, "And that kid you been toyin' with . . . cut 'im loose.

An' if you lay a finger on him, I'll be layin' *ten* on you. You gets me?"

"Thanks," Anton said when the call was done. "I appreciate it."

"You owe me," Big T said.

"Nah, I reckon this makes us straight." Anton stood up.

Big T squinted up at him. "You're wrong about all that shit, man. On my nan's eyes, I didn't know."

"It doesn't matter now." Anton shrugged. "Just do yourself a favour and quit messin' with them kids before you end up where I've just been. They ain't like us; they don't know the meaning of loyalty."

"I ain't worried," Big T said. Then, dropping the patois to let Anton know he was talking to him as a mate, he said, "Come back to the crew, bro. We was only just starting out before you left, but things have changed since you've been gone. I'm the don now, and I need my general by my side. Me and you could be running this shit like it *should* be run. I've got the bees, the cars, the soldiers, the girls — you'd never want for nothing."

"I can't." Anton shook his head. "Too much has happened, and I'm done with it." Then, smiling regretfully, he held out his fist. "Stay cool, bro."

"You'll be back," Big T predicted as his old friend headed for the door. "Straight life ain't nothing but the poor life. You and me, we need the buzz of rockin' with the crew."

Anton carried on walking. He had known Trey all his life, and had spent the majority of his teens as his

282

partner in petty crime. He'd have trusted Big T with his life back in the day, but the man had chosen blood over loyalty and had allowed Anton to take the rap for a stabbing that they both knew Trey's cousin had done. That couldn't be forgotten *or* forgiven.

Chantelle had gone home after leaving Anton's, and she'd been pacing the floor ever since; chewing on her nails, and rushing to the door every time she heard a noise. When she heard a knock now, she hurtled out into the hall and yanked it open.

"What happened?" she asked when Anton stepped inside. "Did you find anything out?"

"I've sorted it," he told her. "Your bro should be home any time."

"Oh, thank God!" she gasped, bursting into tears. "I've been so worried."

"Hey, come on." Anton took her in his arms. "It's gonna be cool."

"Sorry." Chantelle suppressed her tears and took a step back. "I'm not usually this hysterical, but I've been thinking all sorts."

"I can imagine." Unsure what to do with his hands now, Anton shoved them into his pockets. "Look, is it all right if I hang around till he gets back?"

"Yeah, course." Chantelle waved him into the living room. "Would you like a drink? Tea? Coffee?"

"Tea, please. White, one sugar."

Chantelle left him to make himself comfortable and rushed into the kitchen to put the kettle on. She felt awkward now — grateful, but awkward. Theirs was

**283**

such a strange relationship, forever bouncing between friendly and spiky, but never quite settling in either.

It was another fifteen minutes before they heard a key in the door. Chantelle jumped up and ran out into the hall, and gasped in horror when she saw the blood on Leon's face. "Oh God, what's happened?" she cried, running to him.

"Get off me," he sobbed, pushing her away when she ran to him.

"Leave it," Anton said, touching Chantelle's arm. "This your room?" he asked Leon then, nodding towards the door they were standing outside. When Leon wiped his nose on his sleeve and nodded, he gave him a rough push. "Inside."

Chantelle had desperately wanted to comfort Leon, and tend to his wounds, but she was out of her depth, so she left Anton to deal with him and went into the living room.

Anton ordered Leon to stop crying and pushed him towards the bed. When they were both seated, he looked at the boy's cut lip and the swelling around his eye. He'd obviously taken a beating, and would be in pain for a few days.

"I take it your crew did this?" he asked. "So, what happened? And I want to know *everything*."

"D-Damo was going to sh-shoot me," Leon sobbed, struggling to bring his tears under control. "He was m-mad at me for getting caught with the gun. He rang this morning and said we was gonna do the job this afternoon, but he went crazy when I told him my sister had seen it. Acky said they was going to kill me, then kill her to stop her from grassing. And he . . . he said they were going to rape her first," he added, wailing again.

"Ain't gonna happen, so quit worrying about it," Anton said angrily, his jaw tightly clenched. "What else?"

"They laid into me," Leon whimpered, rubbing at the sore spots on his arms as he spoke. "But then Damo got a call off Big T and told the others to stop. He t-told me to get lost, and said he'd best not ever see me again or he'd let Acky cut me up bad."

"And you think these are your boys?" Anton asked when he'd finished. "Can you see now that they ain't?"

Leon's little face crumpled and he swiped at his tears with his sleeve. "I thought they liked me."

"That's what they *wanted* you to think," Anton told him bluntly. "They don't give a shit about you; they were just using you to keep their own hands clean. What do you think would have happened if your sis had called the police and told them about that gun? You think they'd have owned up that it was theirs? No, they'd have said they don't know you and left you to carry the can. And if you'd grassed, they'd have gone after Chantelle in revenge. That what you want?"

"No." Leon shook his head and looked down shamefacedly at the floor.

"Where's the knife?" Anton demanded. When Leon slid it out of his pocket, he snatched it from him and yanked the boy's head up by the chin so he could look him in the eye. "You ever threaten your sister like that again, it'll be *me* coming after you," he warned quietly. "Understand?"

Tears still glittering in his eyes, Leon nodded.

"Waving blades around don't make you look tough, it makes you look spineless," Anton went on sternly. "And threatening fam is lower than low. Chantelle is your flesh and blood, and there ain't no one in the *world* who's gonna love you like she does. You think it's easy for her trying to deal with your shit? She don't deserve *none* of it."

"I know," Leon whimpered. "I wouldn't have done it. I was just scared 'cos she wouldn't give me the gun."

"Yeah, well, think yourself lucky I didn't catch you at it," Anton said. "'Cos I'd have kicked your arse to the police station myself. Yeah, that's right . . ." He nodded. "I'd have grassed you up. And you know why? 'Cos you'd have deserved it. Loyalty starts at home, and if you turn on the people who love you, you ain't worth shit."

He gave the boy a few minutes to digest his words. Then, when Leon had finally stopped snivelling, Anton said, "I worded Big T up to make those dudes leave you alone, so I'd better not hear you've been trying to hook up with them again after this. You hear me?"

Leon's eyes widened. He'd always known Anton was a big shot, but if he had influence over Big T he must be badder than bad.

"If you've got a problem in future, you come to me," Anton went on. "But that don't mean we're gonna be buddies," he added quickly. "Your sister told me you've got a mate you used to hang out with; go see him and start getting your shit back together."

"I can't," Leon murmured guiltily. "I threatened him with the knife."

"So, man up and apologise," Anton said firmly. He stood up now and gazed down at the boy. "Are we all straight? You know what you got to do?"

Leon nodded and wiped his nose on his sleeve.

Anton held out his fist, and smiled when the boy eagerly touched his to it. "Behave, or we'll be having another talk," he said. "And I guarantee you won't be liking it second time around. Seen?"

"Seen," Leon agreed.

Chantelle gave Anton a questioning look when he walked into the living room. "Is he okay? Did they hurt him a lot?"

"Enough to make him realise they ain't his friends," said Anton. "But you don't need to be fussing over him," he added firmly. "He needs to remember this fear and pain, or he'll be in another gang in no time."

"I won't fuss," Chantelle promised. "And thank you so much. You were the only one I could think of to ask for help. I'm just sorry I disturbed you and your girlfriend. Hope she wasn't upset with you?"

"It's all good," Anton assured her, backing towards the door. "You know where I am if you need me, yeah?"

Chantelle nodded, and stayed put as he let himself out. Then, jumping when her phone started to ring, she pulled it out of her pocket and sighed when she saw that it was Rob. She wasn't really in the mood to talk but, after all the craziness, she desperately needed to hear a normal friendly voice.

"Don't hang up," Rob blurted out when she answered. "I know you probably don't want to talk to me, and I don't blame you, but I just want a chance to explain."

"It's all right," she said. "I don't blame you, I blame myself. But it still shouldn't have happened, and it can't happen again."

"Absolutely," Rob agreed. "But we can still be friends, can't we?"

"I suppose so," Chantelle said, frowning as she said it, because she knew that it would never be a real friendship. How could it be when it was based on lies?

"Well, as *friends*, can I take you out for a drink tonight?" Rob asked. "Just to talk," he added quickly. "No strings."

Chantelle squeezed her eyes shut and bit her lip. Her mind was telling her that it wasn't safe to meet up with him when they had both admitted to liking each other more than they should, but her heart was urging her to see him again.

Her heart won.

"Okay," she said. "One drink."

# CHAPTER
# TWENTY-ONE

"Who was that?" Yvette asked, coming into the kitchen dressed in a red silk negligee, her blonde hair piled up on her head.

"Adam." Rob sidestepped her and reached into the fridge for a carton of juice.

"Don't tell me . . ." She slid onto a stool. "You've got another meeting? Don't you ever stop?"

"Money doesn't make itself." He took a glass out of the cupboard.

"What about me?"

"Sorry, did you want some?" He held out the carton.

"I didn't mean that, and you know it." Yvette pouted sulkily. "I mean when are you going to make time for me? I've hardly seen you in weeks."

When Rob shrugged and poured his drink, she tutted and slid a cigarette out of her pack. "I should have an affair," she muttered, reaching for her lighter. "I'm wasted on you."

Rob snorted softly and shook his head. Then, downing his juice, he put his glass in the sink and reached for his jacket. "Don't wait up." He kissed her on the forehead. "Might be a late one."

"What's new?" Yvette sniped, sucking hard on her cigarette as he strolled out.

She waited until she heard his car tyres crunching over the gravel outside, and then reached for her phone and pulled up the PI's number. She stared at it for a while, then slammed the phone down on the counter. What was the point? She'd already spent more than a grand having him followed, and the investigator had turned up zilch.

As a wave of self-pity washed over her, she plucked a bottle of wine out of the rack and carried it back up to the bedroom.

After calling in on a couple of people, Rob headed over to the unit from where he and his partner, Adam, controlled their business. He glanced at the dashboard clock as he drove into the industrial estate and saw that he still had forty minutes before he was due to pick up Julia. Just enough time to get what he'd come for, then stop off and pick up a few things for their date. He'd blown it last night by moving too fast, but he wouldn't make that mistake again. She was an attractive girl, and she had an air of innocence about her that he found intriguing. She wasn't the type he usually went for at all, but he'd never been knocked back before, and that had made him want her all the more.

Adam's car was parked up at the side of the unit when Rob pulled in through the gates. He parked beside it and opened the security door with his electronic key. Two skimpily-dressed dark-haired girls were sitting in the corridor outside the office. They both smiled up at him.

"Comfortable?" he asked.

"Yes, thank you," one of them said, batting her long lashes at him.

Rob grinned and walked into the office, closing the door behind him.

Adam was sitting behind his desk. He'd just put the phone down, and he looked up now and nodded hello.

"Where did they come from?" Rob asked, perching on the edge of his own desk.

"Leroy picked them up in Hull." Adam reached for a cigarette and grinned. "Pretty hot, huh?"

"Not bad." Rob caught the fag Adam tossed to him and leaned forward for a light. "But why are they here? Planning on giving them a private audition, were you?"

"Would that I had the time, my boy." Adam snorted softly. "Leroy's just nipped over to Estelle's to sort some stuff out; he'll be taking them over to JT's as soon as he's finished. Which reminds me — I just had Perry on the phone; he wants another one sending over."

"Already?" Rob frowned. "What the fuck is he playing at?"

"You don't expect *me* to ask him, do you?"

"No, *I* will," Rob said, shaking his head. "He needs to ease up. Rate he's going through them, we'll have none left."

"I'll send Leroy over to the Pool after he's dropped the new ones off," Adam suggested. "Get him to pick some more up."

"Why not just send one of them?" Rob nodded towards the door.

"Are you kidding me?" Adam pulled a face. "I'm not wasting those little hotties on a twat like Perry."

"Fair enough." Rob took a drag on his smoke. "Has the delivery come in yet?"

"Nope." Adam shook his head. "Ed's waiting at the airport. I told him to bell me as soon as it arrives."

"They're taking the piss," Rob said irritably. "I was supposed to be taking it to the client later tonight, now I'm going to have to tell him it's been delayed again. He's not going to be happy."

"Nothing we can do about it." Adam shrugged. "You'll just have to offer him a discount to compensate for the inconvenience."

"And who's gonna compensate us for *our* inconvenience?" Rob asked. Then, sighing, he looked at his watch. "Oh, well, suppose I might as well get off if there's nothing here for me."

"I'll call you if it comes in," Adam said.

"Nah, leave it till morning." Rob grinned slyly. "Got a busy night planned."

"Oh, *really?*" Adam gave him a knowing smile. "Well, have a good one, my friend. And when — *if* — you make it home, give the delectable Yvette my best."

"Will do." Rob stubbed out his cigarette, then shook his friend's hand and strolled out, winking goodbye to the girls as he passed them in the corridor.

Chantelle was nervous as she got ready to go out. It touched her that Rob had tried to take the blame for what had happened, but she knew the fault was entirely hers. All he had done was invite her out to dinner, but she had spent the entire night fluttering her eyelashes at him and hanging on his every word, so it was little wonder that he had misread the signals.

No, that wasn't true. He hadn't misread *anything*; he'd simply seen through her pretence of innocence and had taken her up on her unspoken offer. And, yes, he might be the one who was married, but that didn't make her any the less guilty.

Determined not to give Rob the impression that she was trying to make herself look attractive, Chantelle tried on several outfits before settling for a chaste high-necked blouse and trousers combo. She also toyed with the idea of going bare-faced, but decided that was probably a step too far. If Rob were to see her without the usual heavy make-up, he'd be bound to realise that she wasn't as old as she'd told him she was. And if he realised she'd lied about that, he'd wonder if she had lied about anything else, and that could get very tricky. She just wanted to see him this one last time to show there were no hard feelings, and that would be the end of it.

Ready at last, Chantelle slipped her jacket on and went out into the hall. Miguel came out of the bathroom just as she was about to go into the living room.

"Sorry." He stepped aside to let her pass. Then, smiling, he said quietly, "You look very beautiful."

"Don't you ever talk to me again," she hissed, peering coldly into his eyes. "You might have fooled my mum, but we both know what really happened that day."

"I no understand." Miguel cast a guilty glance at the door behind which Mary and Leon were watching TV. "Why you offer help for marry if you no forgive?"

"For my mum, not *you*," Chantelle informed him. Then, brushing past him, she went into the living room. "I'm nipping out," she told Leon. "You'll be okay with mum, won't you?"

"Why wouldn't he be?" Mary twisted around in her seat and scowled up at her. "He's only had a fight, not a bleedin' kidney transplant."

"I know." Chantelle flashed a hooded glance at Leon to tell him to stay quiet about what had really happened. "I just worry about him, that's all."

"Yeah, well, I'm perfectly capable of looking after me own son, thank you," Mary said clippily.

"Never said you weren't," Chantelle conceded. "But while we're on the subject," she added thoughtfully. "I've been thinking about what you said about taking him back to Spain with you, and I reckon it might be a good idea. As long as *you* still want to?" She directed this to Leon.

He shrugged and dropped his gaze, and Chantelle sensed that he wasn't that keen any more. But she *had* thought about it, and she honestly did think it was for the best — even if only temporarily. Anton was confident that the gang stuff was dealt with, but she would rather know for certain that Leon was safe than worry every time he walked out of the door that they might be lying in wait for him.

294

"Okay, we'll talk about it another time," she said now. "See you later."

"Bye, babes." Mary smiled up at her. "Have a nice time."

Chantelle was frowning as she left the flat and walked down the stairs. Her mum was acting strange again; one minute biting her head off, the next calling her babes. But that was her all over: see-sawing from happy to mad and back again in the blink of an eye. It was as frustrating as hell to be the one on the receiving end, as Chantelle generally was; but she supposed she really ought to be used to it by now.

Out on the road, she walked quickly down to the corner where Rob had dropped her off the night before. He pulled up beside her just seconds after she got there, and she smiled when he climbed out and walked around to her with a bunch of red roses in his hand.

"The real thing, as promised," he said, handing them to her. "Complete with grovelling apology."

"Thank you, they're beautiful," Chantelle said shyly. "But there was no need."

"There was every need," Rob insisted, opening the passenger-side door for her. "I behaved badly, and I want you to know that I'm genuinely sorry and it will never happen again."

"I've already said I don't blame you," Chantelle reminded him as she climbed in.

"Well, *I* do," Rob countered. "But I promise I'll be on my best behaviour tonight."

Chantelle laid the roses carefully across her lap. The ends of the stems were wet, and she was hoping they wouldn't leave damp patches on her trousers. But it was the first time anybody had ever bought flowers for her, and they were far too nice to put on the floor.

"Where are we going?" she asked when Rob turned the car around and headed in the opposite direction from town.

"It's a surprise," he said, smiling as he changed the CD that was playing. "It's such a nice night, it seemed wrong to waste it stuck away in a dingy bar. There's a place I like to go when I need some downtime," he went on as Marvin Gaye's "Let's Get It On' began to filter out through the speakers. "But don't worry, it's public, so there are usually other people around."

Chantelle felt a little guilty for having made him feel the need to reassure her like this. She'd completely overreacted last night, and now he was walking on eggshells trying not to upset her again. She wished she was more experienced so she could have handled it like a woman instead of like a silly little virgin. Although it wouldn't have changed the outcome, because she still wouldn't have let anything happen.

They drove out through Chorlton and onto the motorway; and, ten minutes later, they came off again and headed towards Styal. As the roads became narrower and more winding, Chantelle gazed in awe at the houses they were passing. She'd thought Rob's house was a mansion when she'd seen it on the night when she and Bill had first followed him, but these places dwarfed his, and she was sure they must all belong to multimillionaires.

The deeper they went into the countryside, the darker it became, and Chantelle cried out in alarm when a shadowy fox suddenly ran out in front of them. Rob saw it and threw his arm across her as he slammed on the brakes.

"Sorry," he apologised. "Didn't want you to bang your head."

"It's all right," she murmured, conscious of a tingling sensation in her stomach as his fingers brushed her breast. "It just shocked me."

She bit her lip as they set off again and silently scolded herself for having reacted so strongly to his touch. The sultry music wasn't helping, and nor was the heady scent of his aftershave, or the sight of his handsome profile. But he was married, and she needed to get a grip before she made a fool of herself again.

A short while later they turned onto a rough dirt path, and the car bounced along for a good few minutes before they suddenly emerged into a clearing. Chantelle's eyes widened when they came to a stop and she saw the view. They were parked close to the edge of a steep drop and there was a lake down below, its waters glistening like liquid silver in the moonlight.

Rob climbed out and came around to open her door. "What do you think?" he asked, taking her hand to help her out.

"It's incredible," she murmured, gazing down in awe as the cool breeze ruffled her hair.

"Now you know why I love coming here," Rob said as he walked around to the boot of the car and took out the blanket he'd bought at the petrol station along with the roses. "My dad used to take me fishing down there when I was a kid," he told her as he laid it out on the ground before going back for the wine and plastic glasses he'd also bought. "It's impossible to drive down to, and too dangerous to try walking to at night. But I like it just fine up here. Shall we . . .?" He waved for her to sit on the blanket.

When Chantelle was settled, he sat beside her and opened the wine. He poured two glasses and handed one to her. "To friends."

"Friends." She smiled and touched her glass to his.

They gazed out over the lake in peaceful silence and sipped on their drinks. Chantelle had lived on the estate her entire life, and before she'd started working for Bill she'd rarely ventured further than a mile or so away from it. Her mum had been on holiday a couple of times, but she'd never had the money to take Chantelle and Leon with her. And they'd never been allowed to go on school camping trips, so Chantelle had never before experienced the unique darkness and quietness of the countryside. She had certainly never seen anything quite as stunning as this, and she couldn't get over how magical it was.

When their glasses were empty, Rob reached for the bottle to refill them. "Thanks for agreeing to see me," he said. "I didn't think you would, but I'm glad you did."

"Stop blaming yourself," Chantelle said quietly. "I had a really nice time, but I drank too much, so it was my fault it ended badly."

298

"I wouldn't say it ended badly," Rob countered. "Naughty, maybe, but definitely not bad. In fact, I'd say it was rather nice." He nudged her with his shoulder now and gave her a cheeky smile as he added, "Don't worry, I'm not angling to do it again; just saying I enjoyed it. We're friends now, and it's against the law to lie to friends. You knew that, right?"

If Chantelle hadn't just finished a full glass of wine and started on her second, her natural paranoia would have reared its head at those words and she'd have been convinced that he knew she'd been lying. But the alcohol had dulled the edges, and so she smiled.

"So, now you know you can get arrested for lying," Rob went on teasingly. "What about you?"

"What about me?"

"Did you enjoy it? And remember, you're under oath."

Chantelle took another sip of wine. "Yes, I enjoyed it," she admitted, wishing he didn't have such sexy eyes. "But it's not going to happen again, so we shouldn't be talking about it."

Rob peered into her eyes for several long moments. Then, quietly, he said, "Look, I know you don't want to go there because I'm married, and I promise I didn't bring you here to try and get it on with you again. I just really needed to see a friendly face tonight." He paused now and took a sip of his own drink before continuing. "Truth is, me and Yvette aren't getting on too well at the moment. I'm not blaming her," he added quickly. "We're both at fault. But it doesn't matter who caused it, the fact is it's on the rocks; has been for a while."

"That's so sad," Chantelle said, struggling to contain the giggle that had just risen into her throat. It wasn't that she was happy to hear that his marriage was in a bad way, she was just feeling extremely tipsy all of a sudden, and probably would have laughed if he'd told her that his mother had dropped down dead.

"It *is* sad," Rob agreed, gazing wistfully down at the lake. "But sometimes you've got to be honest and admit it's not working — for everybody's sake. We've been drifting for a long time, but we're so far apart now I can't see us recovering." He turned his head and looked into her eyes again. "I wasn't looking for someone else when I met you, and I know I've only seen you a few times, but there's no point denying I'm attracted to you. I totally respect that you don't want to get involved; I just wanted you to know."

Chantelle felt as if she was being sucked right into his eyes, and it was a struggle to keep her body from leaning towards him. "I'm really sorry it's not working out for you," she murmured, unable to break the gaze. "It must be awful."

"It is." Rob's voice was soft and low. "But it's helped being able to get it off my chest. You're special, Julia. I feel like I can really talk to you."

"I'm glad," she whispered, giving up the fight and resting her head on his shoulder.

Her heart started to pound in her chest when he cupped her face in his hand and kissed her gently. She tasted the sweet combination of cigarette smoke and alcohol as he slid his tongue between her lips and

**300**

moaned softly as he pushed her slowly down onto her back.

"You're so beautiful," he said huskily, moving his lips to her throat as he ran his hand down her thigh.

Chantelle arched her back and ran her fingers through his hair as the heat spread through her body like wildfire. This was so wrong, but it felt too good to stop now.

# CHAPTER
# TWENTY-TWO

Bill gave Chantelle a curious look when she climbed into the car the following night.

"What's up?" Chantelle asked, immediately self-conscious.

"Nothing." Bill shrugged. "You just look different."

Chantelle blushed and looked down as she clicked her seat belt into place. "In what way?"

"Oh, I don't know." Bill smiled as she put the old car into gear and set off. "You just have a sort of glow about you. Is there anything you'd like to tell me?"

"Like what?"

"Like, that some handsome prince has finally had the sense to scoop you up and carry you away on his majestic white stallion," said Bill. She glanced at Chantelle out of the corner of her eye now, and chuckled when she saw the girl squirming in her seat. "Well, it's about time," she said approvingly, convinced that she had guessed correctly. "And I'm sure he must be wonderful, because you're far too bright to pick a bad apple."

Chantelle couldn't help but smile. There was no way she could ever tell Bill who the prince was, but the old woman was right about Rob being wonderful. She'd read loads of magazine articles in the past advising girls not to be disappointed if the earth didn't move the first time they had sex. They reckoned it was supposed to be really painful, but Rob had been so gentle, and she'd been so ready, that it hadn't hurt a bit. In fact, it had been wonderful, and her stomach tingled all over again now as the memory washed over her afresh.

It seemed crazy when she'd only known him a short time, but she was really falling for him. And she was sure he felt the same way about her, because he'd been texting all day telling her how much he'd enjoyed himself, and how beautiful she'd looked as they lay in each other's arms after they had made love. She did still feel a bit guilty about his wife, but Rob had said that Yvette knew it was over and they were going to separate as soon as they'd got their affairs in order, so it wasn't like they were really betraying her.

The only blot on the landscape of the beautiful future that Chantelle had been daydreaming about ever since it had happened was the thought of one day having to tell Rob that she had lied to him about who she really was. It was a terrifying prospect, but she knew she would have to do it eventually. She just hoped he would understand why she'd had to deceive him.

But she still couldn't tell Bill. *Ever*.

The club they were going to tonight was over in Wilmslow. It was packed to the rafters, but it didn't take Chantelle long to locate her suspect. It was his stag do, and he and his friends had taken over one whole side of the room.

When she'd heard that it was his fiancée who had hired them, Chantelle had wondered why the woman was bothering to go ahead with the wedding if she suspected he was a cheat. But she guessed she understood why the woman wanted to keep hold of him when she saw the suspect in the flesh, because he was way more handsome in real life than in his picture. Tall, muscular, and black, his stunning smile was noticeable from all the way across the room. And, judging by the way the lights were dancing off the stud in his ear, Chantelle guessed that the huge diamond was real, so he obviously had money.

The party was roped off from the general customers, so Chantelle knew she wouldn't be able to get too close; but she figured she'd be able to get some reasonably clear footage from the far end of the bar. There were a lot of girls hanging around down there, most of whom were even more scantily-dressed than the girls Chantelle had seen at the other clubs she'd visited. There were a lot of fake tans and hair extensions on display, and more fake boobs than she'd ever seen in her life before.

As she made her way to that end of the bar, she felt the crackle of competitiveness in the air, as if each girl was vying to be more noticeable than the rest. Wondering why they were trying so hard to attract the man's attention when it was clear that he was about to get married, Chantelle ordered a drink and was about to get the videophone out of her bag when two girls sidled up to her.

"You a wag?" one of them demanded while the other looked her up and down.

"Sorry?" Chantelle frowned.

"You shagging one of the guys in the team?"

"What team?"

"The footy team." The girl nodded towards the party. Then, sneering, she said, "Oh, forget it, you're obviously too thick to know what I'm talking about. Just stay out of the way when they start letting us in, 'cos if you get in and we don't, you've had it."

"I can assure you I don't *want* to go in," Chantelle informed her. "And I'm waiting for my boyfriend, so why don't you and your friend go and bother someone else?"

"Who d'ya think you're talking to, you cheeky cow?" the girl retorted indignantly.

"Leave it, Shell," her friend said quietly, unnerved by the icy look in Chantelle's eyes. "Let's go see if we can sneak under the rope."

Chantelle shook her head in disgust when the girls went on their way. As *if she* looked like the kind of tart who would fight to get at a footballer . . . how insulting.

Drink in hand, she distanced herself from the other hopefuls and settled in a dark corner from where she could just about see her target.

Bill was dozing with the dog on her lap when Chantelle came back to the car at 1.30 a.m. She woke in a flash when Chantelle tapped on the window, and unlocked the door. Then, trying to rouse the dog, she said, "Come on, old girl. Off into the back with you." When the dog didn't respond, she shook it, saying, "*Mitzy!* Bed."

For a split second as she climbed into the passenger seat, Chantelle thought the dog was dead. And judging by the look of panic in her boss's sleepy eyes, she guessed Bill did too. But the dog suddenly yawned, and then stretched, before wriggling through the gap between the seats and flopping down on top of its blanket on the back seat.

Bill exhaled shakily, and muttered, "Daft bugger's going to give me a heart attack one of these days." Then, shaking the dread feeling off, she turned to Chantelle. "How did you get on?"

"Bit of a shaky start, but I think I got some usable stuff." Chantelle handed the phone over. "Not sure what the client will make of the lap-dance he got off the stripper, but I think she'll be livid about the other girls."

"Girls?" Bill repeated, placing emphasis on the "s".

"There were loads of them," Chantelle told her. "Did you know he was a professional footballer?"

"I don't ask for details of occupation unless it's relevant to the case." Bill yawned and leaned forward to slot the phone into the glove compartment. She was far too tired to be bothered with reviewing the footage now, but she trusted that Chantelle would have done a good job, as usual. "So, what happened?" she asked, starting the engine and setting off.

"More like what *didn't* happen," Chantelle snorted. "I thought the girls round my way were bad, but

**306**

they've got nothing on that lot in there. They were all over him like a pack of dogs."

"Bitches," Bill corrected her, chuckling softly.

"*Total* bitches," Chantelle agreed, missing her point. "I just don't get what they think will come of it. I mean, they must know he's about to get married."

"Probably hoping to be the one to steal his heart at the eleventh hour," Bill said jadedly. "It's the way of the modern world, unfortunately. Everything is a competition, and to the victor the spoils — however soiled they may be."

Chantelle shook her head and gazed out of the window. The footballer had been one of the most handsome men she had ever seen, but she personally wouldn't have touched him with a bargepole. Rob was different; his marriage was all but over. But if tonight's client decided to go ahead with the wedding after seeing the footage, she would never have a moment's peace knowing that unscrupulous girls were prepared to do absolutely anything to get with her man — including give him oral sex under a table in public, as Chantelle had caught one girl doing on film before she left the club.

Chantelle was greeted by silence when she let herself into the flat a short time later and, guessing that they had all gone to bed, she eased Leon's bedroom door open to check on him. It was the first time in a while that he hadn't wedged it shut, and she smiled when she saw him curled up in his bed. His young face was battered, but he was sleeping deeply, obviously free of the recent stress he'd been under.

Anton had done him a massive favour, and Chantelle hoped he appreciated it and would stay away from gangs in future. There was still a chance that those lads would come after him, and that was why she thought it was a good idea for him to go to Spain with her mum and Miguel when they went back after the wedding. He didn't have to stay for ever, but even a short break would do him good, she was sure.

Still smiling, she closed Leon's door and went quietly into her own room. But the smile disappeared as soon as she turned the light on, and she stared around in disbelief, gasping, "What the *hell* . . . ?" The wardrobe door was standing wide open, her neatly hung clothes strewn around the floor; and the dresser drawers had been tipped out onto the bed.

As anger replaced the initial shock, she marched into her mum's room and gritted her teeth when she saw that the bed was empty. Then, a horrible feeling stirring in the pit of her stomach, she turned and rushed into the kitchen.

"No . . . " she cried when she saw that the cupboard beneath the sink was open, and all the bottles of cleaning fluids which had been neatly stored were scattered around the floor. The jar which had contained her savings was lying amongst them, empty, its lid off. She grabbed it and shook it, as if that would make the missing money reappear, and then sank to her knees, wailing, "You bitch! You absolute *bitch*!"

"'S up?" Leon appeared in the doorway, rubbing at his eyes.

"Where's Mum?" Chantelle asked, pushing herself back up to her feet with the empty jar in her hand.

"Dunno." Leon shrugged. "They went out not long after you. She went on a mad one looking for her purse, so I went to my room to listen to music."

"Looking for *my* purse, more like," Chantelle said angrily. "She's pinched all my money."

"Really?" Leon frowned.

"Yes, really," snapped Chantelle. "She must have been planning this for days, the bitch."

"Where are you going?" Leon asked, following her when she marched out into the hall.

"Tracey's."

"Do you want me to come with you?"

"No — stay here," Chantelle ordered, yanking the door open. "I'm going to get my money back before they blow it on drugs and booze, and then I'm going to kill her."

Tracey's flat was in darkness when Chantelle got there, but she hammered on the door anyway, and yelled through the letter box, "I know you're in there, and I'm not leaving till I get my money back! I mean it, Mum — you had no right to take it, and you're not getting away with it!"

As she started rapping on the knocker again, a light went on next door and, seconds later, the door opened and a man's sleepy head poked out.

"Oi, pack it in," he hissed when he saw her. "It's two in the fuckin' morning; you're gonna wake the whole block."

"I don't care," Chantelle snarled.

"Has someone died?" the man asked. "No? Well, fuck off, before I set the missus on you."

Chantelle was so angry she'd have fought with anyone who tried to tackle her right then. But her conscience kicked in and told her that she was being unreasonable. However furious she might be, it didn't give her the right to disturb innocent people.

"I'm sorry for waking you," she muttered, backing off.

"So you should be," he spat, giving her a dirty look as she walked past, before slamming his door shut.

Leon was sitting at the kitchen table when Chantelle got home. "Did you find her?" he asked.

She shook her head and slumped down on the chair facing his.

"Sorry," he murmured guiltily.

"What are *you* apologising for?" She frowned. "You've done nothing wrong."

"I should have stopped her."

"You weren't to know what she was doing."

"No, but I should have sussed she was up to something when she started mooching round in your room the other night. She said she was checking out your clothes in case she wanted to borrow something for the reception, and asked me not to tell you in case you went mad."

**310**

"Cheeky bitch," Chantelle spat. Then, sighing, she rubbed her hands over her face and said, "It's not your fault, so don't beat yourself up about it. I thought she was acting too nice. I'm so stupid."

"No, you're not," Leon blurted out defensively. "You're dead clever. *She's* the stupid one, and I hate her."

In the past, Chantelle would have told him not to talk about their mum like that, but she couldn't do it this time because she felt the same.

"Well, she'll have to come back sooner or later, 'cos she'll need her stuff for the wedding."

"If she hasn't already took it," Leon said knowingly. "Wouldn't put it past her."

Chantelle jumped up when he said this, and rushed back into her mum's room. She hadn't even thought to check if anything was missing when she'd gone in there the first time, but it was immediately obvious that most of the stuff they had brought home from Spain with them was gone.

"You were right," she said, traipsing miserably back into the kitchen and sitting down. "They've done one."

"Well, she needn't think I'm going to her stupid wedding after this," Leon declared. "And I'm not going to Spain with 'em, neither. I'm stopping here with you. You're more of a mum to me than she's ever been."

Touched by his loyalty, Chantelle gave him a grateful smile. "Why don't you go back to bed?" she suggested. "There's no point both of us sitting here fretting."

Leon shook his head. "I don't want to leave you on your own while you're upset. You might do something daft, like when Mum . . ."

He trailed off, but Chantelle knew exactly what he'd been about to say, and it saddened her to think that he was scared she might try to kill herself.

"Don't be daft." She reached across the table and clutched his hand in hers. "It's only money, and I'm angry, not upset. I would never, *ever* do something like that. Mum might come and go, but I would *never* leave you. Do you understand?"

Chin wobbling, Leon nodded and sniffed. Chantelle squeezed his hand. "Go on, go back to bed. I'll be fine. I'm just going to clean up, then I'll go to bed too. Okay?"

"I can help, if you want?" Leon offered.

"No." Chantelle smiled and shook her head. "Thanks, but it'll help clear my head if I do it on my own. Anyway, you hate cleaning."

"Yeah, I know." Leon shrugged. "But you do loads for me, so I should help you, innit?" He chewed on his lip for a moment now, before adding quietly, "Sorry about all that stuff I said, and threatening you with the knife, and that. I wouldn't have done it really."

Chantelle was stunned that he'd apologised, but she guessed she had Anton to thank for that. Whatever he'd said, it had obviously had a massive impact on Leon. It remained to be seen if this change in attitude would last, but even if Leon reverted back to being his usual cheeky self she doubted that things would ever be as bad as they had been lately.

"Thanks," she said. "I really appreciate that." Then, grinning to lift the heavy atmosphere, she said, "Now piss off and let me get on with sorting this lot out."

"Ah . . ." Leon's eyes lit up when she cursed. "You swore. I'm gonna tell."

Chantelle laughed, and waved him on his way. Then, pushing her sleeves up, she set about cleaning up the mess her thieving mother had left behind.

# CHAPTER
# TWENTY-THREE

When three days had passed with no sign of her mum and no answer to any of the texts she'd sent or calls she'd tried to make, Chantelle guessed that they wouldn't be seeing her again in a hurry. And her suspicions were confirmed when she caught Tracey getting off a bus one morning.

"Before you start, it had nowt to do with me," Tracey said, backing away with her hands out in front of her as if she thought Chantelle was about to attack her. "I didn't get any of your money, and I told your mam she was bang out of order for pissing off back to Spain without telling you."

"She's gone back to Spain?" Chantelle hadn't expected that. "I thought they were supposed to be getting married?"

"They did," Tracey told her. "Yesterday, at the registry office. I was a witness," she added guiltily. "I didn't want to do it after what she did to you and your Leon, but she didn't have no one else."

Chantelle snorted, and shook her head in disgust. Then, shrugging, she said, "Oh, well . . . good luck to her. She's going to need it."

"Are we all right, then?" Tracey asked hesitantly, wringing her hands together. "You're not gonna keep having a go at me every time you see me?"

"Wouldn't waste my breath," Chantelle sniped, giving her a dirty look before walking away.

As a shamefaced Tracey scuttled off in search of a drink to settle her nerves, Chantelle shoved her hands deep into her pockets and walked home, her calm expression masking the fury that was twisting her stomach into a tight knot. Her mum had really outdone herself this time, but as pissed-off as Chantelle was about the money she'd lost she was more upset about her mum abandoning Leon again after having geed him up to think she wanted him to share her new life in Spain. Leon swore blind that he hadn't wanted to go, but Chantelle knew he'd been excited when the subject had initially been raised, and it hurt to think that their mum had sold him out for money. Money she'd probably already spent, knowing her.

The bitch had crossed a million and one lines during Chantelle's lifetime, but this was the last time she would ever get away with it. Even if she turned up tomorrow begging for forgiveness, she was dead as far as Chantelle was concerned. Leon was her priority now — along, of course, with her job, and Rob. She was just glad her mum hadn't got her hands on the fifty quid she'd made that night, or she'd have been back at square one: worrying how she was going to feed Leon and keep the electric on. Fortunately, Bill had called with another job the very next morning, so she'd known that they would be okay. But she was never going to allow herself to be put in that position again.

More jobs came in over the following weeks, and Chantelle was relieved when her savings began to grow again. But she was careful to put the money straight into the bank now, wary of leaving it in the flat in case her mum decided to make an unannounced reappearance.

She didn't like leaving Leon on his own after everything he'd been through, but they needed the money, so it had to be done. It wasn't so easy to justify leaving him when she went out with Rob, but Leon insisted that he didn't mind, and she trusted that he meant it when he promised not to go out or answer the door while she was gone.

Before they knew it, the holidays were over, and Chantelle sat Leon down the night before he was due to go back to school to have a talk with him.

"I'm not going to nag," she said. "But I need to know that you're going to behave yourself. You can't get into any kind of trouble, or we'll have the social workers sniffing around again in no time."

"I know," Leon agreed. "And I'm not gonna do nothing. I'll do what the teachers tell me, and if anyone tries to fight with me I'll walk away."

Amused by the sincerity in his eyes, Chantelle smiled. "As long as you try," she said, sure that it wouldn't be as easy as he thought it was going to be. He'd always been cheeky, but his defiant streak intensified a thousandfold when he got bored, and he wasn't the best at keeping his mouth shut once he got started.

"Nah, I mean it," he insisted. "Anton says I'll never get anywhere if I don't do good at school, so I'm gonna do my best this year."

Chantelle raised an eyebrow in surprise. She didn't even know that he'd spoken with Anton again since that day when it had blown up with the gun; but she wasn't about to object, because his words had obviously hit the spot again.

"Right — you, bed," she said, seeing no need to say anything else, because Leon seemed to have got it. "Your uniform's hanging in your wardrobe, so all you have to do is get up when I tell you in the morning, and have a wash."

"And brush me teeth," Leon reminded her, grinning as he headed to his room.

"Wow!" Chantelle laughed. "Never thought I'd hear you volunteer to do *that*."

"Anton says girls don't like bad breath," Leon informed her. "Oh, and can you get me some Lynx next time you go shopping, 'cos they don't like BO, neither."

Chantelle shook her head in amazement. She hadn't seen much of Anton herself lately, so she hadn't really had a chance to speak to him. But she would stop him next time she saw him and thank him, because she doubted that her brother would be being so agreeable without his intervention.

With everything falling into place at last, the stress began to fall away from Chantelle, and Bill wasn't slow to notice the change in her.

"That young man of yours is doing wonders for you," she remarked as she drove Chantelle home from a job one night a couple of weeks after Leon had gone back to school. "Just remember to give me ample warning when you set a date for the wedding, because it'll take an age to find a hat for Mitzy."

Chantelle laughed, but she wasn't laughing inside. She and Rob were still seeing each other in secret, and she yearned for the day when they could come out into the open, as he kept promising they would. But two enormous obstacles still stood in their way: the first being that Chantelle still hadn't told Rob the truth about herself. She desperately wanted to, and had tried on a few occasions. But fear of his reaction always made the words stick in her throat, and the longer it went on the harder it became.

The second obstacle was his wife Yvette who, despite knowing that he wanted a divorce, was still flatly refusing to move out of the house. Rob had told Chantelle that they had been having furious arguments about it, and her heart went out to him because she knew how much it was stressing him out. He said he felt like selling the house, even though the market had dropped so steeply since he bought it that he'd end up getting much less than he still owed on it.

"I'll be paying it off for years," he said one night as they lay entwined in each other's arms after making love. "But it'd be worth it to get rid of her and be with you."

"Don't do anything daft," Chantelle urged. "She'll give up eventually."

**318**

"You reckon?" He snorted softly. "She's already said she's going to fleece me, but my solicitor reckons she'll get a fraction of what she's after, 'cos I'm the one who earned it while she just sat on her arse spending it."

"Well, that's good, isn't it?" Chantelle asked.

"Yeah, so long as she doesn't find out about us before it goes to court." Rob sighed. "If we get landed with a sympathetic judge, and Yvette's able to prove infidelity, she'll waltz off with the lot."

"Well, she hasn't got any proof, so you're all right," Chantelle murmured, unable to tell him how she knew that his wife had nothing on him.

"Yeah, but I can't take any chances until it's done and dusted," Rob said. "That's why we can't come out into the open just yet," he added, a regretful look on his face as he gazed into her eyes. "I hope you understand, and that you'll wait for me?"

"Of course I'll wait," Chantelle assured him.

And she'd meant it when she said it, but it was hard to see a light at the end of the tunnel while Yvette continued to string things out. It was so unfair that she was holding Rob hostage when he was the one who had made an effort to make their marriage work while she swanned off to spas with her girlfriends and treated herself to manicures, pedicures, expensive haircuts and facials. Any guilt Chantelle had once felt about seeing Rob behind her back was long gone, and she now loathed the selfish, greedy bitch with a passion.

# CHAPTER
# TWENTY-FOUR

September started out dull but quickly turned into a blazing Indian summer, and Chantelle found herself inundated with jobs in the weeks following Leon's return to school. All great for her bank balance but not so great for her relationship, as it became more and more difficult to hook up with Rob, who was equally busy. They had been talking on the phone every night, but it wasn't the same as seeing him, and so Chantelle had been delighted when they had finally found a night when they were both going to be free.

They were meeting at nine p.m. but Chantelle had started to get ready as soon as she got up that morning. After a long soak in the bath, she'd spent the rest of the day pampering herself: moisturising her skin, curling her hair, and agonising over what to wear.

She had just applied her make-up and was about to start painting her nails when her phone rang at 8.30, and she smiled when she saw Rob's name on the screen.

"Hey . . . I was just thinking about you. Can't wait to see you."

"I'm so sorry," Rob said apologetically, "but I've got to cancel. Something's come up, and I can't get away."

"Aw, no," Chantelle moaned. "I'm nearly ready."

"And I bet you look gorgeous," he said quietly. Then, "Look, I can't really talk right now. I've just nipped out of a meeting to call you, and I don't want any of the guys to come out and catch me."

"In case they report you to Yvette?"

"Oh, come on, don't be like that. You know I'd come if I could."

"I know." Chantelle sighed. "Sorry, I'm just disappointed that I won't be seeing you."

"I'll make it up to you," Rob promised. "But I've got to go now."

"When will I see you?"

"I'll ring you. Ciao for now."

Chantelle looked at the phone when it went dead in her hand and willed it to ring again, but it didn't.

Leon was watching TV when she walked into the living room. "Thought you were going out?" he said, glancing up at her.

"So did I." She flopped down into a chair. "But it looks like I'll be watching telly with you again. What's on?"

"*Top Gear.*"

"Great."

They sat in silence for a while, Leon's gaze riveted to the action on the screen, Chantelle staring right through it. She was gutted that she wouldn't be seeing Rob, and wondered if this was how Yvette had used to feel when she'd accused him of working too hard. But where *she* had used it as an excuse to nag him, Chantelle would never do that to him.

"Chan . . . *Chan!*"

Chantelle heard Leon call her name and snapped out of her thoughts. "What?"

"Your phone's ringing. You'd best hurry, or you'll miss it."

Chantelle leapt up, ran into her bedroom and threw herself across the bed. Scared that it was about to cut off, she snatched up the phone and answered without looking to see who was calling. "Hello, Rob . . .?"

"Ah, so Prince Charming has an actual name, does he?"

Chantelle grimaced when she heard Bill's voice. "Er, no, I thought it was my mum's boyfriend," she lied, praying that her boss wouldn't put two and two together. "He called earlier, but she was out, so he said he'd call back later."

"Oh, well, sorry to disappoint," said Bill. "But we've had a last-minute booking — if you're free?"

"What, tonight?"

"If you can manage it? I know it's incredibly short notice, so I'll understand if you can't."

Chantelle wasn't really in the mood. But she was already dressed up, so she figured she might as well put her efforts to good use.

"It's fine. What time?"

"Nine," Bill said. "And thank you. You're an angel."

Chantelle gritted her teeth as an unwelcome memory of Miguel popped into her mind. That was what *he* had called her on the day he'd tried to have sex with her behind her mum's back, the sleazy pig. Still, he was

322

gone now, so at least she would never have to see his greasy face again.

Rob had just finished his call and pulled his jacket on when Yvette walked into the bedroom and flopped down on the bed.

"You look nice," she said tartly. "Hope she appreciates the effort."

"Don't start," Rob muttered, reaching for the comb and turning to face the mirror.

"Oh, so you're trying to tell me you get dressed up like this for your male friends?" Yvette raised an eyebrow.

"Do I tell you how to dress for business?" Rob asked, slamming the comb down on the dresser when he'd finished and turning back to her. "But then, you wouldn't know anything about that, would you, seeing as you haven't lifted a finger since I put that ring on it."

"I do a lot, actually," Yvette retorted indignantly. "Who do you think keeps this house going while you're swanning around playing Mr Big?"

"The cleaner," Rob sniped, snatching his cigarettes off the dresser and striding towards the door. "Don't know when I'll be back, so —"

"*Don't wait up*," Yvette mimicked sarcastically. Then, rolling her eyes in disgust, she reached for the bottle of wine that was sitting on her bedside table and sloshed a large measure into the glass that was sitting beside it.

Rob glanced back at her from the doorway and shook his head before walking out. She'd been drinking a lot lately and was obviously starting earlier by the day, because she was often stoned when he came home from work in the evening. She denied she had a problem but he thought otherwise. Still, there was nothing he could do about it right now, because he had more urgent things to deal with.

He was supposed to have been taking Julia out tonight, but had been forced to cancel at the last minute after a phone call from Adam telling him that Perry had turned up at the unit demanding to see him.

Out in his car now, Rob called JT on his mobile as he waited for the gate to slide shut behind him.

"I'm coming for that thing that was dropped off the other day," he said cagily when his call was answered. "Make sure it's ready."

"Might take a while," the woman on the other end of the line said. Then, "Hang on a minute . . ."

Rob grimaced at the sound of her coughing up what sounded like a year's worth of phlegm. "I'll be there in half an hour," he said when she'd finished. "And get yourself some Benylin, for fuck's sake. You're going to lose a lung at this rate."

He rang Adam now and asked, "Have you got any of that stuff left?" When he got an affirmative, he said, "Right, well, fill your flask, then take Perry down to the club. Keep him sweet, and don't tell him where you're going till you get there in case he makes a call. I'll be there in an hour."

He cut the call now and set off, but as he turned onto the road, he sighed when he caught a glimpse of Yvette silhouetted at the bedroom window. He'd been a bit rough on her lately, so it was little wonder she'd been drinking so much. There was nothing he could do about it right now, but once this business with Perry was sorted he would treat her to something nice. Maybe a holiday or something sparkly, to let her know that he did appreciate her, even if he didn't always show it.

The pub where tonight's suspect was supposed to have been going was dead when Chantelle arrived at 9.15, and she felt uncomfortable as she noticed the few people who were there casting hooded glances in her direction. It was a dark, dingy place, and she was completely over-dressed, but she had a horrible feeling that her clothes had nothing to do with the way they were looking at her. She suspected it was because she was black, and her sense of unease increased as she made her way to the bar and ordered a drink.

Chantelle had grown up in a multicultural community so she hadn't really experienced overt racism before. Her instincts were screaming at her to get the hell out of there, but she told herself that she was just being paranoid and tried to push the feelings aside as she took a seat in a quiet corner.

It was an hour before more people started to arrive, and her fear increased when she saw that it was a gang of bikers. Her suspect wasn't amongst them, so she stuck it out for another twenty minutes. But when another gang arrived the atmosphere took a nosedive, and she was contemplating calling it a night when a glass went flying past her head. On her feet in a flash, she ran out just as a mass brawl kicked off — and didn't stop running until she reached the safety of the car.

"Oh, well, at least you're okay, that's the main thing," Bill said when Chantelle explained what had happened. "But, for future reference, if you *ever* feel uneasy like that again, get the hell out of there *immediately*. Our instincts are designed to protect us, and they must never be ignored. Do you understand?"

"Yeah." Thoroughly chastened, Chantelle nodded and settled back in her seat as they set off.

Still mulling over what might have happened if she hadn't left the pub when she did, she was gazing out of the window when Bill turned onto Deansgate a few minutes later. As they passed the road where the club in which she'd first seen Rob was situated, her heart leapt at the sight of a familiar figure. It was only a fleeting glimpse, but she just knew it was Rob. And he'd been with a woman.

"Something wrong?" Bill asked, sensing a shift in her mood.

"No." Chantelle shook her head and forced a smile. "I, er, think I just saw my friend. Would you mind dropping me here?"

Bill pulled over and handed Chantelle's fee to her. Then, smiling as the girl climbed out, she said, "Try to forget about that nonsense back there and have a good night. I'll call you when the next job comes in."

"Thanks," Chantelle murmured, quickly closing the door as the dog wheezed its way through the gap and plopped onto her vacated seat.

**326**

She waved Bill off. Then, head down, she quickly crossed the road, telling herself as she walked that she must have been mistaken. Rob had said he was working and he had no reason to lie, so it must just have been someone who looked like him.

When she reached the corner and spotted Rob's car parked down at the dark end of the road, she knew she'd been right. But that didn't necessarily mean he'd lied, she reasoned. His meeting might have finished earlier than expected, and he'd decided to meet up with his friends for a drink. There was no harm in that.

But why would he choose to see his friends rather than come to see her, when they hadn't seen each other for ages and he knew she'd been dying to see him?

Unless *he* didn't want to see *her?*

Sickened to think that he might have changed his mind about their relationship, Chantelle stared at the club door. She couldn't just march inside and confront him, because it would be too humiliating if she'd got it all wrong. Anyway, he'd want to know how she'd known he was there, and there was no easy way of explaining it without making him think she'd been spying on him. But she couldn't go home without knowing where she stood, either.

Desperate for answers, she pulled her phone out of her pocket.

"Hey . . ." Rob said when he answered after several rings. "What's up?"

"Just wanted to hear your voice," Chantelle lied. "How's it going? Meeting finished yet?"

"No," Rob said quietly. "Still dragging on."

"Oh, I see." Chantelle's heart sank. "Well, I hope you've been out for something to eat and drink?"

"Chance would be a fine thing," Rob snorted. "These things can go on all night. And the rate this one's going, I'll be lucky if I get home before it's time to come back tomorrow."

"Poor you," Chantelle murmured. Then, gritting her teeth when she heard a woman's voice in the background, she said, "Who's that?"

"Probably one of the secretaries," Rob said. "I'd best go, but I'll ring you in the morning. Love you."

When he abruptly cut off, Chantelle stared at the club door again. Rob had not only lied about where he was, but also about the woman he was with. And why would he do that if there was nothing going on?

Determined to find out, Chantelle pulled her collar up to hide her face and walked quickly down the road. Halfway down, she found a narrow alleyway between two buildings from where she could see the club doorway and the car. She stepped inside and pressed herself back into the shadows. Then, holding her mobile phone in her hand, her finger poised over the camera's record button, she waited.

Rob had used Chantelle's call as an excuse to go out onto the smoking patio at the back of the club. He took a last drag on his cigarette now and stubbed it out before heading back inside.

"Sorry about that," he apologised, smiling as he sat back down. "Bit of business I'd forgotten about."

328

"What's the betting it was monkey business?" Perry smirked, nudging Adam. "Man only grins like that when he's on a promise, eh?"

Adam gave an insincere little laugh. Perry was obnoxious at the best of times, but he became even more crude and disrespectful when he had a drink inside him — or five, which was how many Adam had counted him necking since they'd got here.

The girl Rob had picked up from JT's house was sitting beside Adam on the banquette seat, directly opposite Perry. She'd already been spaced out when he collected her, but she looked like she was in another world now thanks to the cocktail Adam had just given her, and Rob was filled with regret as he looked at her. She was absolutely stunning, and it was a crying shame that she was going to be wasted on a monster like Perry when any one of their other clients would have snatched his hand off to have her. But he'd needed something special to tempt Perry into seeing reason, and she was as special as they came.

"So, what do you think?" he asked Perry, giving a surreptitious nod in the girl's direction.

"Fuckable," Perry said, a lusty light in his eyes. "But I ain't paying, 'cos you owe me *big* time after that last skank you dumped on me."

"Of course," Rob agreed. "But we will need to talk before I hand her over."

"Too right we will," said Perry, his eyes narrowing as he reached for his glass. "I've been a fucking good customer, but I'm starting to think you've got me down as some kind of soft touch. Big mistake that, boys, *very* big mistake. You think I got where I am today by letting people mug me off?"

"Not at all," Rob said evenly. "And, believe me, nobody's trying to mug you off. We appreciate your business — don't we, Ad?"

"Absolutely," Adam agreed, shifting nervously in his seat. He hadn't had a chance to speak with Rob in private yet, so he had no clue how his friend intended to deal with the man. But, one way or another, this had to get resolved tonight, because his nerves couldn't take much more.

"Why don't you go and get the man another drink?" Rob said, giving Adam a pointed look when Perry had drained his glass. "And get the lady another while you're there."

"Righto." Adam stood up and made his way to the bar.

"So, what did you want to talk about?" Perry asked, eyeing the girl's breasts as they strained against the tight, low neckline of her dress.

Rob straightened his trousers and casually crossed his legs. "This has got to stop," he said bluntly, keeping his voice low so the people at the nearby tables wouldn't hear. "We run a tight operation, and we've had no problem with any of our other clients."

"But you're saying you've got a problem with me?" Perry sneered. "What . . . just 'cos I won't let you fob me off with substandard goods?"

"Our goods are top quality," Rob replied coolly. "A lot of hard work goes into making sure of that. The problem lies in the way you handle them."

**330**

"Bollocks," Perry retorted angrily. "There's nowt wrong with the way I handle them. Least, there *wouldn't* be if you didn't keep sending me duds. I don't mind paying for quality, but when I'm paying through the nose for diseased tramps who can't take a bit of action without keeling over, that's where I draw the line, fella."

Rob inhaled deeply and bit down hard on the retort that sprang to the tip of his tongue. They had been supplying Perry for a year now, but unlike the owners of the private clubs and massage parlours they also supplied, who were savvy enough to realise that they were never going to make back the money they had shelled out if they allowed the girls to be treated too badly, Perry was a sadistic cunt who got a kick out of torturing them. He also had an unfortunate habit of killing them, and that was where it got messy.

Rob couldn't care less what he did to the girls when they were alive; it was what he did with their bodies after he'd killed them that worried Rob. If they weren't disposed of properly, it would only be a matter of time before somebody stumbled across one of the corpses. And if that happened, the police would have no trouble tracing it back to Perry, who would undoubtedly have deposited his DNA in every conceivable hole before he got rid. And if *he* went down, he'd made it clear that he would be taking Rob and Adam down with him.

That was the kind of remorseless bastard they were dealing with, and he'd been holding them ransom with that threat for months. And that was why he had to go.

331

This had been his last chance to see sense, but he clearly wasn't going to, so it was time to get serious.

Chantelle had been standing in the alley for almost two hours before Rob, the woman, and two men came out of the club. Her legs were aching from having stood still for so long, but she forgot the pain in an instant when the woman stepped beneath the light above the door and she got her first clear look at her. Just like the one she'd seen with Rob and his friends on that first night, this one had long black hair, a stunning face, and a fantastic figure. She was clearly drunk, and fury coursed through Chantelle like a wave of red-hot lava when she looped her arms around Rob's neck and rested her head on his shoulder.

Hands shaking, Chantelle trained her camera on the pair and gritted her teeth when, laughing, Rob put his arm around the woman's waist and planted a kiss on her lips. One of the men in the group looked equally as drunk as the woman, and the other man held him up as the group made their way down the road. Chantelle kept her gaze firmly on the phone screen, watching as Rob, his arm around the woman, caressed her backside as she stumbled and giggled her way to the car. When they reached it, he propped her against the back door and walked around to the boot. But as soon as he opened it and leaned his head inside to get something, the drunken man made a lunge for the girl; and when she squealed, Rob ran back around and slammed him up against the wall.

**332**

Chantelle was upset as she watched the men tussle. She'd never seen this violent side of Rob before, and the fact that he was doing it in defence of the woman — who the other man had bundled into the back of the car by now — hurt her even more.

Just as Rob punched the man in the gut, dropping him to his knees, the phone screen went black in Chantelle's hand. Terrified that it signalled an incoming call, she stepped quickly back into the shadows and desperately tried to turn it onto silent, only to find that the battery had died. Relieved, but shaking more than ever, she edged back out in time to see Rob and the man who was still standing shove the fallen one into the back of the car beside the woman, before climbing quickly into the front.

When the headlights came on a second later, Chantelle stayed put and hid until the car had driven past. Then, after waiting a few minutes to make sure that they had gone, she stepped out of the alley and made her way home.

"He is bleeding," the woman whined, pressing herself up against the back door of the car and looking with a mixture of horror and disgust at the man who was slouched beside her. "I think he is dying, no?"

"Shut her up," Rob muttered to Adam, his gaze fixed firmly on the road.

Adam reached into his pocket and pulled out a hip flask. "Here." He twisted around in his seat and handed it to the woman. "Have a drink and relax." He grinned now, his teeth glinting in the strobe of the street lights as he watched her take a long swig. "There you go — soon be back in la-la land."

The woman drained the flask and rested her cheek against the cold glass of the window. "Are you taking me to house?" she asked when, a few minutes later, her eyelids began to droop.

"Yeah, that's right, sweetheart," Adam said. "Won't be too long now."

They drove on in silence for the next few miles, then Adam glanced back to see how the woman was getting on. "Flat out," he said when he saw that her eyes were closed and her head had lolled forward onto her chest.

"What about him?" Rob asked.

Adam reached through the gap between the seats and shook Perry's leg. When the man's head rolled to one side and Adam saw his lifeless eyes and his tongue protruding from between his grey lips, he grimaced and quickly withdrew his hand.

"Gone."

"Thank fuck for that."

"I didn't know you were going to knife him," Adam said reproachfully. "Did you even check if anyone was around?"

"Of course I did," Rob said testily. "And what else was I supposed to do? I gave him a chance, but he, wasn't going to budge. He must've had guts of fucking steel to still be standing after the amount of shit you put in his drinks, so there was no other way around it."

"Yeah, but now we'll have to get rid of him, and that's not going to be easy."

"Maybe not, but anything's better than waiting for that axe he's been holding over our heads to fall."

"What about her?" Adam asked.

"She'll have to go," Rob said quietly. "Shame," he added regretfully. "But she's seen too much, so we can't take any chances."

# CHAPTER
# TWENTY-FIVE

Chantelle barely slept that night for thinking about Rob's betrayal. She had watched the short film over and over again after charging her phone, searching for signs that she'd got it wrong: that Rob had only been holding the drunken woman up; that he hadn't kissed her or fondled her bottom. But he had, and the proof — albeit shadowy, and unsteady, thanks to how badly her hands had been shaking — was right there in her phone.

Her eyes were so badly swollen when she dragged herself out of bed the next morning that Leon was concerned when she woke him.

"What's wrong?" he asked, getting up without his usual grumbling and following her into the kitchen.

"Nothing," Chantelle lied, keeping her face turned from him as she poured cereal and milk into a bowl and placed it on the table.

"Something's up," Leon persisted, sitting down and reaching for his spoon. "Have you had a fight with that lad you've been seeing? 'Cos if he's touched you, I'll —"

"I haven't had a fight with anyone. It's just hay fever."

"Since when have you had hay fever?"

"Since I was a kid." Chantelle turned her back to make herself a strong coffee. "Don't worry about it; it never lasts long."

Leon wasn't sure if he believed her, but he decided not to push it. His sister wasn't stupid enough to let a lad push her around, but if he ever found out different, he'd tell Anton. Anton liked her, so he'd soon sort the lad out.

After seeing Leon off to school, Chantelle got dressed and made herself another coffee, then sat on her bed with her phone in her hand, waiting for Rob to call as he'd promised. Despite all the evidence to the contrary, she still desperately wanted to believe that he must have had a good reason to lie to her, and she had decided to give him one last chance to tell her the truth. If he took it, great; if not . . . Well, she'd cross that bridge when she came to it.

Rob rang at 8.45, and Chantelle guessed that he must be on his way to work.

"Hey," she said, forcing herself to sound happy. "How are you?"

"Knackered," he said. "Meeting ran over, so I've only had a couple of hours' sleep."

"Poor thing," Chantelle murmured. "I hope you took a break?"

"Nah, we were pretty much stuck in there all night," Rob told her. "Hope you weren't too upset with me for cancelling our date?" he said now.

"I'll survive," Chantelle replied through gritted teeth. Then, desperate to get off the phone now that she'd had her answer, she picked up one of her shoes and rapped the heel on the side of her wardrobe.

"That the door?" Rob asked.

"Yeah. Best go."

"Okay, I'll call you later. Love you."

Chantelle clenched her hand so tightly that her nails almost pierced her flesh. "Love you, too," she muttered, before quickly disconnecting.

"*Bastard!*" She hurled the phone down on the bed and buried her face in her hands. How could he lie to her like that? All right, so she had been lying to him as well; but that was totally different. She hadn't lied about her feelings for him, and she would never, ever have cheated on him. His wife had been right about him all along.

At the thought of his wife, it occurred to Chantelle that Rob had probably been lying about *her* as well. He'd said that he and Yvette were sleeping in separate rooms, and that it was virtual warfare whenever their paths crossed. Yvette was supposed to be the one who was holding up the divorce, but Chantelle was beginning to wonder if the woman even knew anything about it.

As the cold harsh reality of the situation settled over her, Chantelle couldn't believe how stupid she had been. She'd drifted through the last few months on a cloud of denial, telling herself that she was doing nothing wrong, that it was Yvette's fault that Rob had looked elsewhere for love. But it wasn't true. Rob had played her — exactly like he had probably played that woman last night, and God only knew how many others. She was such a fool. She had always thought she was too clever to be taken in by a sweet-talking man, and had vowed that she would *never* go near a married one. But she had proved that she was every bit as stupid and amoral as her mum, and she couldn't have been more disgusted with herself.

Determined not to let Rob get away with it, Chantelle snatched up her phone and watched the footage again. It was nowhere near as clear as it would have been if she'd filmed it on Bill's camera, but Rob's and the woman's faces were clear in the shots under the light, so there was no way he'd be able to deny it was him. It was Yvette's business what she chose to do with it, but if she had a scrap of sense she would do what Rob had been using as an excuse for why he couldn't be with Chantelle, and take him for everything he owned in the divorce courts.

Bill's office was on the first floor of the shabby block that stood beside the cafe where Chantelle had first met her. Chantelle had only been there a few times but the elderly doorman, Arnold, never forgot a face, and he smiled when he saw her through the glass door now.

"Morning, pet," he said, limping back to his chair behind the reception desk after letting her in and relocking the door behind her. "How's you?"

"I'm okay, thanks," Chantelle lied. "You?"

"Not too bad." He sat down, with a puff. "My knees are playing up again, but the doc's decided I'm not suffering enough for replacement, so I'll just have to struggle on, eh?"

"Hope you feel better soon," Chantelle said, smiling as she backed towards the stairs. He was a nice old man, but he was likely to start talking about the good old days if she hung around for too long, and she had more pressing things on her mind.

"Come," Bill called when she heard a tap at the door. Her eyebrows rose when Chantelle walked in. "Well, that's a surprise. I thought you were Arnold." She sat back in her seat now and looped her hands together over her stomach. "What brings you here on this fine day?"

Chantelle bit her lip. All the way here she'd been to-ing and fro-ing; one minute determined to go through with it, the next telling herself not to give up on Rob so easily. Now she was actually here, she was uncertain again.

*He lied to your face and said he'd been in the office all night*, a little voice in her head reminded her. *And he's probably still been sleeping with Yvette, and God knows who else, the whole time he's been sleeping with you.*

"I saw something after you dropped me off last night," she said, pulling her phone out of her bag. "And I thought you should see it."

"Oh, yes?" Bill waved for her to pull up a chair.

"Me and my friend went for a drink," Chantelle said, sitting down. "But when I was on my way home I saw a man we were hired to follow a while back — the one who said he could set me up with the model agent."

"Mmmm?"

"Well, he came out of the same club I first saw him at," Chantelle said, gritting her teeth as she added, "With a woman. I didn't think anything of it, because I'd seen him with women before and nothing had happened. But when I saw him kiss her, I started filming them on my phone."

When Bill held out her hand, Chantelle passed her phone over and twisted her fingers together in her lap. Her boss wasn't stupid, and she was scared that the old woman would see straight through her lies. But she wasn't about to admit to anything unless she absolutely had to.

Bill attached the phone to her laptop and downloaded the footage, then rested her elbows on the desktop to watch it.

"What do you think?" Chantelle asked when she'd viewed it twice.

"Not a lot," Bill said non-committally. "Could be his wife, for all we know."

"It's not," Chantelle said. Then, realising her mistake, she blushed deeply and lowered her gaze.

Bill narrowed her eyes and peered at her thoughtfully. "Anything you'd like to tell me?"

"I don't know what you mean," Chantelle murmured, trying but failing to look her in the eye.

"Oh, I think you do," Bill said quietly. "I've been in this business for a very long time, Chantelle, and my instincts are as sharp as they ever were. I know a rat when I smell one, and this stinks to high heaven."

She pursed her lips when Chantelle still didn't speak, and said, "Going to make me work it out for myself, are you? Okay, let's see how I get on . . . You saw a *friend* as we were driving home last night and asked me to drop you off. Then, after going for a drink with said *friend*, you claim to have stumbled upon an old suspect and, suspecting that he was up to no good, spent some considerable time filming him on your phone. How am I doing so far?"

Chantelle's cheeks were blazing, and she gave a shamefaced little shrug.

"My dear, even *I* would be hard pushed to recognise a suspect after several weeks," Bill went on reprovingly. "So how *you* managed it, in the dark and from such a distance, is beyond me. Unless you've seen him since we called time on that particular job?"

She gazed at Chantelle now and waited for an answer. Then, sighing when she saw a tear trickle slowly down her cheek, she said, "Oh, you silly girl."

"I'm sorry," Chantelle sobbed. "I didn't mean to; it just happened."

"You know the rules, and I'd have thought by now that you would understand the importance of adhering to them," Bill scolded. "If a suspect we've outed were to find out who we are and where to find us, we'd be extremely vulnerable."

"I haven't told him anything," Chantelle said truthfully. "He still thinks my name's Julia, and he doesn't know where I live."

"How long has it been going on?"

"A few months. He rang me a week after that night at the Hilton and asked me to do him a favour and go to dinner with him and a client."

342

"And you didn't think to tell me?"

"He offered to pay me, so I thought it was just business," Chantelle said guiltily. "We met at the restaurant, but his client rang to say he couldn't come, so —"

"*Really?*" Bill interrupted sarcastically. "Well, there's a surprise. Didn't that strike you as a familiar pattern?"

"I didn't think of it like that at the time," Chantelle admitted. "We just had dinner, and then he dropped me off down the road from mine. I'd had a bit too much to drink, and I let him kiss me, but then I felt guilty and went home."

"But he called and persuaded you to meet up again, and it's been going on ever since?" Bill shook her head when Chantelle nodded. "And, let me guess . . . he said he loved you, and promised to leave his wife for you? Oldest lines in the bloody book, and you fell for it," she finished disappointedly. "I honestly thought you had more sense."

"I believed him," Chantelle said plaintively. "He's been so lovely to me."

Bill plucked a tissue out of a pack in her drawer and passed it over the desk. Then, tutting when something popped into her mind, she said, "*Rob* . . . I should have guessed when you answered my call the other day and thought it was him. If only you'd told me."

"I couldn't," Chantelle croaked. "I was scared you'd sack me. But I guess you will now, anyway."

"I haven't decided what I'm going to do with you yet," Bill informed her. "I need time to think it over."

"I am sorry," Chantelle murmured. "I never wanted to lie to you, but once I started, I didn't know how to stop."

"Am I right to assume the affair, or whatever you'd like to call it, is over?"

"Absolutely." Chantelle nodded. "I've seen my mum get cheated on my whole life, and I always vowed I'd never let it happen to me. I feel so stupid."

"And now you want to punish him by letting wifey know what he's been up to?"

Chantelle gave a little shrug, unable to deny it but ashamed to admit it, because it sounded so petty.

"Can't say I blame you," Bill said. Then, pushing her seat back, she stood up and waved Chantelle towards the door. "Go home. I'll call you when I've decided what I'm going to do with you."

The guilt weighed heavily on Chantelle's shoulders as she made her way out. There were many years between her and Bill in age, but she genuinely liked and respected the woman and truly enjoyed working with her. But if this was the end, she had nobody but herself to blame.

# CHAPTER
# TWENTY-SIX

Yvette Knight was lying on a bed in the treatment room of her favourite salon when her mobile phone rang that afternoon. It was her fourth wedding anniversary, and after making love to her that morning Rob had presented her with a beautiful bunch of roses. His thoughtfulness had been so unexpected, and so welcome after their recent ups and downs, that she had decided to surprise him in return by giving him a night of passion that would totally blow his mind.

As soon as he'd left for work she had booked herself in for a full top-to-toe treatment. Her hair was now covered in strips of foil, her finger- and toenails were beautifully painted in his favourite shade of scarlet, and one of the girls had just applied wax to her bikini line, while another was injecting Botox into her frown lines.

When she heard her phone ringing now, she smiled up at another girl who had just brought her a fresh glass of wine, and said, "Get that for me, sweetie."

The girl reached into Yvette's handbag, which was sitting on the make-up ledge, and took out the ringing phone.

"Who is it?" Yvette asked, hoping that it wasn't Rob. He'd only guess what she was doing if he knew where she was, and that would ruin her surprise.

"It says 'Pix'," the girl told her, reading the name on the screen.

"Give it to me." No longer smiling, Yvette sat bolt upright and dropped her feet to the floor.

"Wait," the wax-girl said when she headed for the door. "That leads back onto the shop floor, and you're naked down there."

Yvette snatched the sheet off the bed and wrapped it around her waist before rushing from the room and into the toilet.

"Why are you calling me?" she asked in a whisper when she was able to talk. "Have you any idea how much trouble you'd have caused if my husband had answered my phone?"

"Please accept my apologies," Bill said evenly, resisting the temptation to remind the woman that she hadn't been so reticent about receiving calls in the past.

"What do you want?" Yvette demanded. "I know you received your payment, because I checked my account."

"That's all in order," Bill assured her. "I just thought you might like to know that I am in possession of additional information concerning the subject of our previous communications."

"What are you talking about?" Yvette squawked. "I didn't authorise you to carry on following him, so don't think you're going to hit me with a massive bill. I'll sue you before I pay you another penny!"

"Highly unlikely," Bill said bluntly, guessing that the woman wouldn't risk exposing their arrangement in a public arena. "But I've decided to waive the follow-up fee, so there will be nothing to pay."

"Oh, I see," Yvette replied, anger quashed, curiosity roused. "So, what do you have for me?"

"If you still have the pin number you may use it to access the latest pictures," Bill told her. "The quality is nowhere near that of the first batch, but you should still be able to gauge what's happening in them."

Yvette felt the blood drain from her face. "Are you saying you've got proof that Rob's cheating on me?"

"Review the pictures and decide for yourself, dear."

Yvette felt sick to her stomach when the line went dead, and her head started to spin. She stumbled against the wall and looked at her reflection in the mirror. Her skin was deathly pale, and her unmade-up eyes were bugging out at her. It couldn't be true . . . Rob couldn't be cheating. Not on their anniversary.

Desperate to get home so that she could view the pictures in private, she rushed out of the toilets and back into the treatment room.

"Get this crap off my hair," she ordered. "And hurry up. I've got to go."

"But it won't be properly developed yet," the girl told her.

"I don't *CARE!*" screeched Yvette. Then, tugging at the foil strips, she said, "Oh, forget it. I'll do it myself."

The receptionist looked up and smiled when Yvette, now dressed, came hurtling out of the treatment room. But when the woman ran straight past and yanked the door open, she called, "Excuse me, Mrs Knight . . . you haven't paid."

"Send me the bill," Yvette yelled back over her shoulder.

Rob was relaxed when he arrived home at six that evening. With his recent problems now taken care of, and a new high-paying client on board, the future was starting to look bright again, and he was whistling as he strolled into the kitchen. But he stopped in his tracks and drew his head back in alarm when he saw Yvette standing there with a glass of wine in her hand and a wild look in her eyes.

"Whoa! What the fuck have you done to your hair? It's bright orange."

"Never mind my fucking hair," Yvette screamed, hurling the glass at him.

He ducked just in time, and it sailed past his head and smashed against the wall behind him. "What the hell was that for?" he demanded, looking at his wife as if she'd lost her mind.

"You tell me!" Yvette launched herself at him and slapped him around the face. "Go on — *tell* me! Tell me about the whore you've been fucking behind my back! *TELL ME!*"

"I don't know what you're talking about," Rob said, batting her hand away when she went to hit him again. "I haven't been fucking anyone."

"*Liar!*" Yvette sobbed, tears cascading down her face as she raked his cheek with her nails.

"Pack it in," he barked, shoving her roughly away and holding a hand to his stinging cheek. When he looked at his hand and saw blood, he scowled. "Look what you've done."

"You deserved it," she gasped, holding herself up against the counter top. "I've known for *months*, but you were never going to tell me, were you? *I'm working ... I'm in a meeting ... you're crazy ...*" she mimicked. "Well, I'm not crazy, am I? I was right all along, and now I've got the pictures to prove it."

"What pictures?" Rob sneered, certain that she had nothing on him. The only woman he'd fucked behind her back recently was Julia, and they always went over to the lake to do the business so he'd have known if anyone had been spying on them.

"Oh, you want to see them, do you?" Yvette snatched up the copies she had printed off and threw them at him.

"*Here* ... And don't bother ripping them up, because I'll just print more."

Rob picked up the scattered photographs and stared at them with narrowed eyes for several moments. Then, voice low, he asked, "Where did you get these?"

"It doesn't matter *where* I got them, it just matters that I *have* got them," Yvette said angrily. "Do you know what it's been like for me, sitting here night after night wondering what you were doing — *who* you were doing? Why couldn't you just tell me, instead of sneaking around behind my back, making a mockery of our marriage? Well, this is the last time, Rob. I can't go through this again. I want a divorce."

Rob had been studying the pictures again as she spoke. He looked up now and said, "I asked you where you got them?"

"And I said it doesn't matter," Yvette repeated, furious that he cared more about that than he did about the fact that he'd been caught and she'd asked for a divorce. "Oh, I get it," she spat as another thought occurred to her. "The bitch is married, and you're scared her husband will see the pictures and come after you. I'm right, aren't I?"

When Rob strode across to her and gripped her by the arm, she cried out in pain. "Get off me! You're hurting me."

"Where did you get them?" Rob asked again, tightening his grip.

"A private investigator," she informed him defiantly.

"You've had me followed?" Rob stared down at her in disbelief. "How long for?"

"Long enough to know *that* bitch wasn't the first," Yvette said, wincing as his fingernails dug into her flesh. "I'm not the one in the wrong here, so I don't see why you're acting like this," she went on angrily. "You're the one who's been screwing around, so if anyone's entitled to be mad, it's m —"

Rob clapped his hand over her mouth before she finished speaking, and her eyes widened with panic as she struggled to breathe. He held on tight for several long moments, then asked, "Ready to tell me what I want to know?"

She nodded frantically, and gasped for breath when he withdrew his hand. She and Rob had fought in the past, but he'd never been as violent as this. She'd really thought he'd been going to suffocate her just then, and she didn't understand why he was so angry. By rights, he ought to be on his knees begging for forgiveness.

"I want a name and address," Rob said again. "And don't fuck around, 'cos I haven't got time for this."

"She didn't give me an address," Yvette croaked truthfully. "I found her online and only ever talked to her on the phone."

"So how did you get the pictures?"

"She put them on her database and sent me a pin number after I paid. I'm sorry!" she squealed when she saw the rage in his eyes, raising her hands to protect her face in case he hit her. "I love you, and I didn't want to lose you. What else was I supposed to do?"

"Show me the pictures." Rob shoved her towards the laptop that was sitting at the other end of the ledge. "All of them."

Yvette's hands were shaking as she unclipped the lid and brought up the PI's website. "There's nothing else on there," she told him as she typed in the code. "All I've got is the pin, and her phone number."

Rob didn't speak. He just stared at the screen and waited for the pictures to appear. When they came up a few seconds later, he scrolled through them until he reached the last batch, and leaned forward to study them. They were still grainy, but much clearer on the screen than in the printed versions, and his jaw clenched when he saw the details he'd missed first time around.

"What are you doing?" Yvette asked when he slammed the lid down and yanked the plug out of the wall.

"Getting rid of this shit," he said. "And I'll have that number while I'm at it." He snatched up her phone. "What's it listed as?"

"Pix. But don't ring her," Yvette begged, scared that he was going to cause trouble with the woman and everyone would find out that their marriage was on the rocks. "She was only doing her job. It's my fault, not hers."

"Yes, it is," Rob agreed, scrolling through her contact list until he found the number he wanted.

"I just needed to know the truth," Yvette whimpered, wiping her nose on the back of her hand as fresh tears began to fall. "I love you so much, I couldn't bear the thought of losing you."

She winced when Rob reached out and cupped her face in his hand, but he peered down into her eyes and said quietly, "And I love you, too, or I wouldn't still be here. But you've got to learn to keep your nose out of my business."

"I do try," she said plaintively, holding onto his hand with both of hers. "But it's hard when I know you're seeing someone else."

"I'm not seeing anyone," Rob lied. "Those women weren't with me, they were with my client. And that's why I need to get rid of these pictures and make sure they can't reappear, because he'll blame me if it gets out and his wife finds out."

"That's his problem," Yvette said unsympathetically, grasping at his story because it was infinitely better than believing that Rob was the cheat.

"No, it's *ours*," said Rob. "He's our biggest client, and if he puts word out that we can't be trusted it'll totally fuck the business up. That what you want? No money coming in; lose this house and everything we've ever worked for?"

"No." Yvette shook her head.

"Yeah, well, that's what'll happen if I don't get it sorted," Rob said.

"I'm sorry," Yvette murmured shamefacedly. "I didn't think."

"Forget it." Rob sighed. Then, giving her a disappointed look, he said, "I really thought you'd got over all that jealousy shit. I told you I'd never hurt you like that again, and I meant it, so you should have trusted me. You're the one I love. And, here, if you don't believe me . . ." He reached into his pocket and took out a small gift-wrapped box.

"What is it?" Yvette gazed up at him tearfully.

"You didn't think I was just going to give you flowers on our anniversary, did you?"

"But . . ."

"Sshhh." Rob lowered his head and kissed her softly on the lips. "We'll talk when I get back."

Yvette gulped back her tears when he walked out and tore the wrapping from the box. When she opened it and saw the diamond earrings twinkling up at her, she stared at them in wonder. They were each a full carat, and they were absolutely flawless, and suddenly the sight of that stupid woman pawing Rob seemed trivial. As he'd said, *she* was the one he loved, and the proof was right here in her hand.

Adam was on the phone when Rob walked into the office. He finished his call and, grinning, sat back in his chair. "What are you doing back here? Thought you were supposed to be doing the old anniversary tango?"

"We've got a problem," Rob told him, laying the laptop down on the desk.

"What kind of problem?" Adam asked, no longer smiling as he saw the serious look on his partner's face.

"A big one." Rob opened the screen and turned it to face him.

Adam looked at the pictures and drew his head back. "Oh. I see. Where did you get these?"

"Yvette's had a private investigator following me," Rob told him, tossing a cigarette to him and lighting one for himself. "Can you hack into the database and wipe it?"

"Doubt it," Adam said, leaning forward for a light. "These kinds of agencies tend to have everything locked down as tight as tight can be."

"We've got to do something," Rob said, pacing the floor. "It's all we've got, apart from a phone number."

Adam took a drag on his cigarette and gazed thoughtfully down at the laptop screen again. "Ring it," he said after a while. "Tell them you want to have your wife followed, and arrange for them to send someone over to the old warehouse. I doubt they go to these things mob-handed but we can take Leroy, just in case."

"No." Rob shook his head. "This is messy enough without him getting involved. It's supposed to be a woman, so even if she's got a bloke with her we should be able to handle them between the two of us."

Adam nodded and reached into his drawer for the mobile phone they used whenever they needed to make calls that couldn't be traced back to them. He handed it over to Rob, then sat back as his friend made the call.

Bill was sitting at her desk, staring at the flickering figures on her laptop screen. Clients had been coming in hard and fast over the last few weeks and she'd had little time to catch breath between handling her own cases and running Chantelle around on hers. And when she *had* managed to snatch any time to herself she'd been too exhausted to tackle the mundane tasks like bringing her accounts up to date.

Too exhausted, or too lazy?

She pondered that thought with pursed lips and decided that neither description was particularly accurate. But each was infinitely preferable to admitting that she was simply getting too old for this lark. She had been toying with the idea of training Chantelle to take over the reins when the time came to call it a day, but in light of recent events she was no longer sure that it was such a good idea.

Bill sighed and stared at the screen again, only to find that the numbers had begun to merge together. It was almost seven p.m. so she decided to give up the

355

fight and go home. The accounts could wait until morning.

She had just closed the laptop down and slipped it into its carry-case when the phone rang.

"Is this the private investigator?" a man asked when she answered.

"It is," Bill confirmed, holding the phone between her cheek and her shoulder as she reached for her handbag. "How may I help you?"

"Sorry, I've never done anything like this before." The caller sounded nervous. "I, er, want someone to follow my wife. Do you do that sort of thing?"

"We do."

"Oh, good. So, um, how does it work?"

"If you decide to go ahead," Bill said, taking her keys out of her bag and standing up to slip her coat on, "you'll be charged by the hour, and payment will be taken in full via debit or credit card before any evidence is released to you — regardless of the outcome."

"Yeah, that's fine," the man agreed. "So, when can you start? Only, I could really do with you getting onto it tonight, if possible?"

"*Tonight?*"

"Is that a problem?"

"No, no problem." Bill rolled her eyes and sat back down. She had been looking forward to an early night, but work was work so she wasn't about to turn it down. "I'll just take a few details," she said, sliding the laptop back out of its case. "And I'll need you to email me a recent photograph of your wife . . ."

# CHAPTER
# TWENTY-SEVEN

It was 8.45 when Bill turned onto the road where the client had told her his wife worked. It was way out on the outskirts of Salford, and it had been a good few miles since she'd seen any sign of life. The street lamps had become more spaced out the further out she'd come, and there were none at all in sight now, so she felt as if she'd entered tumbleweed territory as her headlights picked out the silhouetted rubbish that lined the dark undergrowth on both sides of the road.

She slowed down when she saw a low white building up ahead and peered out at it as she drew alongside the chained-up gate. There were no lights showing at the metal-grilled windows, and no sign of any vehicles in the enclosure.

Bill drove on a little way and reversed into a dark lay-by. When she had parked up she checked the address again. It was the right place, and she frowned as she gazed back across the road. The client had said that his wife worked here, and that she left at nine p.m. each night. She was supposed not to have been getting home until gone eleven and he wanted Bill to follow her to see if she'd been going for after-work drinks — and more — with her boss, as he suspected. But there was obviously some mistake here. Either he had accidentally given her the wrong address, or she'd been sent on a wild-goose chase. It wouldn't be the first time.

"Oh, well, looks like we'll be getting that early night after all," she said to Mitzy, who was lying on the passenger seat. "Want to do your business before we go?"

When the dog sat up Bill unclipped her seat belt and climbed stiffly out of the car. When the dog waddled off in search of a suitable spot, Bill stretched her aching back and strolled across to the warehouse gates. She'd just reached them when she heard a loud yelp behind her.

"Mitzy?" She turned and walked quickly back to the car. "What's the matter, girl? Have you stood on something sharp? Come to momma, let me take a look."

When no sound came back to her, Bill's heart leapt into her throat and she moved forward slowly, dreading with every step that she was about to find the dog badly injured — or worse. When she saw something move from the corner of her eye, she snapped her head around and squinted into the pitch darkness. "Mitzy . . .? Is that you, girl?"

Chantelle hadn't been able to settle after leaving Bill's office earlier that morning and she'd been wandering around like a lost soul ever since: one minute regretting her decision to expose Rob; the next, glad that she'd done it and desperate to know if he'd got his comeuppance.

His wife had to know by now, because Bill had called this afternoon to say that she had decided to send the pictures to her. She had also said that she still hadn't made up her mind about keeping Chantelle on after her breaching of the rules. But, as gutted as she would be if she was fired, Chantelle just wanted to know what was happening with Rob and Yvette. It was nine p.m. now, and Rob hadn't called since this morning. That was unusual, because he'd usually have called a couple of times by now, or at least have messaged her. She just hoped his silence meant that he had been busted.

Irritated by Chantelle's constant pacing and frenetic cleaning, Leon had taken himself off to his room after dinner to listen to music in peace. He was keeping his volume down, but Chantelle could still hear the throb of the bass through the wall and it was grating on her nerves. She'd already polished and scrubbed everything twice over, so she sat down now and switched the TV on, desperate for something to take her mind off Rob. In no mood for light-hearted programmes, she turned on the local news, and chewed on her thumbnail as she gazed at the screen.

Ten minutes passed, and she hadn't heard a single word the presenter had been saying. But when a picture flashed up on the screen now, she jerked out of her reverie and quickly turned up the volume.

"... *Twenty-year-old Mariska was reported as missing by her parents, who became concerned when she failed to contact them after leaving her home in*

**359**

Latvia to start a new life in Manchester. They believed that she had secured a job as an au pair, but police have as yet been unable to locate the couple who were set to be her new employers."

The picture changed now, and Chantelle stared at the CCTV shot of a woman who seemed to be walking through a crowded airport terminal.

"We know from this footage taken at Manchester Airport on Monday night that Mariska arrived in the country, but there have been no sightings of her since," the presenter went on. "If you have seen her, or have any information about her whereabouts, Detective Inspector Ian Peterson of Greater Manchester Police would like to hear from you on the number being displayed at the foot of the screen. There are concerns that Mariska's disappearance may be connected to that of three similar cases . . ."

When photographs of three more dark-haired girls popped up on the screen, Chantelle gasped and reached for her phone. Bill's mobile rang several times before going to voicemail and Chantelle guessed that her boss must be out on a job, because she always kept it on silent when she was working. Irritated, because she desperately wanted to speak to her, Chantelle waited for the beep and then garbled out her message.

Taken by surprise when two shadowy figures suddenly leapt out from behind a bush and rushed at her, Bill cried out in alarm and stumbled backwards, losing her footing and banging her head on the wing of the car as she went down. Dazed, she peered up at the man who was looming over her as the other one circled the car.

"What do you want?" she croaked, her heart thudding painfully in her chest. "I haven't got any money."

"I don't want your fucking money," he hissed. "I want the film."

"What film?" Bill's confusion quickly cleared when the man squatted down and she got her first good look at his face.

"You know what I'm talking about," he said. "You sent the photographs to my wife, but I want the original film they came off."

"I haven't got it," Bill said, desperately trying to appear calm. She'd been confronted by disgruntled spouses in the past and had always managed to talk them down. But she sensed that it wasn't going to be so easy this time, because Rob Knight wouldn't have gone to the trouble of luring her to this remote location if he just wanted to talk.

"So where *is* it?" Rob yelled, lashing her across the face with the back of his fist.

Bill cried out in pain, and tears spilled from her eyes as blood began to trickle from her nose. "I deleted it," she lied, grimacing as another, sharper pain rippled through her chest.

"I don't believe you." Rob seized her by the hair. "It's too convenient. Last chance — where *is* it?"

"I haven't got it," Bill repeated, her breath ragged now as she clutched a hand to her breast. "But *someone*, has," she added, looking him in the eye. "And if you kill me, the police investigation will inevitably involve them accessing my files. And how . . ." She paused and took a pained breath, before continuing through gritted teeth, "How long do you suppose it will be before they get round to questioning you?"

"Who's got it?" Rob demanded.

"I'm not telling you," Bill said bravely. "And nothing you say or do will make —" The rest of the sentence was left hanging as another agonising pain tore through her body and her teeth clamped together.

Rob watched as her eyes rolled and spittle formed bubbles at the corners of her mouth. He let go of her hair when she started to convulse, and moved back as she slid to the floor. Her legs jerked a few times, and then, releasing a sound that reminded him of a deflating bicycle tyre, she was still, her unseeing eyes staring into the darkness above his head.

"*Shit!*" Adam ran over and looked down at her. "We were supposed to do her in *after* we got it, not before, you idiot."

Rob pushed himself back up to his feet and, raking his fingers through his hair, backed away from the body. "I didn't do anything. I think she's had a fucking heart attack."

A glow of light coming from inside the car caught his eye just then, and he snapped his head around. When he saw that it was coming from a mobile phone lying on the passenger seat he yanked the door open and snatched it up.

"Voicemail," he said when he saw the message on the screen. "Probably one of her colleagues checking up on

362

her. We'd best get out of here before they come looking for her."

Adam nodded and leaned inside the car. He saw the laptop lying on the back seat and grabbed it, then did a quick search under the seats and in the glove compartment.

"Here, take this," Rob said, walking back around the car holding the jerrycan he'd just found in the boot. "Doesn't feel like there's much in it, but it should be enough to get it going. Wait till I get her behind the wheel and put some on her," he added, squatting behind the body and shoving his hands under her limp arms. "Then douse the seats and shit."

"What's that?" Adam asked when something fell from the woman's pocket as Rob hauled her up off the ground.

"How should I know?" Rob snapped, panting as he heaved the body towards the door. "You could have helped. She weighs a fucking ton."

Adam reached for the fallen item and turned it over in his hand. "Looks like one of those video recorders they sell at Bowlers," he said. "The ones that are disguised to look like mobile phones. Bloody cheap one, though; wouldn't fool me for a minute."

"Probably the one they use for surveillance," Rob said, exhaling loudly after shoving the woman's body into the driver's seat and wiping his hands on his trousers. "With any luck, the film might still be on it."

Adam slid the phone into his pocket. Then, taking the lid off the petrol can, he doused the body before shaking the rest out haphazardly around the interior of the car. He threw the can inside when he was done and stepped back as Rob sparked his lighter and touched the flame to the woman's skirt before kicking the door shut.

They waited a couple of minutes to make sure she was properly alight, then turned and ran back through the field from which they had come, at the far side of which was the secluded lane where Rob had parked his car.

Back at the unit, Rob poured two glasses of Scotch and handed one to Adam. Then, lighting a cigarette, he paced the office floor while Adam opened the PI's laptop and switched it on.

"Well?" he asked after Adam had tapped away at the keys for a while.

"Patience," his friend said quietly, a deep frown creasing his brow. "As I thought, it's password-protected and encrypted, so it may take a while. Here, check this while you're waiting." He took the videophone out of his pocket and tossed it to Rob.

Rob turned it over in his hand. "How the fuck do you switch it on?"

"Same as you'd switch on a real mobile."

Rob found the button and pressed it. The screen lit up, but his relief was short-lived when he discovered that it was empty.

"She probably downloaded the footage as soon as she'd finished a job," Adam mused. "They've got way more memory than a phone, but not enough to store a whole heap of shit *and* film new stuff. But that's good, because it means the only copy must be on here. Unless," he added grimly, "the company has a bank of computers which all receive the same data."

"Fucking hope not," Rob said worriedly. "If they have, we're screwed."

"Speaking optimistically," said Adam, his focus back on the laptop, "I'd hazard a guess that it was a one-woman operation. No respectable agency would hire an old boot like her. She had to have been a lone wolf."

"She said someone else had the footage," Rob reminded him.

"Probably bluffing."

"What about the voicemail? There must be at least one other person working with her."

"Not necessarily. Could have been her hubby wondering why she wasn't home yet. But there's only one way to find out."

Rob pulled the mobile out of his pocket and listened to the voicemail.

"*Bill, it's Chantelle,*" a girl's voice machine-gunned down his ear. "*I know you're still annoyed with me, but I've just been watching the news and they showed some pictures of missing women. I know it sounds crazy, but I'm sure I've seen two of them with Rob; one last night, and the other on the first job. Please call me back when you get this.*"

"What the *fuck* . . ." Rob pulled the phone away from his ear and stared at it in disbelief.

"What's up, bud?" Adam looked up as he slotted a password-retrieval disc into the laptop's CD drive.

"No, that can't be right." Rob shook his head. Then, looking at his friend, he said, "It sounded exactly like Julia — that girl I've been seeing."

"Really?" Adam frowned. "Are you sure?"

"Course I'm not fucking sure," Rob snapped. "I said it *sounds* like her."

"Play it again, on loudspeaker," Adam said, reaching for a pen. As the message began to play, he wrote down the number of the sender and pushed it across the desk. "Check it against Julia's."

Rob pulled his own phone out of his pocket and compared the numbers. "It fucking *is* her," he said, the blood draining from his face when he saw that they matched. "Only her name's not Julia, it's Chantelle. *Bitch!*" He spat the word out. "I've been seeing her for *months;* treated her like a fucking princess, and all the time she's been *spying* on me. Christ, she reeled me right in with that sweet and innocent act. And here's the best bit," he added indignantly. "When I first saw her I was planning on bringing her into the ring. But I liked her, so I changed my fucking mind."

"Oh, my," Adam murmured. "Seems the player has been well and truly played."

"Yeah, very funny," Rob said angrily. "Now what the fuck are we supposed to do? You heard her — she saw those tarts on the news. And how would she have recognised them if she hadn't seen them? I thought she sounded weird when she rang me at the club last night. She must have been outside, waiting to catch me out."

"All right, calm down," Adam said, reaching for his drink. He took a swig and wiped his mouth on the back of his hand. "Right, if it *was* her, then she must have filmed you on her phone, because the quality of those last shots is terrible compared with the earlier ones. Chances are she'll still have it, so we need to get it off her."

"How?" Rob demanded. "I never even got her fucking address. What an idiot!" he hissed, slapping his forehead with his hand. "I thought I was being clever, keeping things casual, but I played right into her hands."

"Ring her," said Adam. "Arrange to meet her."

"She's not going to take my calls now she thinks I'm involved with those girls going missing," Rob reminded him. "And she definitely won't meet me — she's not that stupid."

"Okay, well, she's waiting for the investigator to call her back," Adam said thoughtfully. "Call her on *that* phone."

"What, and pretend to be a woman?" Rob gave him a *get real* look.

"Text her, then," said Adam. "Tell her you can't talk because you're still working, then ask her what's going on."

Chantelle jumped when her phone's text alert suddenly beeped, and when she saw Bill's name on the screen she snatched it up.

*Just got your message, but can't talk yet, still busy,* the text read. *What's happened?*

*I saw some girls on the news,* Chantelle replied, repeating what she'd already said in the voicemail.

*They've been reported missing, and the police think
they're connected to a few more cases. One looked like
the girl Rob was with last night, and another like the
first girl I saw him with. What should we do?*

*Nothing!* Bill's answer came through quickly. *I'll look
into it, and if I think you're right I'll call the police.
Probably turn out to be nothing, but I'll need your
phone in case they want to see the film. You have still
got it, haven't you?*

*Yeah, was going to delete it, but forgot. Where do
you want to meet? Chorlton Road or office?*

*Chorlton Road. And don't tell anybody anything.*

*I won't. I know I was stupid about the whole Rob
thing, but it'll never happen again, I promise. You can
trust me.*

*Hope so. See you in 20.*

Chantelle was glad that Bill had taken her seriously,
although she was already starting to doubt that the girls
she'd seen on TV could be the ones she'd seen with
Rob because it just seemed too far-fetched. Even if they
were, she seriously doubted that Rob had anything to
do with their disappearance. As much as it hurt to
know that he'd used her, he had always been an
absolute gentleman so there was no way he could be
involved in something like that. More likely he'd met
them and charmed his way into their knickers — just as
he had with her. They probably weren't even missing
but had just decided not to bother taking the jobs they
had come over for, choosing instead to let rich men like
Rob pay their way.

Annoyed with herself for letting her imagination run away with her, Chantelle went out into the hall and pulled her boots on. Then, tapping on Leon's door, she popped her head around and gave him a guilty smile when she saw him lying on his bed with his arms behind his head.

"Sorry for chasing you out before," she apologised. "I've been in a weird mood all day, but I'm going for a walk to shake myself out of it. Will you be all right while I'm gone? Shouldn't be too long."

"Yeah, I'm cool," Leon grunted, adding under his breath, "So long as you've cheered up when you get back. Can't be doing with all these girly mood swings."

Amused that he was putting her moodiness down to hormones, Chantelle let herself out of the flat and walked quickly down the stairs.

She had almost reached the end of the road and was about to cross over to the corner where Bill always picked her up. When she saw an all-too-familiar car sitting directly opposite, she stopped in her tracks. Oh, no, what was he doing here? Had he been trying to call her to let her know that he wanted to meet up, and she hadn't heard it because she was walking?

Chantelle slid her phone out of her pocket to check, and was confused when she saw that there were no missed calls or texts. She'd told Rob that she lived behind the shops he was facing, but he surely couldn't just be sitting there on the off chance that she might walk past?

Unless Yvette had kicked him out and he'd left his phone behind and hadn't been able to call her?

In which case, had he come to tell her that he was now free to be with her, or had he somehow found out that she was behind the photographs being sent to his wife?

Rob suddenly turned his head and looked straight at her, the hairs on the back of Chantelle's neck stood on end when she saw the rage in his eyes. And when his headlights immediately came on and she heard the roar of his engine as he pressed his foot to the floor, her instincts screamed at her to run — and, remembering Bill's warning never to ignore her instincts, she turned and fled back the way she'd come.

Terrified when she realised he was really close behind, Chantelle detoured down an alley between the houses she was passing and raced through the backstreets. In her panic, she dived down another alley, but this one was blocked off at the other end. It was too late to go back out into the open, so she forced her way through a half-open back gate into a pitch-dark yard and squatted down in the shadows.

A couple of minutes later she heard footsteps walking past slowly and bit down on her hand when she heard Rob calling softly, "Julia . . .? Where are you?"

The footsteps faded as he walked to the other end of the alley, but then became louder again as he came back. They stopped a short distance away from the yard and Chantelle squeezed her eyes shut and prayed that he would think he'd lost her and go. When his phone suddenly started to ring, she held her breath and cocked her head to listen.

"Yeah, I saw her, but she did a runner," he said quietly. "She can't have got far, though, 'cos I was right behind her." He paused now, obviously listening to what his caller was saying. Then, sounding jubilant, he said, "Oh, you fucking genius!"

When his footsteps moved briskly away now, Chantelle stayed put, afraid that he was trying to lure her out of her hiding place by making her think he'd gone. She heard a car door slam shut in the near distance, but decided to give it a few more minutes before she risked breaking cover.

"Right, what is it?" Rob asked when he'd started the car and had the sat-nav ready to type in the address that Adam had found after finally managing to hack into the PI's laptop.

"Four thirty Mayfield Court," Adam told him. "What are you going to do?"

"Go and get her," said Rob, peering at the sat-nav screen. "Christ, it's literally around the corner," he said when the route had been calculated. "No wonder I couldn't find her, she was probably already home."

"You can't just go round there," Adam cautioned. "She told you she lived alone, but she's lied about everything else, so she could live with mummy, daddy, and four strapping brothers, for all we know."

"So what am I supposed to do?" Rob asked irritably. "I can't just leave her with that film, or we can kiss goodbye to everything."

Adam thought it over for a minute, then said, "Okay, she thought she was supposed to be meeting her boss to hand her phone over, so text her again . . ."

Chantelle was about to come out of hiding when her phone beeped. Trembling all over at the thought of what would have happened if Rob had still been standing outside the yard, she pulled the phone out of her pocket and saw that it was a text from Bill.

*Sorry couldn't get there, still working,* it read. *Are you okay?*

*I am now,* Chantelle answered. *Rob saw me and chased me, but I got away. About to go home, but don't want to risk coming out again tonight in case he's still hanging about. Can we meet in morning instead?*

*Of course. Have you called police?*

*No. Do you think I should?*

*Absolutely not!* came the quick reply. *We need to know what we're dealing with first. Is anyone going to be with you when you get home?*

*My little brother, but Rob doesn't know address, so we'll be okay.*

*Good! Stay safe, see you in morning x*

Chantelle smiled when she read the last message. It was the first time Bill had ever put a kiss at the end of a text, and it was nice to know that the woman cared about her as a person and not just as an employee. She was so glad that Bill wasn't still angry with her for flouting the rules, and she prayed that she would get the chance to work with her again so she could make it up to her.

She checked the time now and then slid the phone back into her pocket. Rob had been gone for a few minutes, but she would wait a few more to make sure that he wasn't still driving around.

# CHAPTER
# TWENTY-EIGHT

Leon turned his music down when he heard a knock at the front door and crept out into the hall. He hadn't seen Damo and Acky since that day with the gun, and Anton had promised that it was sorted. But Chantelle wasn't the only one who was scared that they might just be biding their time, and so he was always nervous whenever he was alone in the flat at night.

He peeped out through the spyhole and called, "Who is it?" when he saw a white man he'd never seen before on the step.

Rob had been looking around to make sure that no one was watching. He turned to face the door when he heard the voice and, expression serious, said, "Sorry to call round so late, son, but does Chantelle live here? Only there's been an accident, and —"

Leon yanked the door open before the man could finish his sentence and gazed at him in dread. "Is she all right? What's happened?"

"She was hit by a car," Rob told him, assessing that he was around ten or eleven years of age. "Look, is there anyone else here?" he asked, needing to make sure that Chantelle had been telling the truth about the kid being alone. "Mum or dad?"

"No, just me." Leon was visibly shaking. "Where is she?"

"She's been taken to hospital," Rob told him. "I'm Detective Inspector Jones." He pulled out his wallet and quickly flashed his credit cards, sure that the boy wouldn't be able to see any details in the dim light. "I'll be going over there in a minute, but she asked for somebody to come and let you know. I can take you over there, if you like."

"Thanks," Leon said without hesitation, his concern for his sister overriding any suspicion that he might have ordinarily felt about a stranger turning up in the middle of the night and claiming to be a copper. "I'll just get my shoes and coat."

Rob took another look around when the boy rushed back inside to get his things. Nobody was about, and he was pretty sure there were no CCTV cameras covering the area. Adam was a genius for telling him to ask Julia, or rather *Chantelle*, if she'd be alone when she got home. Left to his own devices, Rob would have dived in head first and potentially got himself slaughtered. But once he'd heard that the boy was alone it was simply a matter of getting to the flat before her. She obviously had no intention of facing him, and would probably have called the police by now if her boss hadn't told her not to — and no doubt *would* call them as soon as her boss's body was discovered, which could be any time now. But if she realised that her brother was in danger she wouldn't dare open her trap. Rob just had to get her to come to him so there would be no witnesses when she handed the phone over.

Leon's eyes widened when he and the detective walked out from under the block a couple of minutes later and he saw the car they were heading for. "Is that *yours?*"

"Sure is," Rob said, smiling when he heard the awe in the boy's voice. "I take it you like cars?"

"Love them," Leon affirmed, looking the car over as Rob unlocked the doors. "It's *mint*. Must have cost a bomb."

"Probably," said Rob, opening the passenger-side door for him. "Luckily, I didn't have to pay for it, because the force picks up the tab," he added after closing the boy's door and going around to the other side.

"Wow, I'm gonna be a copper if they give you motors like this to drive," Leon said, awed all over again by the car's luxurious interior.

"Good for you," Rob said approvingly as he locked the doors.

"Which hospital's she at?" Leon asked when they set off.

"Trafford General," Rob lied, smiling as he drove away from the flats. Nobody had seen him and the boy together, he was sure, so it wouldn't be long before this whole sorry mess was cleared up and he and Adam could get back to business.

Chantelle missed Rob's car by just seconds as she scuttled around the corner with her head down and walked quickly towards the flats. Her heart was beating wildly as she rushed up the stairs, and she was flooded with relief when she let herself in. She slammed the door shut and then leaned her back against it for several moments to catch her breath.

Leon's bedroom door was open, the light spilling out into the otherwise dark hall. Calmer now, Chantelle popped her head inside to check on him. He wasn't there and, guessing that he must be in the bathroom, she walked up the hall and tapped on the door.

"Are you going to be long in there, 'cos I really need the loo."

When no answer came, she tried the door, and was surprised when it opened. After going to the toilet, she went into the living room to see if Leon was in there. When she saw that he wasn't, she checked the kitchen, and then her own and her mum's bedrooms, before going back to Leon's room.

"Are you hiding?" she asked, looking around. Then, frowning, she said, "Leon, just come out, this isn't funny any more."

When he didn't pop out of the wardrobe, and she heard no give-away giggles, she began to feel scared. Leon had hardly left the flat since all that stuff with the gang, apart from to go to and from school, and he still hadn't made up with Kermit, so she couldn't think where he might have gone. She just hoped he hadn't taken it into his head to go looking for her. Rob wouldn't know him if he saw him, but there were plenty of freaks out there who would love to get their hands on a cute kid like him.

"Okay, stop it," she scolded herself as her imagination began to run away with her. Leon was young but he wasn't stupid, so there was no way he would be wandering the streets at this time of night. If he was worried about her, he would probably have gone to see Anton, she reasoned. The man was his hero, so it was the logical place to start looking for him.

Anton was in bed but not yet asleep. He'd been out earlier, playing snooker with the lads. But he was working in the morning, so when they had gone on to a club in town he had opted to come home instead.

Thinking that it was probably Shotz when he heard a knock at the front door, he pulled on his dressing gown before going to let him in. His friend had been pretty wrecked when he'd left him, so the dude was bound to be smashed out of his skull by now and in need of a place to crash, because he wouldn't want to face his ma while he was in a state.

He drew his head back in surprise when he saw that it was Chantelle and not Shotz. He had seen her a couple of times since he'd helped her and her brother out that day, but only in passing, so it was a pleasant surprise to see her now.

"Hey." He smiled. "Long time no see, stranger."

"Sorry, am I disturbing you?" Chantelle asked when she saw that he was dressed for bed.

"Not at all." He stepped back. "Come in."

"Thanks." She walked into the hall.

Anton closed the door and gave her a questioning look when he saw the worry in her eyes. "You okay?"

"Not really," Chantelle said quietly. "I can't find Leon. You haven't seen him, have you?"

"Not for a while, no," Anton told her. "When did he go out?"

"Not long ago," Chantelle said, her concerns growing. "I went for a walk, and he was in his room when I left, but he was gone when I got back. I just hope he hasn't gone looking for me." She exhaled shakily now, and bit her lip. Then, figuring that there was no point keeping Anton from his bed, she said, "I'd best go and look for him. Sorry for getting you up."

"It's no problem," Anton assured her. Then, glancing at his watch, he said, "Look, give me a minute to get dressed and I'll come with you. It's too late for you to be walking around on your own."

"No, it's all right." Chantelle shook her head. "Honestly, I'll be fine."

"I insist," Anton said firmly, giving her a stern look to let her know that he wasn't taking no for an answer.

Chantelle didn't want to put him out, but she couldn't deny that she would feel safer with him by her side in light of what had just happened with Rob. So, smiling gratefully, she said, "Okay, thanks."

Anton had just turned to go to his room when her phone rang. She slid it out of her pocket and was relieved to see Bill's name on the screen, and not Rob's, as she had half expected.

"Hi, Bill," she said wearily. "Look, I'm really sorry, but can I call you back in a bit? Only my brother's gone missing, and I need to find him."

"Don't worry about Leon, he's quite safe," Rob said smoothly.

Chantelle was so shocked that she let out a little cry and almost dropped her phone. Anton heard it and turned back. "*You all right?*" he mouthed.

She nodded quickly and, taking a deep breath, croaked, "How did you get Bill's phone?"

"You're a smart girl, I'm sure you'll figure it out," Rob said. "Now listen carefully, because I'm only going to say this once. I've got Leon, and if you ever want to see him again you're going to have to come and get him."

"Where is he?" Chantelle's face had completely drained of colour by now. "What have you done to him?"

"Nothing — *yet*," said Rob. "But if you don't give me what I want, I'll kill him."

"Don't you dare touch him," Chantelle cried. "I've called the police. They'll be here any minute."

"No, you haven't," Rob said calmly. "Who do you think sent you those texts telling you not to? Anyway, enough of the small talk. I want that film, so be a good girl and fetch it to me, and I'll think about letting little brother come home."

"What film?" Chantelle asked, fear for Leon making her temporarily forget what had precipitated this nightmare.

"Don't play games with me!" Rob yelled, losing patience. "You've got it on your fucking phone, and I want it. Now, you either do as you're told, or I swear to God your brother and your boss won't be the only ones who die tonight!"

"Okay!" Chantelle cried. "I'll bring it. Where are you?"

"Usual place, half an hour," Rob told her. "But I'll be watching before I pick you up, to make sure you haven't done anything stupid. Do you understand?"

"Yes, and I won't — I promise."

When the phone went dead in her hand now, Chantelle turned and fumbled with the door lock.

"Hey, wait up," Anton said, rushing to her. He had no clue who she'd been talking to just now, but it was clear from what she had said that the caller was connected to Leon having gone missing, and he wasn't about to let her go running off into danger if she was being threatened.

"I've got to go," Chantelle insisted, still trying to open the door.

"Not until you tell me what's going on," Anton said, holding her by the shoulders and looking down into her tear-filled eyes.

"I can't," she sobbed. "It's too dangerous."

Anton's brow was deeply furrowed by now. "Is this something to do with that gang? 'Cos if it is, I'll —"

"It's nothing to do with them," she blurted out. "It's . . ." She trailed off and shook her head, still struggling to take it in herself. "Look, all I can tell you is he's got Leon and my boss, and he won't let them go until I do as he says."

"Right, well, I'm definitely not letting *you* go until you fill me in properly," said Anton. "Whatever's going down, it sounds like heavy shit, and you can't deal with it on your own."

Chantelle squeezed her eyes shut and bit down hard on her lip. He was right: this was too heavy for her to deal with. But Rob had Leon and Bill, and she couldn't take the risk of calling the police because he'd said that he would kill them both if she did. Rob obviously knew that she was behind those pictures getting to his wife, but there had to be more to it than that because this was way too drastic to be just about the film.

"Talk to me." Anton's soft voice cut into her thoughts.

Chantelle gazed up at him. She could see that he was worried about her, and if she insisted on leaving he would probably only follow her, which would make everything ten times worse because Rob was bound to see him. So, hoping that he would understand why she had to do this alone, she told him the whole story, her cheeks flaring with shame when she reached the part about having started an affair with Rob behind his wife's back.

"That's why I've got to go," she said when she'd finished. "So please just let me do this."

"No chance," Anton said fiercely. "There's no way you're meeting up with the dude on your own."

"You're not listening," Chantelle said with desperation in her voice. "He'll kill Leon and Bill if I don't go to him. All I have to do is give him my phone and this will all be over."

"You don't believe that any more than I do."

"Okay, fine!" Chantelle flapped her hands in a gesture of exasperation. "So, what do you want me to do? Call the police?"

"Absolutely not." Anton gave a derisive snort. "Those fuckers wouldn't have a clue how to deal with this."

"Oh, but I suppose *you* would?" Chantelle was getting angry now. He was trying to help, but he was just delaying her, and she couldn't bear to think what might happen to Leon and Bill if she didn't meet Rob in time.

"Not on my own," said Anton.

He took her by the arm now, to make sure she didn't do a runner while his back was turned, and led her into his bedroom. Then, after sitting her down on the bed, he picked his phone up off the bedside table and reached for his jeans, dialling Shotz's number with one hand as he pulled his pants on with the other.

"Yo, it's me," he said when his friend answered after several rings. "Where you at, bro?"

"Barney's," Shotz told him, shouting over the loud drum 'n' bass music that Anton could hear in the background. "Place is poppin' with *nuff* g'yal dem. You shoulda come, bro."

"Nah, I've got work tomorrow," Anton reminded him.

"So, wha's up?" Shotz asked.

"Nothing," Anton lied. "Just thought you might have got home by now. I'll see you tomorrow, yeah?"

He cut Shotz off now and brought up another number, then stared at it for several seconds before jabbing his thumb down on the call button.

"Wha'pp'n, blud?" Big T drawled when he answered.

"I need a favour," Anton told him straight out. "And I need it fast."

"Oh yeah?"

Anton squeezed his eyes shut. There was going to be a huge price to pay for this, but what choice did he have?

"I need wheels and backup."

"When?" Big T asked without hesitation.

"Now," said Anton. "I'll explain when you get here."

# CHAPTER
# TWENTY-NINE

"Nice place," Big T said when he walked into Anton's living room fifteen minutes later. Then, his gaze falling on Chantelle who was chewing her nails on one of the beanbags, he gave her a slow smile. "Hey, pretty lady, how you doin'?"

"She's scared shitless for her bro," Anton answered for her, sensing that she wasn't in the mood to make small talk with an enormous stranger. "We haven't got much time," he went on. Then, frowning when he noticed Jacko giving him a sly look, he said, "Yo, if you've got a problem being here, you can fuck off, bro."

"He ain't got a problem," Big T drawled, lighting a fat spliff he'd just pulled out of his pocket. "You're back where you belong, and if anyone got beef, they best be tekkin' it up with me," he added, confirming Anton's fear that the fee for helping him out was for Anton to come back into the crew. "Anyone got anything to say?" he asked now, looking from one to the other of the four soldiers he'd brought along.

"Nah, we's all cool," a lad called Foxy said, grinning as he touched fists with Anton. "Good to have you back, bruv."

After the others, Jacko included, had shown their respect for Anton, Big T said, "So, what's the score?"

Anton briefly explained the situation, ending with, "She's to meet the dude in ten minutes down by the Whalley, and he's going to be watching out for five-o, so we can't be seen."

"No problem," said Big T. Then, gazing down at Chantelle again, he said, "We got your back, darlin', so don't be frettin' about your bro no more. Me and Ant go *way* back, and any friend of his is a friend of ours. This dude won't know what 'it 'im by the time we done."

"I just don't want Leon and Bill to get hurt," Chantelle croaked, already scared that it was all going to go horribly wrong.

"They won't," Anton assured her, squatting in front of her and pulling her into his arms. "Trust us," he whispered as he held her. "We've got this."

He sounded so confident — Chantelle desperately wanted to believe him. "Okay." She nodded. "Just tell me what to do."

Rob was drumming his fingers on the steering wheel, but he stopped abruptly when he spotted a figure in the distance. He squinted out through the window and muttered, "About fucking time" when he saw that it was Chantelle.

He had parked in a completely different place than the last time and knew that she couldn't see him as he watched her cross the road and make her way to the corner where he'd said he would pick her up. There was

**386**

a fair bit of traffic on the roads tonight, but he'd been sitting here for a while now and he hadn't seen any police cars. Still, he stayed put now — just to be on the safe side.

Unaware that Rob was staring at her from his hiding place on the other side of the road, Chantelle was shivering from head to toe as she waited on the corner. Anton and his friends had promised that they would be nearby, but she couldn't see them anywhere and she was terrified that they would miss Rob picking her up and lose her.

When ten minutes had passed she started to feel sick. Scared that Rob had somehow guessed that she'd told somebody and had decided not to come for her, she pulled her phone out of her pocket. But just as she was about to ring him, he suddenly pulled up alongside her.

"Get in," he ordered, pushing open the passenger door.

Chantelle swallowed hard and cast a surreptitious glance back up the road. She still couldn't see Anton's friend's Range Rover, but she had no choice but to go ahead and get into the car.

Rob locked the doors when she was in and quickly set off, his gaze flicking from the wing mirrors to the rear-view, on the alert for suspicious-looking vehicles that might be following.

Chantelle pressed herself up against the door and nervously twisted her hands together in her lap. Rob looked furious, and she was sure that he would probably beat her once they had reached wherever he was taking her. But that was okay, so long as he didn't hurt Leon or Bill. She deserved it, they didn't.

"I'm sorry," she murmured as he drove out through Chorlton and headed towards Stretford.

"Too late," Rob replied icily, his gaze fixed on the road ahead.

"I only did it because you hurt me," she said quietly. "I saw you with that girl, and just wanted to get back at you."

"Don't make me laugh." Rob gave a contemptuous snort. "You've been stringing me along for months, so don't pretend it was some great love affair. Sleeping with suspects part of your job description, was it?"

"No!" Chantelle protested. "You were the only one. I've never slept with anyone else," she added, blushing fiercely even though he wasn't looking at her.

Rob gave a humourless laugh. "Oh, that's fucking classic, that is. So now you're claiming you were a virgin?"

"I was," Chantelle said truthfully. "I really loved you."

"Yeah, you loved me so much you thought you'd fuck me right over."

"I'm sorry."

"Oh, shut up, I'm sick of listening to you," Rob snapped. "Never noticed how whiny your voice is before, but it's like fingernails on a fucking chalkboard."

Chantelle fell silent and glanced surreptitiously in the wing mirror as Rob drove on. Her heart lurched when she saw a large vehicle some way behind, and she said a silent prayer to God to *please* let it be Anton and his friends.

"Hurry up," Anton said, struggling to keep the car they were following in his sights as Trey nonchalantly allowed another car to cut in front of them.

"Want me to get right up his arse and blow our cover?" Big T asked, sticking to the speed he'd been doing all along.

Anton inhaled deeply and shook his head. "Nah. Sorry, just freaking out."

"Chill, bro." Big T passed over the spliff he'd been smoking.

Anton wasn't in the mood for getting wrecked, but he needed something to calm him down or he was going to go crazy.

"Yo, he's indicating to go left," Jacko piped up from the back seat, where he was squashed up against the door behind Anton's seat.

"Me can see," Big T drawled. "Seckle down an' let me concentrate."

They drove on for a few more miles, keeping a fair distance between them and the car that was carrying Chantelle. But when the car suddenly swerved into an industrial estate Big T drove straight on.

"Yo, what you doing?" Anton demanded, staring at Big T in disbelief when the man turned onto a side road some way further down and turned the car around before cutting the lights. "We're gonna lose them."

"There's only one way in and out of that place," Big T told him unconcernedly. "He might've turned off to shake us, so we'll sit here for a minute to make sure he don't come back out. If he don't, we'll know where he is — seen?"

"Seen." Anton nodded and blew out an agitated breath. He was already edgy, and it wasn't helping that he could feel Jacko burning holes into the back of his head with dirty looks. The others were cool with him, but Jacko had taken against him big time after he left the crew and his hatred had obviously increased after Anton had faced him down outside Trey's house that day. But the guy was going to have to suck it up quick style, because they would be seeing a lot of each other from here on in.

His heart sinking all over again at the thought that he'd effectively sold his soul to Trey, Anton gazed out through the windscreen and reminded himself of why he'd done it. Chantelle and Leon were in danger, and there was no one else to help them.

The industrial estate was deserted, and Chantelle's fear increased as they drove past all the closed-up units. There were few street lights, and those which were actually working cast just a dim orange glow on the ground beneath them. There were no other cars in sight and she guessed that Anton's friend must have lost them a while back. Without them she was as good as dead, and the realisation settled over her like a lead weight.

All she could think about was Leon, and his future was flashing before her eyes in exactly the way that she'd heard a dying person's life flashed before theirs.

**390**

He acted tough but he was just a baby, and he would be totally lost without Chantelle to look after him. The authorities would probably contact their mum to let her know, but they would never give her custody of Leon once they found out that she had abandoned him. He would go from home to home from now until he was sixteen, and everyone knew that was a one-way street for kids like him. Angry and upset, he would be written off as a problem child — and that would inevitably turn him into one.

Chantelle snapped out of her dread thoughts when Rob suddenly pulled to a stop. She saw that they were outside a unit at the far end of the industrial estate and she shivered when he pressed a key fob and the gates began to slide back. Before they were halfway open, a bright light suddenly sliced through the darkness, and she was flooded with relief when she saw a vehicle in the distance heading their way.

"You fucking bitch," Rob gasped, his mouth falling open when he too saw the lights.

Chantelle cried out in fear when he reached under his seat and pulled out a long knife. "*No!*" she screamed, making a grab for it as he thrust it towards her. She screamed again as the knife sliced through the flesh of her hand and blood spurted out.

"I should slit your fucking throat," Rob hissed, glaring at her. Then, glancing back at the car that was hurtling towards them, he realised it was too late and leapt out of the car.

# CHAPTER
# THIRTY

Adam was in the office when he heard the commotion. Terrified that Perry's boys had come looking for their boss when he checked the CCTV monitor and saw several men heading for the door, with Rob being dragged along behind, he grabbed his keys and ran to the back door. But his hands were shaking so badly that he dropped the keys on his first attempt, and by the time he'd picked them up and found the right one again the men were inside.

"It wasn't me," he yelped, dropping to his knees and covering his head with his arms when the door burst open behind him and two men rushed into the hallway. "It was Rob. He killed Perry and the girl! I told him not to, but I couldn't stop him — you've got to believe me."

"That right?" A sly smile lifted Big T's lips as his huge frame filled the doorway. This had started out as a favour to Anton, but it was starting to sound like a way to earn himself a heap of hush money. He strolled up to the cowering man now and, reaching down, yanked him back up to his feet. "Start singing, blud!"

It was fifteen minutes before Rob regained consciousness. He'd been so convinced that it was the police

392

when he saw the vehicle coming at them that he had jumped out of the car and started legging it. But he had stood no chance of getting away and the last thing he remembered before he went down was a tremendous, blinding pain as he was struck by something hard on the back of the head.

His head was throbbing painfully now, and he groaned as he peeled his eyes open. The room was spinning and it took several seconds before his vision steadied enough for him to recognise that he was in his office. That confused him, because he'd been sure that he would either be in hospital or a police cell.

The overhead light was switched off, and the only illumination was coming from Adam's desk lamp. When he saw a silhouetted figure in the shadows on the other side of the desk, he licked his dry lips and croaked, "That you, Adam?"

"'Fraid not."

Alarmed to hear a voice he didn't recognise, Rob tried to move but realised quickly that he was tied to the chair he was sitting on.

"What's going on?" he asked, straining against the cord that was binding his hands. "Who are you?"

"That don't concern you," Anton said quietly.

"Where's Adam?"

"Gone."

Rob gave a sneering smile. "Big mistake, that. He'll be back any minute with backup."

"Wouldn't bank on it," Anton said unconcernedly as he rose from his seat and walked around the desk. "See, your mate seemed to think we were looking for someone called Perry and he totally gave you up. We know all about the dude you stabbed, the girl you OD'd, *and* the old bird you set on fire. You're quite the little serial killer, innit?"

"Where is he?" Rob demanded furiously. "I'll kill him!"

"Probably on his way to the airport, if he's got any sense."

"So, what are you going to do with me?"

"Dunno." Anton shrugged. "Haven't decided yet."

"Well, I suggest you hurry up," Rob said through gritted teeth as he tried again to free his hands.

"Yo, chill out!" Anton warned. "Don't wanna go cutting your wrists now, do you?"

Rob glared up at him. "You do know you're dead when I get out of here, don't you?"

"And what makes you think you're getting out?" Anton goaded.

Rob held his stare for several long moments. Then, inhaling deeply to regain composure, he said, "All right, what are you after? Money? I can give you money. How much? Name it!"

"Behave!" Anton kissed his teeth in disgust. "I don't need your money, man. That ain't got nutt'n to do with this."

"Oh, I see . . ." Rob's lip curled up when it suddenly occurred to him what was really going on here. "It's *her*, isn't it? So, what is she? Your bird?"

"Nah, man, she's my homegirl," Anton informed him.

"*Homegirl?*" Rob repeated, sneering up at the boy. "You lot crack me up, you really do. You strut around like gangsters, trying to put the fear of God into us *whiteys*, but one sniff of pussy and you roll over like dogs in heat. And I wouldn't even mind if she was worth it." He paused and gave the youth a sly grin before adding, "You do know *I've* had her, right? And if I snapped my fingers she'd come running without giving you a second thought. Know why? 'Cos I'm everything you *wish* you were."

Anton stepped directly in front of the chair and leaned down to look Rob square in the eye. "Finished?"

Rob gave a slow smile when he saw the sweat beads trickling down the boy's face. He'd thought it was the police coming after him when he'd first seen the car, but Julia, or Chantelle, or whoever she was, had obviously had her puppy dog following them all along. And now the kid was playing the hero defending the honour of the damsel in distress.

"You seem like a smart lad," he said, changing tack and playing for time. "And I'm guessing you've got ambitions beyond just being a big fish on whatever piss-puddle estate you come from."

"What you on about?" Anton demanded.

"I'm on about you wising up before this goes too far," said Rob. "I get why you're doing this, and I kind of admire you for having the balls to try and pull it off. But you haven't really thought it through, have you? I mean, you've got me here — but what now? You gonna kill me? Then what?"

**395**

Anton raised his foot and gave the chair a shove, sending it and Rob thudding to the floor. Then, stepping forward, he stood over his captive who lay winded beneath him, a grimace of pain on his face as his full weight pressed down on his bound hands.

"Know your problem, mate? You give it too much of that." Anton made a chatterbox gesture with his hand. "Blokes like you think money can talk you out of anything, but your dosh don't mean klish to me."

"So what *do* you fucking want?" Rob yelled. "I'm getting fucking sick of this, so just do what you're going to do, or get smart and let me go. But make it quick, 'cos I'm sure we've both got better things to do than argue the toss over a tart."

Anton peered down at him thoughtfully for several long moments. Then, pushing his lips out, he said, "Yeah, you're right."

"Hallelujah!" Rob exhaled wearily. Then, giving Anton a questioning look when he didn't move, he said, "Untie me, then."

Anton carried on looking down at him as if he was giving the command consideration. Then, shaking his head, he reached into his pocket, and said, "Nah . . . I don't think so."

# CHAPTER
# THIRTY-ONE

"That's all for now," the police officer said, closing his notebook and pushing it into his top pocket. "But we will need you to come to the station to make a full statement at some point. Someone will contact you in the next few days to arrange it."

He stood up now and nodded down at Chantelle's hand, which a paramedic had bandaged a short time earlier. "Good luck with that."

"Thanks," she murmured, smiling wanly as he nodded goodbye and jumped out of the back of the ambulance.

Anton had been standing outside with Leon while Chantelle was being interviewed. They both hopped in now and Anton took the officer's vacated seat while Leon went and sat beside his sister.

"They said we can come to the hospital with you," he told her. "How are you feeling?"

"Okay," Chantelle lied, looping her uninjured arm around Leon's shoulders. "They reckon I need stitches, but it's nothing compared to what could have happened."

"*BITCH!*" Rob's furious voice shot through the ambulance's open back doors just then, and Chantelle cried out in fear when she looked round and saw two officers escorting him to a waiting van.

"You're going to pay for this!" Rob yelled, straining against his handcuffs as his captors dragged him past. "However long it takes, I swear to God you're going to fucking pay!"

"Shut it!" one of the officers barked, elbowing him in the ribs before hurling him into the back of the van.

"Ignore him," Anton said, reaching over and putting a reassuring hand on Chantelle's knee. "He ain't going to be out for a long time."

Chantelle nodded and hugged Leon tightly to her.

Anton gazed at them and smiled sadly. They had been through so much in the short time he'd known them, and he couldn't get his head around the fact that Chantelle had been struggling along on her own for all that time. Their mother needed stringing up for abandoning them like that, but at least they still had each other.

Chantelle looked up just then and blushed when she saw the way he was looking at her. Then, casting a quick glance outside, to make sure that none of the officers were standing within hearing distance, she whispered, "Where did your friends go?"

"Don't worry about them," Anton replied quietly. "Your man's mate gave them a whole heap of cash and drugs in exchange for letting him go, so I told them to get off. There's tons of shit stored in there, so even if the dude gets off with the other shit — which he *won't* — he'll get life for supplying half of Manchester with gear."

He paused now and looked from Chantelle to Leon before adding, more quietly still, "Just don't forget what I said when the police question you: I followed you on my own when he dragged you into his car, and I knocked him out and tied him up. You didn't see no one else. Yeah?"

When Chantelle and Leon both nodded, Anton pushed himself to his feet. "Right, I'm going to have a quick fag and I'll check if they're ready to go yet while I'm at it. He's wiped." He nodded towards Leon, whose eyes were beginning to close.

"I know." Chantelle's chin wobbled as she stroked Leon's hair. "He's had a rough night, poor thing. I'm just so glad he didn't get hurt."

"He's tougher than you think." Anton reached down and gently stroked a tear from her cheek. "Stop worrying. It's all going to be okay — I promise."

Chantelle closed her eyes when Anton hopped out of the ambulance and wandered off to have his smoke. She had been so sure that Rob was going to kill her when he pulled out that knife, and, after hearing what his friend had said when Anton and his friends had caught him trying to escape, she knew that he would have done it. She was still shocked to the core to know that Rob had cold-bloodedly killed three people, and it broke her heart to know that Bill had been one of them.

Fresh tears began to stream from her closed eyes as she thought about how terrified her friend must have been. She wished she could tell Bill that she was sorry for getting her involved in this mess, and she'd have given anything to be able to tell her how much she admired and respected her. Bill had been a strange woman, but her gruff, scruffy exterior had hidden a razor-sharp mind and a heart of gold. Chantelle had never met anybody quite like her before, and she doubted she ever would again.

Anton was another one who had earned her absolute respect and gratitude tonight, and she couldn't believe how badly she had misjudged him. For months she had dismissed him as a handsome face with a bad heart, but she couldn't have been more wrong. She had thought that Rob, with his fancy suits, flash car and charming ways, was everything she desired in a man; but no amount of money or sweet-talk could ever compare with the generosity that Anton had displayed towards her and Leon. And just when she had thought that he might revert to type and harm Rob back there, he had acted responsibly and called the police instead. That was the act of a *real* man, and deserved real respect.

"All right?" Anton asked, climbing back into the ambulance just then.

"Yeah, fine." Chantelle sighed and opened her eyes. "Just can't wait for this night to be over."

"I bet," said Anton. "Anyway, we'll be setting off in a minute. And no arguing," he added, giving her a stern look, "you two are staying at mine tonight. But you'll have to share my bed, I'm afraid, 'cos I haven't got a spare yet."

"No, we can't take your bed," Chantelle protested. "You've got work in the morning. We'll be all right."

Anton gave her a mock-pained look. "For God's sake, woman, just do as you're told for once in your life, can't you?"

Amused, Chantelle couldn't help but smile. "Okay," she agreed. Then, more seriously, "Thanks, Anton; I really don't know what I would have done without you tonight. You're a good friend, and I'll never forget what you've done for us."

Anton had never wanted a girl as badly as he wanted Chantelle. He'd fancied her ever since she had stood up for the old pervert that his friends had been hassling outside the shops that first night and, as hard as he had tried to push her out of his mind, his attraction to her had only grown progressively stronger. But she didn't feel the same about him, and those words were the final nail in the coffin of his hopes. She considered him a *friend*, and if he'd been in any doubt before she couldn't have made it clearer that that was all they were ever going to be.

"Any time." Anton forced a smile. Then, winking at her, he sat back for the ride as the paramedics closed the door and the ambulance set off for the hospital.

# EPILOGUE

Anton was worn out when he arrived home from work. It had been a shitty day, and he'd twice had to pull himself up short as the temptation to lamp his arrogant boss threatened to overcome him. He'd bitten his tongue so hard that he'd been in danger of chomping right through the damn thing, and it was only the thought that it would soon be over that had kept him going.

There were only a few weeks left before his probation came to an end, and it couldn't come fast enough as far as he was concerned. He knew it wouldn't be easy to find another job, but he would rather starve and lose the flat than carry on working for that wanker Abdul for one second longer than he had to.

Still, walking out of the job was going to be a doddle compared with getting out of the gang. It was a week since he'd had to call on Trey for help, and his old friend had welcomed him back into the fold with open arms. Anton couldn't deny that it had been good to chill with the boys and talk about the old days, but he'd known that the peace was about to come to an end when they heard whispers that a rival crew from Longsight were planning on muscling in on Big T's

**405**

crack-dealing territory. When Trey had immediately started to plot a pre-emptive strike, Anton had known that it was time to get out, because they would all be packing steel and he would either end up getting shot or having to shoot someone.

It hadn't been easy to ask his friend to cut him loose so soon after accepting the crew's help. But Trey had got himself a shitload of money and drugs off Rob Knight's partner in exchange for letting him go that night, so he had finally agreed to call it quits — on condition that Anton never set himself up as a dealer on his territory, because that would mean instant war. Anton had assured him that he need have no worries on that score; one spell inside was more than enough for one lifetime, and he was determined to walk a straight line from here on in.

He was thinking about the future now as he stepped out of the shower; wondering if he ought to do some kind of training in order to get a better-paid job. Maybe forklift-truck driving, or plastering? He'd just wrapped a towel around his waist and was about to go to his bedroom to dry off when someone knocked at the door. Hoping that it was Shotz, because he was out of weed and could really do with one of his friend's killer spliffs to wipe the edge off his mood, he was grinning as he answered the door.

"Yo, am I glad to see you, 'cos I really need a big . . ." He trailed off when he saw Chantelle and said, "Oh, sorry. Thought it was my mate."

"No, I'm sorry," Chantelle said, averting her gaze when she saw the towel. "Shall I come back later?"

"Don't be daft." Anton stepped back and waved for her to come in. "It won't take me a minute to get dressed. Go make yourself comfortable. Or, better still, make yourself useful and put the kettle on," he said, giving her a cheeky grin — the kind that *friends* gave each other.

"Tea or coffee?" Chantelle asked, still not looking at him as she went into the kitchen.

"Tea," he called, already heading for the bedroom. "White —"

"One sugar," Chantelle finished for him.

"All right, smart-arse." Anton laughed, tickled that she'd remembered how he liked his tea.

In the bedroom he dressed quickly. He hadn't seen Chantelle since she and Leon had gone home the morning after the Rob business. He'd been working every day since, and she'd been . . . Well, he wasn't actually sure *what* she'd been doing, because he hadn't seen her to ask. He had thought about calling round to see how they were doing but he'd decided to give them some space, figuring they had probably seen more than enough of him lately.

As he joined her in the kitchen now, he thought she looked more beautiful than ever. But he kept his thoughts to himself and asked instead, "So, how's the hand?"

"Still sore, but getting better." Chantelle handed one of the cups to him and went over to the sink to rinse the spoon under the tap. "I went to the police station this afternoon," she told him over her shoulder.

"Oh yeah?" Anton took a sip of the tea. "What did they say?"

"They caught up with Rob's friend a couple of days ago and he's told them absolutely everything. So they said they won't need me to go to court if I don't want to, because they've got more than enough to convict him."

"That's good." Anton leaned back against the ledge.

"Yes, it's a massive relief, 'cos I really didn't want to have to see him again," Chantelle said, wiping her hand on her thigh and reaching for her own cup. "I met Bill's niece while I was there," she went on, her tone suddenly wistful. "She lives in Ireland and hadn't seen Bill in years, apparently. She asked if I'll be going to the funeral after they release Bill's body. I said I will, but I'm really dreading it."

"I think it'll be a good chance to lay your guilt to rest," Anton said softly. "You couldn't have known what was going to happen, and there's no way she'd be blaming you for any of it."

"Maybe not, but *I* do," Chantelle murmured. Then, smiling sadly, she shrugged and said, "Anyway, it's good news about Rob, 'cos I was convinced he was going to talk his way out of it. But there's no way he's walking free once this goes to court. I just can't believe he was kidnapping and drugging girls the whole time I was with him. To think that was probably what he was doing all those times when he said he couldn't see me. It makes me feel sick just thinking about it."

"Then don't," Anton said simply. "It's in the past, so just put it out of your head and get on with your life."

"That's what Immy said." Chantelle sighed. "But it's not that easy."

"Immy?" Anton gave her a blank look.

"My friend," Chantelle told him. "You'll have seen her loads of times at school, but you probably didn't notice her. Like you didn't notice me," she added, giving him a teasing smile. "She's been practically stalking you since she found out you were working at Abdul's. But don't you dare tell her I told you that, or I'll never speak to you again."

Anton looked confused for a few seconds. Then, a light coming on in his eyes, he said, "Not the little blonde with the bright red lipstick?"

"That's her."

"Yeah, I see what you mean about the stalking." Anton laughed. "She must come into the shop about ten times a day. But she's wasting her time if it's me she's after, 'cos she's not my type."

Chantelle lowered her gaze when he said this, and inhaled deeply. She had been battling her feelings for him ever since she and Leon had slept in his bed, and she couldn't deny that she'd have been gutted if he'd said he was interested in Immy. Not that she stood a chance with him herself any more. He might have liked her in that way once but, if her cold behaviour of the last few months hadn't been enough to put him off, the revelation that she was the kind of girl who slept with married men definitely would have. And she wouldn't blame him if he had lost all respect for her, because she was still thoroughly disgusted with herself.

Anton had been watching her as the thoughts swirled around her head. She still looked so troubled, and he could only imagine how tough she must be finding it to carry on as normal.

"How's Leon getting on?" he asked — at the exact same time as Chantelle said, "I've spoken to my mum."

"Sorry." He laughed. "You first."

"I've spoken to my mum," she said again, gripping her cup a little tighter because she was about to say something that had brought her to tears every time she had thought about it today. "I made Tracey give me her number and called her last night, and she's agreed to let Leon go and stay with them. We'll be flying over as soon as I've sorted the passports and tickets."

"*What?*" Anton felt as if someone had punched him in the gut and knocked all the wind out of him. "How long for?"

"I don't know?" Chantelle said quietly. "At least until Leon's settled. I don't want to go," she went on miserably, "but I don't see I've got any choice. Leon should be with his mum, and it's not fair to put it off just because I don't want to lose him."

"You don't have to lose him," said Anton, desperately hoping that she would reconsider. "He's better off with you, if you want my honest opinion. You've done a great job of looking after him."

"Thanks." Chantelle gave him a sad smile. "But we both know that's not true. I couldn't stop him from getting involved with that gang, could I? And then I nearly got him killed."

"That wasn't your fault," Anton argued.

"Yes, it was," Chantelle said flatly. "I'm the one who had the affair and then sent those pictures to Rob's wife."

"Yeah, but that's all done now."

"Maybe so, but we can't carry on like this indefinitely, can we?" Chantelle gave a helpless little shrug. "It was all right when I had a job, but that's gone now. And my mum's got no intention of coming back, so, sooner or later, the council are going to find out she's not here and repossess the flat. We'd have to leave eventually, so I just figured we might as well jump before we're pushed. At least this way Leon won't get taken into care again."

Anton pursed his lips as, shoulders sagging, Chantelle took a sip of her tea. He had been determined to respect her wish to stay just friends, but this changed everything. He could just about have coped with not being able to have her as long as he could still see her around from time to time, but the thought of never seeing her again was unbearable.

"Don't go," he said. "Move in here with me."

"What?" Chantelle looked up, a deep frown on her brow. "Don't be daft."

"I mean it," Anton insisted. "I *want* you to stay."

"I don't understand." Chantelle's heart was beginning to race.

"Yes, you do." Anton put his cup down on the ledge and then took hers out of her hand. "You know how I feel about you, I can see it in your eyes. And you feel the same, don't you?"

As a deep blush began to spread across her cheeks, Chantelle couldn't bring herself to meet his gaze. "Yes," she whispered. "But —"

She didn't get to finish what she'd been about to say as Anton pulled her into his arms and kissed her. It totally took her breath away, and she knew that her legs would have given way if he hadn't been holding her up. Rob was the first man she had ever kissed, and she had thought that was the best it could ever be. But this was in a different league, and she realised that the difference was that this was genuine.

"Oh, sweet Lord!" Anton laughed when they broke apart at last. "If you knew how long I've wanted to do that, but I thought I stood no chance."

"I've always liked you," Chantelle admitted. "I just thought . . ." She trailed off and shrugged. "I won't lie, I thought you were a player."

"I was," Anton confessed. "But I've changed since I came home. I used to think keeping it casual was enough, but it isn't. *This* is what I want." He gazed down into her eyes. "*You're* what I want."

Chantelle bit her lip. She desperately wanted to say that, yes, she would stay. But it just wasn't going to be that easy. The reality of looking after a ten-year-old boy would soon take its toll, and Anton would regret ever asking them to move in.

"It wouldn't work," she said, pulling away from him. "I couldn't expect you to take us on; it's too much to ask. Anyway, I really think it's best if Leon goes to live with my mum. I don't want him to grow up round here and risk him getting into trouble again. I'll sort myself out once I know he's safe."

"All right — if you won't stay, then I'll come with you," said Anton as the impetuous idea took hold and offered a solution not just to Chantelle's troubles but to his own as well. "Just give me a few weeks till my probation's finished, then we'll go to Spain so Leon can see your mum, if that's what he wants. But then we're coming back and making a fresh start somewhere away from here — and Leon's coming with us."

"Are you serious?" Chantelle gave him a questioning look.

"Deadly."

"But you've got your job, and the flat. You can't just up and leave everything."

"I can, and I will." Anton peered down into her eyes. "In case you haven't got it yet, I love you. I'm *in* love with you, have been for months. And now I've finally got you there's no way I'm letting you go again."

Chantelle was staring up at him in wonder. "You really are serious, aren't you?"

"I just said so, didn't I?"

"You're crazy."

"Yeah, crazy for *you*," Anton said huskily. "So do as you're told and say yes."

"Yes," Chantelle whispered, tears of joy glistening in her eyes as Anton pulled her back into his arms and kissed her deeply.

ISIS publish a wide range of books in large print, from fiction to biography. Any suggestions for books you would like to see in large print or audio are always welcome. Please send to the Editorial Department at:

**ISIS Publishing Limited**
7 Centremead
Osney Mead
Oxford OX2 0ES

A full list of titles is available free of charge from:

**Ulverscroft Large Print Books Limited**

**(UK)**
The Green
Bradgate Road, Anstey
Leicester LE7 7FU
Tel: (0116) 236 4325

**(Australia)**
P.O. Box 314
St Leonards
NSW 1590
Tel: (02) 9436 2622

**(USA)**
P.O. Box 1230
West Seneca
N.Y. 14224-1230
Tel: (716) 674 4270

**(Canada)**
P.O. Box 80038
Burlington
Ontario L7L 6B1
Tel: (905) 637 8734

**(New Zealand)**
P.O. Box 456
Feilding
Tel: (06) 323 6828

Details of **ISIS** complete and unabridged audio books are also available from these offices. Alternatively, contact your local library for details of their collection of **ISIS** large print and unabridged audio books.